Finished by H. Rider Haggard

Sir Henry Rider Haggard, KBE was born on June 22nd, 1856 at Bradenham in Norfolk, England.

After his education he was pushed towards an Army career but failed the entrance exam. Next Haggard was positioned to work for the British Foreign Office but he seems not to have sat that exam. Using family connections, he was sent to Southern Africa by his father in search of a further opportunity of a career.

Haggard spent six years there before a return to England and marriage. He had begun to write and publish some non-fiction in Africa but it was only after studying Law in the hope it might prove to be the proper career his father wanted for him that Haggard began to write fiction, using his African experiences as the basis.

His first fiction was published in 1885 and the following year King Solomon's Mines was published. It was a phenomenal success. His career was set.

Haggard wrote well and wrote often. He managed to sympathise with the local populations even though they were exploited and manipulated by Europeans intent on amassing fortunes in money, people and resources. His writing career covered the great sprint to Empire of several European powers and both reflects and criticizes these events through his well-loved characters including Allan Quatermain and Ayesha.

In his later years Haggard pursued much in the way social reform as well as standing for Parliament and writing a great many letters to The Times.

Henry Rider Haggard died on May 14th, 1925 at the age of 68. His ashes were buried at Ditchingham Church.

Index of Contents

DEDICATION

Ditchingham House, Norfolk, May, 1917.

My dear Roosevelt,—

You are, I know, a lover of old Allan Quatermain, one who understands and appreciates the views of life and the aspirations that underlie and inform his manifold adventures.

Therefore, since such is your kind wish, in memory of certain hours wherein both of us found true refreshment and companionship amidst the terrible anxieties of the World's journey along that bloodstained road by which alone, so it is decreed, the pure Peak of Freedom must be scaled, I dedicate to you this tale telling of the events and experiences of my youth.

Your sincere friend,

H. RIDER HAGGARD.

To COLONEL THEODORE ROOSEVELT, Sagamore Hill, U.S.A.

INTRODUCTION

This book, although it can be read as a separate story, is the third of the trilogy of which Marie and Child of Storm are the first two parts. It narrates, through the mouth of Allan Quatermain, the consummation of the vengeance of the wizard Zikali, alias The Opener of Roads, or "The-Thing-that-should-never-have-been-born," upon the royal Zulu House of which Senzangacona was the founder and Cetewayo, our enemy in the war of 1879, the last representative who ruled as a king. Although, of course, much is added for the purposes of romance, the main facts of history have been adhered to with some faithfulness.

With these the author became acquainted a full generation ago, Fortune having given him a part in the events that preceded the Zulu War. Indeed he believes that with the exception of Colonel Phillips, who, as a lieutenant, commanded the famous escort of twenty-five policemen, he is now the last survivor of the party who, under the leadership of Sir Theophilus Shepstone, or Sompseu as the natives called him from the Zambesi to the Cape, were concerned in the annexation of the Transvaal in 1877. Recently also he has been called upon as a public servant to revisit South Africa and took the opportunity to travel through Zululand, in order to refresh his knowledge of its people, their customs, their mysteries, and better to prepare himself for the writing of this book. Here he stood by the fatal Mount of Isandhlawana which, with some details of the battle, is described in these pages, among the graves of many whom once he knew, Colonels Durnford, Pulleine and others. Also he saw Ulundi's plain where the traces of war still lie thick, and talked with an old Zulu who fought in the attacking Impi until it crumbled away before the fire of the Martinis and shells from the heavy guns. The battle of the Wall of Sheet Iron, he called it, perhaps because of the flashing fence of bayonets.

Lastly, in a mealie patch, he found the spot on which the corn grows thin, where King Cetewayo breathed his last, poisoned without a doubt, as he has known for many years. It is to be seen at the Kraal, ominously named Jazi or, translated into English, "Finished." The tragedy happened long ago, but even now the quiet-faced Zulu who told the tale, looking about him as he spoke, would not tell it all. "Yes, as a young man, I was there at the time, but I do not remember, I do not know—the Inkoosi Lundanda (i.e., this Chronicler, so named in past years by the Zulus) stands on the very place where the king died—His bed was on the left of the door-hole of the hut," and so forth, but no certain word as to the exact reason of this sudden and violent death or by whom it was caused. The name of that destroyer of a king is for ever hid.

In this story the actual and immediate cause of the declaration of war against the British Power is represented as the appearance of the white goddess, or spirit of the Zulus, who is, or was, called Nomkubulwana or Inkosazana-y-Zulu, i.e., the Princess of Heaven. The exact circumstances which led to this decision are not now ascertainable, though it is known that there was much difference of opinion among the Zulu Indunas or great captains, and like the writer, many believe that King Cetewayo was personally averse to war against his old allies, the English.

The author's friend, Mr. J. Y. Gibson, at present the representative of the Union in Zululand, writes in his admirable history: "There was a good deal of discussion amongst the assembled Zulu notables at Ulundi, but of how counsel was swayed it is not possible now to obtain a reliable account."

The late Mr. F. B. Fynney, F.R.G.S., who also was his friend in days bygone, and, with the exception of Sir Theophilus Shepstone, who perhaps knew the Zulus and their language better than any other official of his day, speaking of this fabled goddess wrote: "I remember that just before the Zulu War Nomkubulwana appeared revealing something or other which had a great effect throughout the land."

The use made of this strange traditional Guardian Angel in the following tale is not therefore an unsupported flight of fancy, and the same may be said of many other incidents, such as the account of the reading of the proclamation annexing the Transvaal at Pretoria in 1877, which have been introduced to serve the purposes of the romance.

Mameena, who haunts its pages, in a literal as well as figurative sense, is the heroine of Child of Storm, a book to which she gave her own poetic title.

1916. THE AUTHOR.

CHAPTER I

ALLAN QUATERMAIN MEETS ANSCOMBE

You, my friend, into whose hand, if you live, I hope these scribblings of mine will pass one day, must well remember the 12th of April of the year 1877 at Pretoria. Sir Theophilus Shepstone, or Sompseu, for I prefer to call him by his native name, having investigated the affairs of the Transvaal for a couple of months or so, had made up his mind to annex that country to the British Crown. It so happened that I, Allan Quatermain, had been on a shooting and trading expedition at the back of the Lydenburg district where there was plenty of game to be killed in those times. Hearing that great events were toward I made up my mind, curiosity being one of my weaknesses, to come round by Pretoria, which after all was not very far out of my way, instead of striking straight back to Natal. As it chanced I reached the town about eleven o'clock on this very morning of the 12th of April and, trekking to the Church Square, proceeded to outspan there, as was usual in the Seventies. The place was full of people, English and Dutch together, and I noted that the former seemed very elated and were talking excitedly, while the latter for the most part appeared to be sullen and depressed.

Presently I saw a man I knew, a tall, dark man, a very good fellow and an excellent shot, named Robinson. By the way you knew him also, for afterwards he was an officer in the Pretoria Horse at the time of the Zulu war, the corps in which you held a commission. I called to him and asked what was up.

"A good deal, Allan," he said as he shook my hand. "Indeed we shall be lucky if all isn't up, or something like it, before the day is over. Shepstone's Proclamation annexing the Transvaal is going to be read presently."

I whistled and asked,

"How will our Boer friends take it? They don't look very pleased."

"That's just what no one knows, Allan. Burgers the President is squared, they say. He is to have a pension; also he thinks it the only thing to be done. Most of the Hollanders up here don't like it, but I doubt whether they will put out their hands further than they can draw them back. The question is— what will be the line of the Boers themselves? There are a lot of them about, all armed, you see, and more outside the town."

"What do you think?"

"Can't tell you. Anything may happen. They may shoot Shepstone and his staff and the twenty-five policemen, or they may just grumble and go home. Probably they have no fixed plan."

"How about the English?"

"Oh! we are all crazy with joy, but of course there is no organization and many have no arms. Also there are only a few of us."

"Well," I answered, "I came here to look for excitement, life having been dull for me of late, and it seems that I have found it. Still I bet you those Dutchmen do nothing, except protest. They are slim and know that the shooting of an unarmed mission would bring England on their heads."

"Can't say, I am sure. They like Shepstone who understands them, and the move is so bold that it takes their breath away. But as the Kaffirs say, when a strong wind blows a small spark will make the whole veld burn. It just depends upon whether the spark is there. If an Englishman and a Boer began to fight for instance, anything might happen. Goodbye, I have got a message to deliver. If things go right we might dine at the European tonight, and if they don't, goodness knows where we shall dine."

I nodded sagely and he departed. Then I went to my wagon to tell the boys not to send the oxen off to graze at present, for I feared lest they should be stolen if there were trouble, but to keep them tied to the trek-tow. After this I put on the best coat and hat I had, feeling that as an Englishman it was my duty to look decent on such an occasion, washed, brushed my hair—with me a ceremony without meaning, for it always sticks up—and slipped a loaded Smith & Wesson revolver into my inner poacher pocket. Then I started out to see the fun, and avoiding the groups of surly-looking Boers, mingled with the crowd that I saw was gathering in front of a long, low building with a broad stoep, which I supposed, rightly, to be one of the Government offices.

Presently I found myself standing by a tall, rather loosely-built man whose face attracted me. It was clean-shaven and much bronzed by the sun, but not in any way good-looking; the features were too irregular and the nose was a trifle too long for good looks. Still the impression it gave was pleasant and the steady blue eyes had that twinkle in them which suggests humour. He might have been thirty or thirty-five years of age, and notwithstanding his rough dress that consisted mainly of a pair of trousers held up by a belt to which hung a pistol, and a common flannel shirt, for he wore no coat, I guessed at once that he was English-born.

For a while neither of us said anything after the taciturn habit of our people even on the veld, and indeed I was fully occupied in listening to the truculent talk of a little party of mounted Boers behind us. I put my pipe into my mouth and began to hunt for my tobacco, taking the opportunity to show the hilt of my revolver, so that these men might see that I was armed. It was not to be found, I had left it in the wagon.

"If you smoke Boer tobacco," said the stranger, "I can help you," and I noted that the voice was as pleasant as the face, and knew at once that the owner of it was a gentleman.

"Thank you, Sir. I never smoke anything else," I answered, whereon he produced from his trousers pocket a pouch made of lion skin of unusually dark colour.

"I never saw a lion as black as this, except once beyond Buluwayo on the borders of Lobengula's country," I said by way of making conversation.

"Curious," answered the stranger, "for that's where I shot the brute a few months ago. I tried to keep the whole skin but the white ants got at it."

"Been trading up there?" I asked.

"Nothing so useful," he said. "Just idling and shooting. Came to this country because it was one of the very few I had never seen, and have only been here a year. I think I have had about enough of it, though. Can you tell me of any boats running from Durban to India? I should like to see those wild sheep in Kashmir."

I told him that I did not know for certain as I had never taken any interest in India, being an African elephant-hunter and trader, but I thought they did occasionally. Just then Robinson passed by and called to me—

"They'll be here presently, Quatermain, but Sompseu isn't coming himself."

"Does your name happen to be Allan Quatermain?" asked the stranger. "If so I have heard plenty about you up in Lobengula's country, and of your wonderful shooting."

"Yes," I replied, "but as for the shooting, natives always exaggerate."

"They never exaggerated about mine," he said with a twinkle in his eye. "Anyhow I am very glad to see you in the flesh, though in the spirit you rather bored me because I heard too much of you. Whenever I made a particularly bad miss, my gun-bearer, who at some time seems to have been yours, would say, 'Ah! if only it had been the Inkosi Macumazahn, how different would have been the end!' My name is Anscombe, Maurice Anscombe," he added rather shyly. (Afterwards I discovered from a book of reference that he was a younger son of Lord Mountford, one of the richest peers in England.)

Then we both laughed and he said—

"Tell me, Mr. Quatermain, if you will, what those Boers are saying behind us. I am sure it is something unpleasant, but as the only Dutch I know is 'Guten Tag' and 'Vootsack' (Good-day and Get out) that takes me no forwarder."

"It ought to," I answered, "for the substance of their talk is that they object to be 'vootsacked' by the British Government as represented by Sir Theophilus Shepstone. They are declaring that they won the land 'with their blood' and want to keep their own flag flying over it."

"A very natural sentiment," broke in Anscombe.

"They say that they wish to shoot all damned Englishmen, especially Shepstone and his people, and that they would make a beginning now were they not afraid that the damned English Government, being angered, would send thousands of damned English rooibatjes, that is, red-coats, and shoot them out of evil revenge."

"A very natural conclusion," laughed Anscombe again, "which I should advise them to leave untested. Hush! Here comes the show."

I looked and saw a body of blackcoated gentlemen with one officer in the uniform of a Colonel of Engineers, advancing slowly. I remember that it reminded me of a funeral procession following the corpse of the Republic that had gone on ahead out of sight. The procession arrived upon the stoep opposite to us and began to sort itself out, whereon the English present raised a cheer and the Boers behind us cursed audibly. In the middle appeared an elderly gentleman with whiskers and a stoop, in whom I recognized Mr. Osborn, known by the Kaffirs as Malimati, the Chief of the Staff. By his side was a tall young fellow, yourself, my friend, scarcely more than a lad then, carrying papers. The rest stood to right and left in a formal line. You gave a printed document to Mr. Osborn who put on his glasses and began to read in a low voice which few could hear, and I noticed that his hand trembled. Presently he grew confused, lost his place, found it, lost it again and came to a full stop.

"A nervous-natured man," remarked Mr. Anscombe. "Perhaps he thinks that those gentlemen are going to shoot."

"That wouldn't trouble him," I answered, who knew him well. "His fears are purely mental."

That was true since I know that this same Sir Melmoth Osborn as he is now, as I have told in the book I called Child of Storm, swam the Tugela alone to watch the battle of Indondakasuka raging round him, and on another occasion killed two Kaffirs rushing at him with a right and left shot without turning a hair. It was reading this paper that paralyzed him, not any fear of what might happen.

There followed a very awkward pause such as occurs when a man breaks down in a speech. The members of the Staff looked at him and at each other, then behold! you, my friend, grabbed the paper from his hand and went on reading it in a loud clear voice.

"That young man has plenty of nerve," said Mr. Anscombe.

"Yes," I replied in a whisper. "Quite right though. Would have been a bad omen if the thing had come to a stop."

Well, there were no more breakdowns, and at last the long document was finished and the Transvaal annexed. The Britishers began to cheer but stopped to listen to the formal protest of the Boer Government, if it could be called a government when everything had collapsed and the officials were being paid in postage stamps. I can't remember whether this was read by President Burgers himself or by the officer who was called State Secretary. Anyway, it was read, after which there came an awkward pause as though people were waiting to see something happen. I looked round at the Boers who were muttering and handling their rifles uneasily. Had they found a leader I really think that some of the wilder spirits among them would have begun to shoot, but none appeared and the crisis passed.

The crowd began to disperse, the English among them cheering and throwing up their hats, the Dutch with very sullen faces. The Commissioner's staff went away as it had come, back to the building with blue gums in front of it, which afterwards became Government House, that is all except you. You started across the square alone with a bundle of printed proclamations in your hand which evidently you had been charged to leave at the various public offices.

"Let us follow him," I said to Mr. Anscombe. "He might get into trouble and want a friend."

He nodded and we strolled after you unostentatiously. Sure enough you nearly did get into trouble. In front of the first office door to which you came, stood a group of Boers, two of whom, big fellows, drew together with the evident intention of barring your way.

"Mynheeren," you said, "I pray you to let me pass on the Queen's business."

They took no heed except to draw closer together and laugh insolently. Again you made your request and again they laughed. Then I saw you lift your leg and deliberately stamp upon the foot of one of the Boers. He drew back with an exclamation, and for a moment I believed that he or his fellow was going to do something violent. Perhaps they thought better of it, or perhaps they saw us two Englishmen behind and noticed Anscombe's pistol. At any rate you marched into the office triumphant and delivered your document.

"Neatly done," said Mr. Anscombe.

"Rash," I said, shaking my head, "very rash. Well, he's young and must be excused."

But from that moment I took a great liking to you, my friend, perhaps because I wondered whether in your place I should have been daredevil enough to act in the same way. For you see I am English, and I like to see an Englishman hold his own against odds and keep up the credit of the country. Although, of course, I sympathized with the Boers who, through their own fault, were losing their land without a blow struck. As you know well, for you were living near Majuba at the time, plenty of blows were struck afterwards, but of that business I cannot bear to write. I wonder how it will all work out after I am dead and if I shall ever learn what happens in the end.

Now I have only mentioned this business of the Annexation and the part you played in it, because it was on that occasion that I became acquainted with Anscombe. For you have nothing to do with this story which is about the destruction of the Zulus, the accomplishment of the vengeance of Zikali the wizard at the kraal named Finished, and incidentally, the love affairs of two people in which that old wizard took a hand, as I did to my sorrow.

It happened that Mr. Anscombe had ridden on ahead of his wagons which could not arrive at Pretoria for a day or two, and as he found it impossible to get accommodation at the European or elsewhere, I offered to let him sleep in mine, or rather alongside in a tent I had. He accepted and soon we became very good friends. Before the day was out I discovered that he had served in a crack cavalry regiment, but resigned his commission some years before. I asked him why.

"Well," he said, "I came into a good lot of money on my mother's death and could not see a prospect of any active service. While the regiment was abroad I liked the life well enough, but at home it bored me. Too much society for my taste, and that sort of thing. Also I wanted to travel; nothing else really amuses me."

"You will soon get tired of it," I answered, "and as you are well off, marry some fine lady and settle down at home."

"Don't think so. I doubt if I should ever be happily married, I want too much. One doesn't pick up an earthly angel with a cast-iron constitution who adores you, which are the bare necessities of marriage, under every bush." Here I laughed. "Also," he added, the laughter going out of his eyes, "I have had enough of fine ladies and their ways."

"Marriage is better than scrapes," I remarked sententiously.

"Quite so, but one might get them both together. No, I shall never marry, although I suppose I ought as my brothers have no children."

"Won't you, my friend," thought I to myself, "when the skin grows again on your burnt fingers."

For I was sure they had been burnt, perhaps more than once. How, I never learned, for which I am rather sorry for it interests me to study burnt fingers, if they do not happen to be my own. Then we changed the subject.

Anscombe's wagons were delayed for a day or two by a broken axle or a bog hole, I forget which. So, as I had nothing particular to do until the Natal post-cart left, we spent the time in wandering about Pretoria, which did not take us long as it was but a little dorp in those days, and chatting with all and sundry. Also we went up to Government House as it was now called, and left cards, or rather wrote our names in a book for we had no cards, being told by one of the Staff whom we met that we should do so. An hour later a note arrived asking us both to dinner that night and telling us very nicely not to mind if we had no dress things. Of course we had to go, Anscombe rigged up in my second best clothes that did not fit him in the least, as he was a much taller man than I am, and a black satin bow that he had bought at Becket's Store together with a pair of shiny pumps.

I actually met you, my friend, for the first time that evening, and in trouble too, though you may have forgotten the incident. We had made a mistake about the time of dinner, and arriving half an hour too soon, were shown into a long room that opened on to the verandah. You were working there, being I believe a private secretary at the time, copying some despatch; I think you said that which gave an account of the Annexation. The room was lit by a paraffin lamp behind you, for it was quite dark and the window was open, or at any rate unshuttered. The gentleman who showed us in, seeing that you were very busy, took us to the far end of the room, where we stood talking in the shadow. Just then a door opened opposite to that which led to the verandah, and through it came His Excellency the Administrator, Sir Theophilus Shepstone, a stout man of medium height with a very clever, thoughtful face, as I have always thought, one of the greatest of African statesmen. He did not see us, but he caught sight of you and said testily—

"Are you mad?" To which you answered with a laugh—

"I hope not more than usual, Sir, but why?"

"Have I not told you always to let down the blinds after dark? Yet there you sit with your head against the light, about the best target for a bullet that could be imagined."

"I don't think the Boers would trouble to shoot me, Sir. If you had been here I would have drawn the blinds and shut the shutters too," you answered, laughing again.

"Go to dress or you will be late for dinner," he said still rather sternly, and you went. But when you had gone and after we had been announced to him, he smiled and added something which I will not repeat to you even now. I think it was about what you did on the Annexation day of which the story had come to him.

I mention this incident because whenever I think of Shepstone, whom I had known off and on for years in the way that a hunter knows a prominent Government official, it always recurs to my mind, embodying as it does his caution and appreciation of danger derived from long experience of the country, and the sternness he sometimes affected which could never conceal his love towards his friends. Oh! there was greatness in this man, although they did call him an "African Talleyrand." If it had not been so would every native from the Cape to the Zambesi have known and revered his name, as perhaps that of no other white man has been revered? But I must get on with my tale and leave historical discussions to others more fitted to deal with them.

We had a very pleasant dinner that night, although I was so ashamed of my clothes with smart uniforms and white ties all about me, and Anscombe kept fidgeting his feet because he was suffering agony from his new pumps which were a size too small. Everybody was in the best of spirits, for from all directions came the news that the Annexation was well received and that the danger of any trouble had passed away. Ah! if we had only known what the end of it would be!

It was on our way back to the wagon that I chanced to mention to Anscombe that there was still a herd of buffalo within a few days' trek of Lydenburg, of which I had shot two not a month before.

"Are there, by Jove!" he said. "As it happens I never got a buffalo; always I just missed them in one sense or another, and I can't leave Africa with a pair of bought horns. Let's go there and shoot some."

I shook my head and replied that I had been idling long enough and must try to make some money, news at which he seemed very disappointed.

"Look here," he said, "forgive me for mentioning it, but business is business. If you'll come you shan't be a loser."

Again I shook my head, whereat he looked more disappointed than before.

"Very well," he exclaimed, "then I must go alone. For kill a buffalo I will; that is unless the buffalo kills me, in which case my blood will be on your hands."

I don't know why, but at that moment there came into my mind a conviction that if he did go alone a buffalo or something would kill him and that then I should be sorry all my life.

"They are dangerous brutes, much worse than lions," I said.

"And yet you, who pretend to have a conscience, would expose me to their rage unprotected and alone," he replied with a twinkle in his eye which I could see even by moonlight. "Oh! Quatermain, how I have been mistaken in your character."

"Look here, Mr. Anscombe," I said, "it's no use. I cannot possibly go on a shooting expedition with you just now. Only to-day I have heard from Natal that my boy is not well and must undergo an operation which will lay him up for quite six weeks, and may be dangerous. So I must get down to Durban before it takes place. After that I have a contract in Matabeleland whence you have just come, to take charge of a trading store there for a year; also perhaps to try to shoot a little ivory for myself. So I am fully booked up till, let us say, October, 1878, that is for about eighteen months, by which time I daresay I shall be dead."

"Eighteen months," replied this cool young man. "That will suit me very well. I will go on to India as I intended, then home for a bit and will meet you on the 1st of October, 1878, after which we will proceed to the Lydenburg district and shoot those buffalo, or if they have departed, other buffalo. Is it a bargain?"

I stared at him, thinking that the Administrator's champagne had got into his head.

"Nonsense," I exclaimed. "Who knows where you will be in eighteen months? Why, by that time you will have forgotten all about me."

"If I am alive and well, on the 1st of October, 1878, I shall be exactly where I am now, upon this very square in Pretoria, with a wagon, or wagons, prepared for a hunting trip. But as not unnaturally you have doubts upon that point, I am prepared to pay forfeit if I fail, or even if circumstances cause you to fail."

Here he took a cheque-book from his letter-case and spread it out on the little table in the tent, on which there were ink and a pen, adding—

"Now, Mr. Quatermain, will it meet your views if I fill this up for £250?"

"No," I answered; "taking everything into consideration the sum is excessive. But if you do not mind facing the risks of my non-appearance, to say nothing of your own, you may make it £50."

"You are very moderate in your demands," he said as he handed me the cheque which I put in my pocket, reflecting that it would just pay for my son's operation.

"And you are very foolish in your offers," I replied. "Tell me, why do you make such crack-brained arrangements?"

"I don't quite know. Something in me seems to say that we shall make this expedition and that it will have a very important effect upon my life. Mind you, it is to be to the Lydenburg district and nowhere else. And now I am tired, so let's turn in."

Next morning we parted and went our separate ways.

CHAPTER II

MR. MARNHAM

So much for preliminaries, now for the story.

The eighteen months had gone by, bringing with them to me their share of adventure, weal and woe, with all of which at present I have no concern. Behold me arriving very hot and tired in the post-cart from Kimberley, whither I had gone to invest what I had saved out of my Matabeleland contract in a very promising speculation whereof, today, the promise remains and no more. I had been obliged to leave Kimberly in a great hurry, before I ought indeed, because of the silly bargain which I have just recorded. Of course I was sure that I should never see Mr. Anscombe again, especially as I had heard nothing of him during all this while, and had no reason to suppose that he was in Africa. Still I had taken his £50 and he might come. Also I have always prided myself upon keeping an appointment.

The post-cart halted with a jerk in front of the European Hotel, and I crawled, dusty and tired, from its interior, to find myself face to face with Anscombe, who was smoking a pipe upon the stoep!

"Hullo, Quatermain," he said in his pleasant, drawling voice, "here you are, up to time. I have been making bets with these five gentlemen," and he nodded at a group of loungers on the stoep, "as to whether you would or would not appear, I putting ten to one on you in drinks. Therefore you must now consume five whiskies and sodas, which will save them from consuming fifty and a subsequent appearance at the Police Court."

I laughed and said I would be their debtor to the extent of one, which was duly produced.

After it was drunk Anscombe and I had a chat. He said that he had been to India, shot, or shot at whatever game he meant to kill there, visited his relations in England and thence proceeded to keep his appointment with me in Africa. At Durban he had fitted himself out in a regal way with two wagons, full teams, and some spare oxen, and trekked to Pretoria where he had arrived a few days before. Now he was ready to start for the Lydenburg district and look for those buffalo.

"But," I said, "the buffalo probably long ago departed. Also there has been a war with Sekukuni, the Basuto chief who rules all that country, which remains undecided, although I believe some kind of a peace has been patched up. This may make hunting in this neighborhood dangerous. Why not try some other ground, to the north of the Transvaal, for instance?"

"Quatermain," he answered, "I have come all the way from England, I will not say to kill, but to try to kill buffalo in the Lydenburg district, with you if possible, if not, without you, and thither I am going. If you think it unsafe to accompany me, don't come; I will get on as best I can alone, or with some other skilled person if I can find one."

"If you put it like that I shall certainly come," I replied, "with the proviso that should the buffalo prove to be non-existent or the pursuit of them impossible, we either give up the trip, or go somewhere else, perhaps to the country at the back of Delagoa Bay."

"Agreed," he said; after which we discussed terms, he paying me my salary in advance.

On further consideration we determined, as two were quite unnecessary for a trip of the sort, to leave one of my wagons and half the cattle in charge of a very respectable man, a farmer who lived about five miles from Pretoria just over the pass near to the famous Wonder-boom tree which is one of the sights of the place. Should we need this wagon it could always be sent for; or, if we found the Lydenburg hunting-ground, which he was so set upon visiting, unproductive or impossible, we could return to Pretoria over the high-veld and pick it up before proceeding elsewhere.

These arrangements took us a couple of days or so. On the third we started, without seeing you, my friend, or any one else that I knew, since just at that time every one seemed to be away from Pretoria. You, I remember, had by now become the Master of the High Court and were, they informed me at your office, absent on circuit.

The morning of our departure was particularly lovely and we trekked away in the best of spirits, as so often happens to people who are marching into trouble. Of our journey there is little to say as everything went smoothly, so that we arrived at the edge of the high-veld feeling as happy as the country which has no history is reported to do. Our road led us past the little mining settlement of Pilgrim's Rest where a number of adventurous spirits, most of them English, were engaged in washing for gold, a job at which I once took a turn near this very place without any startling success. Of the locality I need only say that the mountainous scenery is among the most beautiful, the hills are the steepest and the roads are, or were, the worst that I have ever travelled over in a wagon.

However, "going softly" as the natives say, we negotiated them without accident and, leaving Pilgrim's Rest behind us, began to descend towards the low-veld where I was informed a herd of buffalo could still be found, since, owing to the war with Sekukuni, no one had shot at them of late. This war had been suspended for a while, and the Land-drost at Pilgrim's Rest told me he thought it would be safe to hunt on the borders of that Chief's country, though he should not care to do so himself.

Game of the smaller sort began to be plentiful about here, so not more than a dozen miles from Pilgrim's Rest we outspanned early in the afternoon to try to get a blue wildebeeste or two, for I had seen the spoor of these creatures in a patch of soft ground, or failing them some other buck. Accordingly, leaving the wagon by a charming stream that wound and gurgled over a bed of granite, we mounted our salted horses, which were part of Anscombe's outfit, and set forth rejoicing. Riding through the scattered thorns and following the spoor where I could, within half an hour we came to a little glade. There, not fifty yards away, I caught sight of a single blue wildebeeste bull standing in the shadow of the trees on the further side of the glade, and pointed out the ugly beast, for it is the most grotesque of all the antelopes, to Anscombe.

"Off you get," I whispered. "It's a lovely shot, you can't miss it."

"Oh, can't I!" replied Anscombe. "Do you shoot."

I refused, so he dismounted, giving me his horse to hold, and kneeling down solemnly and slowly covered the bull. Bang went his rifle, and I saw a bough about a yard above the wildebeeste fall on to its back. Off it went like lightning, whereon Anscombe let drive with the left barrel of the Express, almost at hazard as it seemed to me, and by some chance hit it above the near fore-knee, breaking its leg.

"That was a good shot," he cried, jumping on to his horse.

"Excellent," I answered. "But what are you going to do?"

"Catch it. It is cruel to leave a wounded animal," and off he started.

Of course I had to follow, but the ensuing ride remains among the more painful of my hunting memories. We tore through thorn trees that scratched my face and damaged my clothes; we struck a patch of antbear holes, into one of which my horse fell so that my stomach bumped against its head; we slithered down granite koppies, and this was the worst of it, at the end of each chapter, so to speak, always caught sight of that accursed bull which I fondly hoped would have vanished into space. At length after half an hour or so of this game we reached a stretch of open, rolling ground, and there not fifty yards ahead of us was the animal still going like a hare, though how it could do so on three legs I am sure I do not know. We coursed it like greyhounds, till at last Anscombe, whose horse was the faster, came alongside of the exhausted creature, whereon it turned suddenly and charged.

Anscombe held out his rifle in his right hand and pulled the trigger, which, as he had forgotten to reload it, was a mere theatrical performance. Next second there was such a mix-up that for a while I could not distinguish which was Anscombe, which was the wildebeeste, and which the horse. They all seemed to be going round and round in a cloud of dust. When things settled themselves a little I discovered the horse rolling on the ground, Anscombe on his back with his hands up in an attitude of prayer and the wildebeeste trying to make up its mind which of them it should finish first. I settled the poor thing's doubts by shooting it through the heart, which I flatter myself was rather clever of me under the circumstances. Then I dismounted to examine Anscombe, who, I presumed, was done for. Not a bit of it. There he sat upon the ground blowing like a blacksmith's bellows and panting out—

"What a glorious gallop. I finished it very well, didn't I? You couldn't have made a better shot yourself."

"Yes," I answered, "you finished it very well as you will find out if you will take the trouble to open your rifle and count your cartridges. I may add that if we are going to hunt together I hope you will never lead me such a fool's chase again."

He rose, opened the rifle and saw that it was empty, for although he had never re-loaded he had thrown out the two cartridges which he had discharged in the glen.

"By Jingo," he said, "you must have shot it, though I could have sworn that it was I. Quatermain, has it ever struck you what a strange thing is the human imagination?"

"Drat the human imagination," I answered, wiping away the blood that was trickling into my eye from a thorn scratch. "Let's look at your horse. If it is lamed you will have to ride Imagination back to the wagon which must be six miles away, that is if we can find it before dark."

Sighing out something about a painfully practical mind, he obeyed, and when the beast was proved to be nothing more than blown and a little bruised, made remarks as to the inadvisability of dwelling on future evil events, which I reminded him had already been better summed up in the New Testament.

After this we contemplated the carcass of the wildebeeste which it seemed a pity to leave to rot. Just then Anscombe, who had moved a few yards to the right out of the shadow of an obstructing tree, exclaimed—

"I say, Quatermain, come here and tell me if I have been knocked silly, or if I really see a quite uncommon kind of house built in ancient Greek style set in a divine landscape."

"Temple to Diana, I expect," I remarked as I joined him on the further side of the tree.

I looked and rubbed my eyes. There, about half a mile away, situated in a bay of the sweeping hills and overlooking the measureless expanse of bush-veld beneath, was a remarkable house, at least for those days and that part of Africa. To begin with the situation was superb. It stood on a green and swelling mound behind which was a wooded kloof where ran a stream that at last precipitated itself in a waterfall over a great cliff. Then in front was that glorious view of the bush-veld, at which a man might look for a lifetime and not grow tired, stretching away to the Oliphant's river and melting at last into the dim line of the horizon.

The house itself also, although not large, was of a kind new to me. It was deep, but narrow fronted, and before it were four columns that carried the roof which projected so as to form a wide verandah. Moreover it seemed to be built of marble which glistened like snow in the setting sun. In short in that lonely wilderness, at any rate from this distance, it did look like the deserted shrine of some forgotten god.

"Well, I'm bothered!" I said.

"So am I," answered Anscombe, "to know the name of the Lydenburg district architect whom I should like to employ; though I suspect it is the surroundings that make the place look so beautiful. Hullo! here comes somebody, but he doesn't look like an architect; he looks like a wicked baronet disguised as a Boer."

True enough, round a clump of bush appeared an unusual looking person, mounted on a very good horse. He was tall, thin and old, at least he had a long white beard which suggested age, although his figure, so far as it could be seen beneath his rough clothes, seemed vigorous. His face was clean cut and handsome, with a rather hooked nose, and his eyes were grey, but as I saw when he came up to us, somewhat bloodshot at the corners. His general aspect was refined and benevolent, and as soon as he opened his mouth I perceived that he was a person of gentle breeding.

And yet there was something about him, something in his atmosphere, so to speak, that I did not like. Before we parted that evening I felt sure that in one way or another he was a wrong-doer, not straight; also that he had a violent temper.

He rode up to us and asked in a pleasant voice, although the manner of his question, which was put in bad Dutch, was not pleasant,

"Who gave you leave to shoot on our land?"

"I did not know that any leave was required; it is not customary in these parts," I answered politely in English. "Moreover, this buck was wounded miles away."

"Oh!" he exclaimed in the same tongue, "that makes a difference, though I expect it was still on our land, for we have a lot; it is cheap about here." Then after studying a little, he added apologetically, "You mustn't think me strange, but the fact is my daughter hates things to be killed near the house, which is why there's so much game about."

"Then pray make her our apologies," said Anscombe, "and say that it shall not happen again."

He stroked his long beard and looked at us, for by now he had dismounted, then said—

"Might I ask you gentlemen your names?"

"Certainly," I replied. "I am Allan Quatermain and my friend is the Hon. Maurice Anscombe."

He started and said—

"Of Allan Quatermain of course I have heard. The natives told me that you were trekking to those parts; and if you, sir, are one of Lord Mountford's sons, oddly enough I think I must have known your father in my youth. Indeed I served with him in the Guards."

"How very strange," said Anscombe. "He's dead now and my brother is Lord Mountford. Do you like life here better than that in the Guards? I am sure I should."

"Both of them have their advantages," he answered evasively, "of which, if, as I think, you are also a soldier, you can judge for yourself. But won't you come up to the house? My daughter Heda is away, and my partner Mr. Rodd" (as he mentioned this name I saw a blue vein, which showed above his cheek bone, swell as though under pressure of some secret emotion) "is a retiring sort of a man—indeed some might think him sulky until they came to know him. Still, we can make you comfortable and even give you a decent bottle of wine."

"No, thank you very much," I answered, "we must get back to the wagon or our servants will think that we have come to grief. Perhaps you will accept the wildebeeste if it is of any use to you."

"Very well," he said in a voice that suggested regret struggling with relief. To the buck he made no allusion, perhaps because he considered that it was already his own property. "Do you know your way? I believe your wagon is camped out there to the east by what we call the Granite stream. If you follow this Kaffir path," and he pointed to a track near by, "it will take you quite close."

"Where does the path run to?" I asked. "There are no kraals about, are there?"

"Oh! to the Temple, as my daughter calls our house. My partner and I are labour agents, we recruit natives for the Kimberley Mines," he said in explanation, adding, "Where do you propose to shoot?"

I told him.

"Isn't that rather a risky district?" he said. "I think that Sekukuni will soon be giving more trouble, although there is a truce between him and the English. Still he might send a regiment to raid that way."

I wondered how our friend knew so much of Sekukuni's possible intentions, but only answered that I was accustomed to deal with natives and did not fear them.

"Ah!" he said, "well, you know your own business best. But if you should get into any difficulty, make straight for this place. The Basutos will not interfere with you here."

Again I wondered why the Basutos should look upon this particular spot as sacred, but thinking it wisest to ask no questions, I only answered—

"Thank you very much. We'll bear your invitation in mind, Mr.—"

"Marnham."

"Marnham," I repeated after him. "Good-bye and many thanks for your kindness."

"One question," broke in Anscombe, "if you will not think me rude. What is the name of the architect who designed that most romantic-looking house of yours which seems to be built of marble?"

"My daughter designed it, or at least I think she copied it from some old drawing of a ruin. Also it is marble; there's a whole hill of the stuff not a hundred yards from the door, so it was cheaper to use than anything else. I hope you will come and see it on your way back, though it is not as fine as it appears from a distance. It would be very pleasant after all these years to talk to an English gentleman again."

Then we parted, I rather offended because he did not seem to include me in the description, he calling after us—

"Stick close to the path through the patch of big trees, for the ground is rather swampy there and it's getting dark."

Presently we came to the place he mentioned where the timber, although scattered, was quite large for South Africa, of the yellow-wood species, and interspersed wherever the ground was dry with huge euphorbias, of which the tall finger-like growths and sad grey colouring looked unreal and ghostlike in the waning light. Following the advice given to us, we rode in single file along the narrow path, fearing lest otherwise we should tumble into some bog hole, until we came to higher land covered with the scattered thorns of the country.

"Did that bush give you any particular impression?" asked Anscombe a minute or two later.

"Yes," I answered, "it gave me the impression that we might catch fever there. See the mist that lies over it," and turning in my saddle I pointed with the rifle in my hand to what looked like a mass of cotton wool over which, without permeating it, hung the last red glow of sunset, producing a curious and indeed rather unearthly effect. "I expect that thousands of years ago there was a lake yonder, which is why trees grow so big in the rich soil."

"You are curiously mundane, Quatermain," he answered. "I ask you of spiritual impressions and you dilate to me of geological formations and the growth of timber. You felt nothing in the spiritual line?"

"I felt nothing except a chill," I answered, for I was tired and hungry. "What the devil are you driving at?"

"Have you got that flask of Hollands about you, Quatermain?"

"Oh! those are the spirits you are referring to," I remarked with sarcasm as I handed it to him.

He took a good pull and replied—

"Not at all, except in the sense that bad spirits require good spirits to correct them, as the Bible teaches. To come to facts," he added in a changed voice, "I have never been in a place that depressed me more than that thrice accursed patch of bush."

"Why did it depress you?" I asked, studying him as well as I could in the fading light. To tell the truth I feared lest he had knocked his head when the wildebeeste upset him, and was suffering from delayed concussion.

"Can't tell you, Quatermain. I don't look like a criminal, do I? Well, I entered those trees feeling a fairly honest man, and I came out of them feeling like a murderer. It was as though something terrible had happened to me there; it was as though I had killed someone there. Ugh!" and he shivered and took another pull at the Hollands.

"What bosh!" I said. "Besides, even if it were to come true, I am sorry to say I've killed lots of men in the way of business and they don't bother me overmuch."

"Did you ever kill one to win a woman?"

"Certainly not. Why, that would be murder. How can you ask me such a thing? But I have killed several to win cattle," I reflected aloud, remembering my expedition with Saduko against the chief Bangu, and some other incidents in my career.

"I appreciate the difference, Quatermain. If you kill for cows, it is justifiable homicide; if you kill for women, it is murder."

"Yes," I replied, "that is how it seems to work out in Africa. You see, women are higher in the scale of creation than cows, therefore crimes committed for their sake are enormously greater than those committed for cows, which just makes the difference between justifiable homicide and murder."

"Good lord! what an argument," he exclaimed and relapsed into silence. Had he been accustomed to natives and their ways he would have understood the point much better than he did, though I admit it is difficult to explain.

In due course we reached the wagon without further trouble. While we were shielding our pipes after an excellent supper I asked Anscombe his impressions of Mr. Marnham.

"Queer cove, I think," he answered. "Been a gentleman, too, and still keeps the manners, which isn't strange if he is one of the Marnhams, for they are a good family. I wonder he mentioned having served with my father."

"It slipped out of him. Men who live a lot alone are apt to be surprised into saying things they regret afterwards, as I noticed he did. But why do you wonder?"

"Because as it happens, although I have only just recalled it, my father used to tell some story about a man named Marnham in his regiment. I can't remember the details, but it had to do with cards when high stakes were being played for, and with the striking of a superior officer in the quarrel that ensued, as a result of which the striker was requested to send in his papers."

"It may not have been the same man."

"Perhaps not, for I believe that more than one Marnham served in that regiment. But I remember my father saying, by way of excuse for the person concerned, that he had a most ungovernable temper. I think he added, that he left the country and took service in some army on the Continent. I should rather like to clear the thing up."

"It isn't probable that you will, for even if you should ever meet this Marnham again, I fancy you would find he held his tongue about his acquaintance with your father."

"I wonder what Miss Heda is like," went on Anscombe after a pause. "I am curious to see a girl who designs a house on the model of an ancient ruin."

"Well, you won't, for she's away somewhere. Besides we are looking for buffalo, not girls, which is a good thing as they are less dangerous."

I spoke thus decisively because I had taken a dislike to Mr. Marnham and everything to do with him, and did not wish to encourage the idea of further meetings.

"No, never, I suppose. And yet I feel as though I were certainly destined to see that accursed yellow-wood swamp again."

"Nonsense," I replied as I rose to turn in. Ah! if I had but known!

CHAPTER III

THE HUNTERS HUNTED

While I was taking off my boots I heard a noise of jabbering in some native tongue which I took to be Sisutu, and not wishing to go to the trouble of putting them on again, called to the driver of the wagon to find out what it was. This man was a Cape Colony Kaffir, a Fingo I think, with a touch of Hottentot in him. He was an excellent driver, indeed I do not think I have ever seen a better, and by no means a bad shot. Among Europeans he rejoiced in the name of Footsack, a Boer Dutch term which is generally addressed to troublesome dogs and means "Get out." To tell the truth, had I been his master he would have got out, as I suspected him of drinking, and generally did not altogether trust him. Anscombe, however, was fond of him because he had shown courage in some hunting adventure in Matabeleland, I think it was at the shooting of that very dark-coloured lion whose skin had been the means of making us acquainted nearly two years before. Indeed he said that on this occasion Footsack had saved his life, though from all that I could gather I do not think this was quite the case. Also the man, who had been on many hunting trips with sportsmen, could talk Dutch well and English enough to make himself understood, and therefore was useful.

He went as I bade him, and coming back presently, told me that a party of Basutos, about thirty in number, who were returning from Kimberley, where they had been at work in the mines, under the leadership of a Bastard named Karl, asked leave to camp by the wagon for the night, as they were afraid to go on to "Tampel" in the dark.

At first I could not make out what "Tampel" was, as it did not sound like a native name. Then I remembered that Mr. Marnham had spoken of his house as being called the Temple, of which, of course, Tampel was a corruption; also that he said he and his partner were labour agents.

"Why are they afraid?" I asked.

"Because, Baas, they say that they must go through a wood in a swamp, which they think is haunted by spooks, and they much afraid of spooks;" that is of ghosts.

"What spooks?" I asked.

"Don't know, Baas. They say spook of some one who has been killed."

"Rubbish," I replied. "Tell them to go and catch the spook; we don't want a lot of noisy fellows howling chanties here all night."

Then it was that Anscombe broke in in his humorous, rather drawling voice.

"How can you be so hard-hearted, Quatermain? After the supernatural terror which, as I told you, I experienced in that very place, I wouldn't condemn a kicking mule to go through it in this darkness. Let the poor devils stay; I daresay they are tired."

So I gave in, and presently saw their fires beginning to burn through the end canvas of the wagon which was unlaced because the night was hot. Also later on I woke up, about midnight I think, and heard voices talking, one of which I reflected sleepily, sounded very like that of Footsack.

Waking very early, as is my habit, I peeped out of the wagon, and through the morning mist perceived Footsack in converse with a particularly villainous-looking person. I at once concluded this must be Karl, evidently a Bastard compounded of about fifteen parts of various native bloods to one of white, who, to add to his attractions, was deeply scarred with smallpox and possessed a really alarming squint. It seemed to me that Footsack handed to this man something that looked suspiciously like a bottle of squareface gin wrapped up in dried grass, and that the man handed back to Footsack some small object which he put in his mouth.

Now, I wondered to myself, what is there of value that one who does not eat sweets would stow away in his mouth. Gold coin perhaps, or a quid of tobacco, or a stone. Gold was too much to pay for a bottle of gin, tobacco was too little, but how about the stone? What stone? Who wanted stones? Then suddenly I remembered that these people were said to come from Kimberley, and whistled to myself. Still I did nothing, principally because the mist was still so dense that although I could see the men's faces, I could not clearly see the articles which they passed to each other about two feet lower, where it still lay very thickly, and to bring any accusation against a native which he can prove to be false is apt to destroy authority. So I held my tongue and waited my chance. It did not come at once, for before I was dressed those Basutos had departed together with their leader Karl, for now that the sun was up they no longer feared the haunted bush.

It came later, thus: We were trekking along between the thorns upon a level and easy track which enabled the driver Footsack to sit upon the "voorkisse" or driving box of the wagon, leaving the lad who is called the voorlooper to lead the oxen. Anscombe was riding parallel to the wagon in the hope of killing some guineafowl for the pot (though a very poor shot with a rifle he was good with a shot-gun). I, who did not care for this small game, was seated smoking by the side of Footsack who, I noted, smelt of gin and generally showed signs of dissipation. Suddenly I said to him—

"Show me that diamond which the Bastard Karl gave you this morning in payment for the bottle of your master's drink."

It was a bow drawn at a venture, but the effect of the shot was remarkable. Had I not caught it, the long bamboo whip Footsack held would have fallen to the ground, while he collapsed in his seat like a man who has received a bullet in his stomach.

"Baas," he gasped, "Baas, how did you know?"

"I knew," I replied grandly, "in the same way that I know everything. Show me the diamond."

"Baas," he said, "it was not the Baas Anscombe's gin, it was some I bought in Pilgrim's Rest."

"I have counted the bottles in the case and know very well whose gin it was," I replied ambiguously, for the reason that I had done nothing of the sort. "Show me the diamond."

Footsack fumbled about his person, his hair, his waistcoat pockets and even his moocha, and ultimately from somewhere produced a stone which he handed to me. I looked at it, and from the purity of colour and size, judged it to be a diamond worth £200, or possibly more. After careful examination I put it into my pocket, saying,

"This is the price of your master's gin and therefore belongs to him as much as it does to anybody. Now if you want to keep out of trouble, tell me—whence came it into the hands of that man, Karl?"

"Baas," replied Footsack, trembling all over, "how do I know? He and the rest have been working at the mines; I suppose he found it there."

"Indeed! And did he find others of the same sort?"

"I think so, Baas. At least he said that he had been buying bottles of gin with such stones all the way down from Kimberley. Karl is a great drunkard, Baas, as I am sure, who have known him for years."

"That is not all," I remarked, keeping my eyes fixed on him. "What else did he say?"

"He said, Baas, that he was very much afraid of returning to the Baas Marnham whom the Kaffirs call White-beard, with only a few stones left."

"Why was he afraid?"

"Because the Baas Whitebeard, he who dwells at Tampel, is, he says, a very angry man if he thinks himself cheated, and Karl is afraid lest he should kill him as another was killed, he whose spook haunts the wood through which those silly people feared to pass last night."

"Who was killed and who killed him?" I asked.

"Baas, I don't know," replied Footsack, collapsing into sullen silence in a way that Kaffirs have when suddenly they realize that they have said too much. Nor did I press the matter further, having learned enough.

What had I learned? This: that Messrs. Marnham & Rodd were illicit diamond buyers, I.D.B.'s as they are called, who had cunningly situated themselves at a great distance from the scene of operations practically beyond the reach of civilized law. Probably they were engaged also in other nefarious dealings with Kaffirs, such as supplying them with guns wherewith to make war upon the Whites. Sekukuni had been fighting us recently, so that there would be a very brisk market for rifles. This, too, would account for Marnham's apparent knowledge of that Chief's plans. Possibly, however, he had no knowledge and only made a pretence of it to keep us out of the country.

Later on I confided the whole story and my suspicions to Anscombe, who was much interested.

"What picturesque scoundrels!" he exclaimed, "We really ought to go back to the Temple. I have always longed to meet some real live I.D.B.'s."

"It is probable that you have done that already without knowing it. For the rest, if you wish to visit that den of iniquity, you must do so alone."

"Wouldn't whited sepulchre be a better term, especially as it seems to cover dead men's bones?" he replied in his frivolous manner.

Then I asked him what he was going to do about Footsack and the bottle of gin, which he countered by asking me what I was going to do with that diamond.

"Give it to you as Footsack's master," I said, suiting the action to the word. "I don't wish to be mixed up in doubtful transactions."

Then followed a long argument as to who was the real owner of the stone, which ended in its being hidden away be produced if called for, and in Footsack, who ought have had a round dozen, receiving a scolding from his master, coupled with the threat that if he stole more gin he would be handed over to a magistrate—when we met one.

On the following day we reached the hot, low-lying veld which the herd of buffalo was said to inhabit. Next morning, however, when we were making ready to begin hunting, a Basuto Kaffir appeared who, on being questioned, said that he was one of Sekukuni's people sent to this district to look for two lost oxen. I did not believe this story, thinking it more probable that he was a spy, but asked him whether in his hunt for oxen he had come across buffalo.

He replied that he had, a herd of thirty-two of them, counting the calves, but that they were over the Oliphant's River about five-and-twenty miles away, in a valley between some outlying hills and the rugged range of mountains, beyond which was situated Sekukuni's town. Moreover, in proof of his story he showed me spoor of the beasts heading in that direction which was quite a week old.

Now for my part, as I did not think it wise to get too near to Sekukuni, I should have given them up and gone to hunt something else. Anscombe, however, was of a different opinion and pleaded hard that we should follow them. They were the only herd within a hundred miles, he said, if indeed there were any others this side of the Lebombo Mountains. As I still demurred, he suggested, in the nicest possible manner, that if I thought the business risky, I should camp somewhere with the wagon, while he went on with Footsack to look for the buffalo. I answered that I was well used to risks, which in a sense were my trade, and that as he was more or less in my charge I was thinking of him, not of myself, who was quite prepared to follow the buffalo, not only to Sekukuni's Mountains but over them. Then fearing that he had hurt my feelings, he apologized, and offered to go elsewhere if I liked. The upshot was that we decided to trek to the Oliphant's River, camp there and explore the bush on the other side on horseback, never going so far from the wagon that we could not reach it again before nightfall.

This, then, we did, outspanning that evening by the hot but beautiful river which was still haunted by a few hippopotamus and many crocodiles, one of which we shot before turning in. Next morning, having breakfasted off cold guineafowl, we mounted, crossed the river by a ford that was quite as deep as I liked, to which the Kaffir path led us, and, leaving Footsack with the two other boys in charge of the wagon, began to hunt for the buffalo in the rather swampy bush that stretched from the further bank to the slope of the first hills, eight or ten miles away. I did not much expect to find them, as the Basuto had said that they had gone over these hills, but either he lied or they had moved back again.

Not half a mile from the river bank, just as I was about to dismount to stalk a fine waterbuck of which I caught sight standing among some coarse grass and bushes, my eye fell upon buffalo spoor that from its appearance I knew could not be more than a few hours old. Evidently the beasts had been feeding here during the night and at dawn had moved away to sleep in the dry bush nearer the hills. Beckoning to Anscombe, who fortunately had not seen the waterbuck, at which he would certainly have fired, thereby perhaps frightening the buffalo, I showed him the spoor that we at once started to follow.

Soon it led us into other spoor, that of a whole herd of thirty or forty beasts indeed, which made our task quite easy, at least till we came to harder ground, for the animals had gone a long way. An hour or more later, when we were about seven miles from the river, I perceived ahead of us, for we were now almost at the foot of the hills, a cool and densely-wooded kloof.

"That is where they will be," I said. "Now come on carefully and make no noise."

We rode to the wide mouth of the kloof where the signs of the buffalo were numerous and fresh, dismounted and tied our horses to a thorn, so as to approach them silently on foot. We had not gone two hundred yards through the bush when suddenly about fifty paces away, standing broadside on in the shadow between two trees, I saw a splendid old bull with a tremendous pair of horns.

"Shoot," I whispered to Anscombe, "you will never get a better chance. It is the sentinel of the herd."

He knelt down, his face quite white with excitement, and covered the bull with his Express.

"Keep cool," I whispered again, "and aim behind the shoulder, half-way down."

I don't think he understood me, for at that moment off went the rifle. He hit the beast somewhere, as I heard the bullet clap, but not fatally, for it turned and lumbered off up the kloof, apparently unhurt, whereon he sent the second barrel after it, a clean miss this time. Then of a sudden all about us appeared buffaloes that had, I suppose, been sleeping invisible to us. These, with snorts and bellows, rushed off towards the river, for having their senses about them, they had no mind to be trapped in the kloof. I could only manage a shot at one of them, a large and long-horned cow which I knocked over quite dead. If I had fired again it would have been but to wound, a thing I hate. The whole business was over in a minute. We went and looked at my dead cow which I had caught through the heart.

"It's cruel to kill these things," I said, "for I don't know what use we are going to make of them, and they must love life as much as we do."

"We'll cut the horns off," said Anscombe.

"You may if you like," I answered, "but you will find it a tough job with a sheath knife."

"Yes, I think that shall be the task of the worthy Footsack to-morrow," he replied. "Meanwhile let us go and finish off my bull, as Footsack & Co. may as well bring home two pair of horns as one."

I looked at the dense bush, and knowing something of the habits of wounded buffaloes, reflected that it would be a nasty job. Still I said nothing, because if I hesitated, I knew he would want to go alone. So we started. Evidently the beast had been badly hit, for the blood spoor was easy to follow. Yet it had been able to retreat up to the end of the kloof that terminated in a cliff over which trickled a stream of water. Here it was not more than a hundred paces wide, and on either side of it were other precipitous cliffs. As we went from one of these a war-horn, such as the Basutos use, was blown. Although I heard it, oddly enough, I paid no attention to it at the time, being utterly intent upon the business in hand.

Following a wounded buffalo bull up a tree-clad and stony kloof is no game for children, as these beasts have a habit of returning on their tracks and then rushing out to gore you. So I went on with every sense alert, keeping Anscombe well behind me. As it happened our bull had either been knocked silly or inherited no guile from his parents. When he found he could go no further he stopped, waited behind a bush, and when he saw us he charged in a simple and primitive fashion. I let Anscombe fire, as I wished him to have the credit of killing it all to himself, but somehow or other he managed to miss both barrels. Then, trouble being imminent, I let drive as the beast lowered its head, and was lucky enough to break its spine (to shoot at the head of a buffalo is useless), so that it rolled over quite dead at our feet.

"You have got a magnificent pair of horns," I said, contemplating the fallen giant.

"Yes," answered Anscombe, with a twinkle of his humorous eyes, "and if it hadn't been for you I think that I should have got them in more senses than one."

As the words passed his lips some missile, from its peculiar sound I judged it was the leg off an iron pot, hurtled past my head, fired evidently from a smoothbore gun with a large charge of bad powder. Then I remembered the war-horn and all that it meant.

"Off you go," I said, "we are ambushed by Kaffirs."

We were indeed, for as we tailed down that kloof, from the top of both cliffs above us came a continuous but luckily ill-directed fire. Lead-coated stones, pot legs and bullets whirred and whistled all round us, yet until the last, just when we were reaching the tree to which we had tied our horses, quite harmlessly. Then suddenly I saw Anscombe begin to limp. Still he managed to run on and mount, though I observed that he did not put his right foot into the stirrup.

"What's the matter?" I asked as we galloped off.

"Shot through the instep, I think," he answered with a laugh, "but it doesn't hurt a bit."

"I expect it will later," I replied. "Meanwhile, thank God it wasn't at the top of the kloof. They won't catch us on the horses, which they never thought of killing first."

"They are going to try though. Look behind you."

I looked and saw twenty or thirty men emerging from the mouth of the kloof in pursuit.

"No time to stop to get those horns," he said with a sigh.

"No," I answered, "unless you are particularly anxious to say good-bye to the world pinned over a broken ant-heap in the sun, or something pleasant of the sort."

Then we rode on in silence, I thinking what a fool I had been first to allow myself to be overruled by Anscombe and cross the river, and secondly not to have taken warning from that war-horn. We could not go very fast because of the difficult and swampy nature of the ground; also the great heat of the day told on the horses. Thus it came about that when we reached the ford we were not more than ten minutes ahead of our active pursuers, good runners every one of them, and accustomed to the country. I suppose that they had orders to kill or capture us at any cost, for instead of giving up the chase, as I hoped they would, they stuck to us in surprising fashion.

We splashed through the river, and luckily on the further bank were met by Footsack who had seen us coming and guessed that something was wrong.

"Inspan!" I shouted to him, "and be quick about it if you want to see tomorrow's light. The Basutos are after us."

Off he went like a shot, his face quite green with fear.

"Now," I said to Anscombe, as we let our horses take a drink for which they were mad, "we have got to hold this ford until the wagon is ready, or those devils will get us after all. Dismount and I'll tie up the horses."

He did so with some difficulty, and at my suggestion, while I made the beasts fast, cut the lace of his boot which was full of blood, and soaked his wounded foot, that I had no time to examine, in the cool water. These things done, I helped him to the rear of a thorn tree which was thick enough to shield most of his body, and took my own stand behind a similar thorn at a distance of a few paces.

Presently the Basutos appeared, trotting along close together whereon Anscombe, who was seated behind the tree, fired both barrels of his Express at them at a range of about two hundred yards. It was a foolish thing to do, first because he missed them clean, for he had over-estimated the range and the bullets went above their heads, and secondly because it caused them to scatter and made them careful, whereas had they come on in a lump we could have taught them a lesson. However I said nothing, as I knew that reproaches would only make him nervous. Down went those scoundrels on to their hands and knees and, taking cover behind stones and bushes on the further bank, began to fire at us, for they were all armed with guns of one sort and another, and there was only about a hundred yards of water between us. As they effected this manoeuvre I am glad to say I was able to get two of them, while Anscombe, I think, wounded another.

After this our position grew quite warm, for as I have said the thorn trunks were not very broad, and three or four of the natives, who had probably been hunters, were by no means bad shots, though the rest of them fired wildly. Anscombe, in poking his head round the tree to shoot, had his hat knocked off by a bullet, while a slug went through the lappet of my coat. Then a worse thing happened. Either by chance or design Anscombe's horse was struck in the neck and fell struggling, whereon my beast, growing frightened, broke its riem and galloped to the wagon. That is where I ought to have left them at first, only I thought that we might need them to make a bolt on, or to carry Anscombe if he could not walk.

Quite a long while went by before, glancing behind me, I saw that the oxen that had been grazing at a little distance had at length arrived and were being inspanned in furious haste. The Basutos saw it also, and fearing lest we should escape, determined to try to end the business. Suddenly they leapt from their cover, and with more courage than I should have expected of them, rushed into the river, proposing to storm us, which, to speak truth, I think they would have done had I not been a fairly quick shot.

As it was, finding that they were losing too heavily from our fire, they retreated in a hurry, leaving their dead behind them, and even a wounded man who was clinging to a rock. He, poor wretch, was in mortal terror lest we should shoot him again, which I had not the heart to do, although as his leg was shattered above the knee by an Express bullet, it might have been true kindness. Again and again he called out for mercy, saying that he only attacked us because his chief, who had been warned of our coming "by the White Man," ordered him to take our guns and cattle.

"What white man?" I shouted. "Speak or I shoot."

There was no answer, for at this moment he fainted from loss of blood and vanished beneath the water. Then another Basuto, I suppose he was their captain, but do not know for he was hidden in some bushes, called out—

"Do not think that you shall escape, White Men. There are many more of our people coming, and we will kill you in the night when you cannot see to shoot us."

At this moment, too, Footsack shouted that the wagon was inspanned and ready. Now I hesitated what to do. If we made for the wagon, which must be very slowly because of Anscombe's wounded foot, we had to cross seventy or eighty yards of rising ground almost devoid of cover. If, on the other hand, we stayed where we were till nightfall a shot might catch one of us, or other Basutos might arrive and rush us. There was also a third possibility, that our terrified servants might trek off and leave us in order to save their own lives, which verily I believe they would have done, not being of Zulu blood. I put the problem to Anscombe, who shook his head and looked at his foot. Then he produced a lucky penny which he carried in his pocket and said—

"Let us invoke the Fates. Heads we run like heroes; tails we stay here like heroes," and he spun the penny, while I stared at him open-mouthed and not without admiration.

Never, I thought to myself, had this primitive method of cutting a gordian knot been resorted to in such strange and urgent circumstances.

"Heads it is!" he said coolly. "Now, my boy, do you run and I'll crawl after you. If I don't arrive, you know my people's address, and I bequeath to you all my African belongings in memory of a most pleasant trip."

"Don't play the fool," I replied sternly. "Come, put your right arm round my neck and hop on your left leg as you never hopped before."

Then we started, and really our transit was quite lively, for all those Basutos began what for them was rapid firing. I think, however, that their best shots must have fallen, for not a bullet touched us, although before we got out of their range one or two went very near.

"There," said Anscombe, as a last amazing hop brought him to the wagon rail, "there, you see how wise it is give Providence a chance sometimes."

"In the shape of a lucky penny," I grumbled as I hoisted him up.

"Certainly, for why should not Providence inhabit a penny as much as it does any other mundane thing? Oh, my dear Quatermain, have you never been taught to look to the pence and let the rest take care of itself?"

"Stop talking rubbish and look to your foot, for the wagon is starting," I replied.

Then off we went at a good round trot, for never have I seen oxen more scientifically driven than they were by Footsack and his friends on this occasion, or a greater pace got out of them. As soon as we reached a fairly level piece of ground I made Anscombe lie down on the cartel of the wagon and examined his wound as well as circumstances would allow. I found that the bullet or whatever the missile may have been, had gone through his right instep just beneath the big sinew, but so far as I could judge without injuring any bone. There was nothing to be done except rub in some carbolic ointment, which fortunately he had in his medicine chest, and bind up the wound as best I could with a clean handkerchief, after which I tied a towel, that was not clean, over the whole foot.

By this time evening was coming on, so we ate of such as we had with us, which we needed badly enough, without stopping the wagon. I remember that it consisted of cheese and hard biscuits. At dark we were obliged to halt a little by a stream until the moon rose, which fortunately she did very soon, as she was only just past her full. As soon as she was up we started again, and with a breathing space or two, trekked all that night, which I spent seated on the after part of the wagon and keeping a sharp look out, while, notwithstanding the roughness of the road and his hurt, Anscombe slept like a child upon the cartel inside.

I was very tired, so tired that the fear of surprise was the only thing that kept me awake, and I recall reflecting in a stupid kind of way, that it seemed always to have been my lot in life to watch thus, in one sense or another, while others slept.

The night passed somehow without anything happening, and at dawn we halted for a while to water the oxen, which we did with buckets, and let them eat what grass they could reach from their yokes, since we did not dare to outspan them. Just as we were starting on again the voortrekker, whom I had set to watch at a little distance, ran up with his eyes bulging out of his head, and reported that he had seen a Basuto with an assegai hanging about in the bush, as though to keep touch with us, after which we delayed no more.

All that day we blundered on, thrashing the weary cattle that at every halt tried to lie down, and by nightfall came to the outspan near to the house called the Temple, where we had met the Kaffirs returning from the diamond fields. This journey we had accomplished in exactly half the time it had taken on the outward trip. Here we were obliged to stop, as our team must have rest and food. So we outspanned and slept that night without much fear, since I thought it most improbable that the Basutos would attempt to follow us so far, as we were now within a day's trek of Pilgrim's Rest, whither we proposed to proceed on the morrow. But that is just where I made a mistake.

CHAPTER IV

DOCTOR RODD

I did get a little sleep that night, with one eye open, but before dawn I was up again seeing to the feeding of our remaining horse with some mealies that we carried, and other matters. The oxen we had been obliged to unyoke that they might fill themselves with grass and water, since otherwise I feared that we should never get them on to their feet again. As it was, the poor brutes were so tired that some of them could scarcely eat, and all lay down at the first opportunity.

Having awakened Footsack and the other boys that they might be ready to take advantage of the light when it came, for I was anxious to be away, I drank a nip of Hollands and water and ate a biscuit, making Anscombe do the same. Coffee would have been more acceptable, but I thought it wiser not to light a fire for fear of showing our whereabouts.

Now a faint glimmer in the east told me that the dawn was coming. Just by the wagon grew a fair-sized, green-leaved tree, and as it was quite easy to climb even by starlight, up it I went so as to get above the ground mist and take a look round before we trekked. Presently the sky grew pearly and light began to gather; then the edge of the sun appeared, throwing long level rays across the world. Everywhere the mist lay dense as cotton wool, except at one spot about a mile behind us where there was a little hill or rather a wave of the ground, over which we had trekked upon the preceding evening. The top of this rise was above mist level, and on it no trees grew because the granite came to the surface. Having discovered nothing, I called to the boys to drive up the oxen, some of which had risen and were eating again, and prepared to descend from my tree.

As I did so, out of the corner of my eye I caught sight of something that glittered far away, so far that it would only have attracted the notice of a trained hunter. Yes, something was shining on the brow of the rise of which I have spoken. I stared at it through my glasses and saw what I had feared to see. A body of natives was crossing the rise and the glitter was caused by the rays of dawn striking on their spears and gun-barrels.

I came down out of that tree like a frightened wild cat and ran to the wagon, thinking hard as I went. The Basutos were after us, meaning to attack as soon as there was sufficient light. In ten minutes or less they would be here. There was no time to inspan the oxen, and even if there had been, stiff and weary as the beasts were, we should be overtaken before we had gone a hundred yards on that bad road. What then was to be done? Run for it? It was impossible, Anscombe could not run. My eye fell upon the horse munching the last of his mealies.

"Footsack," I said as quietly as I could, "never mind about inspanning yet, but saddle up the horse. Be quick now."

He looked at me doubtfully, but obeyed, having seen nothing. If he had seen I knew that he would have been off. I nipped round to the end of the wagon, calling to the other two boys to let the oxen be a while and come to me.

"Now, Anscombe," I said, "hand out the rifles and cartridges. Don't stop to ask questions, but do what I tell you. They are on the rack by your side. So. Now put on your revolver and let me help you down. Man, don't forget your hat."

He obeyed quickly enough, and presently was standing on one leg by my side, looking cramped and tottery.

"The Basutos are on us," I said.

He whistled and remarked something about Chapter No. 2.

"Footsack," I called, "bring the horse here; the Baas wishes to ride a little to ease his leg."

He did so, stopping a moment to pull the second girth tight. Then we helped Anscombe into the saddle.

"Which way?" he asked.

I looked at the long slope in front of us. It was steep and bad going. Anscombe might get up it on the horse before the Kaffirs overtook us, but it was extremely problematical if we could do so. I might perhaps if I mounted behind him and the horse could bear us both, which was doubtful, but how about our poor servants? He saw the doubt upon my face and said in his quiet way,

"You may remember that our white-bearded friend told us to make straight for his place in case of any difficulty with the Basutos. It seems to have arisen."

"I know he did," I answered, "but I cannot make up my mind which is the more dangerous, Marnham or the Basutos. I rather think that he set them on to us."

"It is impossible to solve problems at this hour of the morning, Quatermain, and there is no time to toss. So I vote for the Temple."

"It seems our best chance. At any rate that's your choice, so let's go."

Then I sang out to the Kaffirs, "The Basutos are on us. We go to Tampel for refuge. Run!"

My word! they did run. I never saw athletes make better time over the first quarter of a mile. We ran, too, or at least the horse did, I hanging on to the stirrup and Anscombe holding both the rifles beneath his arm. But the beast was tired, also blown out with that morning feed of mealies, so our progress was not very fast. When we were about two hundred yards from the wagon I looked back and saw the Basutos beginning to arrive. They saw us also, and uttering a sort of whistling war cry, started in pursuit.

After this we had quite an interesting time. I scrambled on to the horse behind Anscombe, whereon that intelligent animal, feeling the double weight, reduced its pace proportionately, to a slow tripple, indeed, out of which it could not be persuaded to move. So I slipped off again over its tail and we went on as before. Meanwhile the Basutos, very active fellows, were coming up. By this time the yellow-wood grove in the swamp, of which I have already written, was close to us, and it became quite a question which of us would get there first (I may mention that Footsack & Co. had already attained its friendly shelter). Anscombe kicked the horse with his sound heel and I thumped it with my fist, thereby persuading it to a hand gallop.

As we reached the outlying trees of the wood the first Basuto, a lank fellow with a mouth like a rat trap, arrived and threw an assegai at us which passed between Anscombe's back and my nose. Then he closed and tried to stab with another assegai. I could do nothing, but Anscombe showed himself cleverer than I expected. Dropping the reins, he drew his pistol and managed to send a bullet through that child of nature's head, so that he went down like a stone.

"And you tell me I am a bad shot," he drawled.

"It was a fluke," I gasped, for even in these circumstances truth would prevail.

"Wait and you'll see," he replied, re-cocking the revolver.

As a matter of fact there was no need for more shooting, since at the verge of the swamp the Basutos pulled up. I do not think that the death of their companion caused them to do this, for they seemed to take no notice of him. It was as though they had reached some boundary which they knew it would not be lawful for them to pass. They simply stopped, took the dead man's assegai and shield from the body and walked quietly back towards the wagon, leaving him where he lay. The horse stopped also, or rather proceeded at a walk.

"There!" exclaimed Anscombe. "Did I not tell you I had a presentiment that I should kill a man in this accursed wood?"

"Yes," I said as soon as I had recovered my breath, "but you mixed up a woman with the matter and I don't see one."

"That's true," he replied, "I hope we shan't meet her later."

Then we went on as quickly as we could, which was not very fast, for I feared lest the Basutos should change their minds and follow us. As the risk of this became less our spirits rose, since if we had lost the wagon and the oxen, at least we had saved our lives, which was almost more than we could have expected in the circumstances. At last we came to that glade where we had killed the wildebeeste not a week before. There lay its skeleton picked clean by the great brown kites that frequent the bush-veld, some of which still sat about in the trees.

"Well, I suppose we must go on to Tampel," said Anscombe rather faintly, for I could see that his wound was giving him a good deal of pain.

As he spoke from round the tree whence he had first emerged, appeared Mr. Marnham, riding the same horse and wearing the same clothes. The only difference between his two entries was that the first took place in the late evening and the second in the early morning.

"So here you are again," he said cheerfully.

"Yes," I answered, "and it is strange to meet you at the same spot. Were you expecting us?"

"Not more than I expect many things," he replied with a shrewd glance at me, adding, "I always rise with the sun, and thinking that I heard a shot fired in the distance, came to see what was happening. The Basutos attacked you at daybreak, did they not?"

"They did, but how did you know that, Mr. Marnham?"

"Your servants told me. I met them running to the house looking very frightened. You are wounded, Mr. Anscombe?"

"Yes, a couple of days ago on the border of Sekukuni's country where the natives tried to murder us."

"Ah!" he replied without surprise. "I warned you the trip was dangerous, did I not? Well, come on home where my partner, Rodd, who luckily has had medical experience, will attend to you. Mr. Quatermain can tell me the story as we go."

So we went on up the long slope, I relating our adventures, to which Mr. Marnham listened without comment.

"I expect that the Kaffirs will have looted the wagon and be on the way home with your oxen by now," he said when I had finished.

"Are you not afraid that they will follow us here?" I asked.

"Oh no, Mr. Quatermain. We do business with these people, also they sometimes come to be doctored by Rodd when they are sick, so this place is sacred ground to them. They stopped hunting you when they got to the Yellow-wood swamp where our land begins, did they not?"

"Yes, but now I want to hunt them. Can you give me any help? Those oxen are tired out and footsore, so we might be able to catch them up."

He shook his head. "We have very few people here, and by the time that you could get assistance from the Camp at Barberton, if the Commandant is able and willing to give you any, which I rather doubt, they will be far away. Moreover," he added, dropping his voice, "let us come to an understanding. You are most welcome to any help or hospitality that I can offer, but if you wish to do more fighting I must ask you to go elsewhere. As I have told you, we are peaceful men who trade with these people, and do not wish to be involved in a quarrel with them, which might expose us to attack or bring us into trouble with the British Government which has annexed but not conquered their country. Do I make myself clear?"

"Perfectly. While we are with you we will do nothing, but afterwards we hold ourselves at liberty to act as we think best."

"Quite so. Meanwhile I hope that you and Mr. Anscombe will make yourselves comfortable with us for as long as you like."

In my own mind I came to the conclusion that this would be for the shortest time possible, but I only said—

"It is most kind of you to take in complete strangers thus. No, not complete," I added, looking towards Anscombe who was following on the tired horse a few paces behind, "for you knew his father, did you not?"

"His father?" he said, lifting his eyebrows. "No. Oh! I remember, I said something to that effect the other night, but it was a mistake. I mixed up two names, as one often does after a lapse of many years."

"I understand," I answered, but remembering Anscombe's story I reflected to myself that our venerable host was an excellent liar. Or more probably he meant to convey that he wished the subject of his youthful reminiscences to be taboo.

Just then we reached the house which had a pretty patch of well-kept flower-garden in front of it, surrounded by a fence covered with wire netting to keep out buck. By the gate squatted our three retainers, looking very blown and rather ashamed of themselves.

"Your master wishes to thank you for your help in a dark hour, Footsack, and I wish to congratulate you all upon the swiftness of your feet," I said in Dutch.

"Oh! Baas, the Basutos were many and their spears are sharp," he began apologetically.

"Be silent, you running dog," I said, "and go help your master to dismount."

Then we went through the gate, Anscombe leaning on my shoulder and on that of Mr. Marnham, and up the path which was bordered with fences of the monthly rose, towards the house. Really this was almost as charming to look at near at hand as it had been from far away. Of course the whole thing was crude in detail. Rough, half-shaped blocks of marble from the neighbouring quarry had been built into walls and columns. Nothing was finished, and considered bit by bit all was coarse and ugly. Yet the general effect was beautiful because it was an effect of design, the picture of an artist who did not fully understand the technicalities of painting, the work of a great writer who had as yet no proper skill in words. Never did I see a small building that struck me more. But then what experience have I of buildings, and, as Anscombe reminded me afterwards, it was but a copy of something designed when the world was young, or rather when civilization was young, and man new risen from the infinite ages of savagery, saw beauty in his dreams and tried to symbolize it in shapes of stone.

We came to the broad stoep, to which several rough blocks of marble served as steps. On it in a long chair made of native wood and seated with hide rimpis, sat or rather lolled a man in a dressing-gown who was reading a book. He raised himself as we came and the light of the sun, for the verandah faced to the east, shone full upon his face, so that I saw him well. It was that of a man of something under forty years of age, dark, powerful, and weary—not a good face, I thought. Indeed, it gave me the impression of one who had allowed the evil which exists in the nature of all of us to become his master, or had even encouraged it to do so.

In the Psalms and elsewhere we are always reading of the righteous and the unrighteous until those terms grow wearisome. It is only of late years that I have discovered, or think that I have discovered, what they mean. Our lives cannot be judged by our deeds; they must be judged by our desires or rather by our moral attitude. It is not what we do so much as what we try to do that counts in the formation of character. All fall short, all fail, but in the end those who seek to climb out of the pit, those who strive, however vainly, to fashion failure to success, are, by comparison, the righteous, while those who are content to wallow in our native mire and to glut themselves with the daily bread of vice, are the unrighteous. To turn our backs thereon wilfully and without cause, is the real unforgiveable sin against the Spirit. At least that is the best definition of the problem at which I in my simplicity can arrive.

Such thoughts have often occurred to me in considering the character of Dr. Rodd and some others whom I have known; indeed the germ of them arose in my mind which, being wearied at the time and therefore somewhat vacant, was perhaps the more open to external impressions, as I looked upon the face of this stranger on the stoep. Moreover, as I am proud to record, I did not judge him altogether wrongly. He was a blackguard who, under other influences or with a few added grains of self-restraint and of the power of recovery, might have become a good or even a saintly man. But by some malice of Fate or some evil inheritance from an unknown past, those grains were lacking, and therefore he went not up but down the hill.

"Case for you, Rodd," called out Marnham.

"Indeed," he answered, getting to his feet and speaking in a full voice, which, like his partner's, was that of an educated Englishman. "What's the matter. Horse accident?"

Then we were introduced, and Anscombe began to explain his injury.

"Um!" said the doctor, studying him with dark eyes. "Kaffir bullet through the foot some days ago. Ought to be attended to at once. Also you look pretty done, so don't tire yourself with the story, which I can get from Mr. Quatermain. Come and lie down and I'll have a look at you while they are cooking breakfast."

Then he guided us to a room of which the double French windows opened on to the stoep, a very pretty room with two beds in it. Making Anscombe lie down on one of these he turned up his trouser, undid my rough bandage and examined the wound.

"Painful?" he asked.

"Very," answered Anscombe, "right up to the thigh."

After this he drew off the nether garments and made a further examination.

"Um," he said again, "I must syringe this out. Stay still while I get some stuff."

I followed him from the room, and when we were out of hearing on the stoep inquired what he thought. I did not like the look of that leg.

"It is very bad," he answered, "so bad that I am wondering if it wouldn't be best to remove the limb below the knee and make it a job. You can see for yourself that it is septic and the inflammation is spreading up rapidly."

"Good Heavens!" I exclaimed, "do you fear mortification?"

He nodded. "Can't say what was on that slug or bit of old iron and he hasn't had the best chance since. Mortification, or tetanus, or both, are more than possible. Is he a temperate man?"

"So far as I know," I answered, and stared at him while he thought. Then he said with decision,

"That makes a difference. To lose a foot is a serious thing; some might think almost as bad as death. I'll give him a chance, but if those symptoms do not abate in twenty-four hours, I must operate. You needn't be afraid, I was house surgeon at a London Hospital—once, and I keep my hand in. Lucky you came straight here."

Having made his preparations and washed his hands, he returned, syringed the wound with some antiseptic stuff, and dressed and bandaged the leg up to the knee. After this he gave Anscombe hot milk to drink, with two eggs broken into it, and told him to rest a while as he must not eat anything solid at present. Then he threw a blanket over him, and, signing to me to come away, let down a mat over the window.

"I put a little something into that milk," he said outside, "which will send him to sleep for a few hours. So we will leave him quiet. Now you'll want a wash."

"Where are you going to take Mr. Quatermain?" asked Marnham who was seated on the stoep.

"Into my room," he answered.

"Why? There's Heda's ready."

"Heda might return at any moment," replied the doctor. "Also Mr. Quatermain had better sleep in Mr. Anscombe's room. He will very likely want some one to look after him at night."

Marnham opened his mouth to speak again, then changed his mind and was silent, as a servant is silent under rebuke. The incident was quite trifling, yet it revealed to me the relative attitude of these two men. Without a doubt Rodd was the master of his partner, who did not even care to dispute with him about the matter of the use of his daughter's bedroom. They were a queer couple who, had it not been for my anxiety as to Anscombe's illness, would have interested me very much, as indeed they were destined to do.

Well, I went to tidy up in the doctor's room, and as he left me alone while I washed, had the opportunity of studying it a little. Like the rest of the house it was lined with native wood which was made to serve as the backs of bookshelves and of cupboards filled with medicines and instruments. The books formed a queer collection. There were medical works, philosophical works, histories, novels, most of them French, and other volumes of a sort that I imagine are generally kept under lock and key; also some that had to do with occult matters. There was even a Bible. I opened it thoughtlessly, half in idle curiosity, to see whether it was ever used, only to replace it in haste. For at the very page that my eye fell on, I remember it was one of my favourite chapters in Isaiah, was a stamp in violet ink marked H. M.'s Prison—well, I won't say where.

I may state, however, that the clue enabled me in after years to learn an episode in this man's life which had brought about his ruin. There is no need to repeat it or to say more than that gambling and an evil use of his medical knowledge to provide the money to pay his debts, were the cause of his fall. The strange thing is that he should have kept the book which had probably been given to him by the prison chaplain. Still everybody makes mistakes sometimes. Or it may have had associations for him, and of course he had never seen this stamp upon an unread page, which happened to leap to my eye.

Now I was able to make a shrewd guess at his later career. After his trouble he had emigrated and began to practise in South Africa. Somehow his identity had been discovered; his past was dragged up against him, possibly by rivals jealous of his skill; his business went and he found it advisable to retire to the Transvaal before the Annexation, at that time the home of sundry people of broken repute. Even there he did not stop in a town, but hid himself upon the edge of savagery. Here he foregathered with another man of queer character, Marnham, and in his company entered upon some doubtful but lucrative form of trade while still indulging his love of medicine by doctoring and operating upon natives, over whom he would in this way acquire great influence. Indeed, as I discovered before the day was over, he had quite a little hospital at the back of the house in which were four or five beds occupied by Kaffirs and served by two male native nurses whom he had trained. Also numbers of out-patients visited him, some of whom travelled from great distances, and occasionally, but not often, he attended white people who chanced to be in the neighbourhood.

The three of us breakfasted in a really charming room from the window of which could be studied a view as beautiful as any I know. The Kaffirs who waited were well trained and dressed in neat linen uniforms. The cooking was good; there was real silver on the table, then a strange sight in that part of Africa, and amongst engravings and other pictures upon the walls, hung an oil portrait of a very beautiful young woman with dark hair and eyes.

"Is that your daughter, Mr. Marnham?" I asked.

"No," he replied rather shortly, "it is her mother."

Immediately afterwards he was called from the room to speak to some one, whereon the doctor said—

"A foreigner as you see, a Hungarian; the Hungarian women are very good looking and very charming."

"So I have understood," I answered, "but does this lady live here?"

"Oh, no. She is dead, or I believe that she is dead. I am not sure, because I make it a rule never to pry into people's private affairs. All I know about her is that she was a beauty whom Marnham married late in life upon the Continent when she was but eighteen. As is common in such cases he was very jealous of her, but it didn't last long, as she died, or I understand that she died, within a year of her daughter's birth. The loss affected him so much that he emigrated to South Africa with the child and began life anew. I do not think that they correspond with Hungary, and he never speaks of her even to his daughter, which suggests that she is dead."

I reflected that all these circumstances might equally well suggest several other things, but said nothing, thinking it wisest not to pursue the subject. Presently Marnham returned and informed me that a native had just brought him word that the Basutos had made off homeward with our cattle, but had left the wagon and its contents quite untouched, not even stealing the spare guns and ammunition.

"That's luck," I said, astonished, "but extremely strange. How do you explain it, Mr. Marnham?"

He shrugged his shoulders and answered—

"As every one knows, you are a much greater expert in native habits and customs than I am, Mr. Quatermain."

"There are only two things that I can think of," I said. "One is that for some reason or other they thought the wagon tagati, bewitched you know, and that it would bring evil on them to touch it, though this did not apply to the oxen. The other is that they supposed it, but not the oxen, to belong to some friend of their own whose property they did not wish to injure."

He looked at me sharply but said nothing, and I went on to tell them the details of the attack that had been made upon us, adding—

"The odd part of the affair is that one of those Basutos called out to us that some infernal scoundrel of a white had warned Sekukuni of our coming and that he had ordered them to take our guns and cattle. This Basuto, who was wounded and praying for mercy, was drowned before he could tell me who the white man was."

"A Boer, I expect," said Marnham quietly. "As you know they are not particularly well affected towards us English just now. Also I happen to be aware that some of them are intriguing with Sekukuni against the British through Makurupiji, his 'Mouth' or prime-minister, a very clever old scamp who likes to have two stools to sit on."

"And doubtless will end by falling between them. Well, you see, now that I think of it, the wounded Kaffir only said that they were ordered to take our guns and oxen, and incidentally our lives. The wagon was not mentioned."

"Quite so, Mr. Quatermain. I will send some of our boys to help your servants to bring everything it contains up here."

"Can't you lend me a team of oxen," I asked, "to drag it to the house?"

"No, we have nothing but young cattle left. Both red-water and lung-sickness have been so bad this season that all the horned stock have been swept out of the country. I doubt whether you could beg, borrow or steal a team of oxen this side of Pretoria, except from some of the Dutchmen who won't part."

"That's awkward. I hoped to be able to trek in a day or two."

"Your friend won't be able to trek for a good many days at the best," broke in the doctor, who had been listening unconcernedly, "but of course you could get away on the horse after it has rested."

"You told me you left a span of oxen at Pretoria," said Marnham. "Why not go and fetch them here, or if you don't like to leave Mr. Anscombe, send your driver and the boys."

"Thanks for the idea. I will think it over," I answered.

That morning after Footsack and the voorlooper had been sent with some of the servants from the Temple to fetch up the contents of the wagon, for I was too tired to accompany them, having found that Anscombe was still asleep, I determined to follow his example. Finding a long chair on the stoep, I sat down and slumbered in it sweetly for hours. I dreamt of all sorts of things, then through my dreams it seemed to me that I heard two voices talking, those of our Marnham and Rodd, not on the stoep, but at a distance from it. As a matter of fact they were talking, but so far away that in my ordinary waking state I could never have heard them. My own belief is that the senses, and I may add the semi-spiritual part of us, are much more acute when we lie half bound in the bonds of sleep, than when we are what is called wide awake. Doubtless when we are quite bound they attain the limits of their power and, I think, sail at times to the uttermost ends of being. But unhappily of their experiences we remember nothing when we awake. In half sleep it is different; then we do retain some recollection.

In this curious condition of mind it seemed to me that Rodd said to Marnham—

"Why have you brought these men here?"

"I did not bring them here," he answered. "Luck, Fate, Fortune, God or the Devil, call it what you will, brought them here, though if you had your wish, it is true they would never have come. Still, as they have come, I am glad. It is something to me, living in this hell, to get a chance of talking to English gentlemen again before I die."

"English gentlemen," remarked Rodd reflectively, "Well, Anscombe is of course, but how about that other hunter? After all, in what way is he better than the scores of other hunters and Kaffir traders and wanderers whom one meets in this strange land?"

"In what way indeed?" thought I to myself, in my dream.

"If you can't see, I can't explain to you. But as I happen to know, the man is of blood as good as mine—and a great deal better than yours," he added with a touch of insolence. "Moreover, he has an honest name among white and black, which is much in this country."

"Yes," replied the doctor in the same reflective voice, "I agree with you, I let him pass as a gentleman. But I repeat, Why did you bring them here when with one more word it would have been so easy—" and he stopped.

"I have told you, it was not I. What are you driving at?"

"Do you think it is exactly convenient, especially when we are under the British flag again, to have two people who, we both admit, are English gentlemen, that is, clean, clear-eyed men, considering us and our affairs for an indefinite period, just because you wish for the pleasure of their society? Would it not have been better to tell those Basutos to let them trek on to Pretoria?"

"I don't know what would have been better. I repeat, what are you driving at?

"Heda is coming home in a day or two; she might be here any time," remarked Rodd as he knocked the ashes out of his pipe.

"Yes, because you made me write and say that I wanted her. But what of that?"

"Nothing in particular, except that I am not sure that I wish her to associate with 'an English gentleman' like this Anscombe."

Marnham laughed scornfully. "Ah! I understand," he said. "Too clean and straight. Complications might ensue and the rest of it. Well, I wish to God they would, for I know the Anscombes, or used to, and I know the genus called Rodd."

"Don't be insulting; you may carry the thing too far one day, and whatever I have done I have paid for. But you've not paid—yet."

"The man is very ill. You are a skilled doctor. If you're afraid of him, why don't you kill him?" asked Marnham with bitter scorn.

"There you have me," replied Rodd. "Men may shed much, but most of them never shed their professional honour. I shall do my honest best to cure Mr. Anscombe, and I tell you that he will take some curing."

Then I woke up, and as no one was in sight, wondered whether or no I had been dreaming. The upshot of it was that I made up my mind to send Footsack to Pretoria for the oxen, not to go myself.

CHAPTER V

A GAME OF CARDS

I slept in Anscombe's room that night and looked after him. He was very feverish and the pain in his leg kept him awake a good deal. He told me that he could not bear Dr. Rodd and wished to get away at once. I had to explain to him that this was impossible until his spare oxen arrived which I was going to send for to Pretoria, but of other matters, including that of the dangerous state of his foot, I said nothing. I was thankful when towards two in the morning, he fell into a sound sleep and allowed me to do the same.

Before breakfast time, just as I had finished dressing myself in some of the clean things which had been brought from the wagon, Rodd came and made a thorough and business-like examination of his patient, while I awaited the result with anxiety on the stoep. At length he appeared and said—

"Well, I think that we shall be able to save the foot, though I can't be quite sure for another twenty-four hours. The worst symptoms have abated and his temperature is down by two degrees. Anyway he will have to stay in bed and live on light food till it is normal, after which he might lie in a long chair on the stoep. On no account must he attempt to stand."

I thanked him for his information heartily enough and asked him if he knew where Marnham was, as I wanted to speak to him with reference to the despatch of Footsack to fetch the oxen from Pretoria.

"Not up yet, I think," he answered. "I fancy that yesterday was one of his 'wet' nights, excitement of meeting strangers and so on."

"Wet nights?" I queried, wishing for a clearer explanation.

"Yes, he is a grand old fellow, one of the best, but like most other people he has his little weaknesses, and when the fit is on him he can put away a surprising amount of liquor. I tell you so that you should not be astonished if you notice anything, or try to argue with him when he is in that state, as then his temper is apt to be—well, lively. Now I must go and give him a pint of warm milk; that is his favourite antidote, and in fact the best there is."

I thought to myself that we had struck a nice establishment in which to be tied, literally by the leg, for an indefinite period. I was not particularly flush at the time, but I know I would have paid a £100 to be out of it; before the end I should have been glad to throw in everything that I had. But mercifully that was hidden from me.

Rodd and I breakfasted together and discoursed of Kaffir customs, as to which he was singularly well informed. Then I accompanied him to see his native patients in the little hospital of which I have spoken. Believing the man to be a thorough scamp as I did, it was astonishing to me to note how gentle and forbearing he was to these people. Of his skill I need say nothing, as that was evident. He was going to perform an internal operation upon a burly old savage, rather a serious one I believe; at any rate it necessitated chloroform. He asked me if I would like to assist, but I declined respectfully, having no taste for such things. So I left him boiling his instruments and putting on what looked like a clean nightgown over his clothes, and returned to the stoep.

Here I found Marnham, whose eyes were rather bloodshot, though otherwise, except for a shaky hand, he seemed right enough. He murmured something about having overslept himself and inquired very politely, for his manners were beautiful, after Anscombe and as to whether we were quite comfortable and so forth. After this I consulted him as to the best road for our servants to travel by to Pretoria, and later on despatched them, giving Footsack various notes to ensure the delivery of the oxen to him. Also I gave him some money to pay for their keep and told him with many threats to get back with the beasts as quick as he could travel. Then I sent him and the two other boys off, not without misgivings, although he was an experienced man in his way and promised faithfully to fulfil every injunction to the letter. To me he seemed so curiously glad to go that I inquired the reason, since after a journey like ours, it would have been more natural if he had wished to rest.

"Oh! Baas," he said, "I don't think this Tampel very healthy for coloured people. I am told of some who have died here. That man Karl who gave me the diamond, I think he must have died also, at least I saw his spook last night standing over me and shaking his head, and the boys saw it too."

"Oh! be off with your talk of spooks," I said, "and come back quickly with those oxen, or I promise you that you will die and be a spook yourself."

"I will, Baas, I will!" he ejaculated and departed almost at a run, leaving me rather uncomfortable.

I believed nothing of the tale of the spook of Karl, but I saw that Footsack believed in it, and was afraid lest he might be thereby prevented from returning. I would much rather have gone myself, but it was impossible for me to leave Anscombe so ill in the hands of our strange hosts. And there was no one else whom I could send. I might perhaps have ridden to Pilgrim's Rest and tried to find a white messenger there; indeed afterwards I regretted not having done so, although it would have involved at least a day's absence at a very critical time. But the truth is I never thought of it until too late, and probably if I had, I should not have been able to discover anyone whom I could trust.

As I walked back to the house, having parted from Footsack on the top of a neighbouring ridge whence I could point out his path to him, I met Marnham riding away. He pulled up and said that he was going down to the Granite stream to arrange about setting some one up to watch the wagon. I expressed sorrow that he should have the trouble, which should have been mine if I could have got away, whereon he answered that he was glad of the opportunity for a ride, as it was something to do.

"How do you fill in your time here," I asked carelessly, "as you don't farm?"

"Oh! by trading," he replied, and with a nod set his horse to a canter.

A queer sort of trading, thought I to myself, where there is no store. Now what exactly does he trade in, I wonder?

As it happened I was destined to find out before I was an hour older. Having given Anscombe a look and found that he was comfortable, I thought that I would inspect the quarry whence the marble came of which the house was built, as it had occurred to me that if there was plenty of it, it might be worth exploiting some time in the future. It had been pointed out to me in the midst of some thorns in a gully that ran at right angles to the main kloof not more than a few hundred yards from the house. Following a path over which the stones had been dragged originally, I came to the spot and discovered that a little cavity had been quarried in what seemed to me to be a positive mountain of pure white marble. I examined the place as thoroughly as I could, climbing among some bushes that grew in surface earth which had been washed down from the top, in order to do so.

At the back of these bushes there was a hole large enough for a man to creep through. I crept through with the object of ascertaining whether the marble veins continued. To my surprise I found a stout yellow-wood door within feet of the mouth of the hole. Reflecting that no doubt it was here that the quarrymen kept, or had kept tools and explosives, I gave it a push. I suppose it had been left unfastened accidentally, or that something had gone wrong with the lock; at any rate it swung open. Pursuing my researches as to the depth of the marble I advanced boldly and, the place being dark, struck a match. Evidently the marble did continue, as I could see by the glittering roof of a cavern, for such it was. But the floor attracted my attention as well as the roof, for on it were numerous cases not unlike coffins, bearing the stamp of a well-known Birmingham firm, labelled "fencing iron" and addressed to Messrs. Marnham & Rodd, Transvaal, via Delagoa Bay.

I knew at once what they were, having seen the like before, but if any doubt remained in my mind it was easy to solve, for as it chanced one of the cases was open and half emptied. I slipped my hand into it. As I thought it contained the ordinary Kaffir gun of commerce, cost delivered in Africa, say 35s.; cost delivered to native chief in cash or cattle, say £10, which, when the market is eager, allows for a decent profit. Contemplating those cases, survivors probably of a much larger stock, I understood how it came about that Sekukuni had dared to show fight against the Government. Doubtless it was hence that the guns had come which sent a bullet through Anscombe's foot and nearly polished off both of us.

Moreover, as further matches showed me, that cave contained other stores—item, kegs of gunpowder; item, casks of cheap spirit; item, bars of lead, also a box marked "bullet moulds" and another marked "Percussion caps." I think, too, there were some innocent bags full of beads and a few packages of Birmingham-made assegai blades. There may have been other things, but if so I did not wait to investigate them. Gathering up the ends of my matches and, in case there should be any dust in the place that would show footmarks, flapping the stone floor behind me with my pocket handkerchief, I retired and continued my investigations of that wonderful marble deposit from the bottom of the quarry, to which, having re-arranged the bushes, I descended by another route, leaping like a buck from stone to stone.

It was just as well that I did so, for a few minutes later Dr. Rodd appeared.

"Made a good job of your operation?" I asked cheerfully.

"Pretty fair, thanks," he answered, "although that Kaffir tried to brain the nurse-man when he was coming out of the anesthetic. But are you interested in geology?"

"A little," I replied, "that is if there is any chance of making money out of it, which there ought to be here, as this marble looks almost as good as that of Carrara. But flint instruments are more my line, that is in an ignorant and amateur way, as I think they are in yours, for I saw some in your room. Tell me, what do you think of this. Is it a scraper?" and I produced a stone out of my pocket which I had found a week before in the bush-veld.

At once he forgot his suspicions, of which I could see he arrived very full indeed. This curious man, as it happened, was really fond of flint instruments, of which he knew a great deal.

"Did you find this here?" he asked.

I led him several yards further from the mouth of the cave and pointed out the exact spot where I said I had picked it up amongst some quarry debris. Then followed a most learned discussion, for it appeared that this was a flint instrument of the rarest and most valuable type, one that Noah might have used, or Job might have scraped himself with, and the question was how the dickens had it come among that quarry debris. In the end we left the problem undecided, and having presented the article to Dr. Rodd, a gift for which he thanked me with real warmth, I returned to the house filled with the glow that rewards one who has made a valuable discovery.

Of the following three days I have nothing particular to say, except that during them I was perhaps more acutely bored than ever I had been in my life before. The house was beautiful in its own fashion; the food was excellent; there was everything I could want to drink, and Rodd announced that he no longer feared the necessity of operation upon Anscombe's leg. His recovery was now a mere matter of time, and meanwhile he must not use his foot or let the blood run into it more than could be helped, which meant that he must keep himself in a recumbent position. The trouble was that I had nothing on earth do except study the characters of our hosts, which I found disagreeable and depressing. I might have gone out shooting, but nothing of the sort was allowed upon the property in obedience to the wish of Miss Heda, a mysterious young person who was always expected and never appeared, and beyond it I was afraid to travel for fear of Basutos. I might have gone to Pilgrim's Rest or Lydenburg to make report of the nefarious deeds of the said Basutos, but at best it would have taken one or two days, and possibly I should have been detained by officials who never consider any one's time except their own.

This meant that I should have been obliged to leave Anscombe alone, which I did not wish to do, so I just sat still and, as I have said, was intensely bored, hanging about the place and smoking more than was good for me.

In due course Anscombe emerged on to the stoep, where he lay with his leg up, and was also bored, especially after he had tried to pump old Marnham about his past in the Guards and completely failed. It was in this mood of utter dejection that we agreed to play a game of cards one evening. Not that either of us cared for cards; indeed, personally, I have always detested them because, with various-coloured counters to represent money which never passed, they had formed one of the afflictions of my youth.

It was so annoying if you won, to be handed a number of green counters and be informed that they represented so many hundreds or thousands of pounds, or vice-versa if you lost, for as it cost no one anything, my dear father insisted upon playing for enormous stakes. Never in any aspect of life have I cared for fooling. Anscombe also disliked cards, I think because his ancestors too had played with counters, such as some that I have seen belonging to the Cocoa-Tree Club and other gambling places of a past generation, marked as high as a thousand guineas, which counters must next morning be redeemed in hard cash, whereby his family had been not a little impoverished.

"I fancy you will find they are high-fliers," he said when the pair had left to fetch a suitable table, for the night being very hot we were going to play on the stoep by the light of the hanging paraffin lamp and some candles. I replied to the effect that I could not afford to lose large sums of money, especially to men who for aught I knew might then be engaged in marking the cards.

"I understand," he answered. "Don't you bother about that, old fellow. This is my affair, arranged for my special amusement. I shan't grumble if the fun costs something, for I am sure there will be fun."

"All right," I said, "only if we should happen to win money, it's yours, not mine."

To myself I reflected, however, that with these two opponents we had about as much chance of winning as a snowflake has of resisting the atmosphere of the lower regions.

Presently they returned with the table, which had a green cloth over it that hung down half-way to the ground. Also one of the native boys brought a tray with spirits, from which I judged by various signs, old Marnham, who had already drunk his share at dinner, had helped himself freely on the way. Soon we were arranged, Anscombe, who was to be my partner, opposite to me in his long chair, and the game began.

I forget what particular variant of cards it was we played, though I know it admitted of high and progressive stakes. At first, however, these were quite moderate and we won, as I suppose we were meant to do. After half an hour or so Marnham rose to help himself to brandy and water, a great deal of brandy and very little water, while I took a nip of Hollands, and Anscombe and Rodd filled their pipes.

"I think this is getting rather slow," said Rodd to Anscombe. "I vote we put a bit more on."

"As much as you like," answered Anscombe with a little drawl and twinkle of the eye, which always showed that he was amused. "Both Quatermain and I are born gamblers. Don't look angry, Quatermain, you know you are. Only if we lose you will have to take a cheque, for I have precious little cash."

"I think that will be good enough," replied the doctor quietly—"if you lose."

So the stakes were increased to an amount that made my hair stand up stiffer even than usual, and the game went on. Behold! a marvel came to pass. How it happened I do not know, unless Marnham had brought the wrong cards by mistake or had grown too fuddled to understand his partner's telegraphic signals, which I, being accustomed to observe, saw him make, not once but often, still we won! What is more, with a few set-backs, we went on winning, till presently the sums written down to our credit, for no actual cash passed, were considerable. And all the while, at the end of each bout Marnham helped himself to more brandy, while the doctor grew more mad in a suppressed-thunder kind of a way. For my part I became alarmed, especially as I perceived that Anscombe was on the verge of breaking into open merriment, and his legs being up I could not kick him under the table.

"My partner ought to go to bed. Don't you think we should stop?" I said.

"On the whole I do," replied Rodd, glowering at Marnham, who, somewhat unsteadily, was engaged in wiping drops of brandy from his long beard.

"D—d if I do," exclaimed that worthy. "When I was young and played with gentlemen they always gave losers an opportunity of revenge."

"Then," replied Anscombe with a flash of his eyes, "let us try to follow in the footsteps of the gentlemen with whom you played in your youth. I suggest that we double the stakes."

"That's right! That's the old form!" said Marnham.

The doctor half rose from his chair, then sat down again. Watching him, I concluded that he believed his partner, a seasoned vessel, was not so drunk as he pretended to be, and either in an actual or a figurative sense, had a card up his sleeve. If so, it remained there, for again we won; all the luck was with us.

"I am getting tired," drawled Anscombe. "Lemon and water are not sustaining. Shall we stop?"

"By Heaven! no," shouted Marnham, to which Anscombe replied that if it was wished, he would play another hand, but no more.

"All right," said Marnham, "but let it be for double or quits."

He spoke quite quietly and seemed suddenly to have grown sober. Now I think that Rodd made up his mind that he really was acting and that he really had that card up his sleeve. At any rate he did not object. I, however, was of a different opinion, having often seen drunken men succumb to an access of sobriety under the stress of excitement and remarked that it did not last long.

"Do you really mean that?" I said, speaking for the first time and addressing myself to the doctor. "I don't quite know what the sum involved is, but it must be large."

"Of course," he answered.

Then remembering that at the worst Anscombe stood to lose nothing, I shrugged my shoulders and held my tongue. It was Marnham's deal, and although he was somewhat in the shadow of the hanging lamp and the candles had guttered out, I distinctly saw him play some hocus-pocus with the cards, but in the circumstances made no protest. As it chanced he must have hocus-pocused them wrong, for though his hand was full of trumps, Rodd held nothing at all. The battle that ensued was quite exciting, but the end of it was that an ace in the hand of Anscombe, who really was quite a good player, did the business, and we won again.

In the rather awful silence that followed Anscombe remarked in his cheerful drawl—

"I'm not sure that my addition is quite right; we'll check that in the morning, but I make out that you two gentlemen owe Quatermain and myself £749 10s."

Then the doctor broke out.

"You accursed old fool," he hissed—there is no other word for it—at Marnham. "How are you going to pay all this money that you have gambled away, drunken beast that you are!"

"Easily enough, you felon," shouted Marnham. "So," and thrusting his hand into his pocket he pulled out a number of diamonds which he threw upon the table, adding, "there's what will cover it twice over, and there are more where they came from, as you know well enough, my medical jailbird."

"You dare to call me that," gasped the doctor in a voice laden with fury, so intense that it had deprived him of his reason, "you—you—murderer! Oh! why don't I kill you as I shall some day?" and lifting his glass, which was half full, he threw the contents into Marnham's face.

"That's a nice man for a prospective, son-in-law, isn't he?" exclaimed the old scamp, as, seizing the brandy decanter, he hurled it straight at Rodd's head, only missing him by an inch.

"Don't you think you had both better go to bed, gentlemen?" I inquired. "You are saying things you might regret in the morning."

Apparently they did think it, for without another word they rose and marched off in different directions to their respective rooms, which I heard both of them lock. For my part I collected the I.O.U.'s; also the diamonds which still lay upon the table, while Anscombe examined the cards.

"Marked, by Jove!" he said. "Oh! my dear Quatermain, never have I had such an amusing evening in all my life."

"Shut up, you silly idiot," I answered. "There'll be murder done over this business, and I only hope it won't be on us."

It might be thought that after all this there would have been a painful explanation on the following morning, but nothing of the sort happened. After all the greatest art is the art of ignoring things, without which the world could scarcely go on, even among the savage races. Thus on this occasion the two chief actors in the scene of the previous night pretended that they had forgotten what took place, as I believe, to a large extent truly. The fierce flame of drink in the one and of passion in the other had burnt the web of remembrance to ashes. They knew that something unpleasant had occurred and its main outlines; the rest had vanished away; perhaps because they knew also that they were not responsible for what they said and did, and therefore that what occurred had no right to a permanent niche in their memories. It was, as it were, something outside of their normal selves. At least so I conjectured, and their conduct seemed to give colour to my guess.

The doctor spoke to me of the matter first.

"I fear there was a row last night," he said; "it has happened here before over cards, and will no doubt happen again until matters clear themselves up somehow. Marnham, as you see, drinks, and when drunk is the biggest liar in the world, and I, I am sorry to say, am cursed with a violent temper. Don't judge either of us too harshly. If you were a doctor you would know that all these things come to us with our blood, and we didn't fashion our own clay, did we? Have some coffee, won't you?"

Subsequently when Rodd wasn't there, Marnham spoke also and with that fine air of courtesy which was peculiar to him.

"I owe a deep apology," he said, "to yourself and Mr. Anscombe. I do not recall much about it, but I know there was a scene last night over those cursed cards. A weakness overtakes me sometimes. I will say no more, except that you, who are also a man who perhaps have felt weaknesses of one sort or another, will, I hope, make allowances for me and pay no attention to anything that I may have said or done in the presence of guests; yes, that is what pains me—in the presence of guests."

Something in his distinguished manner caused me to reflect upon every peccadillo that I had ever committed, setting it in its very worst light.

"Quite so," I answered, "quite so. Pray do not mention the matter any more, although—" These words seemed to jerk themselves out of my throat, "you did call each other by such very hard names."

"I daresay," he answered with a vacant smile, "but if so they meant nothing."

"No, I understand, just like a lovers' quarrel. But look here, you left some diamonds on the table which I took to keep the Kaffirs out of temptation. I will fetch them."

"Did I? Well, probably I left some I.O.U.'s also which might serve for pipelights. So suppose we set the one against the other. I don't know the value of either the diamonds or the pipelights, it may be less or more, but for God's sake don't let me see the beastly things again. There's no need, I have plenty."

"I must speak to Anscombe," I answered. "The money at stake was his, not mine."

"Speak to whom you will," he replied, and I noted that the throbbing vein upon his forehead indicated a rising temper. "But never let me see those diamonds again. Throw them into the gutter if you wish, but never let me see them again, or there will be trouble."

Then he flung out of the room, leaving his breakfast almost untasted.

Reflecting that this queer old bird probably did not wish to be cross-questioned as to his possession of so many uncut diamonds, or that they were worth much less than the sum he had lost, or possibly that they were not diamonds at all but glass, I went to report the matter to Anscombe. He only laughed and said that as I had got the things I had better keep them until something happened, for we had both got it into our heads that something would happen before we had done with that establishment.

So I went to put the stones away as safely as I could. While I was doing so I heard the rumble of wheels, and came out just in time to see a Cape cart, drawn by four very good horses and driven by a Hottentot in a smart hat and a red waistband, pull up at the garden gate. Out of this cart presently emerged a neatly dressed lady, of whom all I could see was that she was young, slender and rather tall; also, as her back was towards me, that she had a great deal of auburn hair.

"There!" said Anscombe. "I knew that something would happen. Heda has happened. Quatermain, as neither her venerated parent nor her loving fiance, for such I gather he is, seems to be about, you had better go and give her a hand."

I obeyed with a groan, heartily wishing that Heda hadn't happened, since some sense warned me that she would only add to the present complications. At the gate, having given some instructions to a very stout young coloured woman who, I took it, was her maid, about a basket of flower roots in the cart, she turned round suddenly and we came face to face with the gate between us. For a moment we stared at each other, I reflecting that she really was very pretty with her delicately-shaped features, her fresh, healthy-looking complexion, her long dark eyelashes and her lithe and charming figure. What she reflected about me I don't know, probably nothing half so complimentary. Suddenly, however, her large greyish eyes grew troubled and a look of alarm appeared upon her face.

"Is anything wrong with my father?" she asked. "I don't see him."

"If you mean Mr. Marnham," I replied, lifting my hat, "I believe that Dr. Rodd and he—"

"Never mind about Dr. Rodd," she broke in with a contemptuous little jerk of her chin, "how is my father?"

"I imagine much as usual. He and Dr. Rodd were here a little while ago, I suppose that they have gone out" (as a matter of fact they had, but in different directions).

"Then that's all right," she said with a sigh of relief. "You see, I heard that he was very ill, which is why I have come back."

So, thought I to myself, she loves that old scamp and she—doesn't love the doctor. There will be more trouble as sure as five and two are seven. All we wanted was a woman to make the pot boil over.

Then I opened the gate and took a travelling bag from her hand with my politest bow.

"My name is Quatermain and that of my friend Anscombe. We are staying here, you know," I said rather awkwardly.

"Indeed," she answered with a delightful smile, "what a very strange place to choose to stay in."

"It is a beautiful house," I remarked.

"Not bad, although I designed it, more or less. But I was alluding to its inhabitants."

This finished me, and I am sure she felt that I could think of nothing nice to say about those inhabitants, for I heard her sigh. We walked side by side up the rose-fringed path and presently arrived at the stoep, where Anscombe, whose hair I had cut very nicely on the previous day, was watching us from his long chair. They looked at each other, and I saw both of them colour a little, out of mere foolishness, I suppose.

"Anscombe," I said, "this is—" and I paused, not being quite certain whether she also was called Marnham. "Heda Marnham," she interrupted.

"Yes—Miss Heda Marnham, and this is the Honourable Maurice Anscombe."

"Forgive me for not rising, Miss Marnham," said Anscombe in his pleasant voice (by the way hers was pleasant too, full and rather low, with just a suggestion of something foreign about it). "A shot through the foot prevents me at present."

"Who shot you?" she asked quickly.

"Oh! only a Kaffir."

"I am so sorry, I hope you will get well soon. Forgive me now, I must go to look for my father."

"She is uncommonly pretty," remarked Anscombe, "and a lady into the bargain. In reflecting on old Marnham's sins we must put it to his credit that he has produced a charming daughter."

"Too pretty and charming by half," I grunted.

"Perhaps Dr. Rodd is of the same way of thinking. Great shame that such a girl should be handed over to a medical scoundrel like Dr. Rodd. I wonder if she cares for him?"

"Just about as much as a canary cares for a tom-cat. I have found that out already."

"Really, Quatermain, you are admirable. I never knew anyone who could make a better use of the briefest opportunity."

Then we were silent, waiting, not without a certain impatience, for the return of Miss Heda. She did return with surprising quickness considering that she had found time to search for her parent, to change into a clean white dress, and to pin a single hibiscus flower on to her bodice which gave just the touch of colour that was necessary to complete her costume.

"I can't find my father," she said, "but the boys say he has gone out riding. I can't find anybody. When you have been summoned from a long way off and travelled post-haste, rather to your own inconvenience, it is amusing, isn't it?"

"Wagons and carts in South Africa don't arrive like express trains, Miss Marnham," said Anscombe, "so you shouldn't be offended."

"I am not at all offended, Mr. Anscombe. Now that I know there is nothing the matter with my father I'm—But, tell me, how did you get your wound?"

So he told her with much amusing detail after his fashion. She listened quietly with a puckered up brow and only made one comment. It was,—

"I wonder what white man told those Sekukuni Kaffirs that you were coming."

"I don't know," he answered, "but he deserves a bullet through him somewhere above the ankle."

"Yes, though few people get what they deserve in this wicked world."

"So I have often thought. Had it been otherwise, for example, I should have been—"

"What would you have been?" she asked, considering him curiously.

"Oh! a better shot than Mr. Allan Quatermain, and as beautiful as a lady I once saw in my youth."

"Don't talk rubbish before luncheon," I remarked sternly, and we all laughed, the first wholesome laughter that I had heard at the Temple. For this young lady seemed to bring happiness and merriment with her. I remember wondering what it was of which her coming reminded me, and concluding that it was like the sight and smell of a peach orchard in full bloom stumbled on suddenly in the black desert of the burnt winter veld.

After this we became quite friendly. She dilated on her skill in having produced the Temple from an old engraving, which she fetched and showed to us, at no greater an expense than it would have cost to build an ordinary house.

"That is because the marble was at hand," said Anscombe.

"Quite so," she replied demurely. "Speaking in a general sense one can do many things in life—if the marble is at hand. Only most of us when we look for marble find sandstone or mud."

"Bravo!" said Anscombe, "I have generally lit upon the sandstone."

"And I on the mud," she mused.

"And I on all three, for the earth contains marble and mud and sandstone, to say nothing of gold and jewels," I broke in, being tired of silence.

But neither of them paid much attention to me. Anscombe did say, out of politeness, I suppose, that pitch and subterranean fires should be added, or some such nonsense.

Then she began to tell him of her infantile memories of Hungary, which were extremely faint; of how they came this place and lived first of all in two large Kaffir huts, until suddenly they began to grow rich; of her school days at Maritzburg; of the friends with whom she had been staying, and I know not what, until at last I got up and went out for a walk.

When I returned an hour or so later they were still talking, and so continued to do until Dr. Rodd arrived upon the scene. At first they did not see him, for he stood at an angle to them, but I saw him and watched his face with a great deal of interest. It, or rather its expression, was not pleasant; before now I have seen something like it on that of a wild beast which thinks that it is about to be robbed of its prey by a stronger wild beast, in short, a mixture of hate, fear and jealousy—especially jealousy. At the last I did not wonder, for these two seemed to be getting on uncommonly well.

They were, so to speak, well matched. She, of course, was the better looking of the two, a really pretty and attractive young woman indeed, but the vivacity of Anscombe's face, the twinkle of his merry blue eyes and its general refinement made up for what he lacked—regularity of feature. I think he had just told her one of his good stories which he always managed to make so humorous by a trick of pleasing and harmless exaggeration, and they were both laughing merrily. Then she caught sight of the doctor and her merriment evaporated like a drop of water on a hot shovel. Distinctly I saw her pull herself together and prepare for something.

"How do you do?" she said rapidly, rising and holding out her slim sun-browned hand. "But I need not ask, you look so well."

"How do you do, my dear," with a heavy emphasis on the "dear" he answered slowly. "But I needn't ask, for I see that you are in perfect health and spirits," and he bent forward as though to kiss her.

Somehow or other she avoided that endearment or seal of possession. I don't quite know how, as I turned my head away, not wishing to witness what I felt to be unpleasant. When I looked up again, however, I saw that she had avoided it, the scowl on his face the demureness of hers and Anscombe's evident amusement assured me of this. She was asking about her father; he answered that he also seemed quite well.

"Then why did you write to tell me that I ought to come as he was not at all well?" she inquired, with a lifting of her delicate eyebrows.

The question was never answered, for at that moment Marnham himself appeared.

"Oh! father," she said, and rushed into his arms, while he kissed her tenderly on both cheeks.

So I was not mistaken, thought I to myself, she does really love this moral wreck, and what is more, he loves her, which shows that there must be good in him. Is anyone truly bad, I wondered, or for the matter of that, truly good either? Is it not all a question of circumstance and blood?

Neither then or at any other time have I found an answer to the problem. At any rate to me there seemed something beautiful about the meeting of these two.

The influence of Miss Heda in the house was felt at once. The boys became smarter and put on clean clothes. Vases of flowers appeared in the various rooms; ours was turned out and cleaned, a disagreeable process so far as we were concerned. Moreover, at dinner both Marnham and Rodd wore dress clothes with short jackets, a circumstance that put Anscombe and myself to shame since we had none. It was curious to see how with those dress clothes, which doubtless awoke old associations within him, Marnham changed his colour like a chameleon. Really he might have been the colonel of a cavalry regiment rising to toast the Queen after he had sent round the wine, so polite and polished was his talk. Who could have identified the man with the dry old ruffian of twenty-four hours before, he who was drinking claret (and very good claret too) mixed with water and listening with a polite interest to all the details of his daughter's journey? Even the doctor looked a gentleman, which doubtless he was once upon a time, in evening dress. Moreover, some kind of truce had been arranged. He no longer called Miss Heda "My dear" or attempted any familiarities, while she on more than one occasion very distinctly called him Dr. Rodd.

So much for that night and for several others that followed. As for the days they went by pleasantly and idly. Heda walked about on her father's arm, conversed in friendly fashion with the doctor, always watching him, I noticed, as a cat watches a dog that she knows is waiting an opportunity to spring, and for the rest associated with us as much as she could. Particularly did she seem to take refuge behind my own insignificance, having, I suppose, come to the conclusion that I was a harmless person who might possibly prove useful. But all the while I felt that the storm was banking up. Indeed Marnham himself, at any rate to a great extent, played the part of the cloud-compelling Jove, for soon it became evident to me, and without doubt to Dr. Rodd also, that he was encouraging the intimacy between his daughter and Anscombe by every means in his power.

In one way and another he had fully informed himself as to Anscombe's prospects in life, which were brilliant enough. Moreover he liked the man who, as the remnant of the better perceptions of his youth told him, was one of the best class of Englishmen, and what is more, he saw that Heda liked him also, as much indeed as she disliked Rodd. He even spoke to me of the matter in a round-about kind of fashion, saying that the young woman who married Anscombe would be lucky and that the father who had him for a son-in-law might go to his grave confident of his child's happiness. I answered that I agreed with him, unless the lady's affections had already caused her to form other ties.

"Affections!" he exclaimed, dropping all pretence, "there are none involved in this accursed business, as you are quite sharp enough to have seen for yourself."

"I understood that an engagement was involved," I remarked.

"On my part, perhaps, not on hers," he answered. "Oh! can't you understand, Quatermain, that sometimes men find themselves forced into strange situations against their will?"

Remembering the very ugly name that I had heard Rodd call Marnham on the night of the card party, I reflected that I could understand well enough, but I only said—

"After all marriage is a matter that concerns a woman even more than it does her father, one, in short, of which she must be the judge."

"Quite so, Quatermain, but there are some daughters who are prepared to make great sacrifices for their fathers. Well, she will be of age ere long, if only I can stave it off till then. But how, how?" and with a groan he turned and left me.

That old gentleman's neck is in some kind of a noose, thought I to myself, and his difficulty is to prevent the rope from being drawn tight. Meanwhile this poor girl's happiness and future are at stake.

"Allan," said Anscombe to me a little later, for by now he called me by my Christian name, "I suppose you haven't heard anything about those oxen, have you?"

"No, I could scarcely expect to yet, but why do you ask?"

He smiled in his droll fashion and replied, "Because, interesting as this household is in sundry ways, I think it is about time that we, or at any rate that I, got out of it."

"Your leg isn't fit to travel yet, Anscombe, although Rodd says that all the symptoms are very satisfactory."

"Yes, but to tell you the truth I am experiencing other symptoms quite unknown to that beloved physician and so unfamiliar to myself that I attribute them to the influences of the locality. Altitude affects the heart, does it not, and this house stands high."

"Don't play off your jokes on me," I said sternly. "What do you mean?"

"I wonder if you find Miss Heda attractive, Allan, or if you are too old. I believe there comes an age when the only beauties that can move a man are those of architecture, or scenery, or properly cooked food."

"Hang it all! I am not Methusaleh," I replied; "but if you mean that you are falling in love with Heda, why the deuce don't you say so, instead of wasting my time and your own?"

"Because time was given to us to waste. Properly considered it is the best use to which it can be put, or at any rate the one that does least mischief. Also because I wished to make you say it for me that I might judge from the effect of your words whether it is or is not true. I may add that I fear the former to be the case."

"Well, if you are in love with the girl you can't expect one so ancient as myself, who is quite out of touch with such follies, to teach you how to act."

"No, Allan. Unfortunately there are occasions when one must rely upon one's own wisdom, and mine, what there is of it, tells me I had better get out of this. But I can't ride even if I took the horse and you ran behind, and the oxen haven't come."

"Perhaps you could borrow Miss Marnham's cart in which to run away from her," I suggested sarcastically.

"Perhaps, though I believe it would be fatal to my foot to sit up in a cart for the next few days, and the horses seem to have been sent off somewhere. Look here, old fellow," he went on, dropping his bantering tone, "it's rather awkward to make a fool of oneself over a lady who is engaged to some one else, especially if one suspects that with a little encouragement she might begin to walk the same road. The truth is I have taken the fever pretty bad, worse than ever I did before, and if it isn't stopped soon it will become chronic."

"Oh no, Anscombe, only intermittent at the worst, and African malaria nearly always yields to a change of climate."

"How can I expect a cynic and a misogynist to understand the simple fervour of an inexperienced soul—Oh! drat it all, Quatermain, stop your acid chaff and tell me what is to be done. Really I am in a tight place."

"Very; so tight that I rejoice to think, as you were kind enough to point out, that my years protect me from anything of the sort. I have no advice to give; I think you had better ask it of the lady."

"Well, we did have a little conversation, hypothetical of course, about some friends of ours who found themselves similarly situated, and I regret to say without result."

"Indeed. I did not know you had any mutual acquaintances. What did she say and do?"

"She said nothing, only sighed and looked as though she were going to burst into tears, and all she did was to walk away. I'd have followed her if I could, but as my crutch wasn't there it was impossible. It seemed to me that suddenly I had come up against a brick wall, that there was something on her mind which she could not or would not let out."

"Yes, and if you want to know, I will tell you what it is. Rodd has got a hold over Marnham of a sort that would bring him somewhere near the gallows. As the price of his silence Marnham has promised him his daughter. The daughter knows that her father is in this man's power, though I think she does not know in what way, and being a good girl—"

"An angel you mean—do call her by her right name, especially in a place where angels are so much wanted."

"Well, an angel if you like—she has promised on her part to marry a man she loathes in order to save her parent's bacon."

"Just what I concluded, from what we heard in the row. I wonder which of that pair is the bigger blackguard. Well, Allan, that settles it. You and I are on the side of the angel. You will have to get her out of this scrape and—if she'll have me, I'll marry her; and if she won't, why it can't be helped. Now that's a fair division of labour. How are you going to do it? I haven't an idea, and if I had, I should not presume to interfere with one so much older and wiser than myself."

"I suppose that by the time you appeared in it, the game of heads I win and tails you lose had died out of the world," I replied with an indignant snort. "I think the best thing I can do will be to take the horse and look for those oxen. Meanwhile you can settle your business by the light of your native genius, and I only hope you'll finish it without murder and sudden death."

"I say, old fellow," said Anscombe earnestly, "you don't really mean to go off and leave me in this hideousness? I haven't bothered much up to the present because I was sure that you would find a way out, which would be nothing to a man of your intellect and experience. I mean it honestly, I do indeed."

"Do you? Well, I can only say that my mind is a perfect blank, but if you will stop talking I will try to think the matter over. There's Miss Heda in the garden cutting flowers. I will go to help her, which will be a very pleasant change."

And I went, leaving him to stare after me jealously.

CHAPTER VII

THE STOEP

When I reached Miss Heda she was collecting half-opened monthly roses from the hedge, and not quite knowing what to say I made the appropriate quotation. At least it was appropriate to my thought, and, from her answer, to hers also.

"Yes," she said, "I am gathering them while I may," and she sighed and, as I thought, glanced towards the verandah, though of this I could not be sure because of the wide brim of the hat she was wearing.

Then we talked a little on indifferent matters, while I pricked my fingers helping to pluck the roses. She asked me if I thought that Anscombe was getting on well, and how long it would be before he could travel. I replied that Dr. Rodd could tell her better than myself, but that I hoped in about a week.

"In a week!" she said, and although she tried to speak lightly there was dismay in her voice.

"I hope you don't think it too long," I answered; "but even if he is fit to go, the oxen have not come yet, and I don't quite know when they will."

"Too long!" she exclaimed. "Too long! Oh! if you only knew what it is to me to have such guests as you are in this place," and her dark eyes filled with tears.

By now we had passed to the side of the house in search of some other flower that grew in the shade, I think it was mignonette, and were out of sight of the verandah and quite alone.

"Mr. Quatermain," she said hurriedly, "I am wondering whether to ask your advice about something, if you would give it. I have no one to consult here," she added rather piteously.

"That is for you to decide. If you wish to do so I am old enough to be your father, and will do my best to help."

We walked on to an orange grove that stood about forty yards away, ostensibly to pick some fruit, but really because we knew that there we should be out of hearing and could see any one who approached.

"Mr. Quatermain," she said presently in a low voice, "I am in great trouble, almost the greatest a woman can have. I am engaged to be married to a man whom I do not care for."

"Then why not break it off? It may be unpleasant, but it is generally best to face unpleasant things, and nothing can be so bad as marrying a man whom you do not—care for."

"Because I cannot—I dare not. I have to obey."

"How old are you, Miss Marnham?"

"I shall be of age in three months' time. You may guess that I did not intend to return here until they were over, but I was, well—trapped. He wrote to me that my father was ill and I came."

"At any rate when they are over you will not have to obey any one. It is not long to wait."

"It is an eternity. Besides this is not so much a question of obedience as of duty and of love. I love my father who, whatever his faults, has always been very kind to me."

"And I am sure he loves you. Why not go to him and tell him your trouble?"

"He knows it already, Mr. Quatermain, and hates this marriage even more than I do, if that is possible. But he is driven to it, as I am. Oh! I must tell the truth. The doctor has some hold over him. My father has done something dreadful; I don't know what and I don't want to know, but if it came out it would ruin my father, or worse, worse. I am the price of his silence. On the day of our marriage he will destroy the proofs. If I refuse to marry him, they will be produced and then—"

"It is difficult," I said.

"It is more than difficult, it is terrible. If you could see all there is in my heart, you would know how terrible."

"I think I can see, Miss Heda. Don't say any more now. Give me time to consider. In case of necessity come to me again, and be sure that I will protect you."

"But you are going in a week."

"Many things happen in a week. Sufficient to the day is its evil. At the end of the week we will come to some decision unless everything is already decided."

For the next twenty-four hours I reflected on this pretty problem as hard as ever I did on anything in all my life. Here was a young woman who must somehow be protected from a scoundrel, but who could not be protected because she herself had to protect another scoundrel—to wit, her own father. Could the thing be faced out? Impossible, for I was sure that Marnham had committed a murder, or murders, of which Rodd possessed evidence that would hang him. Could Heda be married to Anscombe at once?

Yes, if both were willing, but then Marnham would still be hung. Could they elope? Possibly, but with the same result. Could I take her away and put her under the protection of the Court at Pretoria? Yes, but with the same result. I wondered what my Hottentot retainer, Hans, would have advised, he who was named Light-in-Darkness, and in his own savage way was the cleverest and most cunning man that I have met. Alas! I could not raise him from the grave to tell me, and yet I knew well what he would have answered.

"Baas," he would have said, "this is a rope which only the pale old man (i.e., death) can cut. Let this doctor die or let the father die, and the maiden will be free. Surely heaven is longing for one or both of them, and if necessary, Baas, I believe that I can point out a path to heaven!"

I laughed to myself at the thought, which was one that a white man could not entertain even as a thought. And I felt that the hypothetical Hans was right, death alone could cut this knot, and the reflection made me shiver.

That night I slept uneasily and dreamed. I dreamed that once more I was in the Black Kloof in Zululand, seated in front of the huts at the end of the kloof. Before me squatted the old wizard, Zikali, wrapped up in his kaross—Zikali, the "Thing-that-should-never-have-been-born," whom I had not seen for years. Near him were the ashes of a fire, by the help of which I knew he had been practising divination. He looked up and laughed one of his terrible laughs.

"So you are here again, Macumazahn," he said, "grown older, but still the same; here at the appointed hour. What do you come to seek from the Opener of Roads? Not Mameena as I think this time. No, no, it is she who seeks you this time, Macumazahn. She found you once, did she not? Far away to the north among a strange people who worshipped an Ivory Child, a people of whom I knew in my youth, and afterwards, for was not their prophet, Harut, a friend of mine and one of our brotherhood? She found you beneath the tusks of the elephant, Jana, whom Macumazahn the skilful could not hit. Oh! do not look astonished."

"How do you know?" I asked in my dream.

"Very simply, Macumazahn. A little yellow man named Hans has been with me and told me all the story not an hour ago, after which I sent for Mameena to learn if it were true. She will be glad to meet you, Macumazahn, she who has a hungry heart that does not forget. Oh! don't be afraid. I mean here beneath the sun, in the land beyond there will be no need for her to meet you since she will dwell ever at your side."

"Why do you lie to me, Zikali?" I seemed to ask. "How can a dead man speak to you and how can I meet a woman who is dead?"

"Seek the answer to that question in the hour of the battle when the white men, your brothers, fall beneath assegai as weeds fall before the hoe—or perhaps before it. But have done with Mameena, since she who never grows more old can well afford to wait. It is not of Mameena that you came to speak to me; it is of a fair white woman named Heddana you would speak, and of the man she loves, you, who will ever be mixing yourself up in affairs of others, and therefore must bear their burdens with no pay save that of honour. Hearken, for the time is short. When the storm bursts upon them bring hither the fair maiden, Heddana, and the white lord, Mauriti, and I will shelter them for your sake. Take them nowhere else. Bring them hither if they would escape trouble. I shall be glad to see you,

Macumazahn, for at last I am about to smite the Zulu House of Senzangacona, my foes, with a bladder full of blood, and oh! it stains their doorposts red."

Then I woke up, feeling afraid, as one does after a nightmare, and was comforted to hear Anscombe sleeping quietly on the other side of the room.

"Mauriti. Why did Zikali call him Mauriti?" I wondered drowsily to myself. "Oh! of course his name is Maurice, and it was a Zulu corruption of a common sort as was Heddana of Heda." Then I dozed off again, and by the morning had forgotten all about my dream until it was brought back to me by subsequent events. Still it was this and nothing else that put it into my head to fly to Zululand on an emergency that was to arise ere long.*

[—For the history of Zikali and Mameena see the book called Child of Storm by H. Rider Haggard.]*

That evening Rodd was absent from dinner, and on inquiring where he might be, I was informed that he had ridden to visit a Kaffir headman, a patient of his who lived at a distance, and would very probably sleep at the kraal, returning early next day. One of the topics of conversation during dinner was as to where the exact boundary line used to run between the Transvaal and the country over which the Basuto chief, Sekukuni, claimed ownership and jurisdiction. Marnham said that it passed within a couple of miles of his house, and when we rose, the moon being very bright, offered to show me where the beacons had been placed years before by a Boer Commission. I accepted, as the night was lovely for a stroll after the hot day. Also I was half conscious of another undefined purpose in my mind, which perhaps may have spread to that of Marnham. Those two young people looked very happy together there on the stoep, and as they must part so soon it would, I thought, be kind to give them the opportunity of a quiet chat.

So off we went to the brow of the hill on which the Temple stood, whence old Marnham pointed out to me a beacon, which I could not see in the dim, silvery bush-veld below, and how the line ran from it to another beacon somewhere else.

"You know the Yellow-wood swamp," he said. "It passes straight through that. That is why those Basutos who were following you pulled up upon the edge of the swamp, though as a matter of fact, according to their ideas, they had a perfect right to kill you on their side of the line which cuts through the middle."

I made some remark to the effect that I presumed that the line had in fact ceased to exist at all, as the Basuto territory had practically become British; after which we strolled back to the house. Walking quietly between the tall rose hedges and without speaking, for each of us was preoccupied with his own thoughts, suddenly we came upon a very pretty scene.

We had left Anscombe and Heda seated side by side on the stoep. They were still there, but much closer together. In fact his arms were round her, and they were kissing each other in a remarkably whole-hearted way. About this there could be no mistake, since the rimpi-strung couch on which they sat was immediately under the hanging lamp—a somewhat unfortunate situation for such endearments. But what did they think of hanging lamps or any other lights, save those of their own eyes, they who were content to kiss and murmur words of passion as though they were as much alone as Adam and Eve in Eden? What did they think either of the serpent coiled about the bole of this tree of knowledge whereof they had just plucked the ripe and maddening fruit?

By a mutual instinct Marnham and I withdrew ourselves, very gently indeed, purposing to skirt round the house and enter it from behind, or to be seized with a fit of coughing at the gate, or to do something to announce our presence at a convenient distance. When we had gone a little way we heard a crash in the bushes.

"Another of those cursed baboons robbing the garden," remarked Marnham reflectively.

"I think he is going to rob the house also," I replied, turning to point to something dark that seemed to be leaping up on to the verandah.

Next moment we heard Heda utter a little cry of alarm, and a man say in a low fierce voice—

"So I have caught you at last, have I!"

"The doctor has returned from his business rounds sooner than was expected, and I think that we had better join the party," I remarked, and made a bee line for the stoep, Marnham following me.

I think that I arrived just in time to prevent mischief. There, with a revolver in his hand, stood Rodd, tall and formidable, his dark face looking like that of Satan himself, a very monument of rage and jealousy. There in front of him on the couch sat Heda, grasping its edge with her fingers, her cheeks as pale as a sheet and her eyes shining. By her side was Anscombe, cool and collected as usual, I noticed, but evidently perplexed.

"If there is any shooting to be done," he was saying, "I think you had better begin with me."

His calmness seemed to exasperate Rodd, who lifted the revolver. But I too was prepared, for in that house I always went armed. There was no time to get at the man, who was perhaps fifteen feet away, and I did not want to hurt him. So I did the best I could; that is, I fired at the pistol in his hand, and the light being good, struck it near the hilt and knocked it off the barrel before the he could press the trigger, if he really meant to shoot.

"That's a good shot," remarked Anscombe who had seen me, while Rodd stared at the hilt which he still held.

"A lucky one," I answered, walking forward. "And now, Dr. Rodd, will you be so good as to tell me what you mean by flourishing a revolver, presumably loaded, in the faces of a lady and an unarmed man?"

"What the devil is that to you," he asked furiously, "and what do you mean by firing at me?"

"A great deal," I answered, "seeing that a young woman and my friend are concerned. As for firing at you, had I done so you would not be asking questions now. I fired at the pistol in your hand, but if there is more trouble next time it shall be at the holder," and I glanced at my revolver.

Seeing that I meant business he made no reply, but turned upon Marnham who had followed me.

"This is your work, you old villain," he said in a low voice that was heavy with hate. "You promised your daughter to me. She is engaged to me, and now I find her in this wanderer's arms."

"What have I to do with it?" said Marnham. "Perhaps she has changed her mind. You had better ask her."

"There is no need to ask me," interrupted Heda, who now seemed to have got her nerve again. "I have changed my mind. I never loved you, Dr. Rodd, and I will not marry you. I love Mr. Anscombe here, and as he has asked me to be his wife I mean to marry him."

"I see," he sneered, "you want to be a peeress one day, no doubt. Well, you never shall if I can help it. Perhaps, too, this fine gentleman of yours will not be so particularly anxious to marry you when he learns that you are the daughter of a murderer."

That word was like a bombshell bursting among us. We looked at each other as people, yet dazed with the shock, might on a battlefield when the noise of the explosion has died and the smoke cleared away, to see who is still alive. Anscombe spoke the first.

"I don't know what you mean or to what you refer," he said quietly. "But at any rate this lady who has promised to marry me is innocent, and therefore if all her ancestors had been murderers it would not in the slightest turn me from my purpose of marrying her."

She looked at him, and all the gratitude in the world shone in her frightened eyes. Marnham stepped, or rather staggered forward, the blue vein throbbing on forehead.

"He lies," he said hoarsely, tugging at his long beard. "Listen now and I will tell you the truth. Once, more than a year ago, I was drunk and in a rage. In this state I fired at a Kaffir to frighten him, and by some devil's chance shot him dead. That's what he calls being a murderer."

"I have another tale," said Rodd, "with which I will not trouble this company just now. Look here, Heda, either you fulfil your promise and marry me, or your father swings."

She gasped and sank together on the seat as though she had been shot. Then I took up my parable.

"Are you the man," I asked, "to accuse others of crime? Let us see. You have spent several months in an English prison (I gave the name) for a crime I won't mention."

"How do you know—" he began.

"Never mind, I do know and the prison books will show it. Further, your business is that of selling guns and ammunition to the Basutos of Sekukuni's tribe, who, although the expedition against them has been temporarily recalled, are still the Queen's enemies. Don't deny it, for I have the proofs. Further, it was you who advised Sekukuni to kill us when we went down to his country to shoot the other day, because you were afraid that we should discover whence he got his guns." (This was a bow drawn at a venture, but the arrow went home, for I saw his jaw drop.) "Further, I believe you to be an illicit diamond buyer, and I believe also that you have again been arranging with the Basutos to make an end of us, though of these last two items at present I lack positive proof. Now, Dr. Rodd, I ask you for the second time whether you are a person to accuse others of crimes and whether, should you do so, you will be considered a credible witness when your own are brought to light?"

"If I had been guilty of any of these things, which I am not, it is obvious that my partner must have shared in all of them, except the first. So if you inform against me, you inform against him, and the father of Heda, whom your friend wishes to marry, will, according to your showing, be proved a gun-runner, a thief and a would-be murderer of his guests. I should advise you to leave that business alone, Mr. Quatermain."

The reply was bold and clever, so much so that I regarded this blackguard with a certain amount of admiration, as I answered—

"I shall take your advice if you take mine to leave another business alone, that of this young lady and her father, but not otherwise."

"Then spare your breath and do your worst; only careful, sharp as you think yourself, that your meddling does not recoil on your own head. Listen, Heda, either you make up your mind to marry me at once and arrange that this young gentleman, who as a doctor I assure you is now quite fit to travel without injury to his health, leaves this house to-morrow with the spy Quatermain—you might lend him the Cape cart to go in—or I start with the proofs to lay a charge of murder against your father. I give you till to-morrow morning to have a family council to think it over. Good-night."

"Good-night," I answered as he passed me, "and please be careful that none of us see your face again before to-morrow morning. As you may happen to have heard, my native name means Watcher-by-Night," and I looked at the revolver in my hand.

When he had vanished I remarked in as cheerful voice as I could command, that I thought it was bedtime, and as nobody stirred, added, "Don't be afraid, young lady. If you feel lonely, you must tell that stout maid of yours to sleep in your room. Also, as the night is so hot I shall take my nap on the stoep, there, just opposite your window. No, don't let us talk any more now. There will be plenty of time for that to-morrow."

She rose, looked at Anscombe, looked at me, looked at her father very pitifully; then with a little exclamation of despair passed into her room by the French window, where presently I heard her call the native maid and tell her that she was to sleep with her.

Marnham watched her depart. Then he too went with his head bowed and staggering a little in his walk. Next Anscombe rose and limped off into his room, I following him.

"Well, young man," I said, "you have put us all in the soup now and no mistake."

"Yes, Allan, I am afraid I have. But on the whole don't you think it rather interesting soup—so many unexpected ingredients, you see!"

"Interesting soup! Unexpected ingredients!" I repeated after him, adding, "Why not call it hell's broth at once?"

Then he became serious, dreadfully serious.

"Look here," he said, "I love Heda, and whatever her family history may be I mean to marry her and face the row at home."

"You could scarcely do less in all the circumstances, and as for rows, that young lady would soon fit herself into any place that you can give her. But the question is, how can you marry her?"

"Oh! something will happen," he replied optimistically.

"You are quite right there. Something will certainly happen, but the point is—what? Something was very near happening when I turned up on that stoep, so near that I think it was lucky for you, or for Miss Heda, or both, that I have learned how to handle a pistol. Now let me see your foot, and don't speak another word to me about all this business to-night. I'd rather tackle it when I am clear-headed in the morning."

Well, I examined his instep and leg very carefully and found that Rodd was right. Although it still hurt him to walk, the wound was quite healed and all inflammation had gone from the limb. Now it was only a question of time for the sinews to right themselves. While I was thus engaged he held forth on the virtues and charms of Heda, I making no comment.

"Lie down and get to sleep, if you can," I said when I had finished. "The door is locked and I am going on to the stoep, so you needn't be afraid of the windows. Good-night."

I went out and sat myself down in such a position that by the light of the hanging lamp, which still burned, I could make sure that no one could approach either Heda's or my room without my seeing him. For the rest, all my life I have been accustomed to night vigils, and the loaded revolver hung from my wrist by a loop of hide. Moreover, never had I felt less sleepy. There I sat hour after hour, thinking.

The substance of my thoughts does not matter, since the events that followed make them superfluous to the story. I will merely record, therefore, that towards dawn a great horror took hold of me. I did not know of what I was afraid, but I was much afraid of something. Nothing was passing in either Heda's or our room, of that I made sure by personal examination. Therefore it would seem that my terrors were unnecessary, and yet they grew and grew. I felt sure that something was happening somewhere, a dread occurrence which it was beyond my power to prevent, though whether it were in this house or at the other end of Africa I did not know.

The mental depression increased and culminated. Then of a sudden it passed completely away, and as I mopped the sweat from off my brow I noticed that dawn was breaking. It was a tender and beautiful dawn, and in a dim way I took it as a good omen. Of course it was nothing but the daily resurrection of the sun, and yet it brought to me comfort and hope. The night was past with all its fears; the light had come with all its joys. From that moment I was certain that we should triumph over these difficulties and that the end of them would be peace.

So sure was I that I ventured to take a nap, knowing that the slightest movement or sound would wake me. I suppose I slept until six o'clock, when I was aroused by a footfall. I sprang up, and saw before me one of our native servants. He was trembling and his face was ashen beneath the black. Moreover he could not speak. All he did was to put his head on one side, like a dead man, and keep on pointing downwards. Then with his mouth open and starting eyes he beckoned to me to follow him.

I followed.

CHAPTER VIII

RODD'S LAST CARD

The man led me to Marnham's room, which I had never entered before. All I could see at first, for the shutters were closed, was that the place seemed large, as bedchambers go in South Africa. When my eyes grew accustomed to the light, I made out the figure of a man seated in a chair with his head bent forward over a table that was placed at the foot of the bed almost in the centre of the room. I threw open the shutters and the morning light poured in. The man was Marnham. On the table were writing materials, also a brandy bottle with only a dreg of spirit in it. I looked for the glass and found it by his side on the floor, shattered, not merely broken.

"Drunk," I said aloud, whereon the servant, who understood me, spoke for the first time, saying in a frightened voice in Dutch—

"No, Baas, dead, half cold. I found him so just now."

I bent down and examined Marnham, also felt his face. Sure enough, he was dead, for his jaw had fallen; also his flesh was chill, and from him came a horrible smell of brandy. I thought for a moment, then bade the boy fetch Dr. Rodd and say nothing to any one else, He went, and now for the first time I noticed a large envelope addressed "Allan Quatermain, Esq." in a somewhat shaky hand. This I picked up and slipped into my pocket.

Rodd arrived half dressed.

"What's the matter now?" he growled.

I pointed to Marnham, saying—

"That is a question for you to answer.

"Oh! drunk again, I suppose," he said. Then he did as I had done, bent down and examined him. A few seconds later he stepped or reeled back, looking as frightened as a man could be, and exclaiming—

"Dead as a stone, by God! Dead these three hours or more."

"Quite so," I answered, "but what killed him?"

"How should I know?" he asked savagely. "Do you suspect me of poisoning him?"

"My mind is open," I replied; "but as you quarrelled so bitterly last night, others might."

The bolt went home; he saw his danger.

"Probably the old sot died in a fit, or of too much brandy. How can one know without a post-mortem? But that mustn't be made by me. I'm off to inform the magistrate and get hold of another doctor. Let the body remain as it is until I return."

I reflected quickly. Ought I to let him go or not? If he had any hand in this business, doubtless he intended to escape. Well, supposing this were so and he did escapee, that would be a good thing for Heda, and really it was no affair of mine to bring the fellow to justice. Moreover there was nothing to show that he was guilty; his whole manner seemed to point another way, though of course he might be acting.

"Very well," I replied, "but return as quickly as possible."

He stood for a few seconds like a man who is dazed. It occurred to me that it might have come into his mind with Marnham's death that he had lost his hold over Heda. But if so he said nothing of it, but only asked—

"Will you go instead of me?"

"On the whole I think not," I replied, "and if I did, the story I should have to tell might not tend to your advantage."

"That's true, damn you!" he exclaimed and left the room.

Ten minutes later he was galloping towards Pilgrim's Rest. Before I departed from the death chamber I examined the place carefully to see if I could find any poison or other deadly thing, but without success. One thing I did discover, however. Turning the leaf of a blotting-book that was by Marnham's elbow, I came upon a sheet of paper on which were written these words in his hand, "Greater love hath no man than this—" that was all.

Either he had forgotten the end of the quotation or changed his mind, or was unable through weakness to finish the sentence. This paper also I put in my pocket. Bolting the shutters and locking the door I returned to the stoep, where I was alone, for as yet no one else was stirring. Then I remembered the letter in my pocket and opened it. It ran—

"Dear Mr. Quatermain,—

"I have remembered that those who quarrel with Dr. Rodd are apt to die soon and suddenly; at any rate life at my age is always uncertain. Therefore, as I know you to be an honest man, I am enclosing my will that it may be in safe keeping and purpose to send it to your room to-morrow morning. Perhaps when you return to Pretoria you will deposit it in the Standard Bank there, and if I am still alive, forward me the receipt. You will see that I leave everything to my daughter whom I dearly love, and that there is enough to keep the wolf from her door, besides my share in this property, if it is ever realized.

"After all that has passed to-night I do not feel up to writing a long letter, so

"Remain sincerely yours,

"H. A. Marnham."

"PS.—I should like to state clearly upon paper that my earnest hope and wish are that Heda may get clear of that black-hearted, murderous, scoundrel Rodd and marry Mr. Anscombe, whom I like and who, I am sure, would make her a good husband."

Thinking to myself this did not look very like the letter of a suicide, I glanced through the will, as the testator seemed to have wished that I should do so. It was short, but properly drawn, signed, and witnessed, and bequeathed a sum of £9,000, which was on deposit at the Standard Bank, together with all his other property, real and personal, to Heda for her own sole use, free from the debts and engagements of her husband, should she marry. Also she was forbidden to spend more than £1,000 of the capital. In short the money was strictly tied up. With the will were some other papers that apparently referred to certain property in Hungary to which Heda might become entitled, but about these I did not trouble.

Replacing these documents in a safe inner pocket in the lining of my waistcoat, I went into our room and woke up Anscombe who was sleeping soundly, a fact that caused an unreasonable irritation in my mind. When at length he was thoroughly aroused I said to him—

"You are in luck's way, my friend. Marnham is dead."

"Oh! poor Heda," he exclaimed, "she loved him. It will half break her heart."

"If it breaks half of her heart," I replied, "it will mend the other half, for now her filial affection can't force her to marry Rodd, and that is where you are in luck's way."

Then I told him all the story.

"Was he murdered or did he commit suicide?" he asked when I had finished.

"I don't know, and to tell you the truth I don't want to know; nor will you if you are wise, unless knowledge is forced upon you. It is enough that he is dead, and for his daughter's sake the less the circumstances of his end are examined into the better."

"Poor Heda!" he said again, "who will tell her? I can't. You found him, Allan."

"I expected that job would be my share of the business, Anscombe. Well, the sooner it is over the better. Now dress yourself and come on to the stoep."

Then I left him and next minute met Heda's fat, half-breed maid, a stupid but good sort of a woman who was called Kaatje, emerging from her mistress's room with a jug, to fetch hot water, I suppose.

"Kaatje," I said, "go back and tell the Missie Heda that I want to speak to her as soon as I can. Never mind the hot water, but stop and help her to dress."

She began to grumble a little in a good-natured way, but something in my eye stopped her and she went back into the room. Ten minutes later Heda was by my side.

"What is it, Mr. Quatermain?" she asked. "I feel sure that something dreadful has happened."

"It has, my dear," I answered, "that is, if death is dreadful. Your father died last night."

"Oh!" she said, "oh!" and sank back on to the seat.

"Bear up," I went on, "we must all die one day, and he had reached the full age of man."

"But I loved him," she moaned. "He had many faults I know, still I loved him."

"It is the lot of life, Heda, that we should lose what we love. Be thankful, therefore, that you have some one left to love."

"Yes, thank God! that's true. If it had been him—no, it's wicked to say that."

Then I told her the story, and while I was doing so, Anscombe joined us, walking by aid of his stick. Also I showed them both Marnham's letter to me and the will, but the other bit of paper I did not speak of or show.

She sat very pale and quiet and listened till I had done. Then she said—

"I should like to see him."

"Perhaps it is as well," I answered. "If you can bear it, come at once, and do you come also, Anscombe."

We went to the room, Anscombe and Heda holding each other by the hand. I unlocked the door and, entering, threw open a shutter. There sat the dead man as I had left him, only his head had fallen over a little. She gazed at him, trembling, then advanced and kissed his cold forehead, muttering,

"Good-bye, father. Oh! good-bye, father."

A thought struck me, and I asked—

"Is there any place here where your father locked up things? As I have shown you, you are his heiress, and if so it might be as well in this house that you should possess yourself of his property."

"There is a safe in the corner," she answered, "of which he always kept the key in his trouser pocket."

"Then with your leave I will open it in your presence."

Going to the dead man I searched his pocket and found in it a bunch of keys. These I withdrew and went to the safe over which a skin rug was thrown. I unlocked it easily enough. Within were two bags of gold, each marked £100; also another larger bag marked "My wife's jewelry. For Heda"; also some papers and a miniature of the lady whose portrait hung in the sitting-room; also some loose gold.

"Now who will take charge of these?" I asked. "I do not think it safe to leave them here."

"You, of course," said Anscombe, while Heda nodded.

So with a groan I consigned all these valuables to my capacious pockets. Then I locked up the empty safe, replaced the keys where I had found them on Marnham, fastened the shutter and left the room with Anscombe, waiting for a while outside till Heda joined us, sobbing a little. After this we got something to eat, insisting on Heda doing the same.

On leaving the table I saw a curious sight, namely, the patients whom Rodd was attending in the little hospital of which I have spoken, departing towards the bush-veld, those of them who could walk well and the attendants assisting the others. They were already some distance away, too far indeed for me to follow, as I did not wish to leave the house. The incident filled me with suspicion, and I went round to the back to make inquiries, but could find no one. As I passed the hospital door, however, I heard a voice calling in Sisutu—

"Do not leave me behind, my brothers."

I entered and saw the man on whom Rodd had operated the day of our arrival, lying in bed and quite alone. I asked him where the others had gone. At first he would not answer, but when I pretended to leave him, called out that it was back to their own country. Finally, to cut the story short, I extracted from him that they had left because they had news that the Temple was going to be attacked by Sekukuni and did not wish to be here when I and Anscombe were killed. How the news reached him he refused, or could not, say; nor did he seem to know anything of the death of Marnham. When I pressed him on the former point, he only groaned and cried for water, for he was in pain and thirsty. I asked him who had told Sekukuni's people to kill us, but he refused to speak.

"Very well," I said, "then you shall lie here alone and die of thirst," and again I turned towards the door.

At this he cried out—

"I will tell you. It was the white medicine-man who lives here; he who cut me open. He arranged it all a few days ago because he hates you. Last night he rode to tell the impi when to come."

"When is it to come?" I asked, holding the jug of water towards him.

"To-night at the rising of the moon, so that it may get far away before the dawn. My people are thirsty for your blood and for that of the other white chief, because you killed so many of them by the river. The others they will not harm."

"How did you learn all this?" I asked him again, but without result, for he became incoherent and only muttered something about being left alone because the others could not carry him. So I gave him some water, after which he fell asleep, or pretended to do so, and I left him, wondering whether he was delirious, or spoke truth. As I passed the stables I saw that my own horse was there, for in this district horses are always shut up at night to keep them from catching sickness, but that the four beasts that had brought Heda from Natal in the Cape cart were gone, though it was evident that they had been kraaled here till within an hour or two. I threw my horse a bundle of forage and returned to the house by the back entrance. The kitchen was empty, but crouched by the door of Marnham's room sat the boy who had found him dead. He had been attached to his master and seemed half dazed. I asked him where the other servants were, to which he replied that they had all run away. Then I asked him where the horses were. He answered that the Baas Rodd had ordered them to be turned out before he rode off that morning. I bade him accompany me to the stoep, as I dared not let him out of my sight, which he did unwillingly enough.

There I found Anscombe and Heda. They were seated side by side upon the couch. Tears were running down her face and he, looking very troubled, held her by the hand. Somehow that picture of Heda has always remained fixed in my mind. Sorrow becomes some women and she was one of them. Her beautiful dark grey eyes did not grow red with weeping; the tears just welled up in them and fell like dewdrops from the heart of a flower.

She sat very upright and very still, as he did, looking straight in front of her, while a ray of sunshine, falling on her head, showed the chestnut-hued lights in her waving hair, of which she had a great abundance.

Indeed the pair of them, thus seated side by side, reminded me of an engraving I had seen somewhere of the statues of a husband and wife in an old Egyptian tomb. With just such a look did the woman of thousands of years ago sit gazing in patient hope into the darkness of the future. Death had made her sad, but it was gone by, and the little wistful smile about her lips seemed to suggest that in this darkness her sorrowful eyes already saw the stirring of the new life to be. Moreover, was not the man she loved the companion of her hopes as he had been of her woes. Such was the fanciful thought that sprang up in my mind, even in the midst of those great anxieties, like a single flower in a stony wilderness of thorns or one star on the blackness of the night.

In a moment it had gone and I was telling them of what I had learned. They listened till I had finished. Then Anscombe said slowly—

"Two of us can't hold this house against an impi. We must get out of it."

"Both your conclusions seem quite sound," I remarked, "that is if yonder old Kaffir is telling the truth. But the question is—how? We can't all three of us ride on one nag, as you are still a cripple."

"There is the Cape cart," suggested Heda.

"Yes, but the horses have been turned out, and I don't know where to look for them. Nor dare I send that boy alone, for probably he would bolt like the others. I think that you had better get on my horse and ride for it, leaving us to take our chance. I daresay the whole thing is a lie and that we shall be in no danger," I added by way of softening the suggestion.

"That I will never do," she replied with so much quiet conviction that I saw it was useless to pursue the argument.

I thought for a moment, as the position was very difficult. The boy was not to be trusted, and if I went with him I should be leaving these two alone and, in Anscombe's state, almost defenceless. Still it seemed as though I must. Just then I looked up, and there at the garden gate saw Anscombe's driver, Footsack, the man whom I had despatched to Pretoria to fetch his oxen. I noted that he looked frightened and was breathless, for his eyes started out of his head. Also his hat was gone and he bled a little from his face.

Seeing us he ran up the path and sat down as though he were tired.

"Where are the oxen?" I asked.

"Oh! Baas," he answered, "the Basutos have got them. We heard from an old black woman that Sekukuni had an impi out, so we waited on the top of that hill about an hour's ride away to see if it was true. Then suddenly the doctor Baas appeared riding, and I ran out and asked him if it were safe to go on. He knew me again and answered—

"'Yes, quite safe, for have I not just ridden this road without meeting so much as a black child. Go on, man; your masters will be glad to have their oxen, as they wish to trek, or will by nightfall.' Then he laughed and rode away.

"So we went on, driving the oxen. But when we came to the belt of thorns at the bottom of the hill, we found that the doctor Baas had either lied to us or he had not seen. For there suddenly the tall grass on either side of the path grew spears; yes, everywhere were spears. In a minute the two voorloopers were assegaied. As for me, I ran forward, not back, since the Kaffirs were behind me, across the path, Baas, driving off the oxen. They sprang at me, but I jumped this way and that way and avoided them. Then they threw assegais—see, one of them cut my cheek, but the rest missed. They had guns in their hands also, but none shot. I think they did not wish to make a noise. Only one of them shouted after me—

"'Tell Macumazahn that we are going to call on him tonight when he cannot see to shoot. We have a message for him from our brothers whom he killed at the drift of the Oliphant's River.'

"Then I ran on here without stopping, but I saw no more Kaffirs. That is all, Baas."

Now I did not delay to cross-examine the man or to sift the true from the false in his story, since it was clear to me that he had run into a company of Basutos, or rather been beguiled thereto by Rodd, and lost our cattle, also his companions, who were either killed as he said, or had escaped some other way.

"Listen, man," I said. "I am going to fetch some horses. Do you stay here and help the Missie to pack the cart and make the harness ready. If you disobey me or run away, then I will find you and you will never run again. Do you understand?"

He vowed that he did and went to get some water, while I explained everything to Anscombe and Heda, pointing out that all the information we could gather seemed to show that no attack was to be made upon the house before nightfall, and that therefore we had the day before us. As this was so I proposed to go to look for the horses myself, since otherwise I was sure we should never find them. Meanwhile Heda must pack and make ready the cart with the help of Footsack, Anscombe superintending everything, as he could very well do since he was now able to walk leaning on a stick.

Of course neither of them liked my leaving them, but in view of our necessities they raised no objection. So off I went, taking the boy with me. He did not want to go, being, as I have said, half dazed with grief or fear, or both, but when I had pointed out to him clearly that I was quite prepared to shoot him if he played tricks, he changed his mind. Having saddled my mare that was now fresh and fat, we started, the boy guiding me to a certain kloof at the foot of which there was a small plain of good grass where he said the horses were accustomed to graze.

Here sure enough we found two of them, and as they had been turned out with their headstalls on, were able to tie them to trees with the riems which were attached to the headstalls. But the others were not there, and as two horses could not drag a heavy Cape cart, I was obliged to continue the search. Oh! what a hunt those beasts gave me. Finding themselves free, for as Rodd's object was that they should stray, he had ordered the stable-boy not to kneel-halter them, after filling themselves with grass they had started off for the farm where they were bred, which, it seemed, was about fifty miles away, grazing as they went. Of course I did not know this at the time, so for several hours I rode up and down the neighbouring kloofs, as the ground was too hard for me to hope to follow them by their spoor.

It occurred to me to ask the boy where the horses came from, a question that he happened to be able to answer, as he had brought them home when they were bought the year before. Having learned in what direction the place lay I rode for it at an angle, or rather for the path that led to it, making the boy run alongside, holding to my stirrup leather. About three o'clock in the afternoon I struck this path, or rather track, at a point ten or twelve miles away from the Temple, and there, just mounting a rise, met the two horses quietly walking towards me. Had I been a quarter of an hour later they would have passed and vanished into a sea of thorn-veld. We caught them without trouble and once more headed homewards, leading them by their riems.

Reaching the glade where the other two were tied up, we collected them also and returned to the house, where we arrived at five o'clock. As everything seemed quiet I put my mare into the stable, slipped its bit and gave it some forage. Then I went round the house, and to my great joy found Anscombe and Heda waiting anxiously, but with nothing to report, and with them Footsack. Very hastily I swallowed some food, while Footsack inspanned the horses. In a quarter of an hour all was ready. Then suddenly, in an inconsequent female fashion, Heda developed a dislike to leaving her father unburied.

"My dear young lady," I said, "it seems that you must choose between that and our all stopping to be buried with him."

She saw the point and compromised upon paying him a visit of farewell, which I left her to do in Anscombe's company, while I fetched my mare. To tell the truth I felt as though I had seen enough of the unhappy Marnham, and not for £50 would I have entered that room again. As I passed the door of the hospital, leading my horse, I heard the old Kaffir screaming within and sent the boy who was with me to find out what was the matter with him. That was the last I saw of either of them, or ever shall see this side of kingdom come. I wonder what became of them?

When I got back to the front of the house I found the cart standing ready at the gate, Footsack at the head of the horses and Heda with Anscombe at her side. It had been neatly packed during the day by Heda with such of her and our belongings as it would hold, including our arms and ammunition. The rest, of course, we were obliged to abandon. Also there were two baskets full of food, some bottles of brandy and a good supply of overcoats and wraps. I told Footsack to take the reins, as I knew him to be a good driver, and helped Anscombe to a seat at his side, while Heda and the maid Kaatje got in behind in order to balance the vehicle. I determined to ride, at any rate for the present.

"Which way, Baas?" asked Footsack.

"Down to the Granite Stream where the wagon stands," I answered.

"That will be through the Yellow-wood Swamp. Can't we take the other road to Pilgrim's Rest and Lydenburg, or to Barberton?" asked Anscombe in a vague way, and as I thought, rather nervously.

"No," I answered, "that is unless you wish to meet those Basutos who stole the oxen and Dr. Rodd returning, if he means to return."

"Oh! let us go through the Yellow-wood," exclaimed Heda, who, I think, would rather have met the devil than Dr. Rodd.

Ah! if I had but known that we were heading straight for that person, sooner would I have faced the Basutos twice over. But I did what seemed wisest, thinking that he would be sure to return with another doctor or a magistrate by the shorter and easier path which he had followed in the morning. It just shows once more how useless are all our care and foresight, or how strong is Fate, have it which way you will.

So we started down the slope, and I, riding behind, noted poor Heda staring at the marble house, which grew ever more beautiful as it receded and the roughness of its building disappeared, especially at that part of it which hid the body of her old scamp of a father whom still she loved. We came down to the glen and once more saw the bones of the blue wildebeeste that we had shot—oh! years and years ago, or so it seemed. Then we struck out for the Granite Stream.

Before we reached the patch of Yellow-wood forest where I knew that the cart must travel very slowly because of the trees and the swampy nature of the ground, I pushed on ahead to reconnoitre, fearing lest there might be Basutos hidden in this cover. Riding straight through it I went as far as the deserted wagon at a sharp canter, seeing nothing and no one. Once indeed, towards the end of the wood where it was more dense, I thought that I heard a man cough and peered about me through the gloom, for here the rays of the sun, which was getting low in the heavens, scarcely penetrated. As I could perceive no one I came to the conclusion that I must have been deceived by my fancy. Or perhaps it was some baboon that coughed, though it was strange that a baboon should have come to such a low-lying spot where there was nothing for it to eat.

The place was eerie, so much so that I bethought me of tales of the ghosts whereby it was supposed to be haunted. Also, oddly enough, of Anscombe's presentiment which he had fulfilled by killing a Basuto. Look! There lay his grinning skull with some patches of hair still on it, dragged away from the rest of the bones by a hyena. I cantered on down the slope beyond the wood and through the scattered thorns to the stream on the banks of which the wagon should be. It had gone, and by the freshness of the trail, within an hour or two. A moment's reflection told me what had happened. Having stolen our oxen the Basutos drove them to the wagon, inspanned them and departed with their loot. On the whole I was glad to see this, since it suggested that they had retired towards their own country, leaving our road open.

Turning my horse I rode back again to meet the cart. As I reached the edge of the wood at the top of the slope I heard a whistle blown, a very shrill whistle, of which the sound would travel for a mile or two on that still air. Also I heard the sound of men's voices in altercation and caught words, such as—"Let go, or by Heaven—!" then a furious laugh and other words which seemed to be—"In five minutes the Kaffirs will be here. In ten you will be dead. Can I help it if they kill you after I have warned you to turn back?" Then a woman's scream.

Rodd's voice, Anscombe's voice and Kaatje's scream—not Heda's but Kaatje's!

Then as I rode furiously round the last patch of intervening trees the sound of a pistol shot. I was out of them now and saw everything. There was the cart on the further side of a swamp. The horses were standing still and snorting. Holding the rein of one of the leaders was Rodd, whose horse also stood close by. He was rocking on his feet and as I leapt from my mare and ran up, I saw his face. It was horrible, full of pain and devilish rage. With his disengaged hand he pointed to Anscombe sitting in the cart and grasping a pistol that still smoked.

"You've killed me," he said in a hoarse, choking voice, for he was shot through the lung, "to get her," and he waved his hand towards Heda who was peering at him between the heads of the two men. "You are a murderer, as her father was, and as David was before you. Well, I hope you won't keep her long. I hope you'll die as I do and break her false heart, you damned thief."

All of this he said in a slow voice, pausing between the words and speaking ever more thickly as the blood from his wound choked him. Then of a sudden it burst in a stream from his lips, and still pointing with an accusing finger at Anscombe, he fell backwards into the slimy pool behind him and there vanished without a struggle.

So horrible was the sight that the driver, Footsack, leapt from the cart, uttering a kind of low howl, ran to Rodd's horse, scrambled into the saddle and galloped off, striking it with his fist, where to I do not know. Anscombe put his hand before his eyes, Heda sank down on the seat in a heap, and the coloured woman, Kaatje, beat her breast and said something in Dutch about being accursed or bewitched. Luckily I kept my wits and went to the horses' heads, fearing lest they should start and drag the trap into the pool. "Wake up," I said. "That fellow has only got what he deserved, and you were quite right to shoot him."

"I am glad you think so," answered Anscombe absently. "It was so like murder. Don't you remember I told you I should kill a man in this place and about a woman?"

"I remember nothing," I answered boldly, "except that if we stop here much longer we shall have those Basutos on us. That brute was whistling to them and holding the horses till they came to kill us. Pull yourself together, take the reins and follow me."

He obeyed, being a skilful whip enough who, as he informed me afterwards, had been accustomed to drive a four-in-hand at home. Mounting my horse, which stood by, I guided the cart out of the wood and down the slope beyond, till at length we came to our old outspan where I proposed to turn on to the wagon track which ran to Pilgrim's Rest. I say proposed, for when I looked up it I perceived about five hundred yards away a number of armed Basutos running towards us, the red light of the sunset shining on their spears. Evidently the scout or spy to whom Rodd whistled, had called them out of their ambush which they had set for us on the Pilgrim's Rest road in order that they might catch us if we tried to escape that way.

Now there was only one thing to be done. At this spot a native track ran across the little stream and up a steepish slope beyond. On the first occasion of our outspanning here I had the curiosity to mount this slope, reflecting as I did so that although rough it would be quite practicable for a wagon. At the top of it I found a wide flat plain, almost high-veld, for the bushes were very few, across which the track ran on. On subsequent inquiry I discovered that it was one used by the Swazis and other natives when they made their raids upon the Basutos, or when bodies of them went to work in the mines.

"Follow me," I shouted and crossed the stream which was shallow between the little pools, then led the way up the stony slope. The four horses negotiated it very well and the Cape cart, being splendidly built, took no harm. At the top I looked back and saw that the Basutos were following us.

"Flog the horses!" I cried to Anscombe, and off we went at a hand gallop along the native track, the cart swaying and bumping upon the rough veld. The sun was setting now, in half an hour it would be quite dark.

Could we keep ahead of them for that half hour?

CHAPTER IX

FLIGHT

The sun sank in a blaze of glory. Looking back by the light of its last rays I saw a single native silhouetted against the red sky. He was standing on a mound that we had passed a mile or more behind us, doubtless waiting for his companions whom he had outrun. So they had not given up the chase. What was to be done? Once it was completely dark we could not go on. We should lose our way; the horses would get into ant-bear holes and break their legs. Perhaps we might become bogged in some hollow, therefore we must wait till the moon rose, which would not be for a couple of hours.

Meanwhile those accursed Basutos would be following us even in the dark. This would hamper them, no doubt, but they would keep the path, with which they were probably familiar, beneath their feet, and what is more, the ground being soft with recent rain, they could feel the wheel spoor with their fingers. I looked about me. Just here another track started off in a nor'-westerly direction from that which we were following. Perhaps it ran to Lydenburg; I do not know. To our left, not more than a hundred yards or so away, the higher veld came to an end and sloped in an easterly direction down to bush-land below.

Should I take the westerly road which ran over a great plain? No, for then we might be seen for miles and cut off. Moreover, even if we escaped the natives, was it desirable we should plunge into civilization just now and tell all our story, as in that case we must do. Rodd's death was quite justified, but it had happened on Transvaal territory and would require a deal of explanation. Fortunately there was no witness of it, except ourselves. Yes, there was though—the driver Footsack, if he had got away, which, being mounted, would seem probable, a man who, for my part, I would not trust for a moment. It would be an ugly thing to see Anscombe in the dock charged with murder and possibly myself, with Footsack giving evidence against us before a Boer jury who might be hard on Englishmen. Also there was the body with a bullet in it.

Suddenly there came into my mind a recollection of the very vivid dream of Zikali which had visited me, and I reflected that in Zululand there would be little need to trouble about the death of Rodd. But Zululand was a long way off, and if we were to avoid the Transvaal, there was only one way of going there, namely through Swaziland. Well, among the Swazis we should be quite safe from the Basutos, since the two peoples were at fierce enmity. Moreover I knew the Swazi chiefs and king very well, having traded there, and could explain that I came to collect debts owing to me.

There was another difficulty. I had heard that the trouble between the English Government and Cetewayo, the Zulu king, was coming to a head, and that the High Commissioner, Sir Bartle Frere, talked of presenting him with an ultimatum. It would be awkward if this arrived while we were in the country, though even so, being on such friendly terms with the Zulus of all classes, I did not think that I, or any with me, would run great risks.

All these thoughts rushed through my brain while I considered what to do. At the moment it was useless to ask the opinion of the others who were but children in native matters. I and I alone must take the responsibility and act, praying that I might do so aright. Another moment and I had made up my mind.

Signing to Anscombe to follow me, I rode about a hundred yards or more down the nor'-westerly path. Then I turned sharply along a rather stony ridge of ground, the cart following me all the time, and came back across our own track, my object being of course to puzzle any Kaffirs who might spoor us. Now we were on the edge of the gentle slope that led down to the bush-veld. Over this I rode towards a deserted cattle kraal built of stones, in the rich soil of which grew sundry trees; doubtless one of those which had been abandoned when Mosilikatze swept all this country on his way north about the year 1838. The way to it was easy, since the surrounding stones had been collected to build the kraal generations before. As we passed over the edge of the slope in the gathering gloom, Heda cried—

"Look!" and pointed in the direction whence we came. Far away a sheet of flame shot upwards.

"The house is burning," she exclaimed.

"Yes," I said, "it can be nothing else;" adding to myself, "a good job too, for now there will be no postmortem on old Marnham."

Who fired the place I never learnt. It may have been the Basutos, or Marnham's body-servant, or Footsack, or a spark from the kitchen fire. At any rate it blazed merrily enough notwithstanding the marble walls, as a wood-lined and thatched building of course would do. On the whole I suspected the boy, who may very well have feared lest he should be accused of having had a hand in his master's death. At least it was gone, and watching the distant flames I bethought me that with it went all Heda's past. Twenty-four hours before her father was alive, the bondservant of Rodd and a criminal. Now he was ashes and Rodd was dead, while she and the man she loved were free, with all the world before them. I wished that I could have added that they were safe. Afterwards she told me that much the same ideas passed through her own mind.

Dismounting I led the horses into the old kraal through the gap in the wall which once had been the gateway. It was a large kraal that probably in bygone days had held the cattle of some forgotten head chief whose town would have stood on the brow of the rise; so large that notwithstanding the trees I have mentioned, there was plenty of room for the cart and horses in its centre. Moreover, on such soil the grass grew so richly that after we had slipped their bits, the horses were able to fill themselves without being unharnessed. Also a little stream from a spring on the brow ran within a few yards whence, with the help of Kaatje, a strong woman, I watered them with the bucket which hung underneath the cart. Next we drank ourselves and ate some food in the darkness that was now complete. Then leaving Kaatje to stand at the head of the horses in case they should attempt any sudden movement, I climbed into the cart, and we discussed things in low whispers.

It was a curious debate in that intense gloom which, close as our faces were together, prevented us from seeing anything of each other, except once when a sudden flare of summer lightning revealed them, white and unnatural as those of ghosts. On our present dangers I did not dwell, putting them aside lightly, though I knew they were not light. But of the alternative as to whether we should try to escape to Lydenburg and civilization, or to Zululand and savagery, I felt it to be my duty to speak.

"To put it plainly," said Anscombe in his slow way when I had finished, "you mean that in the Transvaal I might be tried as a murderer and perhaps convicted, whereas if we vanish into Zululand the probability is that this would not happen."

"I mean," I whispered back, "that we might both be tried and, if Footsack should chance to appear and give evidence, find ourselves in an awkward position. Also there is another witness—Kaatje, and for the matter of that, Heda herself. Of course her evidence would be in our favour, but to make it understood by a jury she would have to explain a great deal of which she might prefer not to speak. Further, at the best, the whole business would get into the English papers, which you and your relatives might think disagreeable, especially in view of the fact that, as I understand, you and Heda intend to marry."

"Still I think that I would rather face it out," he said in his outspoken way, "even if it should mean that I could never return to England. After all, of what have I to be afraid? I shot this scoundrel because I was obliged to do so."

"Yes, but it is of this that you may have to convince a jury who might possibly find a motive in Rodd's past, and your present, relationship to the same lady. But what has she to say?"

"I have to say," whispered Heda, "that for myself I care nothing, but that I could never bear to see all these stories about my poor father raked up. Also there is Maurice to be considered. It would be terrible if they put him in prison—or worse. Let us go to Zululand, Mr. Quatermain, and afterwards get out of Africa. Don't you agree, Maurice?"

"What does Mr. Quatermain think himself?" he answered. "He is the oldest and by far the wisest of us and I will be guided by him."

Now I considered and said—

"There is such a thing as flying from present troubles to others that may be worse, the 'ills we know not of.' Zululand is disturbed. If war broke out there we might all be killed. On the other hand we might not, and it ought to be possible for you to work up to Delagoa Bay and there get some ship home, that is if you wish to keep clear of British law. I cannot do so, as I must stay in Africa. Nor can I take the responsibility of settling what you are to do, since if things went wrong, it would be on my head. However, if you decide for the Transvaal or Natal and we escape, I must tell you that I shall go to the first magistrate we find and make a full deposition of all that has happened. It is not possible for me to live with the charge of having been concerned in the shooting of a white man hanging over me that might be brought up at any time, perhaps when no one was left in the country to give evidence on my behalf, for then, even if I were acquitted my name would always be tarnished. In Zululand, on the other hand, there are no magistrates before whom I could depose, and if this business should come out, I can always say that we went there to escape from the Basutos. Now I am going to get down to see if the horses are all right. Do you two talk the thing over and make up your minds. Whatever you agree on, I shall accept and do my best to carry through." Then, without waiting for an answer, I slipped from the cart.

Having examined the horses, who were cropping all the grass within reach of them, I crept to the wall of the kraal so as to be quite out of earshot. The night was now pitch dark, dark as it only knows how to be in Africa. More, a thunderstorm was coming up of which that flash of sheet lightning had been a presage. The air was electric. From the vast bush-clad valley beneath us came a wild, moaning sound caused, I suppose, by wind among the trees, though here I felt none; far away a sudden spear of lightning stabbed the sky. The brooding trouble of nature spread to my own heart. I was afraid, and not of our present dangers, though these were real enough, so real that in a few hours we might all be dead.

To dangers I was accustomed; for years they had been my daily food by day and by night, and, as I think I have said elsewhere, I am a fatalist, one who knows full well that when God wants me He will take me; that is if He can want such a poor, erring creature. Nothing that I did or left undone could postpone or hasten His summons for a moment, though of course I knew it to be my duty to fight against death and to avoid it for as long as I might, because that I should do so was a portion of His plan. For we are all part of a great pattern, and the continuance or cessation of our lives re-acts upon other lives, and therefore life is a trust.

No, it was of greater things that I felt afraid, things terrible and imminent which I could not grasp and much less understand. I understand them now, but who would have guessed that on the issue of that whispered colloquy in the cart behind me, depended the fate of a people and many thousands of lives? As I was to learn in days to come, if Anscombe and Heda had determined upon heading for the Transvaal, there would, as I believe, have been no Zulu war, which in its turn meant that there would have been no Boer Rebellion and that the mysterious course of history would have been changed.

I shook myself together and returned to the cart.

"Well," I whispered, but there was no answer. A moment later there came another flash of lightning.

"There," said Heda, "how many do you make it?

"Ninety-eight," he answered.

"I counted ninety-nine," she said, "but anyway it was within the hundred. Mr. Quatermain, we will go to Zululand, if you please, if you will show us the way there."

"Right," I answered, "but might I ask what that has to do with your both counting a hundred?"

"Only this," she said, "we could not make up our minds. Maurice was for the Transvaal, I was for Zululand. So you see we agreed that if another flash came before we counted a hundred, we would go to Zululand, and if it didn't, to Pretoria. A very good way of settling, wasn't it?"

"Excellent!" I replied, "quite excellent for those who could think of such a thing."

As a matter of fact I don't know which of them thought of it because I never inquired. But I did remember afterwards how Anscombe had tossed with a lucky penny when it was a question whether we should or should not run for the wagon during our difficulty by the Oliphant's River; also when I asked him the reason for this strange proceeding he answered that Providence might inhabit a penny as well as anything else, and that he wished to give it—I mean Providence—a chance. How much more then, he may have argued, could it inhabit a flash of lightning which has always been considered a divine manifestation from the time of the Roman Jove, and no doubt far before him.

Forty or fifty generations ago, which is not long, our ancestors set great store by the behaviour of lightning and thunder, and doubtless the instinct is still in our blood, in the same way that all our existing superstitions about the moon come down to us from the time when our forefathers worshipped her. They did this for tens of hundreds or thousands of years, and can we expect a few coatings of the veneer that we politely call civilization, which after all is only one of our conventions that vanish in any human stress such as war, to kill out the human impulse it seems to hide? I do not know, though I have my own opinion, and probably these young people never reasoned the matter out. They just acted on an intuition as ancient as that which had attracted them to each other, namely a desire to consult the ruling fates by omens or symbols. Or perhaps Anscombe thought that as his experience with the penny had proved so successful, he would give Providence another "chance." If so it took it and no mistake. Confound it! I don't know what he thought; I only dwell on the matter because of the great results which followed this consultation of the Sybilline books of heaven.

As it happened my speculations, if I really indulged in any at that time, were suddenly extinguished by the bursting of the storm. It was of the usual character, short but very violent. Of a sudden the sky became alive with lightnings and the atmosphere with the roar of winds. One flash struck a tree quite near the kraal, and I saw that tree seem to melt in its fiery embrace, while about where it had been, rose a column of dust from the ground beneath. The horses were so frightened that luckily they stood quite quiet, as I have often known animals to do in such circumstances. Then came the rain, a torrential rain as I, who was out in it holding the horses, became painfully aware. It thinned after a while, however, as the storm rolled away.

Suddenly in a silence between the tremendous echoes of the passing thunder I thought that I heard voices somewhere on the brow of the slope, and as the horses were now quite calm, I crept through the trees to that part of the enclosure which I judged to be nearest to them.

Voices they were sure enough, and of the Basutos who were pursuing us. What was more, they were coming down the slope. The top of the old wall reached almost to my chin. Taking off my hat I thrust my head forward between two loose stones, that I might hear the better.

The men were talking together in Sisutu. One, whom I took to be their captain, said to the others—

"That white-headed old jackal, Macumazahn, has given us the slip again. He doubled on his tracks and drove the horses down the hillside to the lower path in the valley. I could feel where the wheels went over the edge."

"It is so, Father," answered another voice, "but we shall catch him and the others at the bottom if we get there before the moon rises, since they cannot have moved far in this rain and darkness. Let me go first and guide you who know every tree and stone upon this slope where I used to herd cattle when I was a child."

"Do so," said the captain. "I can see nothing now the lightning has gone, and were it not that I have sworn to dip my spear in the blood of Macumazahn who has fooled us again, I would give up the hunt."

"I think it would be better to give it up in any case," said a third voice, "since it is known throughout the land that no luck has ever come to those who tried to trap the Watcher-by-Night. Oh! he is a leopard who springs and is gone again. How many are the throats in which his fangs have met. Leave him alone, I say, lest our fate should be that of the white doctor in the Yellow-wood Swamp, he who set us on this hunt. We have his wagon and his cattle; let us be satisfied."

"I will leave him alone when he sleeps for the last time, and not before," answered the captain, "he who shot my brother in the drift the other day. What would Sekukuni say if we let him escape to bring the Swazis on us? Moreover, we want that white maiden for a hostage in case the English should attack us again. Come, you who know the road, and lead us."

There was some disturbance as this man passed to the front. Then I heard the line move forward. Presently they were going by the wall within a foot or two of me. Indeed by ill-luck just as we were opposite to each other the captain stumbled and fell against the wall.

"There is an old cattle kraal here," he said. "What if those white rats have hidden in it?"

I trembled as I heard the words. If a horse should neigh or make any noise that could be heard above the hiss of the rain! I did not dare to move for fear lest I should betray myself. There I stood so close to the Kaffirs that I could smell them and hear the rain pattering on their bodies. Only very stealthily I drew my hunting knife with my right hand. At that moment the lightning, which I thought had quite gone by, flashed again for the last time, revealing the fat face of the Basuto captain within a foot of my own, for he was turned towards the wall on which one of his hands rested. Moreover, the blue and ghastly light revealed mine to him thrust forward between the two stones, my eyes glaring at him.

"The head of a dead man is set upon the wall!" he cried in terror. "It is the ghost of—"

He got no further, for as the last word passed his lips I drove the knife at him with all my strength deep into his throat. He fell back into the arms of his followers, and next instant I heard the sound of many feet rushing in terror down the hill. What became of him I do not know, but if he still lives, probably he agrees with his tribesman that Macumazahn—Watcher-by-Night, or his ghost "is a leopard who springs and kills and is gone again"; also, that those who try to trap him meet with no luck. I say, or his ghost—because I am sure he thought that I was a spirit of the dead; doubtless I must have looked like one with my white, rain-drowned face appearing there between the stones and made ghastly and livid by the lightning.

Well, they had gone, the whole band of them, not less than thirty or forty men, so I went also, back to the cart where I found the others very comfortable indeed beneath the rainproof tilt. Saying nothing of what had happened, of which they were as innocent as babes, I took a stiff tot of brandy, for I was chilled through by the wet, and while waiting for the moon to rise, busied myself with getting the bits back into the horses' mouths—an awkward job in the dark. At length it appeared in a clear sky, for the storm had quite departed and the rain ceased. As soon as there was light enough I took the near leader by the bridle and led the cart to the brow of the hill, which was not easy under the conditions, making Kaatje follow with my horse.

Then, as there were no signs of any Basutos, we started on again, I riding about a hundred yards ahead, keeping a sharp look-out for a possible ambush. Fortunately, however, the veld was bare and open, consisting of long waves of ground. One start I did get, thinking that I saw men's heads just on the crest of a wave, which turned out to be only a herd of springbuck feeding among the tussocks of grass. I was very glad to see them, since their presence assured me that no human being had recently passed that way.

All night long we trekked, following the Kaffir path for as long as I could see it, and after that going by my compass. I knew whereabouts the drift of the Crocodile River should be, as I had crossed it twice before in my life, and kept my eyes open for a certain tall koppie which stood within half a mile it on the Swazi side of the river. Ultimately to my joy I caught sight of this hill faintly outlined against the sky and headed for it. Half a mile further on I struck a wagon-track made by Boers trekking into Swazi-Land to trade or shoot. Then I knew that the drift was straight ahead of us, and called to Anscombe to flog up the weary horses.

We reached the river just before the dawn. To my horror it was very full, so full that the drift looked dangerous, for it had been swollen by the thunder-rain of the previous night. Indeed some wandering Swazis on the further bank shouted to us that we should be drowned if we tried to cross.

"Which means that the only thing to do is to stay until the water runs down," I said to Anscombe, for the two women, tired out, were asleep.

"I suppose so," he answered, "unless those Basutos—"

I looked back up the long slope down which we had come and saw no one. Then I raised myself in my stirrups and looked along another track that joined the road just here, leading from the bush-veld, as ours led from the high-veld. The sun was rising now, dispersing the mist that hung about the trees after the wet. Searching among these with my eyes, presently I perceived the light gleaming upon what I knew must be the points of spears projecting above the level of the ground vapour.

"Those devils are after us by the lower road," I said to Anscombe, adding, "I heard them pass the old cattle kraal last night. They followed our spoor over the edge of the hill, but in the dark lost it among the stones."

He whistled and asked what was to be done.

"That is for you to decide," I answered. "For my part I'd rather risk the river than the Basutos," and I looked at the slumbering Heda.

"Can we bolt back the way we came, Allan?"

"The horses are very spent and we might meet more Basutos," and again I looked at Heda.

"A hard choice, Allan. It is wonderful how women complicate everything in life, because they are life, I suppose." He thought a moment and went on, "Let's try the river. If we fail, it will be soon over, and it is better to drown than be speared."

"Or be kept alive by savages who hate us," I exclaimed, with my eyes still fixed upon Heda.

Then I got to business. There were hide riems on the bridles of the leaders. I undid these and knotted their loose ends firmly together. To them I made fast the riem of my own mare, slipping a loop I tied in it, over my right hand and saying—

"Now I will go first, leading the horses. Do you drive after me for all you are worth, even if they are swept off their feet. I can trust my beast to swim straight, and being a mare, I hope that the horses will follow her as they have done all night. Wake up Heda and Kaatje."

He nodded, and looking very pale, said—

"Heda my dear, I am sorry to disturb you, but we have to get over a river with a rough bottom, so you and Kaatje must hang on and sit tight. Don't be frightened, you are as safe as a church."

"God forgive him for that lie," thought I to myself as, having tightened the girths, I mounted my mare. Then gripping the riem I kicked the beast to a canter, Anscombe flogging up the team as we swung down the bank to the edge of the foaming torrent, on the further side of which the Swazis shouted and gesticulated to us to go back.

We were in it now, for, as I had hoped, the horses followed the mare without hesitation. For the first twenty yards or so all went well, I heading up the stream. Then suddenly I felt that the mare was swimming.

"Flog the horses and don't let them turn," I shouted to Anscombe.

Ten more yards and I glanced over my shoulder. The team was swimming also, and behind them the cart rocked and bobbed like a boat swinging in a heavy sea. There came a strain on the riem; the leaders were trying to turn! I pulled hard and encouraged them with my voice, while Anscombe, who drove splendidly, kept their heads as straight as he could. Mercifully they came round again and struck out for the further shore, the water-logged cart floating after them. Would it turn over? That was the question in my mind. Five seconds; ten seconds and it was still upright. Oh! it was going. No, a fierce back eddy caught it and set it straight again. My mare touched bottom and there was hope. It struggled forward, being swept down the stream all the time. Now the horses in the cart also found their footing and we were saved.

No, the wet had caused the knot of one of the riems to slip beneath the strain, or perhaps it broke—I don't know. Feeling the pull slacken the leaders whipped round on to the wheelers. There they all stood in a heap, their heads and part of their necks above water, while the cart floated behind them on its side. Kaatje screamed and Anscombe flogged. I leapt from my mare and struggled to the leaders, the water up to my chin. Grasping their bits I managed to keep them from turning further. But I could do no more and death came very near to us. Had it not been for some of those brave Swazis on the bank it would have found us, every one. But they plunged in, eight of them, holding each other's hands, and half-swimming, half-wading, reached us. They got the horses by the head and straightened them out, while Anscombe plied his whip. A dash forward and the wheels were on the bottom again.

Three minutes later we were safe on the further bank, which my mare had already reached, where I lay gasping on my face, ejaculating prayers of thankfulness and spitting out muddy water.

CHAPTER X

NOMBE

The Swazis, shivering, for all these people hate cold, and shaking themselves like a dog when he comes to shore, gathered round, examining me.

"Why!" said one of them, an elderly man who seemed to be their leader, "this is none other than Macumazahn, Watcher-by-Night, the old friend of all us black people. Surely the spirits of our fathers have been with us who might have risked our lives to save a Boer or a half-breed." (The Swazis, I may explain, did not like the Boers for reasons they considered sound.)

"Yes," I said, sitting up, "it is I, Macumazahn."

"Then why," asked the man, "did you, whom all know to be wise, show yourself to have suddenly become a fool?" and he pointed to the raging river.

"And why," I asked, "do you show yourself a fool by supposing that I, whom you know to be none, am a fool? Look across the water for your answer."

He looked and saw the Basutos, fifty or more of them, arriving, just too late.

"Who are these?" he asked.

"They are the people of Sekukuni whom you should know well enough. They have hunted us all night, yes, and before, seeking to murder us; also they have stolen our oxen, thirty-two fine oxen which I give to your king if he can take them back. Now perhaps you understand why we dared the Crocodile River in its rage."

At the name of Sekukuni the man, who it seemed was the captain of some border guards, stiffened all over like a terrier which perceives a rat. "What!" he exclaimed, "do these dirty Basuto dogs dare to carry spears so near our country? Have they not yet learned their lesson?"

Then he rushed into the water, shaking an assegai he had snatched up, and shouted,

"Bide a while, you fleas from the kaross of Sekukuni, till I can come across and crack you between my thumb and finger. Or at the least wait until Macumazahn has time to get his rifle. No, put down those guns of yours; for every shot you fire I swear that I will cut ten Basuto throats when we come to storm your koppies, as we shall do ere long."

"Be silent," I said, "and let me speak."

Then I, too, called across the river, asking where was that fat captain of theirs, as I would talk with him. One of the men shouted back that he had stopped behind, very sick, because of a ghost that he had seen.

"Ah!" I answered, "a ghost who pricked him in the throat. Well, I was that ghost, and such are the things that happen to those who would harm Macumazahn and his friends. Did you not say last night that he is a leopard who leaps out in the dark, bites and is gone again?"

"Yes," the man shouted back, "and it is true, though had we known, O Macumazahn, that you were the ghost hiding in those stones, you should never have leapt again. Oh! that white medicine-man who is dead has sent us on a mad errand."

"So you will think when I come to visit you among your koppies. Go home and take a message from Macumazahn to Sekukuni, who believes that the English have run away from him. Tell him that they will return again and these Swazis with them, and that then he will cease to live and his town will be burnt and his tribe will no more be a tribe. Away now, more swiftly than you came, since the water by which you thought to trap us is falling, and a Swazi impi gathers to make an end of every one of you."

The man attempted no answer, nor did his people so much as fire on us. They turned tail and crept off like a pack of frightened jackals—pursued by the mocking of the Swazis.

Still in a way they had the laugh of us, seeing that they gave us a terrible fright and stole our wagon and thirty-two oxen. Well, a year or two later I helped to pay them back for that fright and even recovered some of the oxen.

When they had gone the Swazis led us to a kraal about two miles from the river, sending on a runner with orders to make huts and food ready for us. It was just as much as we could do to reach it, for we were all utterly worn out, as were the horses. Still we did get there at last, the hot sun warming us as we went. Arrived at the kraal I helped Heda and Kaatje from the cart—the former could scarcely walk, poor dear—and into the guest hut which seemed clean, where food of a sort and fur karosses were brought to them in which to wrap themselves while their clothes dried.

Leaving them in charge of two old women, I went to see to Anscombe, who as yet could not do much for himself, also to the outspanning of the horses which were put into a cattle kraal, where they lay down at once without attempting to eat the green forage which was given to them. After this I gave our goods into the charge of the kraal-head, a nice old fellow whom I had never met before, and he led Anscombe to another hut close to that where the women were. Here we drank some maas, that is curdled milk, ate a little mutton, though we were too fatigued to be very hungry, and stripping off our wet clothes, threw them out into the sun to dry.

"That was a close shave," said Anscombe as he wrapped up in the kaross.

"Very," I answered. "So close that I think you must have been started in life with an extra strong guardian angel well accustomed to native ways."

"Yes," he replied, "and, old fellow, I believe that on earth he goes by the name of Allan Quatermain."

After this I remember no more, for I went to sleep, and so remained for about twenty-four hours. This was not wonderful, seeing that for two days and nights practically I had not rested, during which time I went through much fatigue and many emotions.

When at length I did wake up, the first thing I saw was Anscombe already dressed, engaged in cleaning my clothes with a brush from his toilet case. I remember thinking how smart and incongruous that dressing-bag, made appropriately enough of crocodile hide, looked in this Kaffir hut with its silver-topped bottles and its ivory-handled razors.

"Time to get up, Sir. Bath ready, Sir," he said in his jolly, drawling voice, pointing to a calabash full of hot water. "Hope you slept as well as I did, Sir."

"You appear to have recovered your spirits," I remarked as I rose and began to wash myself.

"Yes, Sir, and why not? Heda is quite well, for I have seen her. These Swazis are very good people, and as Kaatje understands their language, bring us all we want. Our troubles seem to be done with. Old Marnham is dead, and doubtless cremated; Rodd is dead and, let us hope, in heaven; the Basutos have melted away, the morning is fine and warm and a whole kid is cooking for breakfast."

"I wish there were two, for I am ravenous," I remarked.

"The horses are getting rested and feeding well, though some of their legs have filled, and the trap is little the worse, for I have walked to look at them, or rather hopped, leaning on the shoulder of a very sniffy Swazi boy. Do you know, old fellow, I believe there never were any Basutos; also that the venerable Marnham and the lurid Rodd had no real existence, that they were but illusions, a prolonged nightmare—no more. Here is your shirt. I am sorry that I have not had time to wash it, but it has cooked well in the sun, which, being flannel, is almost as good."

"At any rate Heda remains," I remarked, cutting his nonsense short, "and I suppose she is not a nightmare or a delusion."

"Yes, thank God! she remains," he replied with earnestness. "Oh! Allan, I thought she must drown in that river, and if I had lost her, I think I should have gone mad. Indeed, at the moment I felt myself going mad while I dragged and flogged at those horses."

"Well, you didn't lose her, and if she had drowned, you would have drowned also. So don't talk any more about it. She is safe, and now we have got to keep her so, for you are not married yet, my boy, and there are generally more trees in a wood than one can see. Still we are alive and well, which is more than we had any right to expect, and, as you say, let us thank God for that."

Then I put on my coat and my boots which Anscombe had greased as he had no blacking, and crept from the hut.

There, only a few yards away, engaged in setting the breakfast in the shadow of another hut on a tanned hide that served for a tablecloth while Kaatje saw to the cooking close by, I found Heda, still a little pale and sorrowful but otherwise quite well and rested. Moreover, she had managed to dress herself very nicely, I suppose by help of spare clothes in the cart, and therefore looked as charming as she always did. I think that her perfect manners were one of her greatest attractions. Thus on this morning her first thought was to thank me very sweetly for all she was good enough to say I had done for her and Anscombe, thereby, as she put it, saving their lives several times over.

"My dear young lady," I answered as roughly as I could, "don't flatter yourself on that point; it was my own life of which I was thinking."

But she only smiled and, shaking her head in a fascinating way that was peculiar to her, remarked that I could not deceive her as I did the Kaffirs. After this the solid Kaatje brought the food and we breakfasted very heartily, or at least I did.

Now I am not going to set out all the details of our journey through Swazi-Land, for though in some ways it was interesting enough, also as comfortable as a stay among savages can be, for everywhere we were kindly received, to do so would be too long, and I must get on with my story. At the king's kraal, which we did not reach for some days as the absence of roads and the flooded state of the rivers, also the need of sparing our horses, caused us to travel very slowly, I met a Boer who I think was concession hunting.

He told me that things were really serious in Zululand, so serious that he thought there was a probability of immediate war between the English and the Zulus. He said also that Cetewayo, the Zulu king, had sent messengers to stir up the Basutos and other tribes against the white men, with the result that Sekukuni had already made a raid towards Pilgrim's Rest and Lydenburg.

I expressed surprise and asked innocently if he had done any harm. The Boer replied he understood that they had stolen some cattle, killed two white men, if not more, and burnt their house. He added, however, that he was not sure whether the white men had been killed by the Kaffirs or by other white men with whom they had quarrelled. There was a rumour to this effect, and he understood that the magistrate of Barberton had gone with some mounted police and armed natives to investigate the matter.

Then we parted, as, having got his concession to which the king Umbandine had put his mark when he was drunk on brandy that the Boer himself had brought with him as a present, he was anxious to be gone before he grew sober and revoked it. Indeed, he was in so great a hurry that he never stopped to inquire what I was doing in Swazi-Land, nor do I think he realized that I was not alone. Certainly he was quite unaware that I had been mixed up in these Basuto troubles. Still his story as to the investigation concerning the deaths of Marnham and Rodd made me uneasy, since I feared lest he should hear something on his journey and put two and two together, though as a matter of fact I don't think he ever did either of these things.

The Swazis told me much the same story as to the brewing Zulu storm. In fact an old Induna or councillor, whom I knew, informed me that Cetewayo had sent messengers to them, asking for their help if it should come to fighting with the white men, but that the king and councillors answered that they had always been the Queen's children (which was not strictly true, as they were never under English rule) and did not wish to "bite her feet if she should have to fight with her hands." I replied that I hoped they would always act up to these fine words, and changed the subject.

Now once more the question arose as to whether we should make for Natal or press on to Zululand. The rumour of coming war suggested that the first would be our better course, while the Boer's story as to the investigation of Rodd's death pointed the other way. Really I did not know which to do, and as usual Anscombe and Heda seemed inclined to leave the decision to me. I think that after all Natal would have gained the day had it not been for a singular circumstance, not a flash of lightning this time. Indeed, I had almost made up my mind to risk trouble and inquiry as to Rodd's death, remembering that in Natal these two young people could get married, which, being in loco parentis, I thought it desirable they should do as soon as possible, if only to ease me of my responsibilities. Also thence I could attend to the matter of Heda's inheritance and rid myself of her father's will that already had been somewhat damaged in the Crocodile River, though not as much as it might have been since I had taken the precaution to enclose it in Anscombe's sponge bag before we left the house.

The circumstance was this: On emerging from the cart one morning, where I slept to keep an eye upon the valuables, for it will be remembered that we had a considerable sum in gold with us, also Heda's jewels, a Swazi informed me that a messenger wished to see me. I asked what messenger and whence did he come. He replied that the messenger was a witch-doctoress named Nombe, and that she came from Zululand and said that I knew her father.

I bade the man bring her to me, wondering who on earth she could be, for it is not usual for the Zulus to send women as messengers, and from whom she came. However, I knew exactly what she would be like, some hideous old hag smelling horribly of grease and other abominations, with a worn snake skin and some human bones tied about her.

Presently she came, escorted by the Swazi who was grinning, for I think he guessed what I expected to see. I stared and rubbed my eyes, thinking that I must still be asleep, for instead of a fat old Isanusi there appeared a tall and graceful young woman, rather light-coloured, with deep and quiet eyes and a by no means ill-favoured face, remarkable for a fixed and somewhat mysterious smile. She was a witch-doctoress sure enough, for she wore in her hair the regulation bladders and about her neck the circlet of baboon's teeth, also round her middle a girdle from which hung little bags of medicines.

She contemplated me gravely and I contemplated her, waiting till she should choose to speak. At length, having examined me inch by inch, she saluted by raising her rounded arm and tapering hand, and remarked in a soft, full voice—

"All is as the picture told. I perceive before me the lord Macumazahn."

I thought this a strange saying, seeing that I could not recollect having given my photograph to any one in Zululand.

"You need no magic to tell you that, doctoress," I remarked, "but where did you see my picture?"

"In the dust far away," she replied.

"And who showed it to you?"

"One who knew you, O Macumazahn, in the years before I came out of the Darkness, one named Opener of Roads, and with him another who also knew you in those years, one who has gone down to the Darkness."

Now for some occult reason I shrank from asking the name of this "one who had gone down to the Darkness," although I was sure that she was waiting for the question. So I merely remarked, without showing surprise—

"So Zikali still lives, does he? He should have been dead long ago."

"You know well that he lives, Macumazahn, for how could he die till his work was accomplished? Moreover, you will remember that he spoke to you when last moon was but just past her full—in a dream, Macumazahn. I brought that dream, although you did not see me."

"Pish!" I exclaimed. "Have done with your talk of dreams. Who thinks anything of dreams?"

"You do," she replied even more placidly than before, "you whom that dream has brought hither—with others."

"You lie," I said rudely. "The Basutos brought me here."

"The Watcher-by-Night is pleased to say that I lie, so doubtless I do lie," she answered, her fixed smile deepening a little. Then she folded her arms across her breast and remained silent.

"You are a messenger, O seer of pictures in the dust and bearer of the cup of dreams," I said with sarcasm. "Who sends a message by your lips for me, and what are the words of the message?"

"My Lords the Spirits spoke the message by the mouth of the master Zikali. He sends it on to you by the lips of your servant, the doctoress Nombe."

"Are you indeed a doctoress, being so young?" I asked, for somehow I wished to postpone the hearing of that message.

"O Macumazahn, I have heard the call, I have felt the pain in my back, I have drunk of the black medicine and of the white medicine, yes, for a whole year. I have been visited by the multitude of Spirits and seen the shades of those who live and of those who are dead. I have dived into the river and drawn my snake from its mud; see, its skin is about me now," and opening the mantle she wore she showed what looked like the skin of a black mamba, fastened round her slender body. "I have dwelt in the wilderness alone and listened to its voices. I have sat at the feet of my master, the Opener of Roads, and looked down the road and drunk of his wisdom. Yes, I am in truth a doctoress."

"Well, after all this, you should be as wise as you are pretty."

"Once before, Macumazahn, you told a maid of my people that she was pretty and she came to no good end; though to one that was great. Therefore do not say to me that I am pretty, though I am glad that you should think so who can compare me with so many whom you have known," and she dropped her eyes, looking a little shy.

It was the first human touch I had seen about her, and I was glad to have found a weak spot in her armour. Moreover, from that moment she was always my friend.

"As you will, Nombe. Now for your message."

"My Lords the Spirits, speaking through Zikali as one who makes music speak through a pipe of reeds, say—"

"Never mind what the spirits say. Tell me what Zikali says," I interrupted.

"So be it, Macumazahn. These are the words of Zikali: 'O Watcher-by-Night, the time draws on when the Thing-who-should-never-have-been-born will be as though he never had been born, whereat he rejoices. But first there is much for him to do, and as he told you nearly three hundred moons ago, in what must be done you will have your part. Of that he will speak to you afterwards. Macumazahn, you dreamed a dream, did you not, lying asleep in the house that was built of white stone which now is black with fire? I, Zikali, sent you that dream through the arts of a child of mine who is named Nombe, she to whom I have given a Spirit to guide her feet. You did well to follow it, Macumazahn, for had you tried the other path, which would have led you back to the towns of the white men, you and those with you must have been killed, how it does not matter. Now by the mouth of Nombe I say to you, do not follow the thought that is in your mind as she speaks to you and go to Natal, since if you do so, you and those with you will come to much shame and trouble that to you would be worse than death, over the matter of the killing of a certain white doctor in a swamp where grow yellow-wood trees. For there in Natal you will be taken, all of you, and sent back to the Transvaal to be tried before a man who wears upon his head horse's hair stained white. But if you come to Zululand this shadow shall pass away from you, since great things are about to happen which will cause so small a matter to be forgot. Moreover, I Zikali, who do not lie, promise this: That however great may be their dangers here in Zululand, those half-fledged ones whom you, the old night-hawk, cover with your wings, shall in the end suffer no harm; those of whom I spoke to you in your dream, the white lord, Mauriti, and the white lady, Heddana, who stretch out their arms one to another. I wait to welcome you, here at the Black Kloof, whither my daughter Nombe will guide you. Cetewayo, the king, also will welcome you, and so will another whose name I do not utter. Now choose. I have spoken.'"

Having delivered her message Nombe stood quite still, smiling as before, and apparently indifferent as to its effect.

"How do I know that you come from Zikali?" I asked. "You may be but the bait set upon a trap."

From somewhere within her robe she produced a knife and handed it to me, remarking—

"The Master says you will remember this, and by it know that the message comes from him. He bade me add that with it was carved a certain image that once he gave to you at Panda's kraal, wrapped round with a woman's hair, which image you still have."

I looked at the knife and did remember it, for it was one of those of Swedish make with a wooden handle, the first that I had ever seen in Africa. I had made a present of it to Zikali when I returned to Zululand before the war between the Princes. The image, too, I still possessed. It was that of the woman called Mameena who brought about the war, and the wrapping which covered it was of the hair that once grew upon her head.

"The words are Zikali's," I said, returning her the knife, "but why do you call yourself the child of one who is too old to be a father?"

"The Master says that my great-grandmother was his daughter and that therefore I am his child. Now, Macumazahn, I go to eat with my people, for I have servants with me. Then I must speak with the Swazi king, for whom I also have a message, which I cannot do at present because he is still drunk with the white man's liquor. After that I shall be ready to return with you to Zululand."

"I never said that I was going to Zululand, Nombe."

"Yet your heart has gone there already, Macumazahn, and you must follow your heart. Does not the image which was carved with the knife you gave, hold a white heart in its hand, and although it seems to be but a bit of Umzimbeete wood, is it not alive and bewitched, which perhaps is why you could never make up your mind to burn it, Macumazahn?"

"I wish I had," I replied angrily; but having thrown this last spear, with a flash of her unholy eyes Nombe had turned and gone.

A clever woman and thoroughly coached, thought I. Well, Zikali was never one to suffer fools, and doubtless she is another of the pawns whom he uses on his board of policy. Oh! she, or rather he was right; my heart was in Zululand, though not in the way he thought, and I longed to see the end of that great game played by a wizard against a despot and his hosts.

So we went to Zululand because after talking it over we all came to the conclusion that this was the best thing to do, especially as there we seemed to be sure of a welcome. For later in the day Nombe repeated to Anscombe and Heda the invitation which she had delivered to me, assuring them also that in Zululand they would come to no harm.

It was curious to watch the meeting between Heda and Nombe. The doctoress appeared just as we had risen from breakfast, and Heda, turning round, came face to face with her.

"Is this your witch, Mr. Quatermain?" she asked me in her vivacious way. "Why, she is different from what I expected, quite good-looking and, yes, impressive. I am not sure that she does not frighten me a little."

"What does the Inkosikaasi (i.e., the chieftainess) say concerning me, Macumazahn?" asked Nombe.

"Only what I said, that you are young who she thought would be old, and pretty who she thought would be ugly."

"To grow old we must first be young, Macumazahn, and in due season all of us will become ugly, even the Inkosikaasi. But I thought she said also that she feared me."

"Do you know English, Nombe?"

"Nay, but I know how to read eyes, and the Inkosikaasi has eyes that talk. Tell her that she has no reason to fear me who would be her friend, though I think that she will bring me little luck."

It was scarcely necessary, so far as Heda was concerned, but I translated, leaving out the last sentence.

"Say to her that I am grateful who have few friends, and that I will fear her no more," said Heda.

Again I translated, whereon Nombe stretched out her hand, saying—

"Let her not scorn to take it, it is clean. It has brought no man to his death—" Here she looked at Heda meaningly. "Moreover, though she is white and I am black, I like herself am of high blood and come of a race of warriors who did nothing small, and lastly, we are of an age, and if she is beautiful, I am wise and have gifts great as her own."

Once more I interpreted for the benefit of Anscombe, for Heda understood Zulu well enough, although she had pretended not to do so, after which the two shook hands, to Anscombe's amusement and my wonder. For I felt this scene to be strained and one that hid, or presaged, something I did not comprehend.

"This is the Chief she loves?" said Nombe to me, studying Anscombe with her steady eyes after Heda had gone. "Well, he is no common man and brave, if idle; one, too, who may grow tall in the world, should he live, when he has learned to think. But, Macumazahn, if she met you both at the same time why did she not choose you?"

"Just now you said you were wise, Nombe," I replied laughing, "but now I see that, like most of your trade, you are but a vain boaster. Is there a hat upon my head that you cannot see the colour of my hair, and is it natural that youth should turn to age?"

"Sometimes if the mind is old, Macumazahn, which is why I love the Spirits only who are more ancient than the mountains, and with them Zikali their servant, who was young before the Zulus were a people, or so he says, and still year by year gathers wisdom as the bee gathers honey. Inspan your horses, Macumazahn, for I have done my business and am ready to start."

CHAPTER XI

ZIKALI

Ten days had gone by when once more I found myself drawing near to the mouth of the Black Kloof where dwelt Zikali the Wizard. Our journey in Zululand had been tedious and uneventful. It seemed to me that we met extraordinarily few people; it was as though the place had suddenly become depopulated, and I even passed great kraals where there was no one to be seen. I asked Nombe what was the meaning of this, for she and three silent men she had with her were acting as our guides. Once she answered that the people had moved because of lack of food, as the season had been one of great scarcity owing to drought, and once that they had been summoned to a gathering at the king's kraal near Ulundi. At any rate they were not there, and the few who did appear stared at us strangely.

Moreover, I noticed that they were not allowed to speak to us. Also Heda was kept in the cart and Nombe insisted that the rear canvas curtain should be closed and a blanket fastened behind Anscombe who drove, evidently with the object that she should not be seen. Further, on the plea of weariness, from the time that we entered Zulu territory Nombe asked to be allowed to ride in the cart with Kaatje and Heda, her real reason, as I was sure, being that she might keep a watch on them. Lastly we travelled by little-frequented tracks, halting at night in out-of-the-way places, where, however, we always found food awaiting us, doubtless by arrangement.

With one man whom I had known in past days and who recognized me, I did manage to have a short talk. He asked me what I was doing in Zululand at that time. I replied that I was on a visit to Zikali, whereon he said I should be safer with him than with any one else.

Our conversation went no further, for just then one of Nombe's servants appeared and made some remark to the man of which I could not catch the meaning, whereon he promptly turned and deported, leaving me wondering and uneasy.

Evidently we were being isolated, but when I remonstrated with Nombe she only answered with her most unfathomable smile—

"O Macumazahn, you must ask Zikali of all these things. I am no one and know nothing, who only do what the Master tells me is for your good."

"I am minded to turn and depart from Zululand," I said angrily, "for in this low veld whither you have led us there is fever and the horses will catch sickness or be bitten by the tsetse fly and perish."

"I cannot say, Macumazahn, who only travel by the road the Master pointed out. Yet if you will be guided by me, you will not try to leave Zululand."

"You mean that I am in a trap, Nombe."

"I mean that the country is full of soldiers and that all white men have fled from it. Therefore, even if you were allowed to pass because the Zulus love you, Macumazahn, it might well happen that those with you would stay behind, sound asleep, Macumazahn, for which, like you, I should be sorry."

After this I said no more, for I knew that she meant to warn me. We had entered on this business and must see it through to its end, sweet or bitter.

As for Anscombe and Heda their happiness seemed to be complete. The novelty of the life charmed them, and of its dangers they took no thought, being content to leave me, in whom they had a blind faith, to manage everything. Moreover, Heda, who in the joy of her love was beginning to forget the sorrow of her father's death and the other tragic events through which she had just passed, took a great fancy to the young witch-doctoress who conversed with her in Zulu, a language of which, having lived so long in Natal, Heda knew much already. Indeed, when I suggested to her that to be over-trusting was not wise, she fired up and replied that she had been accustomed to natives all her life and could judge them, adding that she had every confidence in Nombe.

After this I held my tongue and said no more of my doubts. What was the use since Heda would not listen to them, and at that time Anscombe was nothing but her echo?

So this, for me, very dull journey continued, till at length, after being held up for a couple of days by a flooded river where there was nothing to do but sit and smoke, as Nombe requested me not to make a noise by shooting at the big game that abounded, we began to emerge from the bush-veld on to the lovely uplands in the neighbourhood of Nongoma. Leaving these on our right we headed for a place called Ceza, a natural stronghold consisting of a flat plain on the top of a mountain, which plain is surrounded by bush. It is at the foot of this stronghold that the Black Kloof lies, being one of the ravines that run up into the mountain.

So thither we came at last. It was drawing towards sunset, a tremendous and stormy sunset, as we approached the place, and lo! it looked exactly as it had done when first I saw it more than a score of years before, forbidding as the mouth of hell, vast and lonesome. There stood the columns of boulders fantastically piled one upon another; there grew the sparse trees upon its steep sides, mingled with aloes that looked like the shapes of men; there was the granite bottom swept almost clean by floods in some dim age, and the little stream that flowed along it. There, too, was the spot where once I had outspanned my wagons on the night when my servants swore that they saw the Imikovu, or wizard-raised spectres, floating past them on the air in the shapes of the Princes and others who were soon to fall at the battle of the Tugela. Up it we went, I riding and Nombe, who had descended from the cart that followed, walking by my side and watching me.

"You seem sad, Macumazahn," she said at length.

"Yes, Nombe, I am sad. This place makes me so."

"Is it the place, Macumazahn, or is it the thought of one whom once you met in the place, one who is dead?"

I looked at her, pretending not to understand, and she went on—

"I have the gift of vision, Macumazahn, which comes at times to those of my trade, and now and again, amongst others, I have seemed to see the spirit of a certain woman haunting this kloof as though she were waiting for some one."

"Indeed, and what may that woman be like?" I inquired carelessly.

"As it chances I can see her now gliding backwards in front of you just there, and therefore am able to answer your question, Macumazahn. She is tall and slender, beautifully made, and light-coloured for one of us black people. She has large eyes like a buck, and those eyes are full of fire that does not come from the sun but from within. Her face is tender yet proud, oh! so proud that she makes me afraid. She wears a cloak of grey fur, and about her neck there is a circlet of big blue beads with which her fingers play. A thought comes from her to me. These are the words of the thought: 'I have waited long in this dark place, watching by day and night till you, the Watcher-by-Night, return to meet me here. At length you have come, and in this enchanted place my hungry spirit can feed upon your spirit for a while. I thank you for coming, who now am no more lonely. Fear nothing, Macumazahn, for by a certain kiss I swear to you that till the appointed hour when you become as I am, I will be a shield upon your arm and a spear in your hand.' Such are the words of her thought, Macumazahn, but she has gone away and I hear no more. It was as though your horse rode over her and she passed through you."

Then, like one who wished to answer no questions, Nombe turned and went back to the cart, where she began to talk indifferently with Heda, for as soon as we entered the kloof her servants had drawn back the curtains and let fall the blanket. As for me, I groaned, for of course I knew that Zikali, who was well acquainted with the appearance of Mameena, had instructed Nombe to say all this to me in order to impress my mind for some reason of his own. Yet he had done it cleverly, for such words as those Mameena might well have uttered could her great spirit have need to walk the earth again. Was such a thing possible, I wondered? No, it was not possible, yet it was true that her atmosphere seemed to cling about this place and that my imagination, excited by memory and Nombe's suggestions, seemed to apprehend her presence.

As I reflected the horse advanced round the little bend in the ever-narrowing cliffs, and there in front of me, under the gigantic mass of overhanging rock, appeared the kraal of Zikali surrounded by its reed fence. The gate of the fence was open, and beyond it, on his stool in front of the large hut, sat Zikali. Even at that distance it was impossible to mistake his figure, which was like no other that I had known in the world. A broad-shouldered dwarf with a huge head, deep, sunken eyes and snowy hair that hung upon his shoulders; the whole frame and face pervaded with an air of great antiquity, and yet owing to the plumpness of the flesh and that freshness of skin which is sometimes seen in the aged, comparatively young-looking.

Such was the great wizard Zikali, known throughout the land for longer than any living man could remember as "Opener of Roads," a title that referred to his powers of spiritual vision, also as the "Thing-that-should-never-have-been-born," a name given to him by Chaka, the first and greatest of the Zulu kings, because of his deformity.

There he sat silent, impassive, staring open-eyed at the red ball of the setting sun, looking more like some unshapely statue than a man. His silent, fierce-faced servants appeared. To me they looked like the same men whom I had seen here three and twenty years before, only grown older. Indeed, I think they were, for they greeted me by name and saluted by raising their broad spears. I dismounted and waited while Anscombe, whose foot was now quite well again, helped Heda from the cart which was led away by the servants. Anscombe, who seemed a little oppressed, remarked that this was a strange place.

"Yes," said Heda, "but it is magnificent. I like it."

Then her eye fell upon Zikali seated before the hut and she turned pale.

"Oh! what a terrible-looking man," she murmured, "if he is a man."

The maid Kaatje saw him also and uttered a little cry.

"Don't be frightened, dear," said Anscombe, "he is only an old dwarf."

"I suppose so," she exclaimed doubtfully, "but to me he is like the devil."

Nombe slid past us. She threw off the kaross she wore and for the first time appeared naked except for the mucha about her middle and her ornaments. Down she went on her hands and knees and in this humble posture crept towards Zikali. Arriving in front of him she touched the ground with her forehead, then lifting her right arm, gave the salute of Makosi, to which as a great wizard he was entitled, being supposed to be the home of many spirits. So far as I could see he took no notice of her. Presently she moved and squatted herself down on his right hand, while two of his attendants appeared from behind the hut and took their stand between him and its doorway, holding their spears raised. About a minute later Nombe beckoned to us to approach, and we went forward across the courtyard, I a little ahead of the others. As we drew near Zikali opened his mouth and uttered a loud and terrifying laugh. How well I remembered that laugh which I had first heard at Dingaan's kraal as a boy after the murder of Retief and the Boers.*

[*—See the book called Marie, by H. Rider Haggard.]

"I begin to think that you are right and that this old gentleman must be the devil," said Anscombe to Heda, then lapsed into silence.

As I was determined not to speak first I took the opportunity to fill my pipe. Zikali, who was watching me, although all the while he seemed to be staring at the setting sun, made a sign. One of the servants dashed away and immediately returned, bearing a flaming brand which he proffered to me as a pipe-lighter. Then he departed again to bring three carved stools of red wood which he placed for us. I looked at mine and knew it again by the carvings. It was the same on which I had sat when first I met Zikali. At length he spoke in his deep, slow voice.

"Many years have gone by, Macumazahn, since you made use of that stool. They are cut in notches upon the leg you hold and you may count them if you will."

I examined the leg. There were the notches, twenty-two or three of them. On the other legs were more notches too numerous to reckon.

"Do not look at those, Macumazahn, for they have nothing to do with you. They tell the years since the first of the House of Senzangacona sat upon that stool, since Chaka sat upon it, since Dingaan and others sat upon it, one Mameena among them. Well, much has happened since it served you for a rest. You have wandered far and seen strange things and lived where others would have died because it was your lot to live, of all of which we will talk afterwards. And now when you are grey you have come back here, as the Opener of Roads told you you would do, bringing with you new companions, you who have the art of making friends even when you are old, which is one given to few men. Where are those with whom you used to company, Macumazahn? Where are Saduko and Mameena and the rest? All gone except the Thing-who-should-never-have-been-born," and again he laughed loudly.

"And who it seems has never learned when to die," I remarked, speaking for the first time.

"Just so, Macumazahn, because I cannot die until my work is finished. But thanks be to the spirits of my fathers and to my own that I live on to glut with vengeance, the end draws near at last, and as I promised you in the dead days, you shall have your share in it, Macumazahn."

He paused, then continued, still staring at the sinking sun, which made his remarks about us, whom he did not seem to see, uncanny—

"That white man with you is brave and well-born, one who loves fighting, I think, and the maiden is fair and sweet, with a high spirit. She is thinking to herself that I am an old wizard whom, if she were not afraid of me, she would ask to tell her her fortune. See, she understands and starts. Well, perhaps I will one day. Meanwhile, here is a little bit of it. She will have five children, of whom two will die and one will give her so much trouble that she will wish it had died also. But who their father will be I do not say. Nombe my child, lead away this White One and her woman to the hut that has been made ready for her, for she is weary and would rest. See, too, that she lacks for nothing which we can give her who is our guest. Let the white lord, Mauriti, accompany her to the hut and be shown that next to it in which he and Macumazahn will sleep, so that he may be sure that she is safe, and attend to the horses if he wills. There is a place to tether them behind the huts, and the men who travelled with you will help him. Afterwards, when I have spoken with him, Macumazahn can join them that they may eat before they sleep."

These directions I translated to Anscombe, who went gladly enough with Heda, for I think they were both afraid of the terrible old dwarf and did not desire his company in the gathering gloom.

"The sun sinks once more, Macumazahn," he said when they were gone, "and the air grows chill. Come with me now into my hut where the fire burns, for I am aged and the cold strikes through me. Also there we can be alone."

So speaking he turned and crawled into the hut, looking like a gigantic white-headed beetle as he did so, a creature, I remembered, to which I had once compared him in the past. I followed, carrying the historic stool, and when he had seated himself on his kaross on the further side of the fire, took up my position opposite to him. This fire was fed with some kind of root or wood that gave a thin clear flame with little or no smoke. Over it he crouched, so closely that his great head seemed to be almost in the flame at which he stared with unblinking eyes as he had done at the sun, circumstances which added to his terrifying appearance and made me think of a certain region and its inhabitants.

"Why do you come here, Macumazahn?" he asked after studying me for a while through that window of fire.

"Because you brought me, Zikali, partly through your messenger, Nombe, and partly by means of a dream which she says you sent."

"Did I, Macumazahn? If so, I have forgotten it. Dreams are as many as gnats by the water; they bite us while we sleep, but when we wake up we forget them. Also it is foolishness to say that one man can send a dream to another."

"Then your messenger lied, Zikali, especially as she added that she brought it."

"Of course she lied, Macumazahn. Is she not my pupil whom I have trained from a child? Moreover, she lied well, it would seem, who guessed what sort of a dream you would have when you thought of turning your steps to Zululand."

"Why do you play at sticks (i.e., fence) with me, Zikali, seeing that neither of us are children?"

"O Macumazahn, that is where you are mistaken, seeing that both of us, old though we be and cunning though we think ourselves, are nothing but babes in the arms of Fate. Well, well, I will tell you the truth, since it would be foolish to try to throw dust into such eyes as yours. I knew that you were down in Sekukuni's country and I was watching you—through my spies. You have been nowhere during all these years that I was not watching you—through my spies. For instance, that Arab-looking man named Harut, whom first you met at a big kraal in a far country, was a spy of mine. He has visited me lately and told me much of your doings. No, don't ask me of him now who would talk to you of other matters—"

"Does Harut still live then, and has he found a new god in place of the Ivory Child?" I interrupted.

"Macumazahn, if he did not live, how could he visit and speak with me? Well, I watched you there by the Oliphant's River where you fought Sekukuni's people, and afterwards in the marble hut where you found the old white man dead in his chair and got the writings that you have in your pocket which concern the maiden Heddana; also afterwards when the white man, your friend, killed the doctor who fell into a mud hole and the Basutos stole his cattle and wagon."

"How do you know all these things, Zikali?"

"Have I not told you—through my spies. Was there not a half-breed driver called Footsack, and do not the Basutos come and go between the Black Kloof and Sekukuni's town, bearing me tidings?"

"Yes, Zikali, and so does the wind and so do the birds."

"True! O Macumazahn, I see that you are one who has watched Nature and its ways as closely as my spies watch you. So I learned these matters and knew that you were in trouble over the death of these white men, and your friends likewise, and as you were always dear to me, I sent that child Nombe to bring you to me, thinking from what I knew of you that you would be more likely to follow a woman who is both wise and good to look at, than a man who might be neither. I told her to say to you that you and the others would be safer here than in Natal at present. It seems that you hearkened and came. That is all."

"Yes, I hearkened and came. But, Zikali, that is not all, for you know well that you sent for me for your own sake, not for mine."

"O Macumazahn, who can prevent a needle from piercing cloth when it is pushed by a finger like yours? Your wits are too sharp for me, Macumazahn; your eyes read through the blanket of cunning with which I would hide my thought. You speak truly. I did send for you for my own sake as well as for yours. I sent for you because I wanted your counsel, Macumazahn, and because Cetewayo the king also wants your counsel, and I wished to see you before you saw Cetewayo. Now you have the whole truth."

"What do you want my counsel about, Zikali?"

He leaned forward till his white locks almost seemed to mingle with the thin flame, through which he glared at me with eyes that were fiercer than the fire.

"Macumazahn, you remember the story that I told you long ago, do you not?"

"Very well, Zikali. It was that you hate the House of Senzangacona which has given all its kings to Zululand. First, because you are one of the Dwandwe tribe whom the Zulus crushed and mocked at. Secondly, because Chaka the Lion named you the 'Thing-that-should-never-have-been-born' and killed your wives, for which crime you brought about the death of Chaka. Thirdly, because you have matched your single wit for many years against all the power of the royal House and yet kept your life in you, notably when Panda threatened you in my presence at the trial of one who has 'gone down,' and you told him to kill you if he dared. Now you would prove that you were right by causing your cunning to triumph over the royal House."

"True, quite true, O Macumazahn. You have a good memory, Macumazahn, especially for anything that has to do with that woman who has 'gone down.' I sent her down, but how was she named, Macumazahn? I forget, I forget, whose mind being old, falls suddenly into black pits of darkness—like her who went down."

He paused and we stared at each other through the veil of fire. Then as I made no answer, he went on—

"Oh! I remember now, she was called Mameena, was she not, a name taken from the wailing of the wind? Hark! It is wailing now."

I listened; it was, and I shivered to hear it, since but a minute before the night had been quite still. Yes, the wind moaned and wailed about the rocks of the Black Kloof.

"Well, enough of her. Why trouble about the dead when there are so many to be sent to join them? Macumazahn, the hour is at hand. The fool Cetewayo has quarrelled with your people, the English, and on my counsel. He has sent and killed women, or allowed others to do so, across the river in Natal. His messengers came to me asking what he should do. I answered, 'Shall a king of the blood of Chaka fear to allow his own wicked ones to be slain because they have stepped across a strip of water, and still call himself king of the Zulus?' So those women were dragged back across the water and killed; and now the Queen's man from the Cape asks many things, great fines of cattle, the giving up of the slayers, and that an end should be made of the Zulu army, which is to lay down its spears and set to hoeing like the old women in the kraals."

"And if the king refuses, what then, Zikali?"

"Then, Macumazahn, the Queen's man will declare war on the Zulus; already he gathers his soldiers for the war."

"Will Cetewayo refuse, Zikali?"

"I do not know. His mind swings this way and that, like a pole balanced on a rock. The ends of the pole are weighted with much counsel, and it hangs so even that if a grasshopper lit on one end or the other, it would turn the scale."

"And do you wish me to be that grasshopper, Zikali?"

"Who else? That is why I brought you to Zululand."

"So you wish me to counsel Cetewayo to lie down in the bed that the English have made for him. If he seeks my advice I will do so gladly, for so I am sure he will sleep well."

"Why do you mock me, Macumazahn? I wish you to counsel Cetewayo to throw back his word into the teeth of the Queen's man and to fight the English."

"And thus bring destruction on the Zulus and death to thousands of them and of my own people, and in return gain nothing but remorse. Do you think me mad or wicked, or both, that I should do this thing?"

"Nay, Macumazahn, you would gain much. I could show you where the king's cattle are hidden. The English will never find them, and after the war you might take as many as you chose. But it would be useless, for knowing you well, I am sure that you would only hand them over to the British Government, as once you handed over the cattle of Bangu, being fashioned that way by the Great-Great, Macumazahn."

"Perhaps I might, but then what should I gain, Zikali?"

"This: you would so bring things about that, being broken by war, the Zulu power could never again menace the white men, which would be a great and good deed, Macumazahn."

"Mayhap—I am not sure. But of this I am sure, that I will not thrust my face into your nest of wasps, that the English hornets may steal the honey when they are disturbed. I leave such matters to the Queen and those who rule under her. So have done with such talk, for you do but waste your breath, Zikali."

"It is as I guessed it would be," he answered, shaking his great head. "You are too honest to prosper in the world, Macumazahn. Well, I must find other means to bring the House of Cetewayo to the end that he deserves, who has been an evil and a cruel king."

All this he said, showing neither surprise nor resentment, which convinced me of what I had suspected throughout, that never for an instant did he believe that I should fall in with his suggestions and try to influence the Zulus to declare war. No, this talk of his was but a blind; there was some deeper scheme at work in his cunning old brain which he was hiding from me. Why exactly had he beguiled me to Zululand? I could not divine, and to ask him would be worse than useless, but then and there I made up my mind that I would get away from the Black Kloof early on the following morning, if that were possible.

He began to speak of other matters in a low, droning voice, like a man who converses with himself. Sad, all of them, such as the haunted death of Saduko who had betrayed his lord, the Prince Umbelazi, because of a woman, every circumstance of which seemed to be familiar to him.

I made no answer, who was waiting for an opportunity to leave the hut, and did not care to dwell on these events. He ceased and brooded for a while, then said suddenly—

"You are hungry and would eat, Macumazahn, and I who eat little would sleep, for in sleep the multitudes of Spirits visit me, bringing tidings from afar. Well, we have spoken together and of that I am glad, for who knows when the chance will come again, though I think that soon we shall meet at Ulundi, Ulundi where Fate spreads its net. What was it I had to say to you? Ah! I remember. There is one who is always in your thoughts and whom you wish to see, one too who wishes to see you. You shall, you shall in payment for the trouble you have taken in coming so far to visit a poor old Zulu doctor whom, as you told me long ago, you know to be nothing but a cheat."

He paused and, why I could not tell, I grew weak with fear of I knew not what, and bethought me of flight.

"It is cold in this hut, is it not?" he went on. "Burn up, fire, burn up!" and plunging his hand into a catskin bag of medicines which he wore, he drew out some powder which he threw upon the embers that instantly burst into bright flame.

"Look now, Macumazahn," he said, "look to your right."

I looked and oh Heaven! there before me with outstretched arms and infinite yearning on her face, stood Mameena, Mameena as I had last seen her after I gave her the promised kiss that she used to cover her taking of the poison. For five seconds, mayhap, she stood thus, living, wonderful, but still as death, the fierce light showing all. Then the flame died down again and she was gone.

I turned and next instant was out of the hut, pursued by the terrible laughter of Zikali.

CHAPTER XII

TRAPPED

Outside in the cool night air I recovered myself, sufficiently at any rate to be able to think, and saw at once that the thing was an illusion for which Zikali had prepared my mind very carefully by means of the young witch-doctoress, Nombe. He knew well enough that this remarkable woman, Mameena, had made a deep impression on me nearly a quarter of a century before, as she had done upon other men with whom she had been associated. Therefore it was probable that she would always be present to my thought, since whatever a man forgets, he remembers the women who have shown him favour, true or false, for Nature has decreed it thus.

Moreover, this was one to be remembered for herself, since she was beautiful and most attractive in her wild way. Also she had brought about a great war, causing the death of thousands, and lastly her end might fairly be called majestic. All these impressions Zikali had instructed Nombe to revivify by her continual allusions to Mameena, and lastly by her pretence that she saw her walking in front of me. Then when I was tired and hungry, in that place which for me was so closely connected with this woman, and in his own uncanny company, either by mesmerism or through the action of the drug he threw upon the fire, he had succeeded in calling up the illusion of her presence to my charmed sight. All this was clear enough, what remained obscure was his object.

Possibly he had none beyond an impish desire to frighten me, which is common enough among practitioners of magic in all lands. Well, for a little while he had succeeded, although to speak truth I remained uncertain whether in a sense I was not more thrilled and rejoiced than frightened. Mameena had never been so ill to look upon, and I knew that dead or living I had nothing to fear from her who would have walked through hell fire for my sake, would have done anything, except perhaps sacrifice her ambition. No, even if this were her ghost I should have been glad to see her again.

But it was not a ghost; it was only a fancy reproduced exactly as my mind had photographed her, almost as my eyes last saw her, when her kiss was still warm upon my lips.

Such were my thoughts as I stood outside that hut with the cold perspiration running down my face, for to tell the truth my nerves were upset, although without reason. So upset were they that when suddenly a silent-footed man appeared out of the darkness I jumped as high as though I had set my foot on a puff-adder, and until I recognized him by his voice as one of Nombe's servants who had accompanied us from Swazi-Land, felt quite alarmed. As a matter of fact he had only come to tell me that our meal was ready and that the other "high White Ones" were waiting for me.

He led me round the fence that encircled Zikali's dwelling-place, to two huts that stood nearly behind it, almost against the face of the rock which, overhanging in a curve, formed a kind of natural roof above them. I thought they must have been built since I visited the place, as I, who have a good memory for such things, did not remember them. Indeed, on subsequent examination I found that they were quite new, for the poles that formed their uprights were still green and the grass of the thatch was scarcely dry. It looked to me as if they had been specially constructed for our accommodation.

In one of these huts, that to the right which was allotted to Anscombe and myself, I found the others waiting for me, also the food. It was good of its sort and well cooked, and we ate it by the light of some candles that we had with us, Kaatje serving us. Yet, although a little while before I had been desperately hungry, now my appetite seemed to have left me and I made but a poor meal. Heda and Anscombe also seemed oppressed and ate sparingly. We did not talk much until Kaatje had taken away the tin plates and gone to eat her own supper by a fire that burned outside the hut. Then Heda broke out, saying that she was terrified of this place and especially of its master, the old dwarf, and felt sure that something terrible was going to happen to her. Anscombe did his best to calm her, and I also told her she had nothing to fear.

"If there is nothing to fear, Mr. Quatermain," she answered, turning on me, "why do you look so frightened yourself? By your face you might have seen a ghost."

This sudden and singularly accurate thrust, for after all I had seen something that looked very like a ghost, startled me, and before I could invent any soothing and appropriate fib, Nombe appeared, saying that she had come to lead Heda to her sleeping-place. After this further conversation was impossible since, although Nombe knew but few words of English, she was a great thought-reader and I feared to speak of anything secret in her presence. So we all went out of the hut, Nombe and I drawing back a little to the fire while the lovers said good-night to each other.

"Nombe," I said, "the Inkosikazi Heddana is afraid. The rocks of this kloof lie heavy on her heart; the face of the Opener of Roads is fearful to her and his laughter grates upon her ears. Do you understand?"

"I understand, Macumazahn, and it is as I expected. When you yourself are frightened it is natural that she, an untried maiden, should be frightened also in this home of spirits."

"It is men we fear, not spirits, now when all Zululand is boiling like a pot," I replied angrily.

"Have it as you will, Macumazahn," she said, and at that moment her quiet, searching eyes and fixed smile were hateful to me. "At least you admit that you do fear. Well, for the lady Heddana fear nothing. I sleep across the door of her hut, and while I who have learned to love her, live, I say—for her fear nothing, whatever may chance or whatever you may see or hear."

"I believe you, but, Nombe, you might die."

"Yes, I may die, but be sure of this, that when I die she will be safe, and he who loves her also. Sleep well, Macumazahn, and do not dream too much of what you heard and saw in Zikali's house."

Then before I could speak she turned and left me.

I did not sleep well; I slept very badly. To begin with, Maurice Anscombe, generally the most cheerful and nonchalant of mortals with a jest for every woe, was in a most depressed condition, and informed me of it several times, while I was getting ready to turn in. He said he thought the place hateful and felt as if people he could not see were looking at him (I had the same sensation but did not mention the fact to him). When I told him he was talking stuff, he only replied that he could not help it, and pointed out that it was not his general habit to be downcast in any danger, which was quite true. Now, he added, he was enjoying much the same sensations as he did when first he saw the Yellow-wood Swamp and got the idea into his head that he would kill some one there, which happened in due course.

"Do you mean that you think you are going to kill somebody else?" I asked anxiously.

"No," he answered, "I think I am going to be killed, or something like it, probably by that accursed old villain of a witch-doctor, who I don't believe is altogether human."

"Others have thought that before now, Anscombe, and to be plain, I don't know that he is. He lives too much with the dead to be like other people."

"And with Satan, to whom I expect he makes sacrifices. The truth is I'm afraid of his playing some of his tricks with Heda. It is for her I fear, not for myself, Allan. Oh! why on earth did you come here?"

"Because you wished it and it seemed the safest thing to do. Look here, my boy, as usual the trouble comes through a woman. When a man's single—you know the rest. You used to be able to laugh at anything, but now that you are practically double you can't laugh any more. Well, that's the common lot of man and you've got to put up with it. Adam was pretty jolly in his garden until Eve was started, but you know what happened afterwards. The rest of his life was a compound of temptation, anxiety, family troubles, remorse, hard labour with primitive instruments, and a flaming sword behind him. If you had left your Eve alone you would have escaped all this. But you see you didn't, and as a matter of fact, nobody ever does who is worth his salt, for Nature has arranged it so."

"You appear to talk with experience, Allan," he retorted blandly. "By the way, that girl Nombe, when she isn't star-gazing or muttering incantations, is always trying to explain to Heda some tale about you and a lady called Mameena. I gather that you were introduced to her in this neighbourhood where, Nombe says, you were in the habit of kissing her in public, which sounds an odd kind of a thing to do; all of which happened before she, Nombe, was born. She adds, according to Kaatje's interpretation, that you met her again this afternoon, which, as I understand the young woman has been long dead, seems so incomprehensible that I wish you would explain."

"With reference to Heda," I said, ignoring the rest as unworthy of notice, "I think you may make your mind easy. Zikali knows that she is in my charge and I don't believe that he wants to quarrel with me. Still, as you are uncomfortable here, the best thing to do will be to get away as early as possible to-morrow morning, where to we can decide afterwards. And now I am going to sleep, so please stop arguing."

As I have already hinted, my attempts in the sleep line proved a failure, for whenever I did drop off I was pursued by bad dreams, which resulted from lying down so soon after supper. I heard the cries of desperate men in their mortal agony. I saw a rain-swollen river; its waters were red with blood. I beheld a vision of one who I knew by his dress to be a Zulu king, although I could not see his face. He was flying and staggering with weariness as he fled. A great hound followed him. It lifted its head from the spoor; it was that of Zikali set upon the hound's body, Zikali who laughed instead of baying. Then one whose copper ornaments tinkled as she walked, entered beside me, whispering into my ear. "A quarter of a hundred years have gone by since we talked together in this haunted kloof," she seemed to whisper, "and before we talk again face to face there remain to pass of years"—

Here she ceased, though naturally I should have liked to hear the number. But that is just where dreams break down. They tell us only of what we know, or can evolve therefrom. Of what it is impossible for us to know they tell us nothing—at least as a general rule.

I woke up with a start, and feeling stifled in that hot place and aggravated by the sound of Anscombe's peaceful breathing, threw a coat about me and, removing the door-board, crept into the air. The night was still, the stars shone, and at a little distance the embers of the fire still glowed. By it was seated a figure wrapped in a kaross. The end of a piece of wood that the fire had eaten through fell on to the red ashes and flamed up brightly. By its light I saw that the figure was Nombe's. The eternal smile was still upon her face, the smile which suggested a knowledge of hidden things that from moment to moment amused her soul. Her lips moved as though she were talking to an invisible companion, and from time to time, like one who acts upon directions, she took a pinch of ashes and blew them, either towards Heda's hut or ours. Yes, she did this when all decent young women should have been asleep, like one who keeps some unholy, midnight assignation.

Talking with her master, Zikali, or trying to cast spells upon us, confound her! thought I to myself, and very silently crept back into the hut. Afterwards it occurred to me that she might have had another motive, namely of watching to see that none of us left the huts.

The rest of the night went by somehow. Once, listening with all my ears, I thought that I caught the sound of a number of men tramping and of some low word of command, but as I heard no more, concluded that fancy had deceived me. There I lay, puzzling over the situation till my head ached, and wondering how we were to get clear of the Black Kloof and Zikali, and out of Zululand which I gathered was no place for white people at the moment.

It seemed to me that the only thing was to make start for Dundee on the Natal border, and for the rest to trust to fortune. If we got into trouble over the death of Rodd, unpleasant as this would be, the matter must be faced out, that was all. For even if any witness appeared against us, the man had been killed in self-defence whilst trying to bring about our deaths at the hands of Basutos. I could see now that I was foolish not to have taken this line from the first, but as I think I have already explained, what weighed with me was the terror of involving these young people in a scandal which might shadow all their future lives. Also some fate inch by inch had dragged me into Zululand. Fortunately in life there are few mistakes, and even worse than mistakes that cannot be repaired, if the wish towards reparation is real and earnest. Were it otherwise not many of us would escape destruction in one form or another.

Thus I reflected until at length light flowing faintly through the smoke-hole of the hut told me that dawn was at hand. Seeing it I rose quietly, for I did not wish to wake Anscombe, dressed and left the hut. My object was to find Nombe, who I hoped would be still sitting by the fire, and send her to Zikali with a message that I wished to speak with him at once. Glancing round me in the grey dawn I saw that she was gone and that as yet no one seemed to be stirring. Hearing a horse snort at a little distance, I made my way towards the sound and in a little bay of the overhanging cliff discovered the cart and near by our beasts tied up with a plentiful supply of forage. Since so far as I could judge in that uncertain light, nothing seemed to be wrong with them except weariness, for three of them were still lying down, I walked on to the gate of the fence which surrounded Zikali's big hut, proposing to wait there until some one appeared by whom I could send my message.

I reached the gate which I tried and found to be fastened on its inner side. Then I sat down, lit my pipe and waited. It was extraordinarily lonesome in that place; at least this was the feeling that came over me. No doubt the sun was up behind the Ceza Stronghold that I have mentioned, which towered high behind me, for the sky above grew light with the red rays of its rising. But all the vast Black Kloof with its huge fantastic rocks was still plunged in gloom, whereof the shadows seemed to oppress my heart, weary as I was with my wakeful night and many anxieties. I was horribly nervous also and, as it proved, not without reason. Presently I heard rustlings on the further side of the fence as of people creeping about cautiously, and the sound of whispering. Then of a sudden the gate was thrown open and through it emerged about a dozen Zulu warriors, all of them ringed men, who instantly surrounded me, seated there upon the ground.

I looked at them and they looked at me for quite a long while, since following my usual rule, I determined not to be the first to speak. Moreover, if they meant to kill me there was no use in speaking. At length their leader, an elderly man with thin legs, a large stomach and a rather pleasant countenance, saluted politely, saying—

"Good morning, O Macumazahn."

"Good morning, O Captain, whose name and business I do not know," I answered.

"The winds know the mountain on which they blow, but the mountain does not know the winds which it cannot see," he remarked with poetical courtesy; a Zulu way of saying that more people are acquainted with Tom Fool than Tom Fool is aware of.

"Perhaps, Captain; yet the mountain can feel the winds," and I might have added, smell them, for the Kloof was close and these Kaffirs had not recently bathed.

"I am named Goza and come on an errand from the king, O Macumazahn."

"Indeed, Goza, and is your errand to cut my throat?"

"Not at present, Macumazahn, that is, unless you refuse to do what the king wishes."

"And what does the king wish, Goza?"

"He wishes, Macumazahn, that you, his friend, should visit him."

"Which is just what I was on my way to do, Goza." (This was not true, but it didn't matter, for, if a lie, in the words of the schoolgirl's definition, is an abomination to the Lord, it is a very present help in time of trouble.) "After we have eaten I and my friends will accompany you to the king's kraal at Ulundi."

"Not so, Macumazahn. The king said nothing about your friends, of whom I do not think he has ever heard any more than we have. Moreover, if your friends are white, you will do well not to mention them, since the order is that all white people in Zululand who have not come here by the king's desire, are to be killed at once, except yourself, Macumazahn."

"Is it so, Goza? Well, as you will have understood, I am quite alone here and have no friends. Only I did not wish to travel so early."

"Of course we understand that you are quite alone and have no friends, is it not so, my brothers?"

"Yes, yes, we understand," they exclaimed in chorus, one of them adding, "and shall so report to the King."

"What kind of blankets do you like; the plain grey ones or the white ones with the blue stripes?" I asked, desiring to confirm them in this determination.

"The grey ones are warmer, Macumazahn, and do not show dirt so much," answered Goza thoughtfully.

"Good, I will remember when I have the chance."

"The promise of Macumazahn is known from of old to be as a tree that elephants cannot pull down and white ants will not eat," said the sententious Goza, thereby intimating his belief that some time or other they would receive those blankets. As a matter of fact the survivors of the party and the families of the others did receive them after the war, for in dealing with natives I have always made a point of trying to fulfil any promise or engagement made for value received.

"And now," went on Goza, "will the Inkosi be pleased to start, as we have to travel far to-day?"

"Impossible," I replied. "Before I leave I must eat, for who can journey upon yesterday's food? Also I must saddle my horse, collect what belongs to me, and bid farewell to my host, Zikali."

"Of meat we have plenty with us, Macumazahn, and therefore you will not hunger on the way. Your horse and everything that is yours shall be brought after you; since were you mounted on that swift beast and minded to escape, how could we catch you with our feet, and did you please to shoot us with your rifle, how could we who have only spears, save ourselves from dying? As for the Opener of Roads, his servants have told us that he means to sleep all to-day that he may talk with spirits in his dreams, and therefore it is useless for you to wait to bid him farewell. Moreover, the orders of the king are that we should bring you to him at once."

After this for a time there was silence, while I sat immovable revolving the situation, and the Zulus regarded me with a benignant interest. Goza took his snuff-box from his ear, shook out some into the palm of his hand and, after offering it to me in vain, inhaled it himself.

"The orders of the king are (sneeze) that we should bring you to him alive if possible, and if not (sneeze) dead. Choose which you will, Macumazahn. Perhaps you may prefer to go to Ulundi dead, which would—ah! how strong is this snuff, it makes me weep like a woman—save you the trouble of walking. But if you prefer that we should carry you, be so good, Macumazahn, first to write the words which will cause the grey blankets to be delivered to us, for we know well that even your bones would desire to keep your promise. Is it not a proverb in the land from the time of the slaying of Bangu when you gave the cattle you had earned to Saduko's wanderers?"

I listened and an idea occurred to me, as perhaps it had to Goza.

"I hear you, Goza," I said, "and I will start for Ulundi on my feet—to save you the trouble of carrying me. But as the times are rough and accidents may always happen; as, too, I wish to make sure that you should get those blankets, and it may chance that I shall arrive there on my back, first I will write words which, if they are delivered to the witch-doctoress Nombe, will, sooner or later, turn into blankets."

"Write the words quickly, Macumazahn, and they will be delivered," said Goza.

So I drew out my pocket-book and wrote—

"DEAR ANSCOMBE,—

"There is treachery afoot and I think that Zikali is at the bottom of it. I am being carried off to Cetewayo at Ulundi, by a party of armed Zulus who will not allow me to communicate with you, probably by Zikali's orders. You must do the best you can for Heda and yourself. Escape to Natal if you are able. Of course I will help if I get the chance, but if war is about to break out Cetewayo may kill me. I think that you can trust Nombe; also that Zikali does not wish to work you any ill unless he is obliged, though I have no doubt that he has trapped us here for some dark purpose of his own. Tell him through Nombe that if harm comes to you I will kill him if I live, and that if I die, I will settle the score with him afterwards. God save and bless you both. Keep up your courage and use your wits.

"Your friend,

"A. Q."

I tore out the sheet, folded, addressed it and presented it to Goza, remarking that although it seemed to be but paper, it really was fourteen blankets—if given at once to Nombe.

He nodded and handed it to one of his men, who departed in the direction of our huts. So, thought I to myself, Nombe knows all about this business, which means that it is being worked by Zikali. That is why she spoke to me as she did last night.

"It is time to start, Macumazahn, and I think you told us that you would prefer to do so on your feet," said Goza, looking suggestively at his spear.

"I am ready," I said, rising because I must. For a moment I contemplated the door in the kraal fence, wondering whether it would be safe to bolt through it and take refuge with Zikali. No, it was not safe, since Zikali sat there in his hut pulling the strings and probably might refuse to see me. Moreover, it was likely enough that before I could find him one of those broad spears would find my heart. There was nothing to be done except submit. Still I did call out in a loud voice—

"Farewell, Zikali. I leave you without a present against my will who am being taken by soldiers to visit the king at Ulundi. When we meet again I will talk all this matter over with you."

There was no answer, and as Goza took the opportunity to say that he disliked the noise of shouting extremely, which sometimes made him do things that he afterwards regretted, I became silent. Then we departed, I in the exact centre of that guard of Zulus, heavy-hearted and filled with fears both for myself and those I left behind me.

Down the Black Kloof we tramped, emerging on the sunlit plain beyond without meeting any one. A couple of miles further on we came to a small stream where Goza announced we would halt to eat. So we ate of cold toasted meat which one of the men produced from a basket he carried, unpalatable food but better than nothing. Just as we had finished I looked up and saw the soldier to whom my note had been given. He was leading my mare that had been saddled. On it were my large saddle-bags packed with my belongings, also my thick overcoat, mackintosh, waterbottle, and other articles down to a bag of tobacco, a spare pipe and a box of wax matches. Moreover, the man carried my double-barrelled Express rifle and a shot-gun that could be used for ball, together with two bags of cartridges. Practically nothing belonging to me had been forgotten.

I asked him who had collected the things. He replied the doctress Nombe had done so and had brought him the horse saddled to carry them. He did not know who saddled the horse as he had seen no one but Nombe to whom he had given the writing which she hid away. In answer to further questions, he said that Nombe had sent me a message. It was—

"I bid farewell to Macumazahn for a little while and wish him good fortune till we meet again. Let him not be afraid in the battle, for even if he is hurt it will not be to death, since those go with him whom he cannot see, and protect him with their shields. Say to Macumazahn that I, Nombe, remember in the morning what I said in the night and that what seems to be quite lost is ofttimes found again. Wish him good fortune and tell him I am sorry that I had not time to cause his spare garments to be cleansed with water, but that I have been careful to find his little box with the white man's medicines."

I could extract nothing more from this soldier, who was either very stupid, or chose to appear so; nor indeed did I dare to put direct questions about the cart and those who travelled in it.

Soon we marched again, for Goza would not allow me to ride the horse, fearing that I should escape on it. Nor would he let me carry either of the guns lest I should make use of them. All day we travelled, reaching the Nongoma heights in the late afternoon. On this beautiful spot we found a kraal situated where afterwards a magistracy was built when we conquered the country, whence there is one of the finest views in Zululand. There was no one in the kraal except two old women who appeared to be deaf and dumb for all I could get out of them. These aged dames, however, or others who were hidden, had made ready for our arrival, since a calf lay skinned and prepared for cooking, and by it big gourds filled with Kaffir beer and "maas" or curdled milk.

In due course we ate of these provisions, and after we had finished I gave Goza a stiff tot of brandy, of which Nombe, or perhaps Anscombe, had thoughtfully sent a bottle with my other baggage. The strong liquor made the old fellow talkative and enabled me to get a good deal of information out of him. Thus I learned that certain demands, as to which he was rather vague, had been made upon Cetewayo by the English Government, and that the King was now considering whether he should accede to them or fight. The Great Council of the nation was summoned to attend at Ulundi within a few days, when the matter would be decided. Meanwhile all the regiments were being gathered, or, as we should say, mobilized; an army, said Goza, greater than any that Chaka had ever led.

I asked him what I had to do with this business, that I, a peaceful traveller and an old friend of the Zulus, should be made prisoner and dragged off to Ulundi. He replied he did not know who was not in the council of the High Ones, but he thought that Cetewayo the king wished to see me because I was their friend, perhaps that he might send me as a messenger to the white people. I asked him how the king knew that I was in the country, to which he replied that Zikali had told him I was coming, he did not know how, whereon he, Goza, was sent at once to fetch me. I could get no more out of him.

I wondered if it would be worth while to make him quite drunk and then attempt to escape on the horse, but gave up the idea. To begin with, his men were at hand and there was not enough brandy to make them all drunk. Also even if I succeeded in winning away here in the heart of Zululand, it would not help Anscombe or Heda and I should probably be cut off and killed before I could get out of the country. So I abandoned the plan and went to sleep instead.

Next morning we left Nongoma early in the hope of reaching Ulundi that evening if the Ivuna and Black Umfolozi Rivers proved fordable. As it chanced, although they were high, we were able to cross them, I seated on the horse which two of the Zulus led. Next we tramped for miles through the terrible Bekameezi Valley, a hot and desolate place which the Zulus swear is haunted. So unhealthy is this valley, which is the home of large game, that whole kraals full of people who have tried to cultivate the rich land, have died in it of fever, or fled away leaving their crops unreaped. Now no man dwells there. After this we climbed a terrible mount to the high land of Mahlabatini, and having eaten, pushed on once more.

At length we sighted the great hill-encircled plain of Ulundi which may be called the cradle of the Zulu race as, politically speaking, it was destined to be its coffin. On the ridge to the west once stood the Nobamba kraal where dwelt Senzangacona, the father of Chaka the Lion. Nearer to the White Umfolozi was Panda's dwelling-place, Nodwengu, which once I knew so well, while on the slope of the hills of the north-east stood the town of Ulundi in which Cetewayo dwelt, bathed in the lights of sunset.

Indeed it and all the vast plain were red as though with blood, red as they were destined to be on the coming day of the last battle of the Zulus.

CHAPTER XIII

CETEWAYO

It was dark when at last we reached the Ulundi kraal, for the growing moon was obscured by clouds. Therefore I could see nothing and was only aware, by the sound of voices and the continual challenging, that we were passing through great numbers of men. At length we were admitted at the eastern gate and I was taken to a hut where I at once flung myself down to sleep, being so weary that I could not attempt to eat. Next morning as I was finishing my breakfast in the little fenced courtyard of this guest-hut, Goza appeared and said that the king commanded me to be brought to him at once, adding that I must "speak softly" to him, as he was "very angry."

So off we went across the great cattle kraal where a regiment of young men, two thousand strong or so, were drilling with a fierce intensity which showed they knew that they were out for more than exercise. About the sides of the kraal also stood hundreds of soldiers, all of them talking and, it seemed to me, excited, for they stamped upon the ground and even jumped into the air to give point to their arguments. Suddenly some of them caught sight of me, whereon a tall, truculent fellow called out—

"What does a white man at Ulundi at such a time, when even John Dunn dare not come? Let us kill him and send his head as a present to the English general across the Tugela. That will settle this long talk about peace or war."

Others of a like mind echoed this kind proposal, with the result that presently a score or so of them made a rush at me, brandishing their sticks, since they might not carry arms in the royal kraal. Goza did his best to keep them off, but was swept aside like a feather, or rather knocked over, for I saw him on his back with his thin legs in the air.

"You must climb out of this pit by yourself," he began, addressing me in his pompous and figurative way. Then somebody stamped on his face, and fixing his teeth in his assailant's heel, he grew silent for a while.

The truculent blackguard, who was about six feet three high and had a mouth like a wolf's throat, arrived in front of me and, bending down, roared out—

"We are going to kill you, White Man."

I had a pistol in my pocket and could perfectly well have killed him, as I was much tempted to do. A second's reflection showed me, however, that this would be useless, and in a sense put me in the wrong, though when the matter came on for argument it would interest me no more. So I just folded my arms and, looking up at him, said—

"Why, Black Man?"

"Because your face is white," he roared.

"No," I answered, "because your heart is black and your eyes are so full of blood that you do not know Macumazahn when you see him."

"Wow!" said one, "it is Watcher-by-Night whom our fathers knew before us. Leave him alone."

"No," shouted the great fellow, "I will send him to watch where it is always night, I who keep a club for white rats," and he brandished his stick over me.

Now my temper rose. Watching my opportunity, I stretched out my right foot and hooked him round the ankle, at the same time striking up with all my force. My fist caught him beneath the chin and over he went backwards sprawling on the ground.

"Son of a dog!" I said, "if a single stick touches me, at least you shall go first," and whipping out my revolver, I pointed it at him.

He lay quiet enough, but how the matter would have ended I do not know, for passion was running high, had not Goza at this moment risen with a bleeding nose and called out—

"O Fools, would you kill the king's guest to whom the king himself has given safe-conduct. Surely you are pots full of beer, not men."

"Why not?" answered one. "This is the Place of Soldiers. The king's house is yonder. Give the old jackal a start of a length of ten assegais. If he reaches it first, he can shake hands with his friend, the king. If not we will make him into medicine."

"Yes, yes, run for it, Jackal," clamoured the others, knocking their shields with their sticks, as men do who would frighten a buck, and opening out to make a road for me.

Now while all this was going on, with some kind of sixth sense I had noted a big man whose face was shrouded by a blanket thrown over his head, who very quietly had joined these drunken rioters, and vaguely wondered who he might be.

"I will not run," I said slowly, "that I may be saved by the king. Nay, I will die here, though some of you shall die first. Go to the king, Goza, and tell him how his servants have served his guest," and I lifted my pistol, waiting till the first stick touched me to put a bullet through the bully on the ground.

"There is no need," said a deep voice that proceeded from the draped man of whom I have spoken, "for the king has come to see for himself."

Then the blanket was thrown back, revealing Cetewayo grown fat and much aged since last I saw him, but undoubtedly Cetewayo.

"Bayete!" roared the mob in salute, while some of those who had been most active in the tumult tried to slip away.

"Let no man stir," said Cetewayo, and they stood as though they were rooted to the ground, while I slipped my pistol back into my pocket.

"Who are you, White Man?" he asked, looking at me, "and what do you here?"

"The King should know Macumazahn," I answered, lifting my hat, "whom Dingaan knew, whom Panda knew well, and whom the King knew before he was a king."

"Yes, I know you," he answered, "although since we spoke together you have shrunk like an oxhide in the sun, and time has stained your beard white."

"And the King has grown fat like the ox on summer grass. As for what I do here, did not the King send for me by Goza, and was I not brought like a baby in a blanket."

"The last time we met," he went on, taking no heed of my words, "was yonder at Nodwengu when the witch Mameena was tried for sorcery, she who made my brother mad and brought about the great battle, in which you fought for him with the Amawombe regiment. Do you not remember how she kissed you, Macumazahn, and took poison between the kisses, and how before she grew silent she spoke evil words to me, saying that I was doomed to pull down my own House and to die as she died, words that have haunted me ever since and now haunt me most of all? I wish to speak to you concerning them, Macumazahn, for it is said in the land that this beautiful witch loved you alone and that you only knew her mind."

I made no reply, who was heartily tired of this subject of Mameena whom no one seemed able to forget.

"Well," he went on, "we will talk of that matter alone, since it is not natural that you should wish to speak of your dead darlings before the world," and with a wave of the hand he put the matter aside. Then suddenly his attitude changed. His face, that had been thoughtful and almost soft, became fierce, his form seemed to swell and he grew terrible.

"What was that dog doing?" he asked of Goza, pointing to the brute whom I had knocked down and who still lay prostrate on his back, afraid to stir.

"O King," answered Goza, "he was trying to kill Macumazahn because he is a white man, although I told him that he was your guest, being brought to you by the royal command. He was trying to kill him by giving him a start of ten spears' length and making him run to the isigodhlo (the king's house) and beating him to death with the sticks of these men if they caught him, which, as he is old and they are young, they must have done. Only the Watcher-by-Night would not run; no, although he is so small he knocked him to the earth with his fist, and there he lies. That is all, O King."

"Rise, dog," said Cetewayo, and the man rose trembling with fear, and, being bidden, gave his name, which I forget.

"Listen, dog," went on the king in the same cold voice. "What Goza says is true, for I saw and heard it all with my eyes and ears. You would have made yourself as the king. You dared to try to kill the king's guest to whom he had given safe-conduct, and to stain the king's doorposts with his blood, thereby defiling his house and showing him to the white people as a murderer of one of them whom he had promised to protect. Macumazahn, do you say how he shall die, and I will have it done."

"I do not wish him to die," I answered, "I think that he and those with him were drunk. Let him go, O King."

"Aye, Macumazahn, I will let him go. See now, we are in the centre of the cattle-kraal, and to the eastern gate is as far as to the isigodhlo. Let this man have a start of ten spears' length and run to the eastern gate, as he would have made Macumazahn run to the king's house, and let his companions, those who would have hunted Macumazahn, hunt him.

"If he wins through to the gate he can go on to the Government in Natal and tell them of the cruelty of the Zulus. Only then, let those who hunted him be brought before me for trial and perhaps we shall see how they can run."

Now the poor wretch caught hold of my hand, begging me to intercede for him, but soldiers who had come up dragged him away and, having measured the distance allowed him, set him on a mark made upon the ground. Presently at a word off he sped like an arrow, and after him went his friends, ten or more of them. I think they caught him just by the gate doubling like a hare, or so the shouts of laughter from the watching regiment told me, for myself I would not look.

"That dog ate his own stomach," said Cetewayo grimly, thereby indicating in native fashion that the biter had been bit or the engineer hoist with his petard. "It is long since there has been a war in the land, and some of these young soldiers who have never used an assegai save to skin an ox or cut the head from a chicken, shout too loud and leap too high. Now they will be quieter, and while you stay here you may walk where you will in safety, Macumazahn," he added thoughtfully.

Then dismissing the matter from his mind, as we white people dismiss any trivial incident in a morning stroll, he talked for a few minutes to the commanding officer of the regiment that was drilling, who ran up to make some report to him, and walked back towards the isigodhlo, beckoning me to follow with Goza.

After waiting for a little while outside the gate in the surrounding fence, a body-servant ordered us to enter, which we did to find the king seated on the shady side of his big hut quite alone. At a sign I also sat myself down upon a stool that had been set for me, while Goza, whose nose was still bleeding, squatted at my side.

"Your manners are not so good as they were once, Macumazahn," said Cetewayo presently, "or perhaps you have been so long away from the royal kraal that you have forgotten its customs."

I stared at him, wondering what he could mean, whereon he added with a laugh—

"What is that in your pocket? Is it not a loaded pistol, and do you not remember that it is death to appear before the king armed? Now I might kill you and have no blame, although you are my guest, for who knows that you are not sent by the English Queen to shoot me?"

"I ask the King's pardon," I said humbly enough. "I did not think about the pistol. Let your servants take it away."

"Perhaps it is safer in your pocket, where I saw you place it in the cattle-kraal, Macumazahn, than in their hands, which do not know how to hold such things. Moreover, I know that you are not one who stabs in the dark, even when our peoples growl round each other like two dogs about to fight, and if you were, in this place your life would have to pay for mine. There is beer by your side; drink and fear nothing. Did you see the Opener of Roads, Goza, and if so, what is his answer to my message?"

"O King, I saw him," answered Goza. "The Father of the doctors, the friend and master of the Spirits, says he has heard the King's word, yes, that he heard it as it passed the King's lips, and that although he is very old, he will travel to Ulundi and be present at the Great Council of the nation which is to be summoned on the eighth day from this, that of the full moon. Yet he makes a prayer of the King. It is that a place may be prepared for him, for his people and for his servants who carry him, away from this town of Ulundi, where he may sojourn quite alone, a decree of death being pronounced against any who attempt to break in upon his privacy, either where he dwells or upon his journey. These are his very words, O King:

"'I, who am the most ancient man in Zululand, dwell with the spirits of my fathers, who will not suffer strangers to come nigh them and who, if they are offended, will bring great woes upon the land. Moreover, I have sworn that while there is a king in Zululand and I draw the breath of life, never again will I set foot in a royal kraal, because when last I did so at the slaying of the witch, Mameena, the king who is dead thought it well to utter threats against me, and never more will I, the Opener of Roads, be threatened by a mortal. Therefore if the King and his Council seek to drink of the water of my wisdom, it must be in the place and hour of my own choosing. If this cannot be, let me abide here in my house and let the King seek light from other doctors, since mine shall remain as a lamp to my own heart.'"

Now I saw that these words greatly disturbed Cetewayo who feared Zikali, as indeed did all the land.

"What does the old wizard mean?" he asked angrily. "He lives alone like a bat in a cave and for years has been seen of none. Yet as a bat flies forth at night, ranging far and wide in search of prey, so does his spirit seem to fly through Zululand. Everywhere I hear the same word. It is—'What says the Opener of Roads?' It is—'How can aught be done unless the Opener of Roads has declared that it shall be done, he who was here before the Black One (Chaka) was born, he who it is said was the friend of Inkosi

Umkulu, the father of the Zulus who died before our great-grandfathers could remember; he who has all knowledge and is almost a spirit, if indeed he be not a spirit?' I ask you, Macumazahn, who are his friend, what does he mean, and why should I not kill him and be done?"

"O King," I answered, "in the days of your uncle Dingaan, when Dingaan slew the Boers who were his guests, and thus began the war between the White and the Black, I, who was a lad, heard the laughter of Zikali for the first time yonder at the kraal Ungungundhlovu, I who rode with Retief and escaped the slaughter, but his face I did not see. Many years later, in the days of Panda your father, I saw his face and therefore you name me his friend. Yet this friend who drew me to visit him, perhaps by your will, O King, has now caused me to be brought here to Ulundi doubtless by your will, O King, but against my own, for who wishes to come to a town where he is well-nigh slain by the first brawler he meets in the cattle kraal?"

"Yet you were not slain, Macumazahn, and perhaps you do not know all the story of that brawler," replied Cetewayo almost humbly, like one who begs pardon, though the rest of what I had said he ignored. "But still you are Zikali's friend, for between you and him there is a rope which enabled him to draw you to Zululand, which rope I have heard called by a woman's name. Therefore by the spirit of that woman, which still can draw you like a rope, I charge you, tell me—what does this old wizard mean, and why should I not kill him and be rid of one who haunts my heart like an evil vision of the night and, as I sometimes think, is an umtakati, an evil-doer, who would work ill to me and all my House, yes, and to all my people?"

"How should I know what he means, O King?" I answered with indignation, though in fact I could guess well enough. "As for killing him, cannot the King kill whom he will? Yet I remember that once I heard you father ask much the same question and of Zikali himself, saying that he was minded to find out whether or no he were mortal like other men. I remember also Zikali answered that there was a saying that when the Opener of Roads came to the end of his road, there would be no more a king of Zululand, as there was none when first he set foot upon his road. Now I have spoken, who am a white man and do not understand your sayings."

"I remember it also, Macumazahn, who was present at the time," he replied heavily. "My father feared this Zikali and his father feared him, and I have heard that the Black One himself, who feared nothing, feared him also. And I, too, fear him, so much that I dare not make up my mind upon a great matter without his counsel, lest he should bewitch me and the nation and bring us to nothing."

He paused, then turning to Goza, asked, "Did the Opener of Roads tell you where he wished to dwell when he comes to visit me here at Ulundi?"

"O King," answered Goza, "yonder in the hills, not further away than an aged man can walk in the half of an hour, is a place called the Valley of Bones, because there in the days of those who went before the King, and even in the King's day, many evildoers have been led to die. Zikali would dwell in this Valley of Bones, and there and nowhere else would meet the King and the Great Council, not in the daylight but after sunset when the moon has risen."

"Why," said Cetewayo, starting, "the place is ill-omened and, they say, haunted, one that no man dares to approach after the fall of darkness for fear lest the ghosts of the dead should leap upon him gibbering."

"Such were the words of the Opener of Roads, O King," replied Goza. "There and nowhere else will he meet the King, and there he demands that three huts should be built to shelter him and his folk and stored with all things needful. If this be not granted to him, then he refuses to visit the King or to give counsel to the nation."

"So be it then," said Cetewayo. "Send messengers to the Opener of Roads, Goza, saying that what he desires shall be done. Let my command go out that under pain of death none spy upon him while he journeys hither or returns. Let the huts be built forthwith, and when it is known that he is coming, let food in plenty be placed in them and afterwards morning by morning taken to the mouth of the valley. Bid him announce his arrival and the hour he chooses for our meeting by messenger. Begone."

Goza leapt up, gave the royal salute, and retreated backwards from the presence of the king, leaving us alone. I also rose to depart, but Cetewayo motioned to me to be seated.

"Macumazahn," he said, "the Great Queen's man who has come to Natal (Sir Bartle Frere) threatens me with war because two evil-doing women were taken on the Natal side of the Tugela and brought back to Zululand and killed by Mehlokazulu, being the wives of his father, Sirayo, which was done without my knowledge. Also two white men were driven away from an island in the Tugela River by some of my soldiers."

"Is that all, O King?" I asked.

"No. The Queen's man says I kill my people without trial, which is a lie told him by the missionaries, and that girls have been killed also who refused to marry those to whom they were given and ran away with other men. Also that wizards are smelt out and slain, which happens but rarely now; all of this contrary to the promises I made to Sompseu when he came to recognize me as king upon my father's death, and some other such small matters."

"What is demanded if you would avoid war, O King?"

"Nothing less than this, Macumazahn: That the Zulu army should be abolished and the soldiers allowed to marry whom and when they please, because, says the Queen's man, he fears lest it should be used to attack the English, as though I who love the English, as those have done who went before me, desire to lay a finger on them. Also that another Queen's man should be sent to dwell here in my country, to be the eyes and ears of the English Government and have power with me in the land; yes, and more demands which would destroy the Zulus as a people and make me, their king, but a petty kraal-head."

"And what will the King answer?" I asked.

"I know not what to answer. The fine of two thousand cattle I will pay for the killing of the women. If it may be, I wish no quarrel with the English, though gladly I would have fought the Dutch had not Sompseu stretched out his arm over their land. But how can I disband the army and make an end of the regiments that have conquered in so many wars? Macumazahn, I tell you that if I did this, in a moon I should be dead. Oh! you white people think there is but one will in Zululand, that of the king. But it is not so, for he is but a single man among ten thousand thousand, who lives to work the people's wish. If he beats them with too thick a stick, or if he brings them to shame or does what the most of them do not wish, then where is the king? Then, I say, he goes a road that was trodden by Chaka and Dingaan who were before me, yes, the red road of the assegai. Therefore today, I stand like a man between two falling cliffs. If I run towards the English the Zulu cliff falls upon me. If I run towards my own people, the English cliff falls upon me, and in either case I am crushed and no more seen. Tell me then, Macumazahn, you whose heart is honest, what must I do?"

So he spoke, wringing his hands, with tears starting to his eyes, and upon my word, although I never liked Cetewayo as I had liked his father, Panda, perhaps because I loved his brother, Umbelazi, whom he killed, and had known him do many cruel deeds, my heart bled for him.

"I cannot tell you, King," I answered, thinking that I must say something, "but I pray you do not make war against the queen, for she is the most mighty One in the whole earth, and though her foot, of which you see but the little toe here in Africa, seems small to you, yet if she is angered, it will stamp the Zulus flat, so that they cease to be."

"Many have told me this, Macumazahn. Yes, even Uhamu, the son of my uncle Unzibe, or, as some say, the son of his spirit, to which his mother was married after Unzibe was dead, and others throughout the land, and in truth I think it myself. But who can hold the army which shouts for war? Ow! the Council must decide, which, means perhaps that Zikali will decide, for now all hang upon his lips."

"Then I am sorry," I exclaimed.

He looked at me shrewdly.

"Are you? So am I. Yet his counsel must be asked, and better that it should be here in my presence than yonder secretly at the Black Kloof. I would kill him if I dared, but I dare not, who am sure—why I may not say—that the same sun will see his death and mine."

He waved his hand to show that the talk on this matter was ended, then added—

"Macumazahn, you are my prisoner for a while, but give me your word that you will not try to escape and you may go where you will within an hour's ride of Ulundi. I would pay you well to stop here with me, but this I know you would never do should there be trouble between us and your people. Therefore I promise you that if war breaks out I will send you safely to Natal, or perhaps sooner, as my messenger, whence doubtless you will return to fight against me. Know that I have given orders that every other white man or woman who is found in Zululand shall be killed as a spy. Even John Dunn has fled or is flying, or so I hear, John Dunn who has fed out of my hand and grown rich on my gifts. You yourself would have been killed as you came from Swazi-Land in your cart, had not command been sent to those chiefs through whose lands you passed that neither they nor their people were so much as to look at you."

Now for one intense moment I thought, as hard as ever I had done in my life. It was evident—unless he dealing very cunningly with me, which I did not believe—that Cetewayo knew nothing of Anscombe and Heda, but thought that I had come into Zululand alone. Should I or should I not tell him and beg his protection for them? If I did so he might refuse or be unable to give it to them far away in the midst of a savage population aflame with the lust of war. As the incident of the morning showed, it was as much as he could do to protect myself, although the Zulus knew me for their friend. On the other hand no one who dwelt under Zikali's blanket, to use the Kaffir idiom, would be touched, because he was looked on as half divine and therefore everything under it down to the rat in his thatch was sacred. Now Zikali by implication and Nombe with emphasis, had promised to safeguard these two. Surely, therefore, they would run less risk in the Black Kloof than here at Ulundi, if ever they got so far.

All this went through my brain in an instant, with the result that I made up my mind to say nothing. As the issue proved, this was a terrible mistake, but who can always judge rightly? Had I spoken out it seems to me probable that Cetewayo would have granted my prayer and ordered that these two should be escorted out of Zululand before hostilities began, although of course they might have been murdered on the way. Also, for a reason that will become evident later, it is possible that there would never have been any hostilities. All I can plead is, that I acted for the best and Fate would have it so. Another moment and the chance was gone.

The gate opened and a body-servant appeared announcing that one of the great captains with some of his officers waited to see the king. Cetewayo made a sign, whereon the servant called out something, and they entered, three or four of them, saluting loudly. Seeing me they stopped and stared, whereon Cetewayo shortly, but with much clearness, repeated to them and to an induna who accompanied them, what he had already said to me, namely that I was his guest, sent for by him that he might use me as a messenger if he thought fit. He added that the man who dared to speak a word against me, or even to look at me askance, should pay the price with his life, however high his station, and he commanded that the heralds should proclaim this his decree throughout Ulundi and the neighbouring kraals. Then he held out his hand to me in token of friendship, bidding me to "go softly" and come to see him whenever I wished, and dismissed me in charge of the induna, one of the captains and some soldiers.

Within five minutes of reaching my hut I heard a loud-voiced crier proclaiming the order of the king and knew that I had no more to fear.

CHAPTER XIV

THE VALLEY OF BONES

The week that followed my interview with Cetewayo was indeed a miserable time for me. For myself, as I have said, I had no fear, for the king's orders were strictly obeyed. Moreover, the tale of what had happened to the brute who wished to hunt me down in the cattle-kraal had travelled far and wide and none sought to share his fate. My hut was inviolate and well supplied with necessary food, as was my mare, and I could wander where I liked and talk with whom I would. I could even ride to exercise the horse, though this I did very sparingly and only in the immediate neighbourhood of the town for fear of exciting suspicion or meeting Zulus whom the king's word had not reached. Indeed on these occasions I was always accompanied by a guard of swift-footed and armed soldiers sent "to protect me," or more probably to kill me if I did anything that seemed suspicious.

In the course of my rambles I met sundry natives whom I had known in the old days, some of them a long while ago. They all seemed glad to see me and were quite ready to talk of past times, but of the present they would say little or nothing, except that they were certain there would be war. Of Anscombe and Heda I could hear nothing, and indeed did not dare to make any direct inquiries concerning them, but several reliable men assured me that the last missionaries and traders having departed, there was not a white man, woman or child left in Zululand except myself. It was "all black" they said, referring to the colour of their people, as it had been before the time of Chaka. So I was forced to eat out my heart with anxiety in silence, hoping and praying that Zikali had played an honest part and sent them away safely.

Why should he not have done so, seeing that it was my presence he had desired, not theirs? They were only taken, or rather snared, because they were with me and could not be separated, or so I believed at the time.

One ray of comfort I did get. About the fifth day after my interview I saw Goza, who told me that the king's messengers were back from the Black Kloof and had brought "a word" for me from Zikali himself. The word was—

"Bid Goza say to Macumazahn that I was sorry not to see him to say good-bye, because that morning I slept heavily. Bid him say that I am glad he has seen the king, since for this purpose I sought his presence in Zululand. Bid him say that he is to fear nothing, and that if his heart is heavy about others whom he loves, he should make it light again, since the Spirits have them in their keeping as they have him, and never were they or he more safe than they are to-day."

Now I looked at Goza and asked if I could see this messenger. He replied, No, as he had already been despatched upon another errand. Then I asked him if the messenger had said anything else. He answered, Yes, one thing that he had forgotten, namely that the writing about blankets should now be in Natal. Then suddenly he changed the subject and asked me if I would like to accompany him to the Valley of Bones where he was ordered to inspect the huts which were being built for Zikali and his people. Of course I said I should, hoping, quite without result, that I might get something more out of him on the road.

Now this town of Cetewayo's stands, or rather stood, for it has long been burnt, on the slope of the hills to the north-east of the plains of Ulundi. Above it these hills grow steeper, and deep in the recesses of one of them is the Valley of Bones. There is nothing particularly imposing about the place; no towering cliffs or pillars of piled granite, as at the Black Kloof. It is just a vale cut out by water, bordered by steep slopes on either side, and a still steeper slope strown with large rocks at its end. Dotted here and there on these slopes grew tall aloes that from a little distance looked like scattered men, whereof the lower leaves were shrivelled and blackened by veld fires. Also there were a few euphorbias, grey, naked-looking things that end in points like fingers on a hand, and among them some sparse thorn trees, struggling to live in an inhospitable soil.

The place has one peculiarity. Jutting into it from the hillside is a ridge or spur, sixty or seventy yards in length by perhaps twenty broad, that ends in a flat point of rock which stands about forty feet above the level of the rest of the little valley. On this ridge also grew tall aloes until near its extremity the soil ceased, or had been washed away from the water-worn core of rock.

It was, and no doubt still is, a desolate-looking spot, at any rate for most of the day when owing to the shadow of the surrounding hills, it receives but little sun. Everything about it, especially when I was there in a time of rain, seemed dank and miserable, although the flat floor of the kloof was clothed with a growth of tall, coarse grass, and weeds that bore an evil-smelling flower. Perhaps some sense of appropriateness had caused the Zulu kings to choose this lonesome, deathly-looking gorge as one of their execution grounds. At any rate many had been slain here, for skulls and the larger human bones, some of them black with age, lay all about among the grass, as they had been scattered by hyenas and jackals. They were particularly thick beneath and around the table-like rock that I have mentioned.

Goza told me that this was because the King's Slayers made a custom of dragging the victim along the projecting tongue to the edge of this rock and hurling him, either dead or living, to the ground beneath; or, in the case of witches; driving them over after they had been blinded.

Such was the spot that Zikali had selected to abide in during his visit to Ulundi. Certainly where privacy was an object it was well chosen, for, as Cetewayo had said and as Goza emphasized to me, it had the repute of being the most thoroughly haunted place in all Zululand, with the sole exception, perhaps, of the ridge opposite to Dingaan's old kraal where once I shot the vultures for my life and those of my companions.* Even in the daytime people gave it a wide berth, and at night nothing would induce them to approach it, at any rate alone.

[*—See the book called Marie, by H. Rider Haggard.]

Here to one side of and near the root of the tongue of land of which I have spoken, the huts that Zikali had demanded for himself and his company were being rapidly built, close to a spring of water, by a large body of men who laboured as though they wished to be done with their task. Also about half way up the donga, for really it was nothing more, at a distance of perhaps five and twenty paces from its flat point whence the condemned were hurled, a circular space of ground had been cleared and levelled which was large enough to accommodate fifty or sixty men. On this space, Goza told me, the King and the Council were to sit when they came to seek light from Zikali.

In my heart I reflected that the light they were likely to get from him would be such as may be supposed to be thrown by hell fire. For be it remembered I knew what these people never seemed to understand, that Zikali was the most bitter of their enemies. To begin with, he was of Undwandwe blood, one of the people whom the great king Chaka had destroyed. Then this same Chaka had robbed him of his wives and murdered his children, in revenge for which he had plotted the slaying of Chaka, as he did that of his brothers, Umhlangana and Dingaan, the latter of whom he involved in a quarrel with the Boers. Subsequently he brought about the war between the princes Cetewayo and Umbelazi, in which I played a part.

Now I was certain that he intended to bring about another war between the English and the Zulus, knowing well that in the end the latter would be destroyed, and with them the royal House of Senzangacona which he had sworn to level with the dust. Had he not told me as much years ago, and was he one to go back upon his word? Had he not used Mameena with her beauty and ambitions as his tool, and when she was of no further service to him, given her to death, as he had used scores of others and in due season given them to death? Was I not myself perhaps one of those tools destined to be thrown into the pit of doom when my turn came, though in what way I could help his plots was more than I could see, since he knew well that I should do my best to oppose him? Oh! I had half a mind to go to Cetewayo and tell him all I knew about Zikali, even if it involved the breaking of confidences.

But stay! Even if I were believed, this far-seeing wizard held hostages for my good behaviour, and if I betrayed him what would happen to those hostages? He sent me messages saying that they were safe, suggesting that they had escaped to Natal. How was I to know that these were true? I was utterly bewildered; I could not guess why I had been beguiled into Zululand, and I dared not step either this way or that for fear lest I should fall into some pit dug by his cunning hands and, what was worse, drag down others with me.

Moreover, was this man quite human, or perhaps an emissary of Satan upon earth who had knowledge denied to other men and a certain mastery over the Powers of Ill? Again I could not say. His term of life seemed to be extraordinarily prolonged, though none knew how old exactly he might be. Also he had a wonderful knowledge of what was passing in the minds of others, and by his arts, as I had experienced only the other day, could summon up apparitions or illusions before their eyes. Further, he was aware of events which had happened at a distance and could send or read dreams, since otherwise how did Nombe know what I had dreamt at Marnham's house? Lastly he could foretell the future, as once he had done in my own case, prophecying that I should be injured by a buffalo with a split horn.

Yet all of this might be nothing more than a mixture of keen observation, clever spying, trickery and mesmerism. I could not say which it was, nor can I with certainty to this hour.

Such were the thoughts that passed through my mind as I walked back from the Vale of Bones by the side of the big-paunched Goza, whom I caught eyeing me from time to time as a curious crow eyes any object that has attracted his attention.

"Goza," I said at last, "do the Zulus really mean to fight the English?"

He turned and pointed to a spot where the hills ran down into the great plain. Here two regiments were manoeuvring. One of these held the slopes of the hill and the other was attacking them from the plain, so fiercely that at a distance their onslaught looked like that of actual warfare.

"That looks like fighting, does it not, Macumazahn?" he replied.

"Yes, Goza, yet it may be but play."

"Quite so, Macumazahn. It may be fighting or it may be but play. Am I a prophet that I should be able to say which it is? Of that there is but one man in Zululand who knows the truth. It is he for whom the new huts are being built up yonder."

"You think he really knows, Goza?"

"No, Macumazahn, I do not think, I am sure. He is the greatest of all wizards, as he was when my father held on to his mother's apron. He pulls the strings and the Great-ones of the country dance. If he wishes war, there will be war. If he wishes peace, there will be peace."

"And which does he wish, Goza?"

"I thought perhaps you could tell me that, Macumazahn, who, he says, are such an old friend of his; also why he chooses to sojourn in a dark hole among the dead instead of in the sunshine among the living, here at Ulundi."

"Well, I cannot, Goza, since the Opener of Roads does not open his heart to me but keeps his secrets to himself. For the rest, those who talk with the dead may prefer to dwell among the dead."

"Now as always you speak truth, Macumazahn," said Goza, looking at me in a way which suggested to me that he believed I spoke anything but the truth.

Indeed I am convinced he thought that I was in the council of Zikali and acquainted with his plans. Also I am sure he knew that I had not come to Zululand alone, the incident of the blankets, which I had promised to him a bribe to keep silence, showed it, and suspected that my companions were parties to some plot together with myself. And yet at the time I could not be quite sure, and therefore dared not ask anything concerning them lest thus I should reveal their existence and bring them to death.

As a matter of fact I need not have been anxious on this point, since if Goza, who I may state, was a kind of secret service officer as well as a head messenger, knew, as I think probable, he had been commanded by Zikali to hold his tongue under penalty of a curse. Perhaps the same was true of the soldiers who had come with him to take me to Ulundi. The hint of Zikali was as powerful as the word of the king, since they, like thousands of others, believed that whereas Cetewayo could kill them, Zikali, like Satan, could blast their spirits as well as their bodies. But how was I to guess all these things at that time?

During the next two days nothing happened, though I heard that there had been one if not two meetings of the Council at the King's House during which the position of affairs was discussed. Cetewayo I did not see, although twice he sent messengers to me bringing gifts of food, who were charged to inquire whether I was well and happy and if any had offered me hurt or insult. To these I answered that I was well and unmolested but not happy, who grew lonesome, being but a solitary white man among so many thousands of the Zulus.

On the third morning, that of the day of the full moon, Goza came and informed me that Zikali had arrived at the Valley of Bones before dawn. I asked him how he, who was so old and feeble, had walked so far. He answered that he had not walked, or so he understood, but had been carried in a litter, or rather in two litters, one for himself and one for his "spirit." This staggered me even where Zikali was concerned, and I inquired what on earth Goza meant.

"Macumazahn, how can I tell you who only know what I myself am told?" he exclaimed. "Such is the report that the Opener of Roads has made himself by messengers to the king. None have seen him, for he journeys only in the night. Moreover, when Zikali passes all men are blind and even women's tongues grow dumb. Perchance by 'his spirit' he means his medicine or the witch-doctoress, Nombe, whom folks say he created, since none have seen her father or her mother, or heard who begat her; or perchance his snake is hid behind the mats of the second litter, if in truth there was one."

"It may be so," I said, feeling that it was useless to pursue the matter. "Now, Goza, I would see Zikali and at once."

"That cannot be, Macumazahn, since he has given out that he will see no one, who rests after his journey, and the king has issued orders that any who attempt to approach the Valley of Bones shall die, even if they be of the royal blood. Yes, if so much as a dog dares to draw near that place, it must die. The soldiers who ring it round have killed one already, so strict are the orders, also a boy who went towards it searching for a calf, which I think a bad omen."

"Then I will send a message to him," I persisted.

"Do so," mocked Goza. "Look, yonder sails a vulture. Ask it to take your message, for nothing else will. Be not foolish, Macumazahn, but have patience, for to-night you shall see the Opener of Roads when he attends the Council of the king in the Valley of Bones. This is the order of the king—that at the rising of the moon I lead you thither, so that you may be present at the Council in case he wishes to ask you any questions about the White People or to give you any message to the Government in Natal. Therefore at sunset I will come for you. Till then, farewell. I have business that cannot wait."

"Can I see the king?" I cried.

"Not so, Macumazahn. All to-day he makes sacrifice to the spirits of his ancestors and must not be approached," Goza called back as he departed.

Availing myself of the permission of the king to go where I would, a little later in the day I walked out of the town towards the Valley of Bones in order to ascertain for myself whether what Goza had told me was true. So it proved, for about three hundred yards from the mouth of the valley, which at that distance looked like a black hole in the hills, I found soldiers stationed about ten paces apart in a great circle which ran right up the hillside and vanished over the crest. Strolling up to one of these, whose face I thought I knew, I asked him if he would let me pass to see my friend, the Opener of Roads.

The man, who was something of a humourist replied—

"Certainly if you wish, Macumazahn. That is to say, I will let your spirit pass, but to do this, if you come one step nearer I must first make a hole in you with my spear out of which it can fly."

I thanked him for his information and gave him some snuff, which he took gratefully, being bored by his long vigil. Then I asked him how many people the great witch-doctor had with him. He said he did not know, but he had seen a number of tall men come to the mouth of the donga to fetch food that had been placed there. Again I inquired if he had seen any women, whereon he replied none, Zikali being, he understood, too old to trouble himself about the other sex. Just then an officer, making his rounds, came up and looked at me so sternly that I thought it well to retreat. Evidently there was no chance of getting through that line.

On my way back I walked as near the fence of the King's House as I dared, and saw witch-doctors passing in and out in their hideous official panoply. This told me that here also Goza had spoken the truth—the king was performing magical ceremonies, which meant that it would be impossible to approach him. In every direction I met with failure. The Fates were against me; it lay over me like a spell. Indeed I grew superstitious and began to think that Zikali had bewitched me, as he was said to have the power to do. Well, perhaps he had, for the mere fact of finding myself opposed by this persistent wall of difficulties and silence convinced me that there was something behind it to be learned.

I went back very dejected to my hut and talked to my mare which whinnied and rubbed its nose against me, for although it was well fed and looked after, the poor beast seemed as lonely as I was myself. No wonder, since like myself it was separated from all its kind and weary of inaction. After this I ate and smoked and finally dozed, no more, for whenever I tried to go to sleep I thought that I heard Zikali laughing at me, as mayhap he was doing yonder in his hut.

At length that wearisome day drew towards its end. The sun began to sink, a huge red ball of fire, now and again veiled by clouds, for the sky was stormy. Its fierce rays, striking upon other clouds, peopled the enormous heavens with fantastic shapes of light which were thickest over the hills wherein was the Valley of Bones. To my strained mind these clouds looked like battling armies, figures of flame warring against figures of darkness. The darkness won; no, the light broke out again and conquered it. And see, there above them both squatted a strange black presence crowned with fire. It might have been that of Zikali magnified ten thousand times, and hark! it laughed with the low reverberating voice of distant thunder.

Suddenly I felt that I was no longer alone and looking round, saw Goza at my side.

"What do you see up there, Macumazahn, that you stare so hard?" he asked, pointing at the sky with his stick.

"Impis fighting," I answered briefly.

"Then you must be a 'heaven-doctor,' Macumazahn, for I only see black and red clouds. Well, it is time to go to learn whether or no the impis will fight, for Zikali awaits us and the Council has started already. By the way, the king says that you will do well to put your pistol in your pocket in case any should seek to harm you in the dark."

"It is there. But, Goza, I pray you to protect me, since in the dark bullets fly wide, and if I began to shoot, one might hit you, Goza."

He smiled, making no answer, but I noticed that during the rest of that night he was careful to keep behind me as much as possible.

Our way led us through the town where everybody seemed to be standing about doing nothing and speaking very little. There was a curious air of expectancy upon their faces. They knew that the crisis was at hand, that their nation's fate hung upon the scales, and they watched my every look and movement as though in them they expected to read an omen. I too watched them out of the corners of my eyes, wondering whether I should escape from their savage company alive. If once the blood lust broke out among them, it seemed to me that I should have about as much chance as a chopped fox among a pack of hungry hounds.

Once out of the town we saw no one until we came to the circle of guards which I have already mentioned, who stood there like an endless line of black statues. In answer to their challenge Goza gave some complicated password in which my name occurred, whereon they opened out and let us through. Then we marched on to the mouth of the kloof. The place was very dark, for now the sun was down in the west and the moon in the east was cut off from us by the hills and would not be visible here for half an hour or more. Presently I saw a spot of light. It was a small fire burning near the tongue of rock which I have described.

At a distance, in front of the fire on the patch of prepared ground, squatted a number of men, between twenty and thirty of them, in a semicircle. They were wrapped up in karosses and blankets, and in their centre sat a large figure on a chair of wood.

"The King and the Great Council," whispered Goza.

One of them looked round and saw us. At some sign from the king he rose, and against the fire I saw that he was the Prime Minister, Umnyamana. He came to me and, with a nod of recognition, conducted me some paces to the right where a euphorbia tree grew among the rank herbage. Here I found a stool placed ready on which I sat down, Goza, who of course was not of the Council, squatting at my side in the grass.

Now I found that I was so situated that I could not well be seen from the fire, or even from the rock above it, while I, by moving my head a little, could see both quite clearly. After this as the last reflection from the sunk sun faded, the darkness increased until nothing remained visible except the fire and the massive outline of the rock behind. The silence was complete, for none of the Council spoke. They were so still that they might have been dead, so still that a beetle suddenly booming past me made me start as though it had been a bullet. The general impression was almost mesmeric. I felt as though I were going to sleep and yet my mind remained painfully awake, so that I was able to think things out.

I understood clearly that the body of men to my left had come together to decide whether there should be peace or war; that there were divisions of opinion among them; that the king was ready to follow the party which should prove itself the strongest, but that the real voice of decision would speak from behind that fire. It was the case of the Delphic Oracle over again with a priest instead of a priestess, and what a priest!

It was evident to me also that Zikali, who knew human nature, and especially savage human nature, had arranged all this with a view to scenic and indeed supernatural effect. Moreover, he had done it very well, since I knew myself that in this place and hour words and occurrences would affect me deeply at which I should have laughed in the sunlight and open plain. Already the Zulus were affected, for I could hear the teeth of some of them chattering, and Goza began to shiver at my side. He muttered that it was cold, and lied for the donga was extremely hot and stuffy.

At length the silver radiance of the moon spread itself on the high curtain of the dark. Then the edge of her orb appeared above the hill and an arrow of white light fell into the little valley. It struck upon and about the jutting rock, revealing a misshapen, white-headed figure squatted between its base and the fire, the figure of Zikali.

CHAPTER XV

THE GREAT COUNCIL

None had seen or heard him come, and though doubtless he had but crept round the rock and taken his place in the darkness, there appeared to be something mysterious about this sudden appearance of Zikali. So the Zulu nobles thought at any rate, for they uttered a low "Ow!" of fear and wonder.

There he sat like a huge ape staring at the sky, for the firelight shone on his deep and burning eyes. The moonlight increased, but now and again it was broken by little clouds which caused strange shadows to appear about the rock. Some of these shadows looked as though veiled figures were approaching the wizard, bending over him and departing again, after giving him their message or counsel.

"His Spirits visit him," whispered Goza, but I made no answer.

This went on for quite a long time, until the full round of the moon appeared above the hill indeed, and, for the while, the clouds had cleared away. Still Zikali sat silent and I, who was acquainted with the habits of this people, knew that I was witnessing a conflict between two they considered to be respectively a spiritual and an earthly king. It is my belief that unless he were first addressed, Zikali would have sat all night without opening his lips. Possibly Cetewayo would have done the same if the impatience of public opinion had allowed him. At any was rate it was he who gave way.

"Makosi, master of many Spirits, on behalf of the Council and the People of the Zulus I, the King, greet you here in the place that you have chosen," said Cetewayo.

Zikali made no answer.

The silence went on as before, till at length, after a pause and some whispering, Cetewayo repeated his salutation, adding—

"Has age made you deaf, O Opener of Roads, that you cannot hear the voice of the King?"

Then at last Zikali answered in his low voice that yet seemed to fill all the kloof—

"Nay, Child of Senzangacona, age has not made me deaf, but my spirit in these latter days floats far from my body. It is like a bladder filled with air that a child holds by a string, and before I can speak I must draw it from the heavens to earth again. What did you say about the place that I have chosen? Well, what better place could I choose, seeing that it was here in this very Vale of Bones that I met the first king of the Zulus, Chaka the Wild Beast, who was your uncle? Why then should I not choose it to meet the last king of the Zulus?"

Now I, listening, knew at once that this saying might be understood in two ways, namely that Cetewayo was the reigning king, or that he was the last king who would ever reign. But the Council interpreted it in the latter and worse sense, for I saw a quiver of fear go through them.

"Why should I not choose it," went on Zikali, "seeing also that this place is holy to me? Here it was, O Son of Panda, that Chaka brought my children to be killed and forced me, sitting where you sit, to watch their deaths. There on the rock above me they were killed, four of them, three sons and a daughter, and the slayers—they came to an evil end, those slayers, as did Chaka—laughed and cast them down from the rock before me. Yes, and Chaka laughed, and I too laughed, for had not the king the right to kill my children and to steal their mothers, and was I not glad that they should be taken from the world and gathered to that of Spirits whence they always talk to me, yes, even now? That is why I did not hear you at first, King, because they were talking to me."

He paused, turning one ear upwards, then continued in a new and tender voice, "What is it you say to me, Noma, my dear little Noma? Oh! I hear you, I hear you."

Now he shifted himself along the ground on his haunches some paces to the right, and began to search about, groping with his long fingers. "Where, where?" he muttered. "Oh, I understand, further under the root, a jackal buried it, did it? Pah! how hard is this soil. Ah! I have it, but look, Noma, a stone has cut my finger. I have it, I have it," and from beneath the root of some fallen tree he drew out the skull of a child and, holding it in his right hand, softly rubbed the mould off it with his left.

"Yes, Noma, it might be yours, it is of the right size, but how can I be sure? What is it you say? The teeth? Ah! now I remember. Only the day before you were taken I pulled out that front tooth, did I not, and beneath it was another that was strangely split in two. If this skull was yours, it will be there. Come to the fire, Noma, and let us look; the moonlight is faint, is it not?"

Back to the fire he shifted himself, and bending towards the blaze, made an examination.

"True, Noma, true! Here is the split tooth, white as when I saw it all those years ago. Oh! dear child of my body, dear child of my spirit, for we do not beget with the body alone, Noma, as you know better than I do to-day, I greet you," and pressing the skull to his lips, he kissed it, then set it down in front of him between himself and the fire with the face part pointing to the king, and burst into one of his eerie and terrible laughs.

A low moan went up from his audience, and I felt the skin of Goza, who had shrunk against me, break into a profuse sweat. Then suddenly Zikali's voice changed one more and became hard and businesslike, if I may call it so, similar to that of other professional doctors.

"You have sent for me, O King, as those who went before you have sent when great things were about to happen. What is the matter on which you would speak to me?"

"You know well, Opener of Roads," answered Cetewayo, rather shakily I thought. "The matter is one of peace or war. The English threaten me and my people and make great demands on me; amongst others that the army should be disbanded. I can set them all out if you will. If I refuse to do as they bid me, then within a few days they will invade Zululand; indeed their soldiers are already gathered at the drifts."

"It is not needful, King," answered Zikali, "since I know what all know, neither more nor less. The winds whisper the demands of the white men, the birds sing them, the hyenas howl them at night. Let us see how the matter stands. When your father died Sompseu (Sir T. Shepstone), the great white chief, came from the English Government to name you king. This he could not do according to our law, since how can a stranger name the King of the Zulus? Therefore the Council of the Nation and the doctors—I was not among them, King—moved the spirit of Chaka the Lion into the body of Sompseu and made him as Chaka was and gave him power to name you to rule over the Zulus. So it came about that to the English Queen through the spirit of Chaka you swore certain things; that slaying for witchcraft should be abolished; that no man should die without fair and open trial, and other matters."

He paused a while, then went on, "These oaths you have broken, O King, as being of the blood you are and what you are, you must do."

Here there was disturbance among the Council and Cetewayo half rose from his seat, then sat down again. Zikali, gazing at the sky, waited till it had died away, then went on—

"Do any question my words? If so, then let them ask of the white men whether they be true or no. Let them ask also of the spirits of those who have died for witchcraft, and of the spirits of the women who have been slain and whose bodies were laid at the cross-roads because they married the men they chose and not the soldiers to whom the king gave them."

"How can I ask the white men who are far away?" broke out Cetewayo, ignoring the rest.

"Are the white men so far away, King? It is true that I see none and hear none, yet I seem to smell one of them close at hand." Here he took up the skull which he had laid down and whispered to it. "Ah! I thank you, my child. It seems, King, that there is a white man here hidden in this kloof, he who is named Macumazahn, a good man and a truthful, known to many of us from of old, who can tell you what his people think, though he is not one of their indunas. If you question my words, ask him."

"We know what the white men think," said Cetewayo, "so there is no need to ask Macumazahn to sing us an old song. The question is—what must the Zulus do? Must they swallow their spears and, ceasing to be a nation, become servants, or must they strike with them and drive the English into the sea, and after them the Boers?"

"Tell me first, King, who dwell far away and alone, knowing little of what passes in the land of Life, what the Zulus desire to do. Before me sits the Great Council of the Nation. Let it speak."

Then one by one the members of the Council uttered their opinions in order of rank or seniority. I do not remember the names of all who were present, or what each of them said. I recall, however, that Sigananda, a very old chief—he must have been over ninety—spoke the first. He told them that he had been friend of Chaka and one of his captains, and had fought in most of his battles. That afterwards he had been a general of Dingaan's until that king killed the Boers under Retief, when he left him and finally sided with Panda in the civil war in which Dingaan was killed with the help of the Boers. That he had been present at the battle of the Tugela, though he took no actual part in the fighting, and afterwards became a councillor of Panda's and then of Cetewayo his son. It was a long and interesting historical recital covering the whole period of the Zulu monarchy which ended suddenly with these words—

"I have noted, O King and Councillors, that whenever the black vulture of the Zulus was content to attack birds of his own feather, he has conquered. But when it has met the grey eagles of the white men, which come from over the sea, he has been conquered, and my heart tells me that as it was in the past, so it shall be in the future. Chaka was a friend of the English, so was Panda, and so has Cetewayo been until this hour. I say, therefore, let not the King tear the hand which fed him because it seems weak, lest it should grow strong and clutch him by the throat and choke him."

Next spoke Undabuko, Dabulamanzi and Magwenga, brothers of the king, who all favoured war, though the two last were guarded in their speech. After these came Uhamu, the king's uncle—he who was said to be the son of a Spirit—who was strong for peace, urging that the king should submit to the demands of the English, making the best terms he could, that he "should bend like a reed before the storm, so that after the storm had swept by, he might stand up straight again, and with him all the other reeds of the people of the Zulus."

So, too, said Seketwayo, chief of the Umdhlalosi, and more whom I cannot recall, six or seven of them. But Usibebu and the induna Untshingwayo, who afterwards commanded at Isandhlwana, were for fighting, as were Sirayo, the husband of the two women who had been taken on English territory and killed, and Umbilini, the chief of Swazi blood whose surrender was demanded by Sir Bartle Frere and who afterwards commanded the Zulus in the battle at Ihlobane. Last of all spoke the Prime Minister, Umnyamana, who declared fiercely that if the Zulu buffalo hid itself in the swamp like a timid calf when the white bull challenged it on the hills, the spirits of Chaka and all his forefathers would thrust its head into the mud and choke it.

When all had finished Cetewayo spoke, saying—

"That is a bad council which has two voices, for to which of them must the Captain listen when the impis of the foe gather in front of him? Here I have sat while the moon climbs high and counted, and what do I find? That one half of you, men of wisdom and renown, say Yes, and that the other half of you, men of wisdom and renown, say No. Which then is it to be, Yes or No? Are we to fight the English, or are we to sit still?"

"That is for the king to decide," said a voice.

"See what it is to be a king," went on Cetewayo with passion. "If I declare for war and we win, shall I be greater than I am? If victory gives me more land, more subjects, more wives and more cattle, what is the use of these things to me who already have enough of all of them? And if defeat should take everything from me, even my life perhaps, then what shall I have gained? I will tell you—the curse of the Zulus upon my name from father to son for ever. They will say, 'Cetewayo, son of Panda, pulled down a House that once was great. Because of some small matter he quarrelled with the English who were always the friends of our people, and brought the Zulus to the dust.' Sintwangu, my messenger, who brought heavy words from the Queen's induna which we must answer with other words or with spears, says that the English soldiers in Natal are few, so few that we Zulus can swallow them like bits of meat and still be hungry. But are these all the soldiers of the English? I am not sure. You are one of that people, Macumazahn," he added, turning his massive shape towards me, "tell us now, how many soldiers has your Queen?"

"King," I answered, "I do not know for certain. But if the Zulus can muster fifty thousand spears, the Queen, if there be need, can send against them ten times fifty thousand, and if she grows angry, another ten times fifty, every one armed with a rifle that will fire five bullets a minute, and to accompany the soldiers, hundreds of cannon whereof a single shot would give Ulundi to the flames. Out of the sea they will come, shipload after shipload, white men from where the sun sets and black men from where the sun rises, so many that Zululand would not hold them."

Now at these words, which I delivered as grandly as I could, something like a groan burst from the Council, though one man cried—

"Do not listen to the white traitor, O King, who is sent here to turn our hearts to water with his lies."

"Macumazahn may lie to us," went on Cetewayo, "though in the past none in the land have ever known him to lie, but he was not sent to do so, for I brought him here. For my part I do not believe that he lies. I believe that these English are as many as the pebbles in a river bed, and that to them Natal, yes, and all the Cape is but as a single, outlying cattle kraal, one cattle kraal out of a hundred. Did not Sompseu once tell us that they were countless, on that day when he came many years ago after the battle of the Tugela to name me to succeed my father Panda, the day when my faction, the Usutu, roared round him for hours like a river in flood, and he sat still like a rock in the centre of a river? Also I am minded of the words that Chaka said when Dingaan and Umbopa had stabbed him and he lay dying at the kraal Duguza, that although the dogs of his own House whom his hand fed, had eaten him up, he heard the sound of the running of the feet of a great white people that should stamp them and the Zulus flat."

He paused; and the silence was so intense that the crackling of Zikali's fire, which kept on burning brightly although I saw no fuel added to it, sounded quite loud. Presently it was broken, first by a dog near at hand, howling horribly at the moon, and next by the hooting of a great owl that flitted across the donga, the shadow of its wide wings falling for a moment on the king.

"Listen!" exclaimed Cetewayo, "a dog that howls! Methinks that it stands upon the roof of the House of Senzangacona. And an owl that hoots. Methinks that owl has its nest in the world of Spirits! Are these good omens, Councillors? I trow not. I say that I will not decide this matter of peace or war. If there is one of my own blood here who will do so, come, let him take my place and let me go away to my own lordship of Gikazi that I had when I was a prince before the witch Mameena who played with all men and loved but one"—here everybody turned and stared towards me, yes, even Zikali whom nothing else had seemed to move, till I wished that the ground would swallow me up—"caused the war between me and my brother Umbelazi whose blood earth will not swallow nor suns dry—"

"How can that be, O King?" broke in Umnyamana the Prime Minister. "How can any of your race sit in your seat while you still live? Then indeed there would be war, war between tribe and tribe and Zulu and Zulu till none were left, and the white hyenas from Natal would come and chew our bones and with them the Boers that have passed the Vaal. See now. Why is this Nyanga (i.e. witch-doctor) here?" and he pointed to Zikali beyond the fire. "Why has the Opener of Roads been brought from the Black Kloof which he has not left for years? Is it not that he may give us counsel in our need and show us a sign that his counsel is good, whether it be for war or peace? Then when he has made divination and given the counsel and shown the sign, then, O King, do you speak the word of war or peace, and send it to the Queen by yonder white man, and by that word we, the people, will abide."

At this suggestion, which I had no doubt was made by some secret agreement between Umnyamana and Zikali, Cetewayo seemed to grasp. Perhaps this was because it postponed for a little while the dreadful moment of decision, or perhaps because he hoped that in the eyes of the nation it would shift the responsibility from his shoulders to those of the Spirits speaking through the lips of their prophet. At any rate he nodded and answered—

"It is so. Let the Opener of Roads open us a road through the forests and the swamps and the rocks of doubt, danger and fear. Let him give us a sign that it is a good road on which we may safely travel, and let him tell us whether I shall live to walk that road and what I shall meet thereon. I promise him in return the greatest fee that ever yet was paid to a doctor in Zululand."

Now Zikali lifted his big head, shook his grey locks, and opening his wide mouth as though he expected manna to fall into it from the sky, he laughed out loud.

"O-ho-ho," he laughed, "Oho-ho-ho-o, it is worth while to have lived so long when life has brought me to such an hour as this. What is it that my ears hear? That I, the Indwande dwarf, I whom Chaka named 'The-Thing-that-never-should-have-been-born,' I, one of the race conquered and despised by the Zulus, am here to speak a word which the Zulus dare not utter, which the King of the Zulus dares not utter. O-ho-ho-ho! And what does the King offer to me? A fee, a great fee for the word that shall paint the Zulus red with blood or white with the slime of shame. Nay, I take no fee that is the price of blood or shame. Before I speak that word unknown—for as yet my heart has not heard it, and what the heart has not heard the lips cannot shape—I ask but one thing. It is an oath that whatever follows on the word, while there is a Zulu left living in the world, I, the Voice of the Spirits, shall be safe from hurt or from reproach, I and those of my House and those over whom I throw my blanket, be they black or be they white. That is my fee, without which I am silent."

"Izwa! We hear you. We swear it on behalf of the people," said every councillor in the semi-circle in front of him; yes, and the king said it also, stretching out his hand.

"Good," said Zikali, "it is an oath, it is an oath, sworn here upon the bones of the dead. Evil-doers you call them, but I say to you that many of those who sit before me have more evil in their hearts than had those dead. Well, let it be proclaimed, O King, and with it this—that ill shall it go with him who breaks the oath, with his family, with his kraal and all with whom he has to do.

"Now what is it you ask of me? First of all, counsel as to whether you should fight the English Queen, a matter on which you, the Great Ones, are evenly divided in opinion, as is the nation behind you. O King, Indunas, and Captains, who am I that I should judge of such a matter which is beyond my trade, a matter of the world above and of men's bodies, not of the world below and of men's spirits? Yet there was one who made the Zulu people out of nothing, as a potter fashions a vessel from clay, as a smith fashions an assegai out of the ore of the hills, yes, and tempers it with human blood.* Chaka the Lion, the Wild Beast, the King among Kings, the Conqueror. I knew Chaka as I knew his father, yes, and his father. Others still living knew him also, say you, Sigananda there for instance," and he pointed to the old chief who had spoken first. "Yes, Sigananda knew him as a boy knows a great man, as a soldier knows a general. But I knew his heart, aye, I shaped his heart, I was its thought. Had it not been for me he would never have been great. Then he wronged me"—here Zikali took up the skull which he said was that of his daughter, and stroked it—"and I left him.

[—The old Zulu smiths dipped their choicest blades in the blood of men.—A. Q.]*

"He was not wise, he should have killed one whom he had wronged, but perhaps he knew that I could not be killed; perhaps he had tried and found that he was but throwing spears at the moon which fell back on his own head. I forget. It is so long ago, and what does it matter? At least I took away from him the prop of my wisdom, and he fell—to rise no more. And so it has been with others. So it has been with others. Yet while he was great I knew his heart who lived in his heart, and therefore I ask myself, had he been sitting where the King sits to-day, what would Chaka have done? I will tell you. If not only the English but the Boers also and with them the Pondos, the Basutos and all the tribes of Africa had threatened him, he would have fought them—yes, and set his heel upon their necks. Therefore, although I give no counsel upon such a matter, I say to you that the counsel of Chaka is—fight—and conquer. Hearken to it or pass it by—I care not which."

He paused and a loud "Ow" of wonder and admiration rose from his audience. Myself I nearly joined in it, for I thought this one of the cleverest bits of statecraft that ever I had heard of or seen. The old wizard had taken no responsibility and given no answer to the demand for advice. All this he had thrust on to the shoulders of a dead man, and that man one whose name was magical to every Zulu, the king whose memory they adored, the great General who had gorged them with victory and power. Speaking as Chaka, after a long period of peace, he urged them once more to lift their spears and know the joys of triumph, thereby making themselves the greatest nation in Southern Africa. From the moment I heard this cunning appeal, I know what the end would be; all the rest was but of minor and semi-personal interest. I knew also for the first time how truly great was Zikali and wondered what he might have become had Fortune set him in different circumstances among a civilized people.

Now he was speaking again, and quickly before the impression died away.

"Such is the word of Chaka spoken by me who was his secret councillor, the Councillor who was seldom seen, and never heard. Does not Sigananda yonder know the voice which amongst all those present echoes in his ears alone?"

"I know it," cried the old chief. Then with his eyes starting almost from his head, Sigananda leapt up and raising his hand, gave the royal salute, the Bayete, to the spirit of Chaka, as though the dead king stood before him.

I think that most of those there thought that it did stand before him, for some of them also gave the Bayete and even Cetewayo raised his arm.

Sigananda squatted down again and Zikali went on.

"You have heard. This captain of the Lion knows his voice. So, that is done with. Now you ask of me something else—that I who am a doctor, the oldest of all the doctors and, it is thought—I know not— the wisest, should be able to answer. You ask of me—How shall this war prosper, if it is made—and what shall chance to the King during and after the war, and lastly you ask of me a sign. What I tell to you is true, is it not so?"

"It is true," answered the Council.

"Asking is easy," continued Zikali in a grumbling voice, "but answering is another matter. How can I answer without preparation, without the needful medicines also that I have not with me, who did not know what would be sought of me, who thought that my opinion was desired and no more? Go away now and return on the sixth night and I will tell you what I can do."

"Not so," cried the king. "We refuse to go, for the matter is immediate. Speak at once, Opener of Roads, lest it should be said in the land that after all you are but an ancient cheat, a stick that snaps in two when it is leant on."

"Ancient cheat! I remember that is what Macumazahn yonder once told me I am, though afterwards— Perhaps he was right, for who in his heart knows whether or not he be a cheat, a cheat who deceives himself and through himself others. A stick that snaps in two when it is leant on! Some have thought me so and some have thought otherwise. Well, you would have answers which I know not how to give, being without medicine and in face of those who are quite ignorant and therefore cannot lend me their thoughts, as it sometimes happens that men do when workers of evil are sought out in the common fashion. For then, as you may have guessed, it is the evil-doer who himself tells the doctor of his crime, though he may not know that he is telling it. Yet there is another stone that I alone can throw, another plan that I alone can practise, and that not always. But of this I would not make use since it is terrible and might frighten you or even send you back to your huts raving so that your wives, yes, and the very dogs fled, from you."

He stopped and for the first time did something to his fire, for I saw his hands going backwards and forwards, as though he warmed them at the flames.

At length an awed voice, I think it was that of Dabulamanzi, asked—

"What is this plan, Inyanga? Let us hear that we may judge."

"The plan of calling one from the dead and hearkening to the voice of the dead. Is it your desire that I should draw water from this fount of wisdom, O King and Councillors?"

Now men began to whisper together and Goza groaned at my side.

"Rather would I look down a live lion's throat than see the dead," he murmured. But I, who was anxious to learn how far Zikali would carry his tricks, contemptuously told him to be silent.

Presently the king called me to him and said—

"Macumazahn, you white men are reported to know all things. Tell me now, is it possible for the dead to appear?"

"I am not sure," I answered doubtfully; "some say that it is and some say that it is not possible."

"Well," said the king. "Have you ever seen one you knew in life after death?"

"No," I replied, "that is—yes. That is—I do not know. When you will tell me, King, where waking ends and sleep begins, then I will answer."

"Macumazahn," he exclaimed, "just now I announced that you were no liar, who perceive that after all you are a liar, for how can you both have seen, and not seen, the dead? Indeed I remember that you lied long ago, when you gave it out that the witch Mameena was not your lover, and afterwards showed that she was by kissing her before all men, for who kisses a woman who is not his lover, or his mother? Return, since you will not tell me the truth."

So I went back to my stool, feeling very small and yet indignant, for how was it possible to be definite about ghosts, or to explain the exact facts of the Mameena myth which clung to me like a Wait-a-bit thorn.

Then after a little consultation Cetewayo said—

"It is our desire, O Opener of Roads, that you should draw wisdom from the fount of Death, if indeed you can do so. Now let any who are afraid depart and wait for us who are not afraid, alone and in silence at the mouth of the kloof."

At this some of the audience rose, but after hesitating a little, sat down again. Only Goza actually took a step forward, but on my remarking that he would probably meet the dead coming up that way, collapsed, muttering something about my pistol, for the fool seemed to think I could shoot a spirit.

"If indeed I can do so," repeated Zikali in a careless fashion. "That is to be proved, is it not? Perhaps, too, it may be better for every one of you if I fail than if I succeed. Of one thing I warn you, should the dead appear stir not, and above all touch not, for he who does either of these things will, I think, never live to look upon the sun again. But first let me try an easier fashion."

Then once again he took up the skull that he said had been his daughter's, and whispered to it, only to lay it down presently.

"It will not serve," he said with a sigh and shaking his locks. "Noma tells me that she died a child, one who had no knowledge of war or matters of policy, and that in all these things of the world she still remains a child. She says that I must seek some one who thought much of them; one, too who still lives in the heart of a man who is present here, if that be possible, since from such a heart alone can the strength be drawn to enable the dead to appear and speak. Now let there be silence—Let there be silence, and woe to him that breaks it."

Silence there was indeed, and in it Zikali crouched himself down till his head almost rested on his knee, and seemed to go to sleep. He awoke again and chanted for half a minute or so in some language I could not understand. Then voices began to answer him, as it seemed to me from all over the kloof, also from the sky or rock above. Whether the effect was produced by ventriloquism or whether he had confederates posted at various points, I do not know.

At any rate this lord of "multitudes of spirits" seemed to be engaged in conversation with some of them. What is more, the thing was extremely well done, since each voice differed from the other; also I seemed to recognize some of them, Dingaan's for instance, and Panda's, yes, and that of Umbelazi the Handsome, the brother of the king whose death I witnessed down by the Tugela.

You will ask me what they said. I do not know. Either the words were confused or the events that followed have blotted them from my brain. All I remember is that each of them seemed to be speaking of the Zulus and their fate and to be very anxious to refer further discussion of the matter to some one else. In short they seemed to talk under protest, or that was my impression, although Goza, the only person with whom I had any subsequent debate upon the subject, appeared to have gathered one that was different, though what it was I do not recall. The only words that remained clear to me must, I thought, have come from the spirit of Chaka, or rather from Zikali or one of his myrmidons assuming that character. They were uttered in a deep full voice, spiced with mockery, and received by the wizard with "Sibonga," or titles of praise, which I who am versed in Zulu history and idiom knew had only been given to the great king, and indeed since his death had become unlawful, not to be used. The words were—

"What, Thing-that-should-never-have-been-born, do you think yourself a Thing-that-should-never-die, that you still sit beneath the moon and weave witchcrafts as of old? Often have I hunted for you in the Under-world who have an account to settle with you, as you have an account to settle with me. So, so, what does it matter since we must meet at last, even if you hide yourself at the back of the furthest star? Why do you bring me up to this place where I see some whom I would forget? Yes, they build bone on bone and taking the red earth, mould it into flesh and stand before me as last I saw them newly dead. Oh! your magic is good, Spell-weaver, and your hate is deep and your vengeance is keen. No, I have nothing to tell you to-day, who rule a greater people than the Zulus in another land. Who are these little men who sit before you? One of them has a look of Dingaan, my brother who slew me, yes, and wears his armlet. Is he the king? Answer not, for I do not care to know. Surely yonder withered thing is Sigananda. I know his eye and the Iziqu on his breast. Yes, I gave it to him after the great battle with Zweede in which he killed five men. Does he remember it, I wonder? Greeting, Sigananda; old as you are you have still twenty and one years to live, and then we will talk of the battle with Zweede. Let me begone, this place burns my spirit, and in it there is a stench of mortal blood. Farewell, O Conqueror!"

These were the words that I thought I heard Chaka say, though I daresay that I dreamt them. Indeed had it been otherwise, I mean had they really been spoken by Zikali, there would surely have been more in them, something that might have served his purpose, not mere talk which had all the inconsequence of a dream. Also no one else seemed to pay any particular attention to them, though this may have been because so many voices were sounding from different places at once, for as I have said, Zikali arranged his performance very well, as well as any medium could have done on a prepared stage in London.

In a moment, as though at a signal, the voices died away. Then other things happened. To begin with I felt very faint, as though all the strength were being taken out of me. Some queer fancy got a hold of me. I don't quite know what it was, but it had to do with the Bible story of Adam when he fell asleep and a rib was removed from him and made into a woman. I reflected that I felt as Adam must have done when he came out of his trance after this terrific operation, very weak and empty. Also, as it chanced, presently I saw Eve—or rather a woman. Looking at the fire in a kind of disembodied way, I perceived that dense smoke was rising from it, which smoke spread itself out like a fan. It thinned by degrees, and through the veil of smoke I perceived something else, namely, a woman very like one whom once I had known. There she stood, lightly clad enough, her fingers playing with the blue beads of her necklace, an inscrutable smile upon her face and her large eyes fixed on nothingness.

Oh! Heaven, I knew her, or rather thought I did at the moment, for now I am almost sure that it was Nombe dressed, or undressed, for the part. That knowledge came with reflection, but then I could have sworn, being deceived by the uncertain light, that the long dead Mameena stood before us as she had seemed to stand before me in the hut of Zikali, radiating a kind of supernatural life and beauty.

A little wind arose, shaking the dry leaves of the aloes in the kloof; I thought it whispered—Hail, Mameena! Some of the older men, too, among them a few who had seen her die, in trembling voices murmured, "It is Mameena!" whereon Zikali scowled at them and they grew silent.

As for the figure it stood there patient and unmoved, like one who has all time at its disposal, playing with the blue beads. I heard them tinkle against each other, which proves that it was human, for how could a wraith cause beads to tinkle, although it is true that Christmas-story ghosts are said to clank their chains. Her eyes roved idly and without interest over the semi-circle of terrified men before her. Then by degrees they fixed themselves upon the tree behind which I was crouching, whereon Goza sank paralyzed to the ground. She contemplated this tree for a while that seemed to me interminable; it reminded me of a setter pointing game it winded but could not see, for her whole frame grew intent and alert. She ceased playing with the beads and stretched out her slender hand towards me. Her lips moved. She spoke in a sweet, slow voice, saying—

"O Watcher-by-Night, is it thus you greet her to whom you have given strength to stand once more beneath the moon? Come hither and tell me, have you no kiss for one from whom you parted with a kiss?"

I heard. Without doubt the voice was the very voice of Mameena (so well had Nombe been instructed). Still I determined not to obey it, who would not be made a public laughing-stock for a second time in my life. Also I confess this jesting with the dead seemed to me somewhat unholy, and not on any account would I take a part in it.

All the company turned and stared at me, even Goza lifted his head and stared, but I sat still and contemplated the beauties of the night.

"If it is the spirit of Mameena, he will come," whispered Cetewayo to Umnyamana.

"Yes, yes," answered the Prime Minister, "for the rope of his love will draw him. He who has once kissed Mameena, must kiss her again when she asks."

Hearing this I grew furiously indignant and was about to break into explanations, when to my horror I found myself rising from that stool. I tried to cling to it, but, as it only came into the air with me, let it go.

"Hold me, Goza," I muttered, and he like a good fellow clutched me by the ankle, whereon I promptly kicked him in the mouth, at least my foot kicked him, not my will. Now I was walking towards that Shape—shadow or woman—like a man in his sleep, and as I came she stretched out her arms and smiled oh! as sweetly as an angel, though I felt quite sure that she was nothing of the sort.

Now I stood opposite to her alongside the fire of which the smoke smelt like roses at the dawn, and she seemed to bend towards me. With shame and humiliation I perceived that in another moment those arms would be about me. But somehow they never touched me; I lost sight of them in the rose-scented smoke, only the sweet, slow voice which I could have sworn was that of Mameena, murmured in my ear—well, words known to her and me alone that I had never breathed to any living being, though of course I am aware now that they must also have been known to somebody else.

"Do you doubt me any longer?" went on the murmuring. "Say, am I Nombe now? Or—or am I in truth that Mameena, whose kiss thrills your lips and soul? Hearken, Macumazahn, for the time is short. In the rout of the great battle that shall be, do not fly with the white men, but set your face towards Ulundi. One who was your friend will guard you, and whoever dies, no harm shall come to you now that the fire which burns in my heart has set all Zululand aflame. Hearken once more. Hans, the little yellow man who was named Light-in-Darkness, he who died among the Kendah people, sends you salutations and gives you praise. He bids me tell you that now of his own accord he renders to me, Mameena, the royal salute, because royal I must ever be; because also he and I who are so far apart are yet one in the love that is our life."

The smoke blew into my face, causing me to reel back. Cetewayo caught me by the arm, saying—

"Tell us, are the lips of the dead witch warm or cold?"

"I do not know," I groaned, "for I never touched her."

"How he lies! Oh! how he lies even about what our eyes saw," said Cetewayo reflectively as I blundered past him back to my seat, on which I sank half swooning. When I got my wits again the figure that pretended to be Mameena was speaking, I suppose in answer to some question of Zikali's which I had not heard. It said—

"O Lord of the Spirits, you have called me from the land of Spirits to make reply as to two matters which have not yet happened upon the earth. These replies I will give but no others, since the mortal strength that I have borrowed returns whence it came. The first matter is, if there be war between the White and Black, what will happen in that war? I see a plain ringed round with hills and on it a strange-shaped mount. I see a great battle; I see the white men go down like corn before a tempest; I see the spears of the impis redden; I see the white soldiers lie like leaves cut from a tree by frost. They are dead, all dead, save a handful that have fled away. I hear the ingoma of victory sung here at Ulundi. It is finished.

"The second matter is—what shall chance to the king? I see him tossed on the Black Water; I see him in a land full of houses, talking with a royal woman and her councillors. There, too, he conquers, for they offer him tribute of many gifts. I see him here, back here in Zululand, and hear him greeted with the royal salute. Last of all I see him dead, as men must die, and hear the voice of Zikali and the mourning of the women of his house. It is finished. Farewell, King Cetewayo, I pass to tell Panda, your father, how it fares with you. When last we parted did I not prophesy to you that we should meet again at the bottom of a gulf? Was it this gulf, think you, or another? One day you shall learn. Farewell, or fare ill, as it may happen!"

Once more the smoke spread out like a fan. When it thinned and drew together again, the Shape was gone.

Now I thought that the Zulus would be so impressed by this very queer exhibition, that they would seek no more supernatural guidance, but make up their minds for war at once. This, however, was just what they did not do. As it happened, among the assembled chiefs, was one who himself had a great repute as a witch-doctor, and therefore burned with jealousy of Zikali who appeared to be able to do things that he had never even attempted. This man leapt up and declared that all which they had seemed to hear and see was but cunning trickery, carried out after long preparation by Zikali and his confederates. The voices, he said, came from persons placed in certain spots, or sometimes were produced by Zikali himself. As for the vision, it was not that of a spirit but of a real woman, in proof of which he called attention to certain anatomical details of the figure. Finally, with much sense, he pointed out that the Council would be mad to come to any decision upon such evidence, or to give faith to prophecies, whereof the truth or falsity could only be known in the future.

Now a fierce debate broke out, the war party maintaining that the manifestations were genuine, the peace party that they were a fraud. In the end, as neither side would give way and as Zikali, when appealed to, sat silent as a stone, refusing any explanation, the king said—

"Must we sit here talking, talking, till daylight? There is but one man who can know the truth, that is Macumazahn. Let him deny it as he will, he was the lover of this Mameena while she was alive, for with my own eyes I saw him kiss her before she killed herself. It is certain, therefore, that he knows if the woman we seemed to see was Mameena or another, since there are things which a man never forgets. I propose, therefore, that we should question him and form our own judgment of his answer."

This advice, which seemed to promise a road out of a blind ally, met with instant acceptance.

"Let it be so," they cried with one voice, and in another minute I was once more conducted from behind my tree and set down upon the stool in front of the Council, with my back to the fire and Zikali, "that his eyes might not charm me."

"Now, Watcher-by-Night," said Cetewayo, "although you have lied to us in a certain matter, of this we do not think much, since it is one upon which both men and women always lie, as every judge will know. Therefore we still believe you to be an honest man, as your dealings have proved for many years. As an honest man, therefore, we beg you to give us a true answer to a plain question. Was the Shape we saw before us just now a woman or a spirit, and if a spirit, was it the ghost of Mameena, the beautiful witch who died near this place nearly the quarter of a hundred years ago, she whom you loved, or who loved you, which is just the same thing, since a man always loves a woman who loves him, or thinks that he does?"

Now after reflection I replied in these words and as conscientiously as I could—

"King and Councillors, I do not know if what we all saw was a ghost or a living person, but, as I do not believe in ghosts, or at any rate that they come back to the world on such errands, I conclude that it was a living person. Still it may have been neither, but only a mere picture produced before us by the arts of Zikali. So much for the first question. Your second is—was this spirit or woman or shadow, that of her whom I remember meeting in Zululand many years ago? King and Councillors, I can only say that it was very like her. Still one handsome young woman often greatly resembles another of the same age and colouring. Further, the moon gives an uncertain light, especially when it is tempered by smoke from a fire. Lastly, memory plays strange tricks with all of us, as you will know if you try to think of the face of any one who has been dead for more than twenty years. For the rest, the voice seemed similar, the beads and ornaments seemed similar, and the figure repeated to me certain words which I thought I alone had heard come from the lips of her who is dead. Also she gave me a strange message from another who is dead, referring to a matter which I believed was known only to me and that other. Yet Zikali is very clever and may have learned these things in some way unguessed by me, and what he has learned, others may have learned also. King and Councillors, I do not think that what we saw was the spirit of Mameena. I think it a woman not unlike to her who had been taught her lesson. I have nothing more to say, and therefore I pray you not to ask me any further questions about Mameena of whose name I grow weary."

At this point Zikali seemed to wake out of his indifference, or his torpor, for he looked up and said darkly—

"It is strange that the cleverest are always those who first fall into the trap. They go along, gazing at the stars at night, and forget the pit which they themselves have dug in the morning. O-ho-ho! Oho-ho!"

Now the wrangling broke out afresh. The peace party pointed triumphantly to the fact that I, the white man who ought to know, put no faith in this apparition, which was therefore without doubt a fraud. The war party on the other hand declared that I was deceiving them for reasons of my own, one of which would be that I did not wish to see the Zulus eat up my people. So fierce grew the debate that I thought it would end in blows and perhaps in an attack on myself or Zikali who all the while sat quite careless and unmoved, staring at the moon. At length Cetewayo shouted for silence, spitting, as was his habit when angry.

"Make an end," he cried, "lest I cause some of you to grow quiet for ever," whereon the recriminations ceased. "Opener of Roads," he went on, "many of those who are present think like Macumazahn here, that you are but an old cheat, though whether or no I be one of these I will not say. They demand a sign of you that none can dispute, and I demand it also before I speak the word of peace or war. Give us then that sign or begone to whence you came and show your face no more at Ulundi."

"What sign does the Council require, Son of Panda?" asked Zikali quietly. "Let them agree on one together and tell me now at once, for I who am old grow weary and would sleep. Then if it can be given I will give it; and if I cannot give it, I will get me back to my own house and show my face no more at Ulundi, who do not desire to listen again to fools who babble like contending waters round a stone and yet never stir the stone because they run two ways at once."

Now the Councillors stared at each other, for none knew what sign to ask. At length old Sigananda said—

"O King, it is well known that the Black One who went before you had a certain little assegai handled with the royal red wood, which drank the blood of many. It was with this assegai that Mopo his servant, who vanished from the land after the death of Dingaan, let out the life of the Black One at the kraal Duguza, but what became of it afterwards none have heard for certain. Some say that it was buried with the Black One, some that Mopo stole it. Others that Dingaan and Umhlagana burned it. Still a saying rose like a wind in the land that when that spear shall fall from heaven at the feet of the king who reigns in the place of the Black One, then the Zulus shall make their last great war and win a victory of which all the world shall hear. Now let the Opener of Roads give us this sign of the falling of the Black One's spear and I shall be content."

"Would you know the spear if it fell?" asked Cetewayo.

"I should know it, O King, who have often held it in my hand. The end of the haft is gnawed, for when he was angry the Black One used to bite it. Also a thumb's length from the blade is a black mark made with hot iron. Once the Black One made a bet with one of his captains that at a distance of ten paces he would throw the spear deeper into the body of a chief whom he wished to kill, than the captain could. The captain threw first, for I saw him with my eyes, and the spear sank to that place on the shaft where the mark is, for the Black One burned it there. Then the Black One threw and the spear went through the body of the chief who, as he died, called to him that he too should know the feel of it in his heart, as indeed he did."

I think that Cetewayo was about to assent to this suggestion, since he who desired peace believed it impossible that Zikali should suddenly cause this identical spear to fall from heaven. But Umnyamana, the Prime Induna, interposed hurriedly—

"It is not enough, O King. Zikali may have stolen the spear, for he was living and at the kraal Duguza at that time. Also he may have put about the prophecy whereof Sigananda speaks, or at least so men would say. Let him give us a greater sign than this that all may be content, so that whether we make war or peace it may be with a single mind. Now it is known that we Zulus have a guardian spirit who watches over us from the skies, she who is called Nomkubulwana, or by some the Inkosazana-y-Zulu, the Princess of Heaven. It is known also that this Princess, who is white of skin and ruddy-haired, appears always before great things happen in our land. Thus she appeared before the Black One died. Also she appeared to a number of children before the battle of the Tugela. It is said, too, that but lately she appeared to a woman near the coast and warned her to cross the Tugela because there would be war, though this woman cannot now be found. Let the Opener of Roads call down Nomkubulwana before our eyes from heaven and we will admit, every man of us, that this is a sign which cannot be questioned."

"And if he does this thing, which I hold no doctor in the world can do, what shall it signify?" asked Cetewayo.

"O King," answered Umnyamana, "if he does so, it shall signify war and victory. If he does not do so, it shall signify peace, and we will bow our heads before the Amalungwana basi bodwe" (i.e., "the little English," used as a term of derision).

"Do all agree?" asked Cetewayo.

"We agree," answered every man, stretching out his hand.

"Then, Opener of Roads, it stands thus: If you can call Nomkubulwana, should there be such a spirit, to appear before our eyes, the Council will take it as a sign that the Heavens direct us to fight the English."

So spoke Cetewayo, and I noted a tone of triumph in his voice, for his heart shrank from this war, and he was certain that Zikali could do nothing of the sort. Still the opinion of the nation, or rather of the army, was so strong in favour of it that he feared lest his refusal might bring about his deposition, if not his death. From this dilemma the supernatural test suggested by the Prime Minister and approved by the Council that represented the various tribes of people, seemed to offer a path of escape. So I read the situation, as I think rightly.

Upon hearing these words for the first time that night Zikali seemed to grow disturbed.

"What do my ears hear?" he exclaimed excitedly. "Am I the Umkulukulu, the Great-Great (i.e., God) himself, that it should be asked of me to draw the Princess of Heaven from beyond the stars, she who comes and goes like the wind, but like the wind cannot be commanded? Do they hear that if she will not come to my beckoning, then the great Zulu people must put a yoke upon their shoulders and be as slaves? Surely the King must have been listening to the doctrines of those English teachers who wear a white ribbon tied about their necks, and tell us of a god who suffered himself to be nailed to a cross of wood, rather than make war upon his foes, one whom they call the Prince of Peace. Times have changed indeed since the days of the Black One. Yes, generals have become like women; the captains of the impis are set to milk the cows. Well, what have I to do with all this? What does it matter to me who am so very old that only my head remains above the level of the earth, the rest of me being buried in the grave, who am not even a Zulu to boot, but a Dwandwe, one of the despised Dwandwe whom the Zulus mocked and conquered?

"Hearken to me, Spirits of the House of Senzangacona"—here he addressed about a dozen of Cetewayo's ancestors by name, going back for many generations. "Hearken to me, O Princess of Heaven, appointed by the Great-Great to be the guardian of the Zulu race. It is asked that you should appear, should it be your wish to signify to these your children that they must stand upon their feet and resist the white men who already gather upon their borders. And should it be your wish that they should lay down their spears and go home to sleep with their wives and hoe the gardens while the white men count the cattle and set each to his work upon the roads, then that you should not appear. Do what you will, O Spirits of the House of Senzangacona, do what you will, O Princess of Heaven. What does it matter to the Thing-that-never-should-have-been-born, who soon will be as though he never had been born, whether the House of Senzangacona and the Zulu people stand or fall?

"I, the old doctor, was summoned here to give counsel. I gave counsel, but it passed over the heads of these wise ones like a shadow of which none took note. I was asked to prophesy of what would chance if war came. I called the dead from their graves; they came in voices, and one of them put on the flesh again and spoke from the lips of flesh. The white man to whom she spoke denied her who had been his love, and the wise ones said that she was a cheat, yes, a doll that I had dressed up to deceive them. This spirit that had put on flesh, told of what would chance in the war, if war there were, and what would chance to the King, but they mock at the prophecy and now they demand a sign. Come then, Nomkubulwana, and give them the sign if you will and let there be war. Or stay away and give them no sign if you will, and let there be peace. It is nought to me, nought to the Thing-that-should-never-have-been-born."

Thus he rambled on, as it occurred to me who watched and listened, talking against time. For I observed that while he spoke a cloud was passing over the face of the moon, and that when he ceased speaking it was quite obscured by this cloud, so that the Vale of Bones was plunged in a deep twilight that was almost darkness. Further, in a nervous kind of way, he did something more to his wizard's fire which again caused it to throw out a fan of smoke that hid him and the execution rock in front of which he sat.

The cloud floated by and the moon came out as though from an eclipse; the smoke of the fire, too, thinned by degrees. As it melted and the light grew again, I became aware that something was materializing, or had appeared on the point of the rock above us. A few seconds later, to my wonder and amazement, I perceived that this something was the spirit-like form of a white woman which stood quite still upon the very point of the rock. She was clad in some garment of gleaming white cut low upon her breast, that may have been of linen, but from the way it shone, suggested that it was of glittering feathers, egrets' for instance. Her ruddy hair was outspread, and in it, too, something glittered, like mica or jewels. Her feet and milk-hued arms were bare and poised in her right hand was a little spear.

Nor did I see alone, since a moan of fear and worship went up from the Councillors. Then they grew silent stared and stared.

Suddenly Zikali lifted his head and looked at them through the thin flame of the fire which made his eyes shine like those of a tiger or of a cornered baboon.

"At what do you gaze so hard, King and Councillors?" he asked. "I see nothing. At what then do you gaze so hard?"

"On the rock above you stands a white spirit in her glory. It is the Inkosazana herself," muttered Cetewayo.

"Has she come then?" mocked the old wizard. "Nay, surely it is but a dream, or another of my tricks; some black woman painted white that I have smuggled here in my medicine bag, or rolled up in the blanket on my back. How can I prove to you that this is not another cheat like to that of the spirit of Mameena whom the white man, her lover, did not know again? Go near to her you must not, even if you could, seeing that if by chance she should not be a cheat, you would die, every man of you, for woe to him whom Nomkubulwana touches. How then, how? Ah! I have it. Doubtless in his pocket Macumazahn yonder hides a little gun, Macumazahn who with such a gun can cut a reed in two at thirty paces, or shave the hair from the chin of a man, as is well known in the land. Let him then take his little gun and shoot at that which you say stands upon the rock. If it be a black woman painted white, doubtless she will fall down dead, as so many have fallen from that rock. But if it be the Princess of Heaven, then the bullet will pass through her or turn aside and she will take no harm, though whether Macumazahn will take any harm is more than I can say."

Now when they heard this many remained silent, but some of the peace party began to clamour that I should be ordered to shoot at the apparition. At length Cetewayo seemed to give way to this pressure. I say seemed, because I think he wished to give way. Whether or not a spirit stood before him, he knew no more than the rest, but he did know that unless the vision were proved to be mortal he would be driven into war with the English. Therefore he took the only chance that remained to him.

"Macumazahn," he said, "I know you have your pistol on you, for only the other day you brought it into my presence, and through light and darkness you nurse it as a mother does her firstborn. Now since the Opener of Roads desires it, I command you to fire at that which seems to stand above us. If it be a mortal woman, she is a cheat and deserves to die. If it be a spirit from heaven it can take no harm. Nor can you take harm who only do that which you must."

"Woman or spirit, I will not shoot, King," I answered.

"Is it so? What! do you defy me, White Man? Do so if you will, but learn that then your bones shall whiten here in this Vale of Bones. Yes, you shall be the first of the English to go below," and turning, he whispered something to two of the Councillors.

Now I saw that I must either obey or die. For a moment my mind grew confused in face of this awful alternative. I did not believe that I saw a spirit. I believed that what stood above me was Nombe cunningly tricked out with some native pigments which at that distance and in that light made her look like a white woman. For oddly enough at that time the truth did not occur to me, perhaps because I was too surprised. Well, if it were Nombe, she deserved to be shot for playing such a trick, and what is more her death, by revealing the fraud of Zikali, would perhaps avert a great war. But then why did he make the suggestion that I should be commanded to fire at this figure? Slowly I drew out my pistol and brought it to the full cock, for it was loaded.

"I will obey, King," I said, "to save myself from being murdered. But on your head be all that may follow from this deed."

Then it was for the first time that a new idea struck me so clearly that I believe it was conveyed direct from Zikali's brain to my own. I might shoot, but there was no need for me to hit. After that everything grew plain.

"King," I said, "if yonder be a mortal, she is about to die. Only a spirit can escape my aim. Watch now the centre of her forehead, for there the bullet will strike!"

I lifted the pistol and appeared to cover the figure with much care. As I did so, even from that distance I thought I saw a look of terror in its eyes. Then I fired, with a little jerk of the wrist sending the ball a good yard above her head.

"She is unharmed," cried a voice. "Macumazahn missed her."

"Macumazahn does not miss," I replied loftily. "If that at which he aimed is unharmed, it is because it cannot be hit."

"O-ho-o!" laughed Zikali, "the White Man who does not know the taste of his own love's lips, says that he has fired at that which cannot be hit. Let him try again. No, let him choose another target. The Spirit is the Spirit, but he who summoned her may still be a cheat. There is another bullet in your little gun, White Man; see if it can pierce the heart of Zikali, that the King and Council may learn whether he be a true prophet, the greatest of all the prophets that ever was, or whether he be but a common cheat."

Now a sudden rage filled me against this old rascal. I remembered how he had brought Mameena to her death, when he thought that it would serve him, and since then filled the land with stories concerning her and me, which met me whatever way I turned. I remembered that for years he had plotted to bring about the destruction of the Zulus, and to further his dark ends, was now engaged in causing a fearful war which would cost the lives of thousands. I remembered that he had trapped me into Zululand and then handed me over to Cetewayo, separating me from my friends who were in my charge, and for aught I knew, giving them to death. Surely the world would be well rid of him.

"Have your will," I shouted and covered him with the pistol.

Then there came into my mind a certain saying—"Judge not that ye be not judged." Who and what was I that I should dare to arraign and pass sentence upon this man who after all had suffered many wrongs? As I was about to fire I caught sight of some bright object flashing towards the king from above, and instantaneously shifted my aim and pressed the trigger. The thing, whatever it might be, flew in two. One part of it fell upon Zikali, the other part travelled on and struck Cetewayo upon the knee.

There followed a great confusion and a cry of "The king is stabbed!" I ran forward to look and saw the blade of a little assegai lying on the ground and on Cetewayo's knee a slight cut from which blood trickled.

"It is nothing," I said, "a scratch, no more, though had not the spear been stopped in its course it might have been otherwise."

"Yes," cried Zikali, "but what was it that caused the cut? Take this, Sigananda, and tell me what it may be," and he threw towards him a piece of red wood.

Sigananda looked at it. "It is the haft of the Black One's spear," he exclaimed, "which the bullet of Macumazahn has severed from the blade."

"Aye," said Zikali, "and the blade has drawn the blood of the Black One's child. Read me this omen, Sigananda; or ask it of her who stands above you."

Now all looked to the rock, but it was empty. The figure had vanished.

"Your word, King," said Zikali. "Is it for peace or war?"

Cetewayo looked at the assegai, looked at the blood trickling from his knee, looked at the faces of the councillors.

"Blood calls for blood," he moaned. "My word is—War!"

CHAPTER XVII

Zikali burst into one of his peals of laughter, so unholy that it caused the blood in me to run cold.

"The King's word is war," he cried. "Let Nomkubulwana take that word back to heaven. Let Macumazahn take it to the White Men. Let the captains cry it to the regiments and let the world grow red. The King has chosen, though mayhap, had I been he, I should have chosen otherwise; yet what am I but a hollow reed stuck in the ground up which the spirits speak to men? It is finished, and I, too, am finished for a while. Farewell, O King! Where shall we meet again, I wonder? On the earth or under it? Farewell, Macumazahn, I know where we shall meet, though you do not. O King, I return to my own place, I pray you to command that none come near me or trouble me with words, for I am spent."

"It is commanded," said Cetewayo.

As he spoke the fire went out mysteriously, and the wizard rose and hobbled off at a surprising pace round the corner of the projecting rock.

"Stay!" I called, "I would speak with you;" but although I am sure he heard me, he did not stop or look round.

I sprang up to follow him, but at some sign from Cetewayo two indunas barred my way.

"Did you not hear the King's command, White Man?" one of them asked coldly, and the tone of his question told me that war having been declared, I was now looked upon as a foe. I was about to answer sharply when Cetewayo himself addressed me.

"Macumazahn," he said, "you are now my enemy, like all your people, and from sunrise to-morrow morning your safe-conduct here ends, for if you are found at Ulundi two hours after that time, it will be lawful for any man to kill you. Yet as you are still my guest, I will give you an escort to the borders of the land. Moreover, you shall take a message from me to the Queen's officers and captains. It is—that I will send an answer to their demands upon the point of an assegai. Yet add this, that not I but the English, to whom I have always been a friend, sought this war. If Sompseu had suffered me to fight the Boers as I wished to do, it would never have come about. But he threw the Queen's blanket over the Transvaal and stood upon it, and now he declares that lands which were always the property of the Zulus, belong to the Boers. Therefore I take back all the promises which I made to him when he came hither to call me King in the Queen's name, and no more do I call him my father. As for the disbanding of my impis, let the English disband them if they can. I have spoken."

"And I have heard," I answered, "and will deliver your words faithfully, though I hold, King, that they come from the lips of one whom the Heavens have made mad."

At this bold speech some of the Councillors started up with threatening gestures. Cetewayo waved them back and answered quietly, "Perhaps it was the Queen of Heaven who stood on yonder rock who made me mad. Or perhaps she made me wise, as being the Spirit of our people she should surely do. That is a question which the future will decide, and if ever we should meet after it is decided, we will talk it over. Now, hamba gachle! (go in peace)."

"I hear the king and I will go, but first I would speak with Zikali."

"Then, White Man, you must wait till this war is finished or till you meet him in the Land of Spirits. Goza, lead Macumazahn back to his hut and set a guard about it. At the dawn a company of soldiers will be waiting with orders to take him to the border. You will go with him and answer for his safety with your life. Let him be well treated on the road as my messenger."

Then Cetewayo rose and stood while all present gave him the royal salute, after which he walked away down the kloof. I remained for a moment, making pretence to examine the blade of the little assegai that had been thrown by the figure on the rock, which I had picked from the ground. This historical piece of iron which I have no doubt is the same that Chaka always carried, wherewith, too, he is said to have killed his mother, Nandie, by the way I still possess, for I slipped it into my pocket and none tried to take it from me.

Really, however, I was wondering whether I could in any way gain access to Zikali, a problem that was settled for me by a sharp request to move on, uttered in a tone which admitted of no further argument.

Well, I trudged back to my hut in the company of Goza, who was so overcome by all the wonders he had seen that he could scarcely speak. Indeed, when I asked him what he thought of the figure that had appeared upon the rock, he replied petulantly that it was not given to him to know whence spirits came or of what stuff they were made, which showed me that he at any rate believed in its supernatural origin and that it had appeared to direct the Zulus to make war. This was all I wanted to find out, so I said nothing more, but gave up my mind to thought of my own position and difficulties.

Here I was, ordered on pain of death to depart from Ulundi at the dawn. And yet how could I obey without seeing Zikali and learning from him what had happened to Anscombe and Heda, or at any rate without communicating with him? Once more only did I break silence, offering to give Goza a gun if he would take a message from me to the great wizard. But with a shake of his big head, he answered that to do so would mean death, and guns were of no good to a dead man since, as I had shown myself that night, they had no power to shoot a spirit.

This closed the business on which I need not have troubled to enter, since an answer to all my questionings was at hand.

We reached the hut where Goza gave me over to the guard of soldiers, telling their officer that none were to be permitted to enter it save myself and that I was not to be to permitted to come out of it until he, Goza, came to fetch me a little before the dawn.

The officer asked if any one else was to be permitted to come out, a question that surprised me, though vaguely, for I was thinking of other things. Then Goza departed, remarking that he hoped I should sleep better than he would, who "felt spirits in his bones and did not wish to kiss them as I seemed to like to do." I replied facetiously, thinking of the bottle of brandy, that ere long I meant to feel them in my stomach, whereat he shook his head again with the air of one whom nothing connected with me could surprise, and vanished.

I crawled into the hut and put the board over the bee-hole-like entrance behind me. Then I began to hunt for the matches in my pocket and pricked my finger with the point of Chaka's historical assegai. While I was sucking it to my amazement I heard the sound of some one breathing on the further side of the hut. At first I thought of calling the guard, but on reflection found the matches and lit the candle, which stood by the blankets that served me as a bed. As soon as it burned up I looked towards the sound, and to my horror perceived the figure of a sleeping woman, which frightened me so much that I nearly dropped the candle.

To tell the truth, so obsessed was I with Zikali and his ghosts that for a few moments it occurred to me that this might be the Shape with which I had talked an hour or two before. I mean that which had seemed to resemble the long-dead lady Mameena, or rather the person made up to her likeness, come here to continue our conversation. At any rate I was sure, and rightly, that here was more of the handiwork of Zikali who wished to put me in some dreadful position for reasons of his own.

Pulling myself together I advanced upon the lady, only to find myself no wiser, since she was totally covered by a kaross. Now what was to be done? To escape, of which of course I had thought at once, was impossible since it meant an assegai in my ribs. To call to the guard for help seemed indiscreet, for who knew what those fools might say? To kick or shake her would undoubtedly be rude and, if it chanced to be the person who had played Mameena, would certainly provoke remarks that I should not care to face. There seemed to be only one resource, to sit down and wait till she woke up.

This I did for quite a long time, till at last the absurdity of the position and, I will admit, my own curiosity overcame me, especially as I was very tired and wanted to go to sleep. So advancing most gingerly, I turned down the kaross from over the head of the sleeping woman, much wondering whom I should see, for what man is there that a veiled woman does not interest? Indeed, does not half the interest of woman lie in the fact that her nature is veiled from man, in short a mystery which he is always seeking to solve at his peril, and I might add, never succeeds in solving?

Well, I turned down that kaross and next instant stepped back amazed and, to tell the truth, somewhat disappointed, for there, with her mouth open, lay no wondrous and spiritual Mameena, but the stout, earthly and most prosaic—Kaatje!

"Confound the woman!" thought I to myself. "What is she doing here?"

Then I remembered how wrong it was to give way to a sense of romantic disappointment at such a time, though as a matter of fact it is always in a moment of crisis or of strained nerves that we are most open to the insidious advances of romance. Also that there was no one on earth, or beyond it, whom I ought more greatly to have rejoiced to see. I had left Kaatje with Anscombe and Heda; therefore Kaatje could tell me what had become of them. And at this thought my heart sank—why was she here in this most inappropriate meeting-place, alone? Feeling that these were questions which must be answered at once, I prodded Kaatje in the ribs with my toe until, after a good deal of prodding, she awoke, sat up and yawned, revealing an excellent set of teeth in her cavernous, quarter-cast mouth. Then perceiving a man she opened that mouth even wider, as I thought with the idea of screaming for help. But here I was first with her, for before a sound could issue I had filled it full with the corner of the kaross, exclaiming in Dutch as I did so—

"Idiot of a woman, do you not know the Heer Quatermain when you see him?"

"Oh! Baas," she answered, "I thought you were some wicked Zulu come to do me a mischief." Then she burst into tears and sobs which I could not stop for at least three minutes.

"Be quiet, you fat fool!" I cried exasperated, "and tell me, where are your mistress and the Heer Anscombe?"

"I don't know, Baas, but I hope in heaven" (Kaatje was some kind of a Christian), she replied between her sobs.

"In heaven! What do you mean?" I asked, horrified.

"I mean, Baas, that I hope they are in heaven, because when last I saw them they were both dead, and dead people must be either in heaven or hell, and heaven, they say, is better than hell."

"Dead! Where did you see them dead?"

"In that Black Kloof, Baas, some days after you left us and went away. The old baboon man who is called Zikali gave us leave through the witch-girl, Nombe, to go also. So the Baas Anscombe set to work to inspan the horses, the Missie Heda helping him, while I packed the things. When I had nearly finished Nombe came, smiling like a cat that has caught two mice, and beckoned to me to follow her. I went and saw the cart inspanned with the four horses all looking as though they were asleep, for their heads hung down. Then after she had stared at me for a long while Nombe led me past the horses into the shadow of the overhanging cliff. There I saw my mistress and the Baas Anscombe lying side by side quite dead."

"How do you know that they were dead?" I gasped. "What had killed them?"

"I know that they were dead because they were dead, Baas. Their mouths and eyes were open and they lay upon their backs with their arms stretched out. The witch-girl, Nombe, said some Kaffirs had come and strangled them and then gone away again, or so I understood who cannot speak Zulu so very well. Who the Kaffirs were or why they came she did not say."

"Then what did you do?" I asked.

I ran back to the hut, Baas, fearing lest I should be strangled also, and wept there till I grew hungry. When I came out of it again they were gone. Nombe showed me a place under a tree where the earth was disturbed. She said that they were buried there by order of her master, Zikali. I don't know what became of the horses or the cart."

"And what happened to you afterwards?"

"Baas, I was kept for several days, I cannot remember how many, and only allowed out within the fence round the huts. Nombe came to see me once, bringing this," and she produced a package sewn up in a skin. "She said that I was to give it to you with a message that those whom you loved were quite safe with One who is greater than any in the land, and therefore that you must not grieve for them whose troubles were over. I think it was two nights after this that four Zulus came, two men and two women, and led me away, as I thought to kill me. But they did not kill me; indeed they were very kind to me, although when I spoke to them they pretended not to understand. They took me a long journey, travelling for the most part in the dark and sleeping in the day. This evening when the sun set they brought me through a Kaffir town and thrust me into the hut where I am without speaking to any one. Here, being very tired, I went to sleep, and that is all."

And quite enough too, thought I to myself. Then I put her through a cross-examination, but Kaatje was a stupid woman although a good and faithful servant, and all her terrible experiences had not sharpened her intelligence. Indeed, when I pressed her she grew utterly confused, began to cry, thereby taking refuge in the last impregnable female fortification, and snivelled out that she could not bear to talk of her dear mistress any more. So I gave it up, and two minutes later she was literally snoring, being very tired, poor thing.

Now I tried to think matters out as well as this disturbance would allow, for nothing hinders thought so much as snores. But what was the use of thinking? There was her story to take or to leave, and evidently the honest creature believed what she said. Further, how could she be deceived on such a point? She swore that she had seen Anscombe and Heda dead and afterwards had seen their graves.

Moreover, there was confirmation in Nombe's message which could not well have been invented, that spoke of their being well in the charge of a "Great One," a term by which the Zulus designate God, with all their troubles finished. The reason and manner of their end were left unrevealed. Zikali might have murdered them for his own purposes, or the Zulus might have killed them in obedience to the king's order that no white people in the land were to be allowed to live. Or perhaps the Basutos from Sekukuni's country, with whom the Zulus had some understanding, had followed and done them to death; indeed the strangling sounded more Basuto than Zulu—if they were really strangled.

Almost overcome though I was, I bethought me of the package and opened it, only to find another apparent proof of their end, for it contained Heda's jewels as I had found them in the bag in the safe; also a spare gold watch belonging to Anscombe with his coat-of-arms engraved upon it. That which he wore was of silver and no doubt was buried with him, since for superstitious reasons the natives would not have touched anything on his person after death. This seemed to me to settle the matter, presumptively at any rate, since to show that robbery was not the cause of their murder, their most valuable possessions which were not upon their persons had been sent to me, their friend.

So this was the end of all my efforts to secure the safety and well-being of that most unlucky pair. I wept when I thought of it there in the darkness of the hut, for the candle had burned out, and going on to my knees, put up an earnest prayer for the welfare of their souls; also that I might be forgiven my folly in leading them into such danger. And yet I did it for the best, trying to judge wisely in the light of such experience of the world as I possessed.

Now alas! when I am old I have come to the conclusion that those things which one tries to do for the best one generally does wrong, because nearly always there is some tricky fate at hand to mar them, which in this instance was named Zikali. The fact is, I suppose, that man who thinks himself a free agent, can scarcely be thus called, at any rate so far as immediate results are concerned. But that is a dangerous doctrine about which I will say no more, for I daresay that he is engaged in weaving a great life-pattern of which he only sees the tiniest piece.

One thing comforted me a little. If these two were dead I could now leave Zululand without qualms. Of course I was obliged to leave in any case, or die, but somehow that fact would not have eased my conscience. Indeed I think that had I believed they still lived, in this way or in that I should have tried not to leave, because I should have thought it for the best to stay to help them, whereby in all human probability I should have brought about my own death without helping them at all. Well, it had fallen out otherwise and there was an end. Now I could only hope that they had gone to some place where there are no more troubles, even if, at the worst, it were a place of rest too deep for dreams.

Musing thus at last I dozed off, for I was so tired that I think I should have slept although execution awaited me at the dawn instead of another journey. I did not sleep well because of that snoring female on the other side of the hut whose presence outraged my sense of propriety and caused me to be invaded by prophetic dreams of the talk that would ensue among those scandalmongering Zulus. Yes, it was of this I dreamed, not of the great dangers that threatened me or of the terrible loss of my friends, perhaps because to many men, of whom I suppose I am one, the fear of scandal or of being the object of public notice, is more than the fear of danger or the smart of sorrow.

So the night wore away, till at length I woke to see the gleam of dawn penetrating the smoke-hole and dimly illuminating the recumbent form of Kaatje, which to me looked most unattractive. Presently I heard a discreet tapping on the doorboard of the hut which I at once removed, wriggling swiftly through the hole, careless in my misery as to whether I met an assegai the other side of it or not. Without a guard of eight soldiers was standing, and with them Goza, who asked me if I were ready to start.

"Quite," I answered, "as soon as I have saddled my horse," which by the way had been led up to the hut.

Very soon this was done, for I brought out most of my few belongings with me and the bag of jewels was in my pocket. Then it was that the officer of the guard, a thin and melancholy-looking person, said in a hollow voice, addressing himself to Goza—

"The orders are that the White Man's wife is to go with him. Where is she?"

"Where a man's wife should be, in his hut I suppose," answered Goza sleepily.

Rage filled me at the words. Seldom do I remember being so angry.

"Yes," I said, "if you mean that Half-cast whom someone has thrust upon me, she is in there. So if she is to come with us, perhaps you will get her out."

Thus adjured the melancholy-looking captain, who was named Indudu, perhaps because he or his father had longed to the Dudu regiment, crawled into the hut, whence presently emerged sounds not unlike those which once I heard when a ringhals cobra followed a hare that I had wounded into a hole, a muffled sound of struggling and terror. These ended in the sudden and violent appearance of Kaatje's fat and dishevelled form, followed by that of the snakelike Indudu.

Seeing me standing there before a bevy of armed Zulus, she promptly fell upon my neck with a cry for help, for the silly woman thought she was going to be killed by them. Gripping me as an octopus grips its prey, she proceeded to faint, dragging me to my knees beneath the weight of eleven stone of solid flesh.

"Ah!" said one of the Zulus not unkindly, "she is much afraid for her husband whom she loves."

Well, I disentangled myself somehow, and seizing what I took to be a gourd of water in that dim light, poured it over her head, only to discover too late that it was not water but clotted milk. However the result was the same, for presently she sat up, made a dreadful-looking object by this liberal application of curds and whey, whereon I explained matters to her to the best of my power. The end of it was that after Indudu and Goza had wiped her down with tufts of thatch dragged from the hut and I had collected her gear with the rest of my own, we set her on the horse straddlewise, and started, the objects of much interest among such Zulus as were already abroad.

At the gate of the town there was a delay which made me nervous, since in such a case as mine delay might always mean a death-warrant. I knew that it was quite possible Cetewayo had changed, or been persuaded to change his mind and issue a command that I should be killed as one who had seen and knew too much. Indeed this fear was my constant companion during all the long journey to the Drift of the Tugela, causing me to look askance at every man we met or who overtook us, lest he should prove to be a messenger of doom.

Nor were these doubts groundless, for as I learned in the after days, the Prime Minister, Umnyamana, and others had urged Cetewayo strongly to kill me, and what we were waiting for at the gate were his final orders on the subject. However, in this matter, as in more that I could mention, the king played the part of a man of honour, and although he seemed to hesitate for reasons of policy, never had any intention of allowing me to be harmed. On the contrary the command brought was that any one who harmed Macumazahn, the king's guest and messenger, should die with all his House.

Whilst we tarried a number of women gathered round us whose conversation I could not help overhearing. One of them said to another—

"Look at the white man, Watcher-by-Night, who can knock a fly off an ox's horn with a bullet from further away than we could see it. He it was who loved and was loved by the witch Mameena, whose beauty is still famous in the land. They say she killed herself for his sake, because she declared that she would never live to grow old and ugly, so that he turned away from her. My mother told me all about it only last night."

Then you have a liar for a mother, thought I to myself, for to contradict such a one openly would have been undignified.

"Is it so?" asked one of her friends, deeply interested. "Then the lady Mameena must have had a strange taste in men, for this one is an ugly little fellow with hair like the grey ash of stubble and a wrinkled face of the colour of a flayed skin that has lain unstretched in the sun. However, I have been told that witches always love those who look unnatural."

"Yes," said Number one, "but you see now that he is old he has to be satisfied with a different sort of wife. She is not beautiful, is she, although she has dipped her head in milk to make herself look white?"

So it went on till at length a runner arrived and whispered something to Indudu who saluted, showing me that it was a royal message, and ordered us to move. Of this I was glad, for had I stopped there much longer, I think I should have personally assaulted those gossiping female idiots.

Of our journey through Zululand there is nothing particular to say. We saw but few people, since most of the men had been called up to the army, and many of the kraals seemed to be deserted by the women and children who perhaps were hidden away with the cattle. Once, however, we met an impi about five thousand strong, that seemed to cover the hillside like a herd of game. It consisted of the Nodwengu and the Nokenke regiments, both of which afterwards fought at Isandhlwana. Some of their captains with a small guard came to see who we were, fine, fierce-looking men. They stared at me curiously, and with one of them, whom I knew, I had a little talk. He said that I was the last white man in Zululand and that I was lucky to be alive, for soon these, and he pointed to the hordes of warriors who were streaming past, would eat up the English to "the last bone." I answered that this remained to be seen, as the English were also great eaters, whereat he laughed, replying, that it was true that the white men had already taken the first bite—a very little one, from which I gathered that some small engagement had happened.

"Well, farewell, Macumazahn," he said, as he turned to go, "I hope that we shall meet in the battle, for I want to see if you can run as well as you can shoot."

This roused my temper and I answered him—

"I hope for your sake that we shall not meet, for if we do I promise that before I run I will show you what you never saw before, the gateway of the world of Spirits."

I mention this conversation because by some strange chance it happened at Isandhlwana that I killed this man, who was named Simpofu.

During all those days of trudging through hot suns and thunderstorms, for I had to give up the mare to Kaatje who was too fat to walk, or said she was, I was literally haunted by thoughts of my murdered friends. Heaven knows how bitterly I reproached myself for having brought them into Zululand. It seemed so terribly sad that these young people who loved each other and had so bright a future before them, should have escaped from a tragic past merely to be overwhelmed by such a fate. Again and again I questioned that lump Kaatje as to the details of their end and of all that went before and followed after the murder.

But it was quite useless; indeed, as time went on she seemed to become more nebulous on the point as though a picture were fading from her mind. But as to one thing she was always quite clear, that she had seen them dead and had seen their new-made grave. This she swore "by God in Heaven," completing the oath with an outburst of tears in a way that would have carried conviction to any jury, as it did to me.

And after all, what was more likely in the circumstances? Zikali had killed them, or caused them to be killed; or possibly they were killed in spite of him in obedience to the express, or general, order of the king, if the deed was not done by the Basutos. And yet an idea occurred to me. How about the woman on the rock that the Zulus thought was their Princess of the Heavens? Obviously this must be nonsense, since no such deity existed, therefore the person must either have been a white woman or one painted up to resemble a white woman; seen from a distance in moonlight it was impossible to say which. Now, if it were a white woman, she might, from her shape and height and the colour of her hair, be Heda herself. Yet it seemed incredible that Heda, whom Kaatje had seen dead some days before, could be masquerading in such a part and make no sign of recognition to me, even when I covered her with my pistol, whereas that Nombe would play it was likely enough.

Only then Nombe must be something of a quick-change artist since but a little while before she was beyond doubt personating the dead Mameena. If it were not so I must have been suffering from illusions, for certainly I seemed to see some one who looked like Mameena, and only Zikali, and through him Nombe, had sufficient knowledge to enable her to fill that role with such success. Perhaps the whole business was an illusion, though if so Zikali's powers must be great indeed. But then how about the assegai that Nomkubulwana, or rather her effigy, had seemed to hold and throw, whereof the blade was at present in my saddle-bag. That at any rate was tangible and real, though of course there was nothing to prove that it had really been Chaka's famous weapon.

Another thing that tormented me was my failure to see Zikali. I felt as though I had committed a crime in leaving Zululand without doing this and hearing from his own lips—well, whatever he chose to tell me. I forget if I said that while we were waiting at the gate where those silly women talked so much nonsense about Mameena and Kaatje, that I made another effort through Goza to get into touch with the wizard, but quite without avail. Goza only answered what he said before, that if I wished to die at once I had better take ten steps towards the Valley of Bones, whence, he added parenthetically, the Opener of Roads had already departed on his homeward journey. This might or might not be true; at any rate I could find no possible way of coming face to face with him, or even of getting a message to his ear. No, I was not to blame; I had done all I could, and yet in my heart I felt guilty. But then, as cynics would, say, failure is guilt.

At length we came to the ford of the Tugela, and as fortunately the water was just low enough, bade farewell to our escort before crossing to the Natal side. My parting with Goza was quite touching, for we felt that it partook of the nature of a deathbed adieu, which indeed it did. I told him and the others that I hoped their ends be easy, and that whether they met them by bullets or by bayonet thrusts, the wounds would prove quickly mortal so that they might not linger in discomfort or pain. Recognizing my kind thought for their true welfare they thanked me for it, though with no enthusiasm. Indudu, however, filled with the spirit of repartee, or rather of "tu quoque", said in his melancholy fashion that if he and I came face to face in war, he would be sure to remember my words and to cut me up in the best style, since he could not bear to think of me languishing on a bed of sickness without my wife Kaatje to nurse me (they knew I was touchy about Kaatje). Then we shook hands and parted. Kaatje, hung round with paraphernalia like the White Knight in "Alice through the Looking-glass," clinging to a cooking-pot and weeping tears of terror, faced the foaming flood upon the mare, while I grasped its tail.

When we were as I judged out of assegai shot, I turned, with the water up to my armpits, and shouted some valedictory words.

"Tell your king," I said, "that he is the greatest fool in the world to fight the English, since it will bring his country to destruction and himself to disgrace and death, as at last, in the words of your proverb, 'the swimmer goes down with the stream.'"

Here, as it happened, I slipped off the stone on which I was standing and nearly went down with the stream myself.

Emerging with my mouth full of muddy water I waited till they had done laughing and continued—

"Tell that old rogue, Zikali, that I know he has murdered my friends and that when we meet again he and all who were in the plot shall pay for it with their lives."

Now an irritated Zulu flung an assegai, and as the range proved to be shorter than I thought, for it went through Kaatje's dress, causing her to scream with alarm, I ceased from eloquence, and we struggled on to the further bank, where at length we were safe.

Thus ended this unlucky trip of mine to Zululand.

CHAPTER XVIII

ISANDHLWANA

We had crossed the Tugela by what is known as the Middle Drift. A mile or so on the further side of it I was challenged by a young fellow in charge of some mounted natives, and found that I had stumbled into what was known as No. 2 Column, which consisted of a rocket battery, three battalions of the Native Contingent and some troops of mounted natives, all under the command of Colonel Durnford, R.E.

After explanations I was taken to this officer's head-quarter tent. He was a tall, nervous-looking man with a fair, handsome face and long side-whiskers. One of his arms, I remember, was supported by a sling, I think it had been injured in some Kaffir fighting. When I was introduced to him he was very busy, having, I understood from some one on his staff, just received orders to "operate against Matshana."

Learning that I had come from Zululand and was acquainted with the Zulus, he at once began to cross-examine me about Matshana, a chief of whom he seemed to know very little indeed. I told him what I could, which was not much, and before I could give him any information of real importance, was shown out and most hospitably entertained at luncheon, a meal of which I partook with gratitude in some garments that I had borrowed from one of the officers, while my own were set in the sun to dry. Well can I recall how much I enjoyed the first whisky and soda that I had tasted since I left "the Temple," and the good English food by which it was accompanied.

Presently I remembered Kaatje, whom I had left outside with some native women, and went to see what had happened to her. I found her finishing a hearty meal and engaged in conversation with a young gentleman who was writing in a notebook. Afterwards I discovered that he was a newspaper correspondent. What she told him and what he imagined, I do not know, but I may as well state the results at once. Within a few days there appeared in one of the Natal papers and, for aught I know, all over the earth, an announcement that Mr. Allan Quatermain, a well-known hunter in Zululand, after many adventures, had escaped from that country, "together with his favourite native wife, the only survivor of his extensive domestic establishment." Then followed some wild details as to the murder of my other wives by a Zulu wizard called "Road Mender, or Sick Ass" (i.e., Opener of Roads, or Zikali), and so on.

I was furious and interviewed the editor, a mild and apologetic little man, who assured me that the despatch was printed exactly as it had been received, as though that bettered the case. After this I commenced an action for libel, but as I was absent through circumstances over which I had no control when it came on for trial, the case was dismissed. I suppose the truth was that they mixed me up with a certain well-known white man in Zululand, who had a large "domestic establishment," but however this may be, it was a long while before I heard the last of that "favourite native wife."

Later in the day I and Kaatje, who stuck to me like a burr, departed from the camp.

The rest of our journey was uneventful, except for more misunderstandings about Kaatje, one of which, wherein a clergyman was concerned, was too painful to relate. At last we reached Maritzburg, where I deposited Kaatje in a boarding-house kept by another half-cast, and with a sigh of relief betook myself to the Plough Hotel, which was a long way off her.

Subsequently she obtained a place as a cook at Howick, and for a while I saw her no more.

At Maritzburg, as in duty bound, I called upon various persons in authority and delivered Cetewayo's message, leaving out all Zikali's witchcraft which would have sounded absurd. It did not produce much impression as, hostilities having already occurred, it was superfluous. Also no one was inclined to pay attention to the words of one who was neither an official nor a military officer, but a mere hunter supposed to have brought a native wife out of Zululand.

I did, however, report the murder of Anscombe and Heda, though in such times this caused no excitement, especially as they were not known to the officials concerned with such matters. Indeed the occurrence never so much as got into the papers, any more than did the deaths of Rodd and Marnham on the borders of Sekukuni's country. When people are expecting to be massacred themselves, they do not trouble about the past killing of others far away. Lastly, I posted Marnham's will to the Pretoria bank, advising them that they had better keep it safely until some claim arose, and deposited Heda's jewels and valuables in another branch of the same bank in Maritzburg with a sealed statement as to how they came into my possession.

These things done, I found it necessary to turn myself to the eternal problem of earning my living. I am a very rich man now as I write these reminiscences here in Yorkshire—King Solomon's mines made me that—but up to the time of my journey to Kukuana Land with my friends, Curtis and Good, although plenty of money passed through my hands on one occasion and another, little of it ever seemed to stick. In this way or that it was lost or melted; also I was not born one to make the best of his opportunities in the way of acquiring wealth. Perhaps this was good for me, since if I had gained the cash early I should not have met with the experiences, and during our few transitory years, experience is of more real value than cash. It may prepare us for other things beyond, whereas the mere possession of a bank balance can prepare us for nothing in a land where gold ceases to be an object of worship as it is here. Yet wealth is our god, not knowledge or wisdom, a fact which shows that the real essence of Christianity has not yet permeated human morals. It just runs over their surface, no more, and for every eye that is turned towards the divine Vision, a thousand are fixed night and day upon Mammon's glittering image.

Now I owned certain wagons and oxen, and just then the demand for these was keen. So I hired them out to the military authorities for service in the war, and incidentally myself with them. I drove what I considered a splendid bargain with an officer who wrote as many letters after his name as a Governor-General, but was really something quite humble. At least I thought it splendid until outside his tent I met a certain transport rider of my acquaintance whom I had always looked upon as a perfect fool, who told me that not half an hour before he had got twenty per cent. more for unsalted oxen and very rickety wagons. However, it did not matter much in the end as the whole outfit was lost at Isandhlwana, and owing to the lack of some formality which I had overlooked, I never recovered more than a tithe of their value. I think it was that I neglected to claim within a certain specified time.

At last my wagons were laden with ammunition and other Government goods and I trekked over awful roads to Helpmakaar, a place on the Highlands not far from Rorke's Drift where No. 3 Column was stationed. Here we were delayed awhile, I and my wagons having moved to a ford of the Buffalo, together with many others. It was during this time that I ventured to make very urgent representations to certain highly placed officers, I will not mention which, as to the necessity of laagering, that is, forming fortified camps, as soon as Zululand was entered, since from my intimate knowledge of its people I was sure that they would attack in force. These warnings of mine were received with the most perfect politeness and offers of gin to drink, which all transport riders were supposed to love, but in effect were treated with the contempt that they were held to deserve. The subject is painful and one on which I will not dwell. Why should I complain when I know that cautions from notable persons such as Sir Melmoth Osborn, and J. J. Uys, a member of one the old Dutch fighting families, met with a like fate.

By the way it was while I was waiting on the banks of the river that I came across an old friend of mine, a Zulu named Magepa, with whom I had fought at the battle of the Tugela. A few days later this man performed an extraordinary feat in saving his grandchild from death by his great swiftness in running, whereof I have preserved a note somewhere or other.

Ultimately on January 11 we received our marching orders and crossed the river by the drift, the general scheme of the campaign being that the various columns were to converge upon Ulundi. The roads, if so they can be called, were in such a fearful state that it took us ten days to cover as many miles. At length we trekked over a stony nek about five hundred yards in width. To the right of us was a stony eminence and to our left, its sheer brown cliffs of rock rising like the walls of some cyclopean fortress, the strange, abrupt mount of Isandhlwana, which reminded me of a huge lion crouching above the hill-encircled plain beyond. At the foot of this isolated mount, whereof the aspect somehow filled me with alarm, we camped on the night of January 21, taking no precautions against attack by way of laagering the wagons. Indeed the last thing that seemed to occur to those in command was that there would be serious fighting; men marched forward to their deaths as though they were going on a shooting-party, or to a picnic. I even saw cricketing bats and wickets occupying some of the scanty space upon the wagons.

Now I am not going to set out all the military details that preceded the massacre of Isandhlwana, for these are written in history. It is enough to say that on the night of January 21, Major Dartnell, who was in command of the Natal Mounted Police and had been sent out to reconnoitre the country beyond Isandhlwana, reported a strong force of Zulus in front of us. Thereon Lord Chelmsford, the General-in-Chief, moved out from the camp at dawn to his support, taking with him six companies of the 24th regiment, together with four guns and the mounted infantry. There were left in the camp two guns and about eight hundred white and nine hundred native troops, also some transport riders such as myself and a number of miscellaneous camp-followers. I saw him go from between the curtains of one of my wagons where I had made my bed on the top of a pile of baggage. Indeed I had already dressed myself at the time, for that night I slept very ill because I knew our danger, and my heart was heavy with fear.

About ten o'clock in the morning Colonel Durnford, whom I have mentioned already, rode up with five hundred Natal Zulus, about half of whom were mounted, and two rocket tubes which, of course, were worked by white men. This was after a patrol had reported that they had come into touch with some Zulus on the left front, who retired before them. As a matter of fact these Zulus were foraging in the mealie fields, since owing to the drought food was very scarce in Zululand that year and the regiments were hungry. I happened to see the meeting between Colonel Pulleine, a short, stout man who was then in command of the camp, and Colonel Durnford who, as his senior officer, took it over from him, and heard Colonel Pulleine say that his orders were "to defend the camp," but what else passed between them I do not know.

Presently Colonel Durnford saw and recognized me.

"Do you think the Zulus will attack us, Mr. Quatermain?" he said.

"I don't think so, Sir," I answered, "as it is the day of the new moon which they hold unlucky. But to-morrow it may be different."

Then he gave certain orders, dispatching Captain George Shepstone with a body of mounted natives along the ridge to the left, where presently they came in contact with the Zulus about three miles away, and making other dispositions. A little later he moved out to the front with a strong escort, followed by the rocket battery, which ultimately advanced to a small conical hill on the left front, round which it passed, never to return again.

Just before he started Colonel Durnford, seeing me still standing there, asked me if I would like to accompany him, adding that as I knew the Zulus so well I might be useful. I answered, Certainly, and called to my head driver, a man named Jan, to bring me my mare, the same that I had ridden out of Zululand, while I slipped into the wagon and, in addition to the beltful that I wore, filled all my available pockets with cartridges for my double-barrelled Express rifle.

As I mounted I gave Jan certain directions about the wagon and oxen, to which he listened, and then to my astonishment held out his hand to me, saying—

"Good-bye, Baas. You have been a kind master to me and I thank you."

"Why do you say that?" I asked.

"Because, Baas, all the Kaffirs declare that the great Zulu impi will be on to us in an hour or two and eat up every man. I can't tell how they know it, but so they swear."

"Nonsense," I answered, "it is the day of new moon when the Zulus don't fight. Still if anything of the sort should happen, you and the other boys had better slip away to Natal, since the Government must pay for the wagons and oxen."

This I said half joking, but it was a lucky jest for Jan and the rest of my servants, since they interpreted it in earnest and with the exception of one of them who went back to get a gun, got off before the Zulu horn closed round the camp, and crossed the river in safety.

Next moment I was cantering away after Colonel Durnford, whom I caught up about a quarter of a mile from the camp.

Now of course I did not see all of the terrible battle that followed and can only tell of that part of it in which I had a share. Colonel Durnford rode out about three and a half miles to the left front, I really don't quite know why, for already we were hearing firing on the top of the Nqutu Hills almost behind us, where Captain Shepstone was engaging the Zulus, or so I believe. Suddenly we met a trooper of the Natal Carabineers whose name was Whitelaw, who had been out scouting. He reported that an enormous impi was just ahead of us seated in an umkumbi, or semi-circle, as is the fashion of the Zulus before they charge. At least some of them, he said, were so seated, but others were already advancing.

Presently these appeared over the crest of the hill, ten thousand of them I should say, and amongst them I recognized the shields of the Nodwengu, the Dududu, the Nokenke and the Ingoba-makosi regiments. Now there was nothing to be done except retreat, for the impi was attacking in earnest. The General Untshingwayo, together with Undabuko, Cetewayo's brother, and the chief Usibebu who commanded the scouts, had agreed not to fight this day for the reason I have given, because it was that of the new moon, but circumstances had forced their hand and the regiments could no longer be restrained. So to the number of twenty thousand or more, say one-third of the total Zulu army, they hurled themselves upon the little English force that, owing to lack of generalship, was scattered here and there over a wide front and had no fortified base upon which to withdraw.

We fell back to a donga which we held for a little while, and then as we saw that there we should presently be overwhelmed, withdrew gradually for another two miles or so, keeping off the Zulus by our fire. In so doing we came upon the remains of the rocket battery near the foot of the conical hill I have mentioned, which had been destroyed by some regiment that passed behind us in its rush on the camp. There lay all the soldiers dead, assegaied through and through, and I noticed that one young fellow who had been shot through the head, still held a rocket in his hands.

Now somewhat behind and perhaps half a mile to the right of this hill a long, shallow donga runs across the Isandhlwana plain. This we gained, and being there reinforced by about fifty of the Natal Carabineers under Captain Bradstreet, held it for a long while, keeping off the Zulus by our terrible fire which cut down scores of them every time they attempted to advance. At this spot I alone killed from twelve to fifteen of them, for if the big bullet from my Express rifle struck a man, he did not live. Messengers were sent back to the camp for more ammunition, but none arrived, Heaven knows why. My own belief is that the reserve cartridges were packed away in boxes and could not be got at. At last our supply began to run short, so there was nothing to be done except retreat upon the camp which was perhaps half a mile behind us.

Taking advantage of a pause in the Zulu advance which had lain down while waiting for reserves, Colonel Durnford ordered a retirement that was carried out very well. Up to that time we had lost only quite a few men, for the Zulu fire was wild and high and they had not been able to get at us with the assegai. As we rode towards the mount I observed that firing was going on in all directions, especially on the nek that connected it with the Nqutu range where Captain Shepstone and his mounted Basutos were wiped out while trying to hold back the Zulu right horn. The guns, too, were firing heavily and doing great execution.

After this all grew confused. Colonel Durnford gave orders to certain officers who came up to him, Captain Essex was one and Lieutenant Cochrane another. Then his force made for their wagons to get more ammunition. I kept near to the Colonel and a while later found myself with him and a large, mixed body of men a little to the right of the nek which we had crossed in our advance from the river. Not long afterwards there was a cry of "The Zulus are getting round us!" and looking to the left I saw them pouring in hundreds across the ridge that joins Isandhlwana Mountain to the Nqutu Range. Also they were advancing straight on to the camp.

Then the rout began. Already the native auxiliaries were slipping away and now the others followed. Of course this battle was but a small affair, yet I think that few have been more terrible, at any rate in modern times. The aspect of those plumed and shielded Zulus as they charged, shouting their war-cries and waving their spears, was awesome. They were mown down in hundreds by the Martini fire, but still they came on, and I knew that the game was up. A maddened horde of fugitives, mostly natives, began to flow past us over the nek, making for what was afterwards called Fugitives' Drift, nine miles away, and with them went white soldiers, some mounted, some on foot. Mingled with all these people, following them, on either side of them, rushed Zulus, stabbing as they ran. Other groups of soldiers formed themselves into rough squares, on which the savage warriors broke like water on a rock. By degrees ammunition ran out; only the bayonet remained. Still the Zulus could not break those squares. So they took another counsel. Withdrawing a few paces beyond the reach of the bayonets, they overwhelmed the soldiers by throwing assegais, then rushed in and finished them.

This was what happened to us, among whom were men of the 24th, Natal Carabineers and Mounted Police. Some had dismounted, but I sat on my horse, which stood quite still, I think from fright, and fired away so long as I had any ammunition. With my very last cartridge I killed the Captain Indudu who had been in charge of the escort that conducted me to the Tugela. He had caught sight of me and called out—

"Now, Macumazahn, I will cut you up nicely as I promised."

He got no further in his speech, for at that moment I sent an Express bullet through him and his tall, melancholy figure doubled up and collapsed.

All this while Colonel Durnford had been behaving as a British officer should do. Scorning to attempt flight, whenever I looked round I caught sight of his tall form, easy to recognize by the long fair moustaches and his arm in a sling, moving to and fro encouraging us to stand firm and die like men. Then suddenly I saw a Kaffir, who carried a big old smooth-bore gun, aim at him from a distance of about twenty yards, and fire. He went down, as I believe dead, and that was the end of a very gallant officer and gentleman whose military memory has in my opinion been most unjustly attacked. The real blame for that disaster does not rest upon the shoulders of either Colonel Durnford or Colonel Pulleine.

After this things grew very awful. Some fled, but the most stood and died where they were. Oddly enough during all this time I was never touched. Men fell to my right and left and in front of me; bullets and assegais whizzed past me, yet I remained quite unhurt. It was as though some Power protected me, which no doubt it did.

At length when nearly all had fallen and I had nothing left to defend myself with except my revolver, I made up my mind that it was time to go. My first impulse was to ride for the river nine miles away. Looking behind me I saw that the rough road was full of Zulus hunting down those who tried to escape. Still I thought I would try it, when suddenly there flashed across my brain the saying of whoever it was that personated Mameena in the Valley of Bones, to the effect that in the great rout of the battle I was not to join the flying but to set my face towards Ulundi and that if I did so I should be protected and no harm would come to me. I knew that all this prophecy was but a vain thing fondly imagined, although it was true that the battle and the rout had come. And yet I acted on it—why Heaven knows alone.

Setting the spurs to my horse I galloped off past Isandhlwana Mount, on the southern slopes of which a body of the 24th were still fighting their last fight, and heading for the Nqutu Range. The plain was full of Zulus, reserves running up; also to the right of me the Ulundi and Gikazi divisions were streaming forward. These, or some of them, formed the left horn of the impi, but owing to the unprepared nature of the Zulu battle, for it must always be remembered that they did not mean to fight that day, their advance had been delayed until it was too late for them entirely to enclose the camp. Thus the road, if it can so be called, to Fugitives' Drift was left open for a while, and by it some effected their escape. It was this horn, or part of it, that afterwards moved on and attacked Rorke's Drift, with results disastrous to itself.

For some hundreds of yards I rode on thus recklessly, because recklessness seemed my only chance. Thrice I met bodies of Zulus, but on each occasion they scattered before me, calling out words that I could not catch. It was as though they were frightened of something they saw about me. Perhaps they thought that I was mad to ride thus among them. Indeed I must have looked mad, or perhaps there was something else. At any rate I believed that I was going to win right through them when an accident happened.

A bullet struck my mare somewhere in the back. I don't know where it came from, but as I saw no Zulu shoot, I think it must have been one fired by a soldier who was still fighting on the slopes of the mount. The effect of it was to make the poor beast quite ungovernable. Round she wheeled and galloped at headlong speed back towards the peak, leaping over dead and dying and breaking through the living as she went. In two minutes we were rushing up its northern flank, which seemed to be quite untenanted, towards the sheer brown cliff which rose above it, for the fighting was in progress on the other side. Suddenly at the foot of this cliff the mare stopped, shivered and sank down dead, probably from internal bleeding.

I looked about me desperately. To attempt the plain on foot meant death. What then was I to do? Glancing at the cliff I saw that there was a gully in it worn by thousands of years of rainfall, in which grew scanty bushes. Into this I ran, and finding it practicable though difficult, began to climb upwards, quite unnoticed by the Zulus who were all employed upon the further side. The end of it was that I reached the very crest of the mount, a patch of bare, brown rock, except at one spot on its southern front where there was a little hollow in which at this rainy season of the year herbage and ferns grew in the accumulated soil, also a few stunted, aloe-like plants.

Into this patch I crept, having first slaked my thirst from a little pool of rain water that lay in a cup-like depression of the rock, which tasted more delicious than any nectar, and seemed to give me new life. Then covering myself as well as I could with grasses and dried leaves from the aloe plants, I lay still.

Now I was right on the brink of the cliff and had the best view of the Isandhlwana plain and the surrounding country that can be imagined. From my lofty eyrie some hundreds of feet in the air, I could see everything that happened beneath. Thus I witnessed the destruction of the last of the soldiers on the slopes below. They made a gallant end, so gallant that I was proud to be of the same blood with them. One fine young fellow escaped up the peak and reached a plateau about fifty feet beneath me. He was followed by a number of Zulus, but took refuge in a little cave whence he shot three or four of them; then his cartridges were exhausted and I heard the savages speaking in praise of him—dead. I think he was the last to die on the field of Isandhlwana.

The looting of the camp began; it was a terrible scene. The oxen and those of the horses that could be caught were driven away, except certain of the former which were harnessed to the guns and some of the wagons and, as I afterwards learned, taken to Ulundi in proof of victory. Then the slain were stripped and Kaffirs appeared wearing the red coats of the soldiers and carrying their rifles. The stores were broken into and all the spirits drunk. Even the medical drugs were swallowed by these ignorant men, with the result that I saw some of them reeling about in agony and others fall down and go to sleep.

An hour or two later an officer who came from the direction in which the General had marched, cantered right into the camp where the tents were still standing and even the flag was flying. I longed to be able to warn him, but could not. He rode up to the headquarters marquee, whence suddenly issued a Zulu waving a great spear. I saw the officer pull up his horse, remain for a moment as though indecisive, then turn and gallop madly away, quite unharmed, though one or two assegais were thrown and many shots fired at him. After this considerable movements of the Zulus went on, of which the net result was, that they evacuated the place.

Now I hoped that I might escape, but it was not to be, since on every side numbers of them crept up Isandhlwana Mountain and hid behind rocks or among the tall grasses, evidently for purposes of observation. Moreover some captains arrived on the little plateau where was the cave in which the soldier had been killed, and camped there. At least at sundown they unrolled their mats and ate, though they lighted no fire.

The darkness fell and in it escape for me from that guarded place was impossible, since I could not see where to set my feet and one false step on the steep rock would have meant my death. From the direction of Rorke's Drift I could hear continuous firing; evidently some great fight was going on there, I wondered vaguely—with what result. A little later also I heard the distant tramp of horses and the roll of gun wheels. The captains below heard it too and said one to another that it was the English soldiers returning, who had marched out of the camp at dawn. They debated one with another whether it would be possible to collect a force to fall upon them, but abandoned the idea because the regiments who had fought that day were now at a distance and too tired, and the others had rushed forward with orders to attack the white men on and beyond the river.

So they lay still and listened, and I too lay still and listened, for on that cloudy, moonless night I could see nothing. I heard smothered words of command. I heard the force halt because it could not travel further in the gloom. Then they lay down, the living among the dead, wondering doubtless if they themselves would not soon be dead, as of course must have happened had the Zulu generalship been better, for if even five thousand men had been available to attack at dawn not one of them could have escaped. But Providence ordained it otherwise. Some were taken and the others left.

About an hour before daylight I heard them stirring again, and when its first gleams came all of them had vanished over the nek of slaughter, with what thoughts in their hearts, I wondered, and to what fate. The captains on the plateau beneath had gone also, and so had the circle of guards upon the slopes of the mount, for I saw these depart through the grey mist. As the light gathered, however, I observed bodies of men collecting on the nek, or rather on both neks, which made it impossible for me to do what I had hoped, and run to overtake the English troops. From these I was utterly cut off. Nor could I remain longer without food on my point of rock, especially as I was sure that soon some Zulus would climb there to use it as an outlook post. So while I was still more or less hidden by the mist and morning shadows, I climbed down it by the same road that I had climbed up, and thus reached the plain.

Not a living man, white or black, was to be seen, only the dead, only the dead. I was the last Englishman to stand upon the plain of Isandhlwana for weeks or rather months to come.

Of all my experiences this was, I think, the strangest, after that night of hell, to find myself alone upon this field of death, staring everywhere at the distorted faces which on the previous morn I had seen so full of life. Yet my physical needs asserted themselves. I was very hungry, who for twenty-four hours had eaten nothing, faint with hunger indeed. I passed a provision wagon that had been looted by the Zulus. Tins of bully beef lay about, also, among a wreck of broken glass, some bottles of Bass's beer which had escaped their notice. I found an assegai, cleaned it in the ground which it needed, and opening one of the tins, lay down in a tuft of grass by a dead man, or rather between him and some Zulus whom he had killed, and devoured its contents. Also I knocked the tops off a couple of the beer bottles and drank my fill. While I was doing this a large rough dog with a silver-mounted collar on its neck, I think of the sort that is called an Airedale terrier, came up to me whining. At first I thought it was an hyena, but discovering my mistake, threw it some bits of meat which it ate greedily. Doubtless it had belonged to some dead officer, though there was no name on the collar. The poor beast, which I named Lost, at once attached itself to me, and here I may say that I kept it till its death, which occurred of jaundice at Durban not long before I started on my journey to King Solomon's Mines. No man ever had a more faithful friend and companion.

When I had eaten and drunk I looked about me, wondering what I should do. Fifty yards away I saw a stout Basuto pony still saddled and bridled, although the saddle was twisted out of its proper position, which was cropping the grass as well as it could with the bit in its mouth. Advancing gently I caught it without trouble, and led it back to the plundered wagon. Evidently from the marks upon the saddlery it had belonged to Captain Shepstone's force of mounted natives.

Here I filled the large saddlebags made of buckskin with tins of beef, a couple more bottles of beer and a packet of tandstickor matches which I was fortunate enough to find. Also I took the Martini rifle from a dead soldier, together with a score or so of cartridges that remained in his belt, for apparently he must have been killed rather early in the fight.

Thus equipped I mounted the pony and once more bethought me of escaping to Natal. A look towards the nek cured me of that idea, for coming over it I saw the plumed heads of a whole horde of warriors. Doubtless these were returning from the unsuccessful attack on Rorke's Drift, though of that I knew nothing at the time. So whistling to the dog I bore to the left for the Nqutu Hills, riding as fast as the rough ground would allow, and in half an hour was out of sight of that accursed plain.

One more thing too I did. On its confines I came across a group of dead Zulus who appeared to have been killed by a shell. Dismounting I took the headdress of one of them and put it on, for I forgot to say that I had lost my hat. It was made of a band of otterskin from which rose large tufts of the black feathers of the finch which the natives call "sakabula." Also I tied his kilt of white oxtails about my middle, precautions to which I have little doubt I owe my life, since from a distance they made me look like a Kaffir mounted on a captured pony.

Then I started on again, whither I knew not.

CHAPTER XIX

Now I have no intention of setting down all the details of that dreadful journey through Zululand, even if I could recall them, which, for a reason to be stated, I cannot do. I remember that at first I thought of proceeding to Ulundi with some wild idea of throwing myself on the mercy of Cetewayo under pretence that I brought him a message from Natal. Within a couple of hours, however, from the top of a hill I saw ahead of me an impi and with it captured wagons, which was evidently heading for the king's kraal. So as I knew what kind of a greeting these warriors would give me, I bore away in another direction with the hope of reaching the border by a circuitous route. In this too I had no luck, since presently I caught sight of outposts stationed upon rocks, which doubtless belonged to another impi or regiment. Indeed one soldier, thinking from my dress that I also was a Zulu, called to me for news from about half a mile away, in that peculiar carrying voice which Kaffirs can command. I shouted back something about victory and that the white men were wiped out, then put an end to the conversation by vanishing into a patch of dense bush.

It is a fact that after this I have only the dimmest recollection of what happened. I remember off-saddling at night on several occasions. I remember being very hungry because all the food was eaten and the dog, Lost, catching a bush buck fawn, some of which I partially cooked on a fire of dead wood, and devoured. Next I remember—I suppose this was a day or two later—riding at night in a thunderstorm and a particularly brilliant flash of lightning which revealed scenery that seemed to be familiar to me, after which came a shock and total unconsciousness.

At length my mind returned to me. It was reborn very slowly and with horrible convulsions, out of the womb of death and terror. I saw blood flowing round me in rivers, I heard the cries of triumph and of agony. I saw myself standing, the sole survivor, on a grey field of death, and the utter loneliness of it ate into my soul, so that with all its strength it prayed that it might be numbered in this harvest. But oh! it was so strong, that soul which could not, would not die or fly away. So strong, that then, for the first time, I understood its immortality and that it could never die. This everlasting thing still clung for a while to the body of its humiliation, the mass of clay and nerves and appetites which it was doomed to animate, and yet knew its own separateness and eternal individuality. Striving to be free of earth, still it seemed to walk the earth, a spirit and a shadow, aware of the hatefulness of that to which it was chained, as we might imagine some lovely butterfly to be that is fated by nature to suck its strength from carrion, and remains unable to soar away into the clean air of heaven.

Something touched my hand and I reflected dreamily that if I had been still alive, for in a way I believed that I was dead, I should have thought it was a dog's tongue. With a great effort I lifted my arm, opened my eyes and looked at the hand against the light, for there was light, to see it was so thin that this light shone through between the bones. Then I let it fall again, and lo! it rested on the head of a dog which went on licking it.

A dog! What dog? Now I remembered; one that I had found on the field of Isandhlwana. Then I must be still alive. The thought made me cry, for I could feel the tears run down my cheeks, not with joy but with sorrow. I did not wish to go on living. Life was too full of struggle and of bloodshed and bereavement and fear and all horrible things. I was prepared to exchange my part in it just for rest, for the blessing of deep, unending sleep in which no more dreams could come, no more cups of joy could be held to thirsting lips, only to be snatched away.

I heard something shuffling towards me at which the dog growled, then seemed to slink away as though it were afraid. I opened my eyes again, looked, and closed them once more in terror, for what I saw suggested that perhaps I was dead after all and had reached that hell which a certain class of earnest Christian promises to us as the reward of the failings that Nature and those who begat us have handed on to us as a birth doom. It was something unnatural, grey-headed, terrific—doubtless a devil come to torment me in the inquisition vaults of Hades. Yet I had known the like when I was alive. How had it been called? I remembered, "The-thing-that-never-should-have-been-born." Hark! It was speaking in that full deep voice which was unlike to any other.

"Greeting, Macumazahn," it said. "I see that you have come back from among the dead with whom you have been dwelling for a moon and more. It is not wise of you, Macumazahn, yet I am glad who have matched my skill against Death and won, for now you will have much to tell me about his kingdom."

So it was Zikali—Zikali who had butchered my friends.

"Away from me, murderer!" I said faintly, "and let me die, or kill me as you did the others."

He laughed, but very softly, not in his usual terrific fashion, repeating the word "murderer" two or three times. Then with his great hand he lifted my head gently as a woman might, saying—

"Look before you, Macumazahn."

I looked and saw that I was in some kind of a cave. Outside the sun was setting and against its brightness I perceived two figures, a white man and a white woman who were walking hand in hand and gazing into each other's eyes. They were Anscombe and Heda passing the mouth of the cave.

"Behold the murdered, O Macumazahn, dealer of hard words."

"It is only a trick," I murmured. "Kaatje saw them dead and buried."

"Yes, yes, I forgot. The fat fool-woman saw them dead and buried. Well, sometimes the dead come to life again and for good purpose, as you should know, Macumazahn, who followed the counsel of a certain Mameena and wandered here instead of rushing onto the Zulu spears."

I tried to think the thing out and could not, so only asked—

"How did I come? What happened to me?"

"I think the sun smote you first who had no covering on your head and the lightning smote you afterwards. Yet all the while that reason had left you, One led your horse and after the Heavens had tried to kill you and failed, perhaps because my magic was too strong for them, One sent that beast which you found, yes, sent it here to lead us to where you lay. There you were discovered and brought hither. Now sleep lest you should go further than even I can fetch you back again."

He held his hands above my head, seeming to grow in stature till his white hair touched the roof of the cave, and in an instant I fancied that I was falling away, deep, deep into a gulf of nothingness.

There followed another period of dreaming, in which dreams I seemed to meet all sorts of people, dead and living, especially Lady Ragnall, a friend of mine with whom I had been concerned in a very strange adventure among the Kendah people* and with whom in days to come I was destined to be concerned again, although of course I knew nothing of this, in a still stranger adventure of what I may call a spiritual order, which I may or may not try to reduce to writing. It seemed to me that I was constantly dining with her tete-a-tete and that she told me all sorts of queer things between the courses. Doubtless these illusions occurred when I was fed.

[*—See the book called The Ivory Child.—EDITOR.]

At length I woke up again, feeling much stronger, and saw the dog, Lost, watching me with its great tender eyes—oh! they talk of the eyes of women, but are they ever as beautiful as those of a loving dog? It lay by my low bed-stead, a rough affair fashioned of poles and strung with rimpis or strings of raw hide, and by it, stroking its head, sat the witch-doctoress, Nombe. I remember how pleasing she looked, a perfect type of the eternal feminine with her graceful, rounded shape and her continual, mysterious smile which suggested so much more than any mortal woman has to give.

"Good-day to you, Macumazahn," she said in her gentle voice, "you have gone through much since last we met on the night before Goza took you away to Ulundi."

Now remembering all, I was filled with indignation against this little humbug.

"The last time we met, Nombe," I said, "was when you played the part of a woman who is dead in the Vale of Bones by the king's kraal."

She regarded me with a kindly commiseration, and answered, shaking her head—

"You have been very ill, Macumazahn, and your spirit still tricks you. I played the part of no woman in any valley by the king's kraal, nor were my eyes rejoiced with the sight of you there or elsewhere till they brought you to this place, so changed that I should scarcely have known you."

"You little liar!" I said rudely.

"Do the white people always name those liars who tell them true things they cannot understand?" she inquired with a sweet innocence. Then without waiting for an answer, she patted my hand as though I were a fretful child and gave me some soup in a gourd, saying, "Drink it, it is good. The lady Heddana made it herself in the white man's fashion."

I drank the soup, which was very good, and as I handed back the gourd, answered—

"Kaatje has told me that the lady Heddana is dead. Can the dead make soup?"

She considered the point while she threw some bits of meat out of the bottom of the gourd to the dog, Lost, then replied—

"I do not know, Macumazahn, or indeed whether the dead eat as we do. Next time my Spirit visits me I will make inquiry and tell you the answer. But I do know that it is very strange that you, who always turn your back upon the truth, are so ready to accept falsehoods. Why should you believe that the lady

Heddana is dead just because Kaatje told you so, when I who am still alive had sworn to you that I would protect her with my life? Nay, speak no more now. To-morrow if you are well enough you shall see and judge for yourself."

She drew up the kaross over me, again patted my hand in her motherly fashion and departed, still smiling, after which I went to sleep again, so dreamlessly that I think there was some native soporific in that soup.

On the following day two of Zikali's servants who did the rougher work of my sick room, if I may so call it, arrived and said that they were going to carry me out of the cave for a while, if that were my will. I who longed to breathe the fresh air again, said that it was very much my will, whereon they grasped the rough bedstead which I have described by either end and very carefully bore me down the cave and through its narrow entrance, where they set the bedstead in the shadow of the overhanging rock without. When I had recovered a little, for even that short journey tired me, I looked about me and perceived that as I had expected, I was in the Black Kloof, for there in front of me were the very huts which we had occupied on our arrival from Swazi-Land.

I lay a while drawing in the sweet air which to me was like a draught of nectar, and wondering whether I were not still in a dream. For instance, I wondered if I had truly seen the figures of Anscombe and Heda pass the mouth of the cave, on that day when I awoke, or if these were but another of Zikali's illusions imprinted on my weakened mind by his will power. For of what he and Nombe told me I believed nothing. Thus marvelling I fell into a doze and in my doze heard whisperings. I opened my eyes and lo! there before me stood Anscombe and Heda. It was she who spoke the first, for I was tongue-tied; I could not open my lips.

"Dear Mr. Quatermain, dear Mr. Quatermain!" she murmured in her sweet voice, then paused.

Now at last words came to me. "I thought you were both dead," I said. "Tell me, are you really alive?"

She bent down and kissed my brow, while Anscombe took my hand.

"Now you know," she answered. "We are both of us alive and well."

"Thank God!" I exclaimed. "Kaatje swore that she saw you dead and buried."

"One sees strange things in the Black Kloof," replied Anscombe speaking for the first time, "and much has happened to us since we were parted, to which you are not strong enough to listen now. When you are better, then we will tell you all. So grow well as soon as you can."

After this I think I fainted, for when I came to myself again I was back in the cave.

Another ten days or so went by before I could even leave my bed, for my recovery was very slow. Indeed for weeks I could scarcely walk at all, and six whole months passed before I really got my strength again and became as I used to be. During those days I often saw Anscombe and Heda, but only for a few minutes at a time. Also occasionally Zikali would visit me, speaking a little, generally about past history, or something of the sort, but never of the war, and go away. At length one day he said to me—

"Macumazahn, now I am sure you are going to live, a matter as to which I was doubtful, even after you seemed to recover. For, Macumazahn, you have endured three shocks, of which to-day I am not afraid to talk to you. First there was that of the battle of Isandhlwana where you were the last white man left alive."

"How do you know that, Zikali?" I asked.

"It does not matter. I do know. Did you not ride through the Zulus who parted this way and that before you, shouting what you could not understand? One of them you may remember even saluted with his spear."

"I did, Zikali. Tell me, why did they behave thus, and what did they shout?"

"I shall not tell you, Macumazahn. Think over it for the rest of your life and conclude what you choose; it will not be so wonderful as the truth. At least they did so, as a certain doll I dressed up yonder in the Vale of Bones told you they would, she whose advice you followed in riding towards Ulundi instead of back to the river where you would have met your death, like so many others of the white people."

"Who was that doll, Zikali?"

"Nay, ask me not. Perhaps it was Nombe, perhaps another. I have forgotten. I am very old and my memory begins to play me strange tricks. Still I recollect that she was a good doll, so like a dead woman called Mameena that I could scarcely have known them apart. Ah! that was a great game I played in the Vale of Bones, was it not, Macumazahn?"

"Yes, Zikali, yet I do not understand why it was played."

"Being so young you still have the impatience of youth, Macumazahn, although your hair grows white. Wait a while and you will understand all. Well, you lay that night on the topmost rock of Isandhlwana, and there you saw and heard strange things. You heard the rest of the white soldiers come and lie down to rest among their dead brothers, and depart again unharmed. Oh! what fools are these Zulu generals nowadays. They send out an impi to attack men behind walls, spears against rifles, and are defeated. Had they kept that impi to fall on the rest of the English when they walked into the trap, not a man of your people would have been left alive. Would that have happened in the time of Chaka?"

"I think not, Zikali. Still I am glad that it did happen."

"I think not too, Macumazahn, but small men, small wit. Also like you I am glad that it did not happen, since it is the Zulus I hate, not the English who have now learned a lesson and will not be caught again. Oh! many a captain in Zululand is to-day flat as a pricked bladder, and even their victory, as they call it, cost them dear. For, mind you, Macumazahn, for every white man they killed two of them died. So, so! In the morning you left the hill—do not look astonished, Macumazahn. Perhaps those captains on the rock beneath you let you go for their own purposes, or because they were commanded, for though weak I can still lift a stone or two, Macumazahn, and afterwards told me all about it. Then you found yourself alone among the dead, like the last man in the world, Macumazahn, and that dog at your side, also a horse came to you. Perhaps I sent them, perhaps it was a chance. Who knows? Not I myself, for as I have said, my memory has grown so bad. That was your first shock, Macumazahn, the shock of standing alone among the dead like the last man in the world. You felt it, did you not?"

"As I hope I shall never feel anything again. It nearly drove me mad," I answered.

"Very nearly indeed, though I have felt worse things and only laughed, as I would tell you, had I the time. Well, then the sun struck you, for at this season of the year it is very hot in those valleys for a white man with no covering to his head, and you went quite mad, though fortunately the dog and the horse remained as Heaven had made them. That was the second shock. Then the storm burst and the lightning fell. It ran down the rifle that you still carried, Macumazahn. I will show it to you and you will see that its stock is shattered. Perhaps I turned the flash aside, for I am a great thunder-herd, or perhaps it was One mightier than I. That was the third shock, Macumazahn. Then you were found, still living—how, the white man, your friend, will tell you. But you should cherish that dog of yours, Macumazahn, for many a man might have served you worse. And being strong, though small, or perhaps because you still have work left to do in the world before you leave it for a while, you have lived through all these things and will in time recover, though not yet."

"I hope so, Zikali, though on the whole I am not sure that I wish to recover."

"Yes, you do, Macumazahn, because the religion of you white men makes you fear death and what may come after it. You think of what you call your sins and are afraid lest you should be tortured because of them, not understanding that the spirit must be judged not by what the flesh has done but by what the spirit desired to do, by will not by deed, Macumazahn. The evil man is he who wishes to do evil, not he who wishes to do good and falls now and again into evil. Oh! I have hearkened to your white teachers and I know, I know."

"Then by your own standard you are evil, Zikali, since you wished to bring about war, and not in vain."

"Oho! Macumazahn, you think that, do you, who cannot understand that what seems to be evil is often good. I wished to bring about war and brought it about, and maybe what bred the wish was all that I have suffered in the past. But say you, who have seen what the Zulu Power means, who have seen men, women and children killed by the thousand to feed that Power, and who have seen, too, what the English Power means, is it evil that I should wish to destroy the House of the Zulu kings that the English House may take its place and that in a time to come the Black people may be free?"

"You are clever, Zikali, but it is of your own wrongs that you think. How about that skull which you kissed in the Vale of Bones?"

"Mayhap, Macumazahn, but my wrongs are the wrongs of a nation, therefore I think of the nation, and at least I do not fear death like you white men. Now hearken. Presently your friends will tell you a story. The lady Heddana will tell you how I made use of her for a certain purpose, for which purpose indeed I drew the three of you into Zululand, because without her I could not have brought about this war into which Cetewayo did not wish to enter. When you have heard that story, do not judge me too hardly, Macumazahn, who had a great end to gain."

"Yet whatever the story may be, I do judge you hardly, Zikali, who tormented me with a false tale, causing the woman Kaatje to lie to me and swear that she saw these two dead before her—how I know not."

"She did not lie to you, Macumazahn. Has not such a one as I the power to make a fat fool think that she saw what she did not see? As to how! How did I make you think in yonder hut of mine that you saw what you did not see—perhaps."

"But why did you mock me in this fashion, Zikali?"

"Truly, Macumazahn, you are blind as a bat in sunlight. When your friends have told you the story, you will understand why. Yet I admit to you that things went wrong. You should have heard that tale before Cetewayo brought you to the Vale of Bones. But the fool-woman delayed and blundered, and when she reached Ulundi the gates were shut against her as a spy, and not opened till too late, so that you only found her when you returned from the Council. I knew this, and that was why I dared to bid you fire at that which stood upon the rock. Had you heard Kaatje's tale you might have aimed straight, as also you would have certainly shot straight at me, out of revenge for the deaths of those you loved, Macumazahn, though whether you could have killed me before all the game is played is another matter. As it was, I was sure that you would not pierce the heart of one who might be a certain white woman, sure also that you would not pierce my heart whose death might bring about her death and that of another."

"You are very subtle, Zikali," I said in astonishment.

"So you hold because I am very simple, who understand the spirit of man—and some other things. For the rest, had you not believed that these two were dead, you would never have left Zululand. You would have tried to escape to get to them and have been killed. Is it not so?"

"Yes, I think I should have tried, Zikali. But why did you keep them prisoner?"

"For the same reason that I still keep them—and you—to hold them back a while from the world of ghosts. Had I sent them away after that night of the declaration of war, they would have been killed before they had gone an hour's journey. Oh! I am not so bad as you think, Macumazahn, and I never break my word. Now I have done."

"How goes the war?" I asked as he shuffled to his feet.

"As it must go, very ill for the Zulus. They have driven back the white men who gather strength from over the Black Water and will come on presently and wipe them out. Umnyamana would have had Cetewayo invade Natal and sweep it clean, as of course he should have done. But I sent him word that if he did so Nomkubulwana, yes, she and no other, had told me that all the spirits would be against him, and he hearkened. When next you think me wicked, remember that, Macumazahn. Now it is but a matter of time, and here you must bide till all is finished. That will be good for you who need rest, though the other two find it wearisome. Still for them it is good also to watch the fruit ripen on their tree of love. It will be the sweeter when they eat it, Macumazahn, and teach them how to live together. Oho! Oho-ho!" and he shambled off.

CHAPTER XX

HEDA'S TALE

That evening when I was lying on my bed outside the cave, I heard the tale of Anscombe and Heda. Up to a certain point he told it, then she went on with the story.

"On the morning after our arrival at this place, Allan," said Anscombe, "I woke up to find you gone from the hut. As you did not come back I concluded that you were with Zikali, and walked about looking for you. Then food was brought to us and Heda and I breakfasted together, after which we went to where we heard the horses neighing and found that yours was gone. Returning, much frightened, we met Nombe, who gave me your note which explained everything, and we inquired of her why this had been done and what was to become of us. She smiled and answered that we had better ask the first question of the king and the second of her master Zikali, and in the meanwhile be at peace since we were quite safe.

"I tried to see Zikali but could not. Then I went to inspan the horses with the idea of following you, only to find that they were gone. Indeed I have not seen them from that day to this. Next we thought of starting on foot, for we were quite desperate. But Nombe intervened and told us that if we ventured out of the Black Kloof we should be killed. In short we were prisoners.

"This went on for some days, during which we were well treated but could not succeed in seeing Zikali. At length one morning he sent for us and we were taken to the enclosure in front of his hut, Kaatje coming with us as interpreter. For a while he sat still, looking very grim and terrible. Then he said—

"'White Chief and Lady, you think ill of me because Macumazahn has gone and you are kept prisoners here, and before all is done you will think worse. Yet I counsel you to trust me since everything that happens is for your good.'

"At this point Heda, who, as you know, talked Zulu fairly well, though not so well as she does now, broke in, and said some very angry things to him."

"Yes," interrupted Heda. "I told him that he was a liar and I believed that he had murdered you and meant to murder us."

"He listened stonily," continued Anscombe, "and answered, 'I perceive, Lady Heddana, that you understand enough of our tongue to enable me to talk to you; therefore I will send away this half-breed woman, since what I have to say is secret.'

"Then he called servants by clapping his hands and ordered them to remove Kaatje, which was done.

"'Now, Lady Heddana,' he said, speaking very slowly so that Heda might interpret to me and repeating his words whenever she did not understand, 'I have a proposal to make to you. For my own ends it is necessary that you should play a part and appear before the king and the Council as the goddess of this land who is called the Chieftainess of Heaven, which goddess is always seen as a white woman. Therefore you must travel with me to Ulundi and there do those things which I shall tell you.'

"'And if I refuse to play this trick,' said Heda, 'what then?'

"'Then, Lady Heddana, this white lord whom you love and who is to be your husband will—die—and after he is dead you must still do what I desire of you, or—die also.'

"'Would he come with me to Ulundi?' asked Heda.

"'Not so, Lady. He would stay here under guard, but quite safe, and you will be brought back to him, safe. Choose now, with death on the one hand and safety on the other. I would sleep a little. Talk the matter over in your own tongue and when it is settled awaken me again,' and he shut his eyes and appeared to go to sleep.

"So we discussed the situation, if you can call it discussion when we were both nearly mad. Heda wished to go. I begged her to let me be killed rather than trust herself into the hands of this old villain. She pointed out that even if I were killed, which she admitted might not happen, she would still be in his hands whence she could only escape by her own death, whereas if she went there was a chance that we might both continue to live, and that after all death was easy to find. So in the end I gave way and we woke up Zikali and told him so.

"He seemed pleased and spoke to us gently, saying, 'I was sure that wisdom dwelt behind those bright eyes of yours, Lady, and again I promise you that neither you nor the lord your lover shall come to any harm. Also that in payment I and my child, Nombe, will protect you even with our lives, and further, that I will bring back your friend, Macumazahn, to you, though not yet. Now go and be happy together. Nombe will tell the lady Heddana when she is to start. Of all this say nothing on your peril to the woman Kaatje, since if you do, it will be necessary that she should be made silent. Indeed, lest she should learn something, to-morrow I shall send her on to await you at Ulundi, therefore be not surprised if you see her go, and take no heed of aught she may say in going. Nombe, my child, will fill her place as servant to the lady Heddana and sleep with her at night that she may not be lonely or afraid.'

"Then he clapped his hands again and servants came and conducted us back to the huts. And now, Allan, Heda will go on with the story."

"Well, Mr. Quatermain," she said, "nothing more happened that day which we spent with bursting hearts. Kaatje did not question us as to what the witch-doctor had said after she was sent away. Indeed I noticed that she was growing very stupid and drowsy, like a person who has been drugged, as I daresay she was, and would insist upon beginning to pack up the things in a foolish kind of way, muttering something about our trekking on the following day. The night passed as usual, Kaatje sleeping very heavily by my side and snoring so much" (here I groaned sympathetically) "that I could get little rest. On the next morning after breakfast as the huts were very hot, Nombe suggested that we should sit under the shadow of the overhanging rock, just where we are now. Accordingly we went, and being tired out with all our troubles and bad nights, I fell into a doze, and so, I think, did Maurice, Nombe sitting near to us and singing all the while, a very queer kind of song.

"Presently, through my doze as it were, I saw Kaatje approaching. Nombe went to meet her, still singing, and taking her hand, led her to the cart, where they seemed to talk to the horses, which surprised me as there were no horses. Then she brought her round the cart and pointed to us, still singing. Now Kaatje began to weep and throw her hands about, while Nombe patted her on the shoulder. I tried to speak to her but could not. My tongue was tied, why I don't know, but I suppose because I was really asleep, and Maurice also was asleep and did not wake at all."

"Yes," said Anscombe, "I remember nothing of all this business."

"After a while Kaatje went away, still weeping, and then I fell asleep in earnest and did not wake until the sun was going down, when I roused Maurice and we both went back to the hut, where I found that Nombe had cooked our evening meal. I looked for Kaatje, but could not find her. Also in searching through my things I missed the bag of jewels. I called to Nombe and asked where Kaatje was, whereon she smiled and said that she had gone away, taking the bag with her. This pained me, for I had always found Kaatje quite honest—"

"Which she is," I remarked, "for those jewels are now in a bank at Maritzburg."

Heda nodded and went on, "I am glad to hear it; indeed, remembering what Zikali had said, I never really suspected her of being a thief, but thought it was all part of some plan. After this things went on as before, except that Nombe took Kaatje's place and was with me day and night. Of Kaatje's disappearance she would say nothing. Zikali we did not see.

"On the third evening after the vanishing of Kaatje, Nombe came and said that I must make ready for a journey, and while she spoke men arrived with a litter that had grass mats hung round it. Nombe brought out my long cape and put it over me, also a kind of veil of white stuff which she threw over my head, so as to hide my face. I think it was made out of one of our travelling mosquito nets. Then she said I must say good-bye to Maurice for a while. There was a scene as you may imagine. He grew angry and said that he would come with me, whereon armed men appeared, six of them, and pushed him away with the handles of their spears. In another minute I was lifted into the litter which Nombe entered with me, and so we were parted, wondering if we should ever see each other more. At the mouth of the kloof I saw another litter surrounded by a number of Zulus, which Nombe said contained Zikali.

"We travelled all that night and two succeeding nights, resting during the day in deserted kraals that appeared to have been made ready for us. It was a strange journey, for although the armed men flitted about us, neither they nor the bearers ever spoke, nor did I see Zikali, or indeed any one else. Only Nombe comforted me from time to time, telling me there was nothing to fear. Towards dawn on the third night we travelled over some hills and I was put into a new hut and told that my journey was done as we had reached a place near Ulundi.

"I slept most of the following day, but after I had eaten towards evening, Zikali crept into the hut, just as a great toad might do, and squatted down in front of me.

"'Lady,' he said, 'listen. To-night, perhaps one hour after sundown, perhaps two, perhaps three, Nombe will lead you, dressed in a certain fashion, from this hut. See now, outside of it there is a tongue of rock up which you may climb unnoted by the little path that runs between those big stones. Look,' and he showed me the place through the door-hole. 'The path ends on a flat boulder at the end of the rock. There you will take your stand, holding in your right hand a little assegai which will be given to you. Nombe will not accompany you to the rock, but she will crouch between the stones at the head of the path and perhaps from time to time whisper to you what to do. Thus when she tells you, you must throw the little spear into the air, so that it falls among a number of men gathered in debate who will be seated about twenty paces from the rock. For the rest you are to stand quite still, saying nothing and showing no alarm whatever you may hear or see. Among the men before you may be your friend, Macumazahn, but you must not appear to recognize him, and if he speaks to you, you must make no answer. Even if he should seem to shoot at you, do not be afraid. Do you understand? If so, repeat what I have told you.' I obeyed him and asked what would happen if I did not do these things, or some of them.

"He answered, 'You will be killed, Nombe will be killed, the lord Mauriti your lover will be killed, and your friend Macumazahn will be killed. Perhaps even I shall be killed and we will talk the matter over in the land of ghosts.'

"On hearing this I said I would do my best to carry out his orders, and after making me repeat them once more, he went away. Later, Nombe dressed me up as you saw me, Mr. Quatermain, put some glittering powder into my hair and touched me beneath the eyes with a dark kind of pigment. Also she gave me the little spear and made me practise standing quite still with it raised in my right hand, telling me that when I heard her say the word 'Throw,' I was to cast it into the air. Then the moon rose and we heard men talking at a distance. At last some one came to the hut and whispered to Nombe, who led me out to the little path between the rocks.

"This must have been nearly two hours after I heard the men begin to talk—"

"Excuse me," I interrupted, "but where was Nombe all those two hours?"

"With me. She never left my side, Mr. Quatermain, and while I was on the rock she was crouched within three paces of me between two big stones at the mouth of the path."

"Indeed," I replied faintly, "this is very interesting. Please continue—but one word, how was Nombe dressed? Did she wear a necklace of blue beads?"

"Just as she always is, or rather less so, for she had nothing on except her moocha, and certainly no blue beads. But why do you ask?"

"From curiosity merely. I mean, I will tell you afterwards, pray go on."

"Well, I stepped forward on to the rock and at first saw nothing, because at that moment the moon was hid by a cloud; indeed Nombe had waited for the cloud to pass over its face, before she thrust me forward. Also some smoke from a fire below was rising straight in front of me. Presently the cloud passed, the smoke thinned, and I saw the circle of those savage men seated beneath, and in their centre a great chief wearing a leopard's skin cloak who I guessed was the king. You I did not see, Mr. Quatermain, because you were behind a tree, yet I felt that you were there, a friend among all those foes. I stood still, as I had been taught to do, and heard the murmur of astonishment and caught the gleam of the moonlight from the white feathers that were sewn upon my robe.

"Then I heard also the voice of Zikali speaking from beneath. He called on you to come out to shoot at me, and the man whom I took to be the king, ordered you to obey. You appeared from behind the tree, and I was certain from the look upon your face that at that distance you did not know who I was in my strange and glittering raiment. You lifted the pistol and I was terribly afraid, for I had seen you shoot with it before on the verandah of the Temple and knew well that you do not miss. Very nearly I screamed out to you, but remembered and was silent, thinking that after all it did not much matter if I died, except for the sake of Maurice here. Also by now I guessed that I was being used to deceive those men before me into some terrible act, and that if I died, at least they would be undeceived.

"I thought that an age passed between the time you pointed the pistol and I saw the flash for which I was waiting."

"You need not have waited, Heda," I interposed, "for if I had really aimed at you you would never have seen that flash, at least so it is said. I too guessed enough to shoot above you, although at the time I did not know that it was you on the rock; indeed I thought it was Nombe painted up."

"Yes, I heard the bullet sing over me. Then I heard the voice of Zikali challenging you to shoot him, and to tell the truth, hoped that you would do so. Just before you fired for the second time, Nombe whispered to me—'Throw' and I threw the little red-handled spear into the air. Then as the pistol went off Nombe whispered—'Come.' I slipped away down the path and back with her into the hut, where she kissed me and said that I had done well indeed, after which she took off my strange robe and helped me to put on my own dress.

"That is all I know, except that some hours later I was awakened from sleep and put into the litter where I went to sleep again, for what I had gone through tired me very much. I need not trouble you with the rest, for we journeyed here in the same way that we had journeyed to Ulundi—by night. I did not see Zikali, but in answer to my questions, Nombe told me that the Zulus had declared war against the English. What part in the business I had played, she would not tell me, and I do not know to this hour, but I am sure that it was a great one.

"So we came back to the Black Kloof, where I found Maurice quite well, and now he had better go on with the tale, for if I begin to tell you of our meeting I shall become foolish."

"There isn't much more to tell," said Anscombe, "except about yourself. While Heda was away I was kept a prisoner and watched day and night by Zikali's people who would not let me stir a yard, but otherwise treated me kindly. Then one day at sunrise, or shortly after it, Heda re-appeared and told me all this story, for the end of which, as you may imagine, I thanked God.

"After that we just lived on here, happily enough since we were together, until one day Nombe told us that there had been a great battle in which the Zulus had wiped out the English, killing hundreds and hundreds of them, although for every soldier that they killed, they had lost two. Of course this made us very sad, especially as we were afraid you might be with our troops. We asked Nombe if you were present at the battle. She answered that she would inquire of her Spirit and went through some very strange performances with ashes and knuckle bones, after which she announced that you had been in the battle but were alive and coming this way with a dog that had silver on it. We laughed at her, saying that she could not possibly know anything of the sort, also that dogs as a rule did not carry silver. Whereon she only smiled and said—'Wait.'

"I think it was three days later that one night towards dawn I was awakened by hearing a dog barking outside my hut, as though it wished to call attention to its presence. It barked so persistently and in a way so unlike a Kaffir dog, that at length about dawn I went out of the hut to see what was the matter. There, standing a few yards away surrounded by some of Zikali's people, I saw Lost and knew at once that it was an English Airedale, for I have had several of the breed. It looked very tired and frightened, and while I was wondering whence on earth it could have come, I noticed that it had a silver-mounted collar and remembered Nombe and her talk about you and a dog that carried silver on it. From that moment, Allan, I was certain that you were somewhere near, especially as the beast ran up to me—it would take no notice of the Kaffirs—and kept looking towards the mouth of the kloof, as though it wished me to follow it. Just then Nombe arrived, and on seeing the dog looked at me oddly.

"'I have a message for you from my master, Mauriti,' she said to me through Heda, who by now had arrived upon the scene, having also been aroused by Lost's barking. 'It is that if you wish to take a walk with a strange dog you can do so, and bring back anything you may find.'"

"The end of it was that after we had fed Lost with milk and meat, I and six of Zikali's men started down the kloof, Lost going ahead of us and now and again running back and whining. At the mouth of the kloof it led us over a hill and down into a bush-veld valley where the thorns grew very thick. When we had gone along the valley for about two miles, one of the Kaffirs saw a Basuto pony still saddled, and caught it. The dog went on past the pony to a tree that had been shattered by lightning, and there within a few yards of the tree we found you lying senseless, Allan, or, as I thought at first, dead, and by your side a Martini rifle of which the stock also seemed to have been broken by lightning.

"Well, we put you on a shield and carried you here, meeting no one, and that is all the story, Allan."

He stopped and we stared at each other. Then I called Lost and patted its head, and the dear beast licked my hand as though it understood that it was being thanked.

"A strange tale," I said, "but God Almighty has put much wisdom into His creatures of which we know nothing. Let us thank Him," and in our hearts we did.

Thus was I rescued from death by the intelligence and fidelity of a four-footed creature. Doubtless in my semi-conscious state that resulted from shock, weariness and sun-stroke, I had all the while headed sub-consciously and without any definite object for the Black Kloof. When I was within a few miles of it I was stunned by the lightning which ran down the rifle to the ground, though not actually struck. Then the dog, which had escaped, played its part, wandering about the country to find help for me, and so I was saved.

Now of the long months that followed I have little to tell. They were not unhappy in their way, for week by week I felt myself growing stronger, though very slowly. There was a path, steep, difficult and secret, which could be gained through one of the caves in the precipice, not that in which I slept. This path ran up a water-cut kloof through a patch of thorns to a flat tableland that was part of the Ceza stronghold. By it, when I had gained sufficient strength, sometimes we used to climb to the plateau, and there take exercise. It was an agreeable change from the stifling atmosphere of the Black Kloof. The days were very dull, for we were as much out of the world as though we had been marooned on a desert island. Still from time to time we heard of the progress of the war through Nombe, for Zikali I saw but seldom.

She told of disasters to the English, of the death of a great young Chief who was deserted by his companions and died fighting bravely—afterwards I discovered that this was the Prince Imperial of France—of the advance of our armies, of defeats inflicted upon Cetewayo's impis, and finally of the destruction of the Zulus on the battlefield of Ulundi, where they hurled themselves by thousands upon the British square, to be swept away by case-shot and the hail of bullets. This battle, by the way, the Zulus call, not Ulundi or Nodwengu, for it was fought in front of Panda's old kraal of that name, but Ocwecweni, which means—"the fight of the sheet-iron fortress." I suppose they give it this name because the hedge of bayonets, flashing in the sunlight, reminded them of sheet-iron. Or it may be because these proved as impenetrable as would have done walls of iron. At any rate they dashed their naked bodies against the storm of lead and fell in heaps, only about a dozen of our men being killed, as the little graveyard in the centre of the square entrenchment, about which still lie the empty cartridge cases, records to-day.

There, then, on that plain perished the Zulu kingdom which was built up by Chaka.

Now it was after this event that I saw Zikali and begged him to let us go. I found him triumphant and yet strangely disturbed and, as I thought, more apprehensive than I had ever seen him.

"So, Zikali," I said, "if what I hear is true, you have had your way and destroyed the Zulu people. Now you should be happy."

"Is man ever happy, Macumazahn, when he has gained that which he sought for years? The two out there sigh and are sad because they cannot be married after their own white fashion, though what there is to keep them apart I do not know. Well, in time they will be married, only to find that they are not so happy as they thought they would be. Oh! a day will come when they will talk to each other and say— 'Those moons which we spent waiting together in the Black Kloof were the true moons of sweetness, for then we had something to gain; now we have gained all—and what is it?'

"So it is with me, Macumazahn. Since the Zulus under Chaka killed out my people, the Ndwandwe, year by year I have plotted and waited to see them wedded to the assegai. Now it has come about. You white men have stamped them flat upon the plain of Ulundi; they are no more a nation. And yet I am not happy, for after all it was the House of Senzangacona and not the people of the Zulus, that harmed me and mine, and Cetewayo still lives. While the queen bee remains there may be a hive again. While an ember still glows in the dead ashes, the forest may yet be fired. Perhaps when Cetewayo is dead, then I shall be happy. Only his death and mine are set by Fate as close together as two sister grains of corn upon the cob."

I turned the subject, again asking his leave to depart to Natal or to join the English army.

"You cannot go yet," he answered sternly, "so trouble me no more. The land is full of wandering bands of Zulus who would kill you and your blood would be on my head. Moreover, if they saw a white woman who had sheltered with me, might they not guess something? To dress a doll for the part of the Inkosazana-y-Zulu is the greatest crime in the world, Macumazahn, and what would happen to the Opener of Roads and all his House if it were even breathed that he had dressed that doll and thus brought about the war which ruined them? When Cetewayo is killed and the dead are buried and peace falls upon the land, the peace of death, then you shall go, Macumazahn, and not before."

"At least, Zikali, send a message to the captains of the English army and tell them that we are here."

"Send a message to the hyenas and tell them where the carcase is; send a message to the hunters and tell them where the buck Zikali crouches on its form! Hearken, Macumazahn, if you do this, or even urge me again to do it, neither you nor your friends shall ever leave the Black Kloof. I have spoken."

Then understanding that the case was hopeless, I left him and he glowered after me, for fear had made him cruel. He had won the long game and success had turned to ashes in his mouth. Or rather, he had not won—yet—since his war was against the House of Senzangacona from which he and his tribe had suffered cruel wrong. To pull it down he must pull down the Zulu nation; it was like burning a city to destroy a compromising letter. He had burnt the city, but the letter still remained intact and might be produced in evidence against him. In other words Cetewayo yet lived. Therefore his vengeance remained quite unslaked and his danger was as great, or perhaps greater than it had ever been before. For was he not the prophet who by producing the Princess of Heaven, the traditional goddess of the Zulus, before the eyes of the king and Council, had caused them to decide for war? And supposing it were so much as breathed that this spirit which they seemed to see, had been but a trick and a fraud, what then? He would be tortured to death if his dupes had time, or torn limb from limb if they had not, that is if he could die like other men—a matter as to which personally I had no doubts.

Shortly after I left Zikali Heda and I ate our evening meal together. Anscombe, as it chanced, had gone by the secret path to the tableland of which I have spoken, where he amused himself, as of course we were not allowed to fire a gun, by catching partridges, with the help of an ingenious system of grass nets which he had invented. There were springs on this tableland that formed little pools of water, at which the partridges, also occasionally guineafowl and bush pheasants, came to drink at sunrise and sunset. Here it was that he set his nets and retired to work them at those hours by means of strings that he pulled from hiding-places. So Heda and I were alone.

I told her of my ill success with Zikali, at which she was much disappointed. Then by an afterthought I suggested that perhaps she might try to do something in the way of getting a message through to the English camp at Ulundi, or elsewhere, by help of the witch-doctoress, Nombe, adding that I would speak to her myself had I not observed that I seemed to be out of favour with her of late. Heda shook her head and answered that she thought it would be useless to try, also too dangerous. Remembering Zikali's threat, on reflection I agreed with her.

"Tell me, Mr. Quatermain," she added, "is it possible for one woman to be in love with another?"

I stared at her and replied that I did not understand what she meant, since women, so far as I had observed them, were generally in love either with a man or with themselves, perhaps more often with the latter than the former. Rather a cheap joke I admit, with just enough truth in it to make it acceptable—in the Black Kloof.

"So I thought," she answered, "but really Nombe behaves in a most peculiar way. As you know she took a fancy to me from the beginning, perhaps because she had never had any other woman with whom to associate, having, so far as I can make out, been brought up here among men from a child. Indeed, her story is that she was one of twins and therefore as the younger, was exposed to die according to the Zulu superstition. Zikali, however, or a servant of his who knew what was happening, rescued and reared her, so practically I am the only female with whom she has ever been intimate. At any rate her affection for me has grown and grown until, although it seems ungrateful to say so, it has become something of a nuisance. She has told me again and again that she would die to protect me, and that if by chance anything happened to me, she would kill herself and follow me into another world. She is continually making divinations about my future, and as these, in which she entirely believes, always show me as living without her, she is much distressed and at times bursts into tears."

"Hysteria! It is very common among the Zulu women, and especially those of them who practise magic arts," I answered.

"Perhaps, but as it results in the most intense jealousy, Nombe's hysteria is awkward. For instance, she is horribly jealous of Maurice."

"The instincts of a chaperone developed early," I suggested again.

"That won't quite do, Mr. Quatermain," answered Heda with a laugh, "since she is even more jealous of you. With reference to Maurice, she explains frankly that if we marry she might, as she puts it, 'continue to sit outside the hut,' but that in your case you live 'in my head,' where she cannot come between you and me."

"Mad," I remarked, "quite mad. Still madness has to be dealt with in this world like other things, and Nombe, being an abnormal person, may suffer from abnormal ideas. It just amounts to this; she has conceived a passionate devotion to you, at which I am sure neither Maurice nor I can wonder."

"Are those the kind of compliments you used to pay in your youth, Mr. Quatermain? I expect so, and now that you are old you cannot stop them. Well, I thank you all the same, because perhaps you mean what you say. But what is to be done about Nombe? Hush! here she comes. I will leave you to reason with her, if you get the chance," and she departed in a hurry.

Nombe arrived, and something in her aspect told me that I was going to get the chance. Her eternal smile was almost gone and her dark, beautiful eyes flashed ominously. Still she began by asking in a mild voice whether the lady Heddana had eaten her supper with appetite. It will be observed that she was not interested in my appetite or whether enough was left for Anscombe when he returned. I replied that so far as I noted she had consumed about half a partridge, with other things.

"I am glad," said Nombe, "since I was not here to attend upon her, having been summoned to speak with the Master."

Then she sat down and looked at me like a thunder storm.

"I nursed you when you were so ill, Macumazahn," she began, "but now I learn that for the milk with which I fed you, you would force me to drink bitter water that will poison me."

I replied I was well aware that without her nursing I should long ago have been dead, which was what caused me to love her like my own daughter. But would she kindly explain? This she did at once.

"You have been plotting to take away from me the lady Heddana who to me is as mother and sister and child. It is useless to lie to me, for the Master has told me all; moreover, I knew it for myself, both through my Spirit and because I had watched you."

"I have no intention of lying to you, Nombe, about this or any other matter, though I think that sometimes in the past you have lied to me. Tell me, do you expect the Inkosi Mauriti, the lady Heddana and myself to pass the rest of our lives in the Black Kloof, when they wish to get married and go across the Black Water to where their home will be, and I wish to attend to my affairs?"

"I do not know what I expect, Macumazahn, but I do know that never while I live will I be parted from the lady Heddana. At last I have found some one to love, and you and the other would steal her away from me."

I studied her for a while, then asked—

"Why do you not marry, Nombe, and have a husband, and children to love?"

"Marry?" she replied. "I am married to my Spirit which does not dwell beneath the sun, and my children are not of earth; moreover, all men are hateful to me," and her eyes added, "especially you."

"That is a calf with a dog's head," I replied in the words of the native proverb, meaning that she said what was not natural. "Well, Nombe, if you are so fond of the lady Heddana, you had better arrange with her and the Inkosi Mauriti to go away with them."

"You know well I cannot, Macumazahn. I am tied to my Master by ropes that are stronger than iron, and if I attempted to break them my Spirit would wither and I should wither with it."

"Dear me! what a dreadful business. That is what comes of taking to magic. Well, Nombe, I am afraid I have nothing to suggest, nor, to tell you the truth, can I see what I have to do with the matter."

Then she sprang up in a rage, saying—

"I understand that not only will you give me no help, but that you also mock at me, Macumazahn. Moreover, as it is with you, so it is with Mauriti, who pretends to love my lady so much, though I love her more with my little finger than he does with all his body and what he calls his soul. Yes, he too mocks at me. Now if you were both dead," she added with sudden venom, "my lady would not wish to go away. Be careful lest a spell should fall upon you, Macumazahn," and without more words she turned and went.

At first I was inclined to laugh; the whole thing seemed so absurd. On reflection, however, I perceived that in reality it was very serious to people situated as we were. This woman was a savage; more, a mystic savage of considerable powers of mind—a formidable combination. Also there were no restraints upon her, since public opinion had as little authority in the Black Kloof as the Queen's Writ. Lastly, it was not unknown for women to conceive these violent affections which, if thwarted, filled them with something like madness. Thus I remembered a very terrible occurrence of my youth which resulted in the death of one who was most dear to me. I will not dwell on it, but this, too, was the work of a passionate creature, woman I can scarcely call her, who thought she was being robbed of one whom she adored.

The end of it was that I did not enjoy my pipe that night, though luckily Anscombe returned after a successful evening's netting, about which he was so full of talk that there was no need for me to say much. So I put off any discussion of the problem until the morrow.

CHAPTER XXI

THE KING VISITS ZIKALI

Next morning, as a result of my cogitations, I went to see Zikali. I was admitted after a good deal of trouble and delay, for although his retinue was limited and, with the exception of Nombe, entirely male, this old prophet kept a kind of semi-state and was about as difficult to approach as a European monarch. I found him crouching over a fire in his hut, since at this season of the year even in that hot place the air was chilly until midday.

"What is it, Macumazahn?" he asked. "As to your going away, have patience. I learn that he who was King of the Zulus is in full flight, with the white men tracking him like a wounded buck. When the buck is caught and killed, then you can go."

"It is about Nombe," I answered, and told him all the story, which did not seem to surprise him at all.

"Now see, Macumazahn," he said, taking some snuff, "how hard it is to dam up the stream of nature. This child, Nombe, is of my blood, one whom I saved from death in a strange way, not because she was of my blood but that I might make an experiment with her. Women, as you who are wise and have seen much will know, are in truth superior to men, though, because they are weaker in body, men have the upper hand of them and think themselves their masters, a state they are forced to accept because they must live and cannot defend themselves. Yet their brains are keener, as an assegai is keener than a hoe; they are more in touch with the hidden things that shape out fate for people and for nations; they are more faithful and more patient, and by instinct if not by reason, more far-seeing, or at least the best of them are so, and by their best, like men, they should be judged. Yet this is the hole in their shield. When they love they become the slaves of love, and for love's sake all else is brought to naught, and for this reason they cannot be trusted. With men, as you know, this is otherwise. They, too, love, by Nature's law, but always behind there is something greater than love, although often they do not understand what that may be. To be powerful, therefore, a woman must be one who does not love too much. If she cannot love at all, then she is hated and has no power, but she must not love too much.

"Once I thought that I had found such a woman; she was named Mameena, whom all men worshipped and who played with all men, as I played with her. But what was the end of it? Just as things were going very well she learned to love too much some man of strange notions, who would have thwarted me and brought everything to nothing, and therefore I had to kill her, for which I was sorry."

Here he paused to take some more snuff, watching me over the spoon as he drew it up his great nostrils, but as I said nothing, went on—

"Now after Mameena was dead I bethought me that I would rear up a woman who could still love but should never love a man and therefore never become mad or foolish, because I believed that it was only man who in taking her heart from woman, would take her wits also. This child, Nombe, came to my hand, and as I thought, so I did. Never mind how I did it, by medicine perhaps, by magic perhaps, by watering her pride and making it grow tall perhaps, or by all three. At least it was done, and this I know of Nombe, she will never care for any man except as a woman may care for a brother.

"But now see what happens. She, the wise, the instructed, the man-despiser, meets a woman of another race who is sweet and good, and learns to love her, not as maids and mothers love, but as one loves the Spirit that she worships. Yes, yes, to her she is a goddess to be worshipped, one whom she desires to serve with all her heart and strength, to bow down before, making offerings, and at the end to follow into death. So it comes about that this Nombe, whose mind I thought to make as the wings of a bird floating on the air while it searches for its prey, has become even madder than other women. It is a disappointment to me, Macumazahn."

"It may be a disappointment to you, Zikali, and all that you say is very interesting. But to us it is a danger. Tell me, will you command Nombe to cease from her folly?"

"Will I forbid the mist to rise, or the wind to blow, or the lightning to strike? As she is, she is. Her heart is filled with black jealousy of Mauriti and of you, as a butcher's gourd is filled with blood, for she is not one who desires that her goddess should have other worshippers; she would keep her for herself alone."

"Then in this way or in that the gourd must be emptied, Zikali, lest we should be forced to drink from it and that black blood should poison us."

"How, unless it be broken, Macumazahn? If Heddana departs and leaves her, she will go mad, and accompany her she cannot, for her Spirit dwells here," and he tapped his own breast. "It would pull her back again and she would become a great trouble to me, for then that Spirit of hers would not suffer me to sleep, with its continual startings in search of what it had lost, and its returnings empty-handed. Well, have no fear, for at the worst the bowl can be broken and the blood poured upon the earth, as I have broken finer bowls than this before; had I all the bits of them they would make a heap so high, Macumazahn!" and he held out his hand on a level with his head, a gesture that made my back creep. "I will tell her this and it may keep her quiet for a while. Of poison you need not be afraid, since unlike mine, her Spirit hates it. Poison is not one of its weapons as it is with mine. But of spells, beware, for her Spirit has some which are very powerful."

Now I jumped up, filled with indignation, saying—

"I do not believe in Nombe's spells, and in any case how am I to guard against them?"

"If you do not believe there is no need to guard, and if you do believe, then it is for you to find out how to guard, Macumazahn. Oh! I could tell you the story of a white teacher who did not believe and would not guard—but never mind, never mind. Good-bye, Macumazahn, I will speak with Nombe. Ask her for a lock of her hair to wear upon your heart after she has enchanted it. The charm is good against spells. O-ho—Oho-o! What fools we are, white and black together! That is what Cetewayo is thinking to-day."

After this Nombe became much more agreeable. That is to say she was very polite, her smile was more fixed and her eyes more unfathomable than ever. Evidently Zikali had spoken to her and she had listened. Yet to tell the truth my distrust of this handsome young woman grew deeper day by day. I recognized that there was a great gulf between her and the normal, that she was a creature fashioned by Zikali who had trained her as a gardener trains a tree, nay, who had done more, who had grafted some foreign growth of exotic and unnatural spiritualism on to her primitive nature. The nature remained the same, but the graft or grafts bore strange flowers and fruit, unholy flowers and poisonous fruit. Therefore she was not to blame—sometimes I wonder whether in this curious world, could one see their past and their future, anybody is to blame for anything—but this did not make her the less dangerous.

Some talks I had with her only increased my apprehensions, for I found that in a way she had no conscience. Life, she told me, was but a dream, and all its laws as evolved by man were but illusions. The real life was elsewhere. There was the distant lake on which the flower of our true existence floated. Without this unseen lake of supernatural water the flower could not float; indeed there would be no flower. Moreover, the flower did not matter; sometimes it would have this shape and colour, sometimes that. It was but a thing destined to grow and bloom and rot, and during its day to be ugly or to be beautiful, to smell sweet or ill, as it might chance, and ultimately to be absorbed back into the general water of Life.

I pointed out to her that all flowers had roots which grew in soil. Looking at an orchid-like plant that crept along the bough of a tree, she answered that this was not true as some grew upon air. But however this might be, the soil, or the moisture in the air, was distilled from thousands of other flower lives that had flourished in their day and been forgotten. It did not matter when they died or how many other flowers they choked that they might live. Yet each flower had its own spirit which always had been and always would be.

I asked her of the end and the object of that spirit. She answered darkly that she did not know and if she did, would not say, but that these were very dreadful.

Such were some of her vague and figurative assertions which I only record to indicate their uncomfortable and indeed but half human nature. I forgot to add that she declared that every flower or life had a twin flower or life, which in each successive growth it was bound to find and bloom beside, or wither to the root and spring again and that ultimately these two would become one, and as one flourish eternally. Of all of which I understood and understand little, except that she had grasped the elements of some truth which she could not express in clear and definite language.

One day I was seated in Zikali's hut whither by permission I had come to ask the latest news, when suddenly Nombe appeared and crouched down before him.

"Who gave you leave to enter here, and what is your business?" he asked angrily.

"Home of Spirits," she replied in a humble voice, "be not angry with your servant. Necessity gave me leave, and my business is to tell you that strangers approach."

"Who are they that dare to enter the Black Kloof unannounced?"

"Cetewayo the King is one of them, the others I do not know, but they are many, armed all of them. They approach your gate; before a man can count two hundred they will be here."

"Where are the white chief and the lady Heddana?" asked Zikali.

"By good fortune they have gone by the secret path to the tableland and will not be back till sunset. They wished to be alone, so I did not accompany them, and Macumazahn here said that he was too weary to do so." (This was true. Also like Nombe I thought that they wished to be alone.)

"Good. Go, tell the king that I knew of his coming and am awaiting him. Bid my servants kill the ox which is in the kraal, the fat ox that they thought is sick and therefore fit food for a sick king," he added bitterly.

She glided away like a startled snake. Then Zikali turned to me and said swiftly—

"Macumazahn, you are in great danger. If you are found here you will be killed, and so will the others whom I will send to warn not to return till this king has gone away. Go at once to join them. No, it is too late, I hear the Zulus come. Take that kaross, cover yourself with it and lie among the baskets and beerpots here near the entrance of the hut in the deepest of the shadows, so that if any enter, perchance you will not be found. I too am in danger who shall be held to account for all that has happened. Perhaps they will kill me, if I can be killed. If so, get away with the others as best you can. Nombe will tell you where your horses are hidden. In that case let Heddana take Nombe with her, for when I am dead she will go, and shake her off in Natal if she troubles her. Whatever chances, remember, Macumazahn, that I have done my best to keep my word to you and to protect you and your friends. Now I go to look on this pricked bladder who was once a king."

He scrambled from the hut with slow, toad-like motions, while I with motions that were anything but slow, grabbed the grey catskin kaross and ensconced myself among the beerpots and mats in such a position that my head, over which I set a three-legged carved stool of Zikali's own cutting, was but a few inches to the left of the door-hole and therefore in the deepest of the shadows. Thence by stretching out my neck a little, I could see through the hole, also hear all that passed outside. Unless a deliberate search of the hut should be made I was fairly safe from observation, even if it were entered by strangers. One fear I had, however, it was lest the dog Lost should get into the place and smell me out. I had left him tied to the centre pole in my own hut, because he hated Zikali and always growled at him. But suppose he gnawed through the cord, or any one let him loose!

Scarcely had Zikali seated himself in his accustomed place before the hut, than the gate of the outer fence opened and approaching through it I saw forty or fifty fierce and way-worn men. In front of them, riding on a tired horse that was led by a servant, was Cetewayo himself. He was assisted to dismount, or rather threw his great bulk into the arms that were waiting to receive him.

Then after some words with his following and with one of Zikali's people, followed by three or four indunas and leaning on the arm of Umnyamana, the Prime Minister, he entered the enclosure, the rest remaining without. Zikali, who sat as though asleep, suddenly appeared to wake up and perceive him. Struggling to his feet he lifted his right arm and gave the royal salute of Bayete, and with it titles of praise, such as "Black One!" "Elephant!" "Earth-Shaker!" "Conqueror!" "Eater-up of the White men!" "Child of the Wild Beast (Chaka) whose teeth are sharper than the Wild Beast's ever were!" and so on, until Cetewayo, growing impatient, cried out—

"Be silent, Wizard. Is this a time for fine words? Do you not know my case that you offend my ears with them? Give us food to eat if you have it, after which I would speak with you alone. Be swift also; here I may not stay for long, since the white dogs are at my heels."

"I knew that you were coming, O King, to honour my poor house with a visit," said Zikali slowly, "and therefore the ox is already killed and the meat will soon be on the fire. Meanwhile drink a sup of beer, and rest."

He clapped his hands, whereon Nombe and some servants appeared with pots of beer, of which, after Zikali had tasted it to show that it was not poisoned, the king and his people drank thirstily. Then it was taken to those outside.

"What is this that my ears hear?" asked Zikali when Nombe and the others had gone, "that the White Dogs are on the spoor of the Black Bull?"

Cetewayo nodded heavily, and answered—

"My impis were broken to pieces on the plain of Ulundi; the cowards ran from the bullets as children run from bees. My kraals are burnt and I, the King, with but a faithful remnant fly for my life. The prophecy of the Black One has come true. The people of the Zulus are stamped flat beneath the feet of the great White People."

"I remember that prophecy, O King. Mopo told it to me within an hour of the death of the Black One when he gave me the little red-handled assegai that he snatched from the Black One's hand to do the deed. It makes me almost young again to think of it, although even then I was old," replied Zikali in a dreamy voice like one who speaks to himself.

Hearing him from under my kaross I bethought me that he had really grown old at last, who for the moment evidently forgot the part which this very assegai had played a few months before in the Vale of Bones. Well, even the greatest masters make such slips at times when their minds are full of other things. But if Zikali forgot, Cetewayo and his councillors remembered, as I could see by the look of quick intelligence that flashed from face to face.

"So! Mopo the murderer, he who vanished from the land after the death of my uncle Dingaan, gave you the little red assegai, did he, Opener of Roads! And but a few months ago that assegai, which old Sigananda knew again, thrown by the hand of the Inkosazana-y-Zulu, drew blood from my body after the white man, Macumazahn, had severed its shaft with his bullet. Now tell me, Opener of Roads, how did it pass from your keeping into that of the spirit Nomkubulwana?"

At this question I distinctly saw a shiver shake the frame of Zikali who realized too late the terrible mistake he had made. Yet as only the great can do, he retrieved and even triumphed over his error.

"Oho-ho!" he laughed, "who am I that I can tell how such things happen? Do you not know, O King, that the Spirits leave what they will and take what they will, whether it be but a blade of grass, or the life of a man"—here he looked at Cetewayo—"or even of a people? Sometimes they take the shadow and sometimes the substance, since spirit or matter, all is theirs. As for the little assegai, I lost it years ago. I remember that the last time I saw it was in the hands of a woman named Mameena to whom I showed it as a strange and bloody thing. After her death I found that it was gone, so doubtless she took it with her to the Under-world and there gave it to the Queen Nomkubulwana, with whom you may remember this Mameena returned from that Under-world yonder in the Bones."

"It may be so," said Cetewayo sullenly, "yet it was no spirit iron that cut my thigh, but what do I know of the ways of Spirits? Wizard, I would speak with you in your hut alone where no ear can hear us."

"My hut is the King's," answered Zikali, "yet let the King remember that those Spirits of which he does not know the ways, can always hear, yes, even the thoughts of men, and on them do judgment."

"Fear not," said Cetewayo, "amongst many other things I remember this also."

Then Zikali turned and crept into the hut, whispering as he passed me—

"Lie silent for your life." And Cetewayo having bidden his retinue to depart outside the fence and await him there, followed after him.

They sat them down on either side of the smouldering fire and stared at each other through the thin smoke there in the gloom of the hut. By turning my head that the foot of the king had brushed as he passed, I could watch them both. Cetewayo spoke the first in a hoarse, slow voice, saying—

"Wizard, I am in danger of my life and I have come to you who know all the secrets of this land, that you may tell me in what place I may hide where the white men cannot find me. It must be told into my ear alone, since I dare not trust the matter to any other, at any rate until I must. They are traitors every man of them, yes, even those who seem to be most faithful. The fallen man has no friends, least of all if he chances to be a king. Only the dead will keep his counsel. Tell me of the place I need."

"Dingaan, who was before you, once asked this same thing of me, O King, when he was flying from Panda your father, and the Boers. I gave him advice that he did not take, but sought a refuge of his own upon a certain Ghost-mountain. What happened to him there that Mopo, of whom you spoke a while ago, can tell you if he still lives."*

[*—See Nada the Lily.—EDITOR.]

"Surely you are an ill-omened night-bird who thus croak to me continually of the death of kings," broke in Cetewayo with suppressed rage. Then calming himself with an effort added, "Tell me now, where shall I hide?"

"Would you know, King? Then hearken. On the south slope of the Ingome Range west of the Ibululwana River, on the outskirts of the great forest, there is a kloof whereof the entrance, which only one man can pass at a time, is covered by a thicket of thorns and marked by a black rock shaped like a great toad with an open mouth, or, as some say, like myself, 'The-Thing-that-should-never-have-been-born.' Near to this rock dwells an old woman, blind of one eye and lacking a hand, which the Black One cut off shortly before his death, because when he killed her father, she saw the future and prophesied a like death to him, although then she was but a child. This woman is of our company, being a witch-doctoress. I will send a Spirit to her, if you so will it, to warn her to watch for you and your company, O King, and show you the mouth of the kloof, where are some old huts and water. There you will never be found unless you are betrayed."

"Who can betray me when none know whither I am going?" asked Cetewayo. "Send the Spirit, send it at once, that this one-armed witch may make ready."

"What is the hurry, King, seeing that the forest is far away? Yet be it as you will. Keep silence now, lest evil should befall you."

Then of a sudden Zikali seemed to go off into one of his trances. His form grew rigid, his eyes closed, his face became fixed as though in death, and foam appeared upon his lips. He was a dreadful sight to look on, there in the gloomy hut.

Cetewayo watched him and shivered. Then he opened his blanket and I perceived that fastened about him by a loop of hide in such a fashion that it could be drawn out in a moment, was the blade of a broad assegai, the shaft of which was shortened to about six inches. His hand grasped this shaft, and I understood that he was contemplating the murder of Zikali. Then it seemed to me that he changed his mind and that his lips shaped the words—"Not yet," though whether he really spoke them I do not know. At least he withdrew his hand and closed the blanket.

Slowly Zikali opened his eyes, staring at the roof of the hut, whence came a curious sound as of squeaking bats. He looked like a dead man coming to life again. For a few moments he turned up his ear as though he listened to the squealing, then said—

"It is well. The Spirit that I summoned has visited her of our company who is named One-hand and returned with the answer. Did you not hear it speaking in the thatch, O King?"

"I heard something, Wizard," answered Cetewayo in an awed voice. "I thought it was a bat."

"A bat it is, O King, one with wide wings and swift. This bat says that my sister, One-hand, will meet you on the third day from now at this hour on the further side of the ford of the Ibululwana, where three milk-trees grow together on a knoll. She will be sitting under the centre milk-tree and will wait for two hours, no more, to show you the secret entrance to the kloof."

"The road is rough and long, I shall have to hurry when worn out with travelling," said Cetewayo.

"That is so, O King. Therefore my counsel is that you begin the journey as soon as possible, especially as I seem to hear the baying of the white dogs not far away."

"By Chaka's head! I will not," growled Cetewayo, "who thought to sleep here in peace this night."

"As the King wills. All that I have is the King's. Only then One-hand will not be waiting and some other place of hiding must be found, since this is known to me only and to her; also that Spirit which I sent will make no second journey, nor can I travel to show it to the King."

"Yes, Wizard, it is known to you and to myself. Methinks it would be better were it known to me alone. I have a spoonful of snuff to share (i.e., a bone to pick) with you, Wizard. It would seem that you set my feet and those of the Zulu people upon a false road, yonder in the Vale of Bones, causing me to declare war upon the white men and thereby bringing us all to ruin."

"Mayhap my memory grows bad, O King, for I do not remember that I did these things. I remember that the spirit of a certain Mameena whom I called up from the dead, prophesied victory to the King, which victory has been his. Also it prophesied other victories to the King in a far land across the water, which victories doubtless shall be his in due season; for myself I gave no 'counsel to the King or to his indunas and generals.'"

"You lie, Wizard," exclaimed Cetewayo hoarsely. "Did you not summon the shape of the Princess of Heaven to be the sign of war, and did she not hold in her hand that assegai of the Black One which you have told me was in your keeping? How did it pass from your keeping into the hand of a spirit?"

"As to that matter I have spoken, O King. For the rest, is Nomkubulwana my servant to come and go at my bidding?"

"I think so," said Cetewayo coldly. "I think also that you who know the place where I purpose to hide, would do well to forget it. Surely you have lived too long, O Opener of Roads, and done enough evil to the House of Senzangacona, which you ever hated."

So he spoke, and once more I saw his hand steal towards the spearhead which was hidden beneath the blanket that he wore.

Zikali saw it also and laughed. "Oho!" he laughed, "forgetting all my warnings, and that the day of my death will be his own, the King thinks to kill me because I am old and feeble and alone and unarmed. He thinks to kill me as the Black One thought, as Dingaan thought, as even Panda thought, yet I live on to this day. Well, I bear no malice since it is natural that the King should wish to kill one who knows the secret of where he would hide himself for his own life's sake. That spearhead which the King is fingering is sharp, so sharp that my bare breast cannot turn its edge. I must find me a shield! I must find me a shield! Fire, you are not yet dead. Awake, make smoke to be my shield!" and he waved his long, monkey-like arms over the embers, from which instantly there sprang up a reek of thin white smoke that appeared to take a vague and indefinite shape which suggested the shadow of a man; for to me it seemed a nebulous and wavering shadow, no more.

"What are you staring at, O King?" went on Zikali in a fierce and thrilling voice. "Who is it that you see? Who has the fire sent to be my shield? Ghosts are so thick here that I do not know. I cannot tell one of them from the other. Who is it? Who, who of all that you have slain and who therefore are your foes?"

"Umbelazi, my brother," groaned Cetewayo. "My brother Umbelazi stands before me with spear raised; he whom I brought to his death at the battle of the Tugela. His eyes flame upon me, his spear is raised to strike. He speaks words I cannot understand. Protect me, O Wizard! Lord of Spirits, protect me from the spirit of Umbelazi."

Zikali laughed wildly and continued to wave his arms above the fire from which smoke poured ever more densely, till the hut was full of it.

When it cleared away again Cetewayo was gone!

"Saw you ever the like of that?" said Zikali, addressing the kaross under which I was sweltering. "Tell me, Macumazahn."

"Yes," I answered, thrusting out my head as a tortoise does, "when in this very hut you seemed to produce the shape, also out of smoke, I think, of one whom I used to know. Say, how do you do it, Zikali?"

"Do it. Who knows? Perchance I do nothing. Perchance I think and you fools see, no more. Or perchance the spirits of the dead who are so near to us, come at my call and take themselves bodies out of the charmed smoke of my fire. You white men are wise, answer your own question, Macumazahn. At least that smoke or that ghost saved me from a spear thrust in the heart, wherewith Cetewayo was minded to pay me for showing him a hiding-place which he desired should be secret to himself alone. Well, well, I can pay as well as Cetewayo and my count is longer. Now lie you still, Macumazahn, for I go out to watch. He will not bide long in this place which he deems haunted and ill-omened. He will be gone ere sunset, that is within an hour, and sleep elsewhere."

Then he crept from the hut and presently, though I could see nothing, for now the gate of the fence was shut, I heard voices debating and finally that of Cetewayo say angrily—

"Have done! It is my will. You can eat your food outside of this place which is bewitched; the girl will show us where are the huts of which the wizard speaks."

A few minutes later Zikali crept back into the hut, laughing to himself.

"All is safe," he said, "and you can come out of your hole, old jackal. He who calls himself a king is gone, taking with him those whom he thinks faithful, most of whom are but waiting a chance to betray him. What did I say, a king? Nay, in all Africa there is no slave so humble or so wretched as this broken man. Oh! feather by feather I have plucked my fowl and by and by I shall cut his throat. You will be there, Macumazahn, you will be there."

"I trust not," I answered as I mopped my brow. "We have been near enough to throat-cutting this afternoon to last me a long while. Where has the king gone?"

"Not far, Macumazahn. I have sent Nombe to guide him to the huts in the little dip five spear throws to the right of the mouth of the kloof where live the old herdsman and his people who guard my cattle. He and all the rest are away with the cattle that are hidden in the Ceza Forest out of reach of the white men, so the huts are empty. Oh! now I read what you are thinking. I do not mean that he should be taken there. It is too near my house and the king still has friends."

"Why did you send Nombe?" I asked.

"Because he would have no other guide, who does not trust my men. He means to keep her with him for some days and then let her go, and thus she will be out of mischief. Meanwhile you and your friends can depart untroubled by her fancies, and join the white men who are near. Tomorrow you shall start."

"That is good," I said with a sigh of relief. Then an idea struck me and I added, "I suppose no harm will come to Nombe, who might be thought to know too much?"

"I hope not," he replied indifferently, "but that is a matter for her Spirit to decide. Now go, Macumazahn, for I am weary."

I also was weary after my prolonged seclusion under that very hot skin rug. For be it remembered I was not yet strong again, and although this was not the real reason why I had stopped behind when the others went to the plateau, I still grew easily tired. My real reason was that of Nombe—that I thought they preferred to be alone. I looked about me and saw with relief that Cetewayo and every man of his retinue were really gone. They had not even waited to eat the ox that had been killed for them, but had carried off the meat with other provisions to their sleeping-place outside the kloof. Having made sure of this I went to my hut and loosed Lost that fortunately enough had been unable to gnaw through the thick buffalo-hide riem with which I had fastened him to the pole.

He greeted me with rapture as though we had been parted for years. Had he belonged to Ulysses himself he could not have been more joyful. When one is despondent and lonesome, how grateful is the whole-hearted welcome of a dog which, we are sometimes tempted to think, is the only creature that really cares for us in the world. Every other living thing has side interests of its own, but that of a dog is centred in its master, though it is true that it also dreams affectionately of dinner and rabbits.

Then with Lost at my feet I sat outside the hut smoking and waiting for the return of Anscombe and Heda. Presently I caught sight of them in the gloaming. Their arms were around one another, and in some remarkable way they had managed to dispose their heads, forgetting that the sky was still light behind them, in such fashion that it was difficult to tell one from the other. I reflected that it was a good thing that at last we were escaping from this confounded kloof and country for one where they could marry and make an end, and became afflicted with a sneezing fit.

Heda asked where Nombe was and why supper was not ready, for Nombe played the part of cook and parlourmaid combined. I told her something of what had happened, whereon Heda, who did not appreciate its importance in the least, remarked that she, Nombe, might as well have put on the pot before she went and done sundry other things which I forget. Ultimately we got something to eat and turned in, Heda grumbling a little because she must sleep alone, for she had grown used to the company of the ever-watchful Nombe, who made her bed across the door-hole of the hut.

Anscombe was soon lost in dreams, if he did dream, but I could not sleep well that night. I was fearful of I knew not what, and so, I think, was Lost, for he fidgeted and kept poking me with his nose. At last, I think it must have been about two hours after midnight, he began to growl. I could hear nothing, although my ears are sharp, but as he went on growling I crept to the door-hole and drew aside the board. Lost slipped out and vanished, while I waited, listening. Presently I thought I heard a soft foot-fall and a whisper, also that I saw the shape of a woman which reminded me of Nombe, shown faintly by the starlight. It vanished in a moment and Lost returned wagging his tail, as he might well have done if it were Nombe who was attached to the dog. As nothing further happened I went back to bed, reflecting that I was probably mistaken, since Nombe had been sent away for some days by Zikali and would scarcely dare to return at once, even if she could do so.

Shortly before daylight Lost began to growl again in a subdued and thunderous fashion. This time I got up and dressed myself more or less. Then I went out. The dawn was just breaking and by its light I saw a strange scene. About fifty yards away in the narrow nek that ran over some boulders to the site of our huts, stood what seemed to be the goddess Nomkubulwana as I had seen her on the point of rock in the Vale of Bones. She wore the same radiant dress and in the dim glow had all the appearance of a white woman. I stood amazed, thinking that I dreamt, when from round the bend emerged a number of Zulus, creeping forward stealthily with raised spears.

They caught sight of the supernatural figure which barred their road, halted and whispered to each other. Then they turned to fly, but before they went one of them, as it seemed to me through sheer terror, hurled his assegai at the figure which remained still and unmoved.

In thirty seconds they were gone; in sixty their footsteps had died away. Then the figure wheeled slowly round and by the strengthening light I perceived that a spear transfixed its breast.

As it sank to the ground I ran up to it. It was Nombe with her face and arms whitened and her life-blood running down the glittering feather robe.

CHAPTER XXII

THE MADNESS OF NOMBE

The dog reached Nombe first and began to lick her face, its tongue removing patches of the white which had not had time to dry. She was lying, her back supported by one of the boulders. With her left hand she patted the dog's head feebly and with her right drew out the assegai from her body, letting it fall upon the ground. Recognizing me she smiled in her usual mysterious fashion and said—

"All is well, Macumazahn, all is very well. I have deserved to die and I do not die in vain."

"Don't talk, let me see your wound," I exclaimed.

She opened her robe and pointed; it was quite a small gash beneath the breast from which blood ebbed slowly.

"Let it be, Macumazahn," she said. "I am bleeding inside and it is mortal. But I shall not die yet. Listen to me while I have my mind. Yesterday when Mauriti and Heddana went up to the plain I wished to go with them because I had news that Zulus were wandering everywhere and thought that I might be able to protect my mistress from danger. Mauriti spoke to me roughly, telling me that I was not wanted. Of that I thought little, for to such words I am accustomed from him; moreover, they are to be forgiven to a man in love. But it did not end there, for my lady Heddana also pierced me with her tongue, which hurt more than this spear thrust does, Macumazahn, for I could see that her speech had been prepared and that she took this chance to throw it at me. She said that I did not know where I should sit; that I was a thorn beneath her nail, and that whenever she wished to talk with Mauriti, or with you, Macumazahn, I was ever there with my ear open like the mouth of a gourd. She commanded me in future to come only when I was called; all of which things I am sure Mauriti had taught her, who in herself is too gentle even to think them—unless you taught her, Macumazahn."

I shook my head and she went on—

"No, it was not you who also are too gentle, and having suffered yourself, can feel for those who suffer, which Mauriti who has never suffered cannot do. Still, you too thought me a trouble, one that sticks in the flesh like a hooked thorn, or a tick from the grass, and cannot be unfastened. You spoke to the Master about it and he spoke to me."

This time I nodded in assent.

"I do not blame you, Macumazahn; indeed now I see that you were wise, for what right has a poor black doctoress to seek the love, or even to look upon the face of the great white lady whom for a little while Fate has caused to walk upon the same path with her? But yesterday I forgot that, Macumazahn, for you see we are all of us, not one self, but many selves, and each self has its times of rule. Nombe alive and well was one woman, Nombe dying is another, and doubtless Nombe dead will be a third, unless, as she prays, she should sleep for ever.

"Macumazahn, those words of Heddana's were to me what gall is to sweet milk. My blood clotted and my heart turned sour. It was not against her that I was angry, because that can never happen, but against Mauriti and against you. My Spirit whispered in my ear. It said, 'If Mauriti and Macumazahn were dead the lady Heddana would be left alone in a strange land. Then she would learn to rest upon you as upon a stick, and learn to love the stick on which she rested, though it be so rough and homely.' But how can I kill them, I asked of my Spirit, and myself escape death?

"'Poison is forbidden to you by the pact between us,' answered my Spirit, 'yet I will show you a way, who am bound to serve you in all things good or ill.'

"Then we nodded to each other in my breast, Macumazahn, and I waited for what should happen who knew that my Spirit would not lie. Yes, I waited for a chance to kill you both, forgetting, as the wicked forget in their madness, that even if I were not found out, soon or late Heddana would guess the truth and then, even if she had learned to love me a thousand times more than she ever could, would come to hate me as a mother hates a snake that has slain her child. Or even if she never learned or guessed in life, after death she would learn and hunt me and spit on me from world to world as a traitoress and a murderer, one who has sinned past pardon."

Here she seemed to grow faint and I turned to seek for help. But she caught hold of my coat and said—

"Hear me out, Macumazahn, or I will run after you till I fall and die."

So thinking it best, I stayed and she went on—

"My Spirit, which must be an evil one since Zikali gave it me when I was made a doctoress, dealt truly with me, for presently the king and his people came. Moreover, my Spirit brought it about that the king would have no other guide but me to lead him to the kraal where he slept last night, and I went as though unwillingly. At the kraal the king sent for me and questioned me in a dark hut, pretending to be alone, but I who am a doctoress knew that two other men were in that hut, taking note of all my words. He asked me of the Inkosazana-y-Zulu who appeared in the Vale of Bones and of the little assegai she held in her hand, and of the magic of the Opener of Roads, and many other things. I said that I knew nothing of the Inkosazana, but that without doubt my Master was a great magician. He did not believe me. He threatened that I should be tortured very horribly and was about to call his servants to torment me till I told the truth. Then my Spirit spoke in my heart saying, 'Now the door is open to you, as I promised. Tell the king of the two white men whom the Master hides, and he will send to kill them, leaving the lady Heddana and you alone together.' So I pretended to be afraid and told him, whereon he laughed and answered—

"'For your sake I am glad, girl, that you have spoken the truth; besides it is useless to torture a witch, since then the spirit in her only vomits lies.'

"Next he called aloud and a man came, who it was I could not see in the dark. The king commanded him to take me to one of the other huts and tie me up there to the roof-pole. The man obeyed, but he did not tie me up; he only blocked the hut with the door-board, and sat with me there in the dark alone.

"Now I grew cunning and began to talk with him, spreading a net of sweet words, as the fowler spreads a net for cranes from which he would tear the crests. Soon by his talk I found out that the king and his people knew more than I guessed. Macumazahn, they had seen the cart which still stands under the overhanging rock by the mouth of the cave. I asked him if that were all, pretending that the cart belonged to my Master, to whom it had been brought from the field of Isandhlwana, that he might be drawn about in it, who was too weak to walk.

"The man said that if I would kiss him he would tell me everything. I bade him tell me first, swearing that then I would kiss him. Yes, Macumazahn, I, whom no man's lips have ever touched, fell as low as this. So he grew foolish and told me. He told me that they had also seen a kappje such as white women wear, hanging on the hut fence, and I remembered that after washing the headdress of my mistress I had set it there to dry in the sun. He told me also that the King suspected that she who wore that kappje was she who had played the part of the Inkosazana in the Vale of Bones. I asked him what the king would do about the matter, at the same time denying that there was any white woman in the Black Kloof. He said that at dawn the king would send and kill these foreign rats, whom the Opener of Roads kept in the thatch of his hut. Now he drew near and asked his pay. I gave it to him—with a knife-point, Macumazahn. Oh! that was a good thrust. He never spoke again. Then I slipped away, for all the others were asleep, and was here a little after midnight."

"I thought I saw you, Nombe," I said, "but was not sure, so I did nothing."

She smiled and answered—

"Ah! I was afraid that the Watcher-by-Night would be watching by night; also the dog ran up to me, but he knew me and I sent him back again. Now while I was coming home, thoughts entered my heart. I saw, as one sees by a lightning flash, all that I had done. The king and his people were not sure that the Master was hiding white folk here and would never have sent back to kill them on the chance. I had made them sure, as indeed, being mad, I meant to do. Moreover, in throwing spears at the kites I had killed my own dove, since it was on the false Inkosazana who had caused them to declare war and brought the land to ruin, that they wished to be avenged, and perchance on him who taught her her part, not on one or two wandering white men. I saw that when Cetewayo's people came, and there were many more of them outside, several hundreds I think, they would shave the whole head and burn the whole tree. Every one in the kloof would be killed.

"How could I undo the knot that I had tied and stamp out the fire that I had lit? That was the question. I bethought me of coming to you, but without arms how could you help? I bethought me of going to the Master, but I was ashamed. Also, what could he do with but a few servants, for the most of his people are away with the cattle? He is too weak to climb the steep path to the plain above, nor was there time to gather folk to carry him. Lastly, even if there were time which there was not, and we went thither they would track us out and kill us. For the rest I did not care, nor for myself, but that the lady Heddana should be butchered who was more to me than a hundred lives, and through my treachery—ah! for that I cared.

"I called on my Spirit to help me, but it would not come. My Spirit was dead in me because now I would do good and not ill. Yet another Spirit came, that of one Mameena whom once you knew. She came angrily, like a storm, and I shrank before her. She said, 'Vile witch, you have plotted to murder Macumazahn, and for that you shall answer to me before another sun has set over this earth of yours. Now you seek a way of escape from your own wickedness. Well, it can be had, but at a price.'

"'What price, O Lady of Death?' I asked.

"'The price of your own life, Witch.'

"I laughed into that ghost face of hers and said—

"'Is this all? Be swift and show me the way, O Lady of Death, and afterwards we will balance our account.'

"Then she whispered into the ear of my heart and was gone. I ran on, for the dawn was near. I whitened myself with lime, I put on the glittering cloak and powdered my hair with the sparkling earth. I took a little stick in my hand since I could find no spear and had no time to search, and just as day began to break, I crept out and stood in the bend of the path. The slayers came, twelve or so of them, but behind were many more. They saw the Inkosazana-y-Zulu barring their way and were much afraid. They fled, but out of his fright one of them threw a spear which went home, as I knew it would. He watched to see if I should fall, but I would not fall. Then he fled faster than the rest, knowing himself accursed who had lifted steel against the Queen of Heaven, and oh! I am glad, I am glad!"

She ceased, exhausted, yet with a great exultation in her beautiful eyes; indeed at that moment she looked a most triumphant creature. I stared at her, thrilled through and through. She had been wicked, no doubt, but how splendid was her end; and, thank Heaven! she was troubled with no thought of what might befall her after that end, although I was sure she believed that she would live again to face Mameena.

I knew not what to do. I did not like to leave her, especially as no earthly power could help her case, since slowly but quite surely she was bleeding to death from an internal wound. By now the sun was up and Zikali's people were about. One of them appeared suddenly and saw, then with a howl of terror turned to fly away.

"Fool! Fool!" I cried, "go summon the lady Heddana and the Inkosi Mauriti. Bid them come swiftly if they would see the doctoress Nombe before she dies."

The man leapt off like a buck, and within a few minutes I saw Heda and Anscombe running towards us, half dressed, and went to meet them.

"What is it?" she gasped.

"I have only time to tell you this," I answered. "Nombe is dying. She gave her life to save you, how I will explain afterwards. The assegai that pierced her was meant for your heart. Go, thank her, and bid her farewell. Anscombe, stop back with me."

We stood still and watched from a little distance. Heda knelt down and put her arms about Nombe. They whispered together into each other's ears. Then they kissed.

It was at this moment that Zikali appeared, leaning on two of his servants. By some occult art or instinct he seemed to know all that had happened, and oh! he looked terrible. He crouched down in front of the dying woman and, toadlike, spat his venom at her.

"You lost your Spirit, did you?" he said. "Well, it came back to me laden with the black honey of your treachery, to me, its home, as a bee comes to its hive. It has told me everything, and well for you, Witch, it is that you are dying. But think not that you shall escape me there in the world below, for thither I will follow you. Curses on you, traitress, who would have betrayed me and brought all my plans to naught. Ow! in a day to come I will pay you back a full harvest for this seed of shame that you have sown."

She opened her eyes and looked at him, then answered quite softly—

"I think your chain is broken, O Zikali, no more my master. I think that love has cut your chain in two and I fear you never more. Keep the spirit you lent to me; it is yours, but the rest of me is my own, and in the house of my heart another comes to dwell."

Then once more she stretched out her arms towards Heda and murmuring, "Sister, forget me not, Sister, who will await you for a thousand years," she passed away.

It was a good ending to a bad business, and I confess I felt glad when it was finished. Only afterwards I regretted very much that I had not found an opportunity to ask her whether or no she had masqueraded as Mameena in the Valley of Bones. Now it is too late.

We buried poor Nombe decently in her own little hut where she used to practise her incantations. Zikali and his people wished apparently to throw her to the vultures for some secret reason that had to do with their superstitions. But Heda, who, now that Nombe was dead, developed a great affection for her not unmixed with a certain amount of compunction for which really she had no cause, withstood him to his face and insisted upon a decent interment. So she was laid to earth still plastered with the white pigment and wrapped in the bloodstained feather robe. I may add that on the following morning one of Zikali's servants informed me solemnly that because of this she had been seen during the night riding up and down the rocks on a baboon as Zulu umtagati are supposed to do. I have small doubt that as soon as we were gone they dug her up again and threw her to the vultures and the jackals according to their first intention.

On this day we at length escaped from the Black Kloof, and in our own cart, for during the night our horses arrived mysteriously from somewhere, in good condition though rather wild. I went to say good-bye to Zikali, who said little, except that we should meet once more after many moons. Anscombe and Heda he would not see at all, but only sent them a message, to the effect that he hoped they would think kindly of him through the long years to come, since he had kept his promise and preserved them safe through many dangers. I might have answered that he had first of all put them into the dangers, but considered it wise to hold my tongue. I think, however, that he guessed my thought, if one can talk of guessing in connection with Zikali, for he said that they had no reason to thank him, since if he had served their turn they had served his, adding—

"It will be strange in the times to be for the lady Heddana to remember that it was she and no other who crumpled up the Zulus like a frostbitten winter reed, since had she not appeared upon the rock in the Valley of Bones, there would have been no war."

"She did not do this, you did it, Zikali," I said, "making her your tool through love and fear."

"Nay, Macumazahn, I did not do it; it was done by what you call God and I call Fate in whose hand I am the tool. Well, say to the lady Heddana that in payment I will hold back the ghost of Nombe from haunting her, if I can. Say also that if I had not brought her and her lover to Zululand they would have been killed."

So we went from that hateful kloof which I have never seen since and hope I shall never see again, two of Zikali's men escorting us until we got into touch with white people. To these we said as little as possible. I think they believed that we were only premature tourists who had made a dash into Zululand to visit some of the battlefields. Indeed none of us ever reported our strange adventures, and after my experience with Kaatje we were particularly careful to say nothing in the hearing of any gentleman connected with the Press. But as a matter of fact there were so many people moving about and such a continual coming and going of soldiers and their belongings, that after we had managed to buy some decent clothes, which we did at the little town of Newcastle, nobody paid any attention to us.

On our way to Maritzburg one amusing thing did happen. We met Kaatje! It was about sunset that we were driving up a steep hill not far from Howick. At least I was driving, but Anscombe and Heda were walking about a hundred yards ahead of the cart, when suddenly Kaatje appeared over a rise and came face to face with them while taking an evening stroll, or as I concluded afterwards, making some journey. She saw, she stared, she uttered one wild yell, and suddenly bundled over the edge of the road. Never would I have believed that such a fat woman could have run so fast. In a minute she was down the slope and had vanished into a dense kloof where, as night was closing in and we were very tired, it was impossible for us to follow her. Nor did subsequent inquiry in Howick tell us where she was living or whence she came, for some months before she had left the place she had taken there as a cook.

Such was the end of Kaatje so far as we were concerned. Doubtless to her dying day she remained, or will remain, a firm believer in ghosts.

Anscombe and Heda were married at Maritzburg as soon as the necessary formalities had been completed. I could not attend the ceremony, which was a disappointment to me and I hope to them, but unfortunately I had a return of my illness and was laid up for a week. Perhaps this was owing to the hot sun that struck me on the neck one afternoon coming down the Town Hill where I was obliged to hang on to the rear of the cart because the brakes had given out. However I was able to send Heda a wedding gift in the shape of her jewels and money that I recovered from the bank, which she had never expected to see again; also to arrange everything about her property.

They went down to Durban for their honeymoon and, some convenient opportunity arising, sailed thence for England. I received an affectionate letter from them both, which I still treasure, thanking me very much for all I had done for them, that after all was little enough. Also Anscombe enclosed a blank cheque, begging me to fill it in for whatever sum I considered he was indebted to me on the balance of account. I thought this very kind of him and a great mark of confidence, but the cheque remained blank.

I never saw either of them again, and though I believe that they are both living, for the most part abroad—in Hungary I think—I do not suppose that I ever shall. When I came to England some years later after King Solomon's mines had made me rich, I wrote Anscombe a letter. He never answered it, which hurt me at the time. Afterwards I remembered that in their fine position it was very natural that they should not wish to renew acquaintance with an individual who had so intimate a knowledge of certain incidents that they probably regarded as hateful, such as the deaths of Marnham and Dr. Rodd, and all the surrounding circumstances. If so, I daresay that they were wise, but of course it may have been only carelessness. It is so easy for busy and fashionable folk not to answer a rather troublesome letter, or to forget to put that answer in the post. Or, indeed, the letter may never have reached them— such things often go astray, especially when people live abroad. At any rate, perhaps through my own fault, we have drifted apart. I daresay they believe that I am dead, or not to be found somewhere in Africa. However, I always think of them with affection, for Anscombe was one of the best travelling companions I ever had, and his wife a most charming girl, and wonder whether Zikali's prophecy about their children will come true. Good luck go with them!

As it chances, since then I passed the place where the Temple stood, though at a little distance. I had the curiosity, however, at some inconvenience, to ride round and examine the spot. I suppose that Heda had sold the property, for a back-veld Boer, who was absent at the time, had turned what used to be Rodd's hospital into his house. Close by, grim and gaunt, stood the burnt-out marble walls of the Temple. The verandah was still roofed over, and standing on the spot whence I had shot the pistol out of Rodd's hand, I was filled with many memories.

I could trace the whole plan of the building and visited that part of it which had been Marnham's room. The iron safe that stood in the corner had been taken away, but the legs of the bedstead remained. Also not far from it, over grown with running plants, was a little heap which I took to be the ashes of his desk, for bits of burnt wood protruded. I grubbed among them with my foot and riding crop and presently came across the remains of a charred human skull. Then I departed in a hurry.

My way took me through the Yellow-wood grove, past the horns of the blue wildebeeste which still lay there, past that mud-hole also into which Rodd had fallen dead. Here, however, I made no more search, who had seen enough of bones. To this day I do not know whether he still lies beneath the slimy ooze, or was removed and buried.

Also I saw the site of our wagon camp where the Basutos attacked us. But I will have done with these reminiscences which induce melancholy, though really there is no reason why they should.

Tout lasse, tout casse, tout passe—everything wears out, everything crumbles, everything vanishes—in the words of the French proverb that my friend Sir Henry Curtis is so fond of quoting, that at last I wrote it down in my pocket-book, only to remember afterwards that when I was a boy I had heard it from the lips of an old scamp of a Frenchman, of the name of Leblanc, who once gave me and another lessons in the Gallic tongue. But of him I have already written in Marie, which is the first chapter in the Book of the fall of the Zulus. That headed Child of Storm is the second. These pages form the third and last.

Ah! indeed, tout lasse, tout casse, tout passe!

CHAPTER XXIII

THE KRAAL JAZI

Now I shall pass over all the Zulu record of the next four years, since after all it has nothing to do with my tale and I do not pretend to be writing a history.

Sir Garnet Wolseley set up his Kilkenny cat Government in Zululand, or the Home Government did it for him, I do not know which. In place of one king, thirteen chiefs were erected who got to work to cut the throats of each other and of the people.

As I expected would be the case, Zikali informed the military authorities of the secret hiding-place in the Ingome Forest where he suggested to Cetewayo that he should refuge. The ex-king was duly captured there and taken first to the Cape and then to England, where, after the disgrace of poor Sir Bartle Frere, an agitation had been set on foot on his behalf. Here he saw the Queen and her ministers, once more conquering, as it had been prophesied that he would by her who wore the shape of Mameena at the memorable scene in the Valley of Bones when I was present. Often I have thought of him dressed in a black coat and seated in that villa in Melbury Road in the suburb of London which I understand is populated by artists. A strange contrast truly to the savage prince receiving the salute of triumph after the Battle of the Tugela in which he won the kingship, or to the royal monarch to whose presence I had been summoned at Ulundi. However, he was brought back to Zululand again by a British man-of-war, re-installed to a limited chieftainship by Sir Theophilus Shepstone, and freed from the strangling embrace of the black coat.

Then of course there was more fighting, as every one knew would happen, except the British Colonial Office; indeed all Zululand ran with blood. For in England Cetewayo and his rights, or wrongs, had, like the Boers and their rights, or wrongs, become a matter of Party politics to which everything else must give way. Often I wonder whether Party politics will not in the end prove the ruin of the British Empire. Well, thank Heaven, I shall not live to learn.

So Cetewayo came back and fought and was defeated by those who once had been his subjects. Now for the last scene, that is all with which I need concern myself.

At the beginning of February, 1884, business took me to Zululand; it had to do with a deal in cattle and blankets. As I was returning towards the Tugela who should I meet but friend Goza, he who had escorted me from the Black Kloof to Ulundi before the outbreak of war, and who afterwards escorted me and that unutterable nuisance, Kaatje, out of the country. At first I thought that we came together by accident, or perhaps that he had journeyed a little way to thank me for the blankets which I had sent to him, remembering my ancient promise, but afterwards I changed my opinion on this point.

Well, we talked over many matters, the war, the disasters that had befallen Zululand, and so forth. Especially did we talk of that night in the Valley of Bones and the things we had seen there side by side. I asked him if the people still believed in the Inkosazana-y-Zulu who then appeared in the moonlight on the rock. He answered that some did and some did not. For his part, he added, looking at me fixedly, he did not, since it was rumoured that Zikali had dressed up a white woman to play the part of the Spirit. Yet he could not be sure of the matter, since it was also said that when some of Cetewayo's people went to kill this white woman in the Black Kloof, Nomkubulwana, the Princess of Heaven herself, rose before them and frightened them away.

I remarked that this was very strange, and then quite casually asked him whom Zikali had dressed up to play the part of the dead Mameena upon that same occasion, since this was a point upon which I always thirsted for definite intelligence. He stared at me and replied that I ought to be able to answer my own question, since I had been much nearer to her who looked like Mameena than any one else, so near indeed that all present distinctly saw her kiss me, as it was well known she had liked to do while still alive. I replied indignantly that they saw wrong and repeated my question. Then he answered straight out—

"O Macumazahn, we Zulus believe that what we saw on that night was not Nombe or another dressed up, but the spirit of the witch Mameena itself. We believe it because we could see the light of Zikali's fire through her, not always, but sometimes; also because all that she said has come true, though everything is not yet finished."

I could get no more out of him about the matter, for when I tried to speak of it again, he turned the subject, telling me of his wonderful escapes during the war. Presently he rose to go and said casually—

"Surely I grow old in these times of trouble, Macumazahn, for thoughts slip through my head like water through the fingers. Almost I had forgotten what I wished to say to you. The other day I met Zikali, the Opener of Roads. He told me that you were in Zululand and that I should meet you—he did not say where, only that when I did meet you, I was to give you a message. This was the message—that when on your way to Natal you came to the kraal Jazi, you would find him there; also another whom you used to know, and must be sure not to go away without seeing him, since that was about to happen in which you must take your part."

"Zikali!" I exclaimed. "I have heard nothing of him since the war. I thought that by now he was certainly dead."

"Oh! no, Macumazahn, he is certainly not dead, but just the same as ever. Indeed it is believed that he and no other has kept all this broth of trouble on the boil, some say for Cetewayo's sake, and some say because he wishes to destroy Cetewayo. But what do I know of such matters who only desire to live in peace under whatever chief the English Queen sends to us, as she has a right to do having conquered us in war? When you meet the Opener of Roads at the kraal Jazi, ask him, Macumazahn."

"Where the devil is the kraal Jazi?" I inquired with irritation. "I never heard of such a place."

"Nor did I, therefore I cannot tell you, Macumazahn. For aught I can say it may be down beneath where dead men go. But wherever it is there certainly you will meet the Opener of Roads. Now farewell, Macumazahn. If it should chance that we never look into each other's eyes again, I am sure you will think of me sometimes, as I shall of you, and of all that we have seen together, especially on that night in the Vale of Bones when the ghost of the witch Mameena prophesied to us and kissed you before us all. She must have been very beautiful, Macumazahn, as indeed I have heard from those who remember her, and I don't wonder that you loved her so much. Still for my part I had rather be kissed by a living woman than by one who is dead, though doubtless it is best to be kissed by none at all. Again, farewell, and be sure to tell the Opener of Roads that I gave you his message, lest he should lay some evil charm upon me, who have seen enough evil of late."

Thus talking Goza departed. I never saw him again, and do not know if he is dead or alive. Well, he was a kindly old fellow, if no hero.

I had almost forgotten the incident of this meeting when a while later I found myself in the neighbourhood of the beautiful but semi-tropical place called Eshowe, which since those days has become the official home of the British Resident in Zululand. Indeed, although the house was not then finished, if it had been begun, Sir Melmoth Osborn already had an office there. I wished to see him in order to give him some rather important information, but when I reached a kraal of about fifty huts some five hundred yards from the site of the present Residency, my wagon stuck fast in the boggy ground. While I was trying to get it out a quiet-faced Zulu, whose name, I remember, was Umnikwa, informed me that Malimati, that is Sir Melmoth Osborn's native name, was somewhere at a little distance from Eshowe, too far away for me to get to him that night. I answered, Very well, I would sleep where I was, and asked the name of the kraal.

He replied, Jazi, at which I started, but only said that it was a strange name, seeing that it meant "Finished," or "Finished with joy." Umnikwa answered, Yes, but that it had been so called because the chief Umfokaki, or The Stranger, who married a sister of the king, was killed at this kraal by his brother,

Gundane, or the Bat. I remarked that it was an ill-omened kind of name, to which the man replied, Yes, and likely to become more so, since the King Cetewayo who had been sheltering there "beneath the armpit" of Malimati, the white lord, for some months, lay in it dying. I asked him of what he was dying, and he replied that he did not know, but that doubtless the father of the witch-doctors, named Zikali, the Opener of Roads, would be able to tell me, as he was attending on Cetewayo.

"He has sent me to bid you to come at once, O Macumazahn," he added casually, "having had news that you were arriving here."

Showing no surprise, I answered that I would come, although goodness knows I was surprised enough, and leaving my servants to get my wagon out of the bog, I walked into the kraal with the messenger. He took me to a large hut placed within a fence about the gate of which some women were gathered, who all looked very anxious and disturbed. Among them I saw Dabuko the king's brother, whom I knew slightly. He greeted me and told me that Cetewayo was at the point of death within the hut, but like Umnikwa, professed ignorance of the cause of his illness.

For a long while, over an hour I should think, I sat there outside the hut, or walked to and fro. Until darkness came I could occupy myself with contemplating the scenery of the encircling hills, which is among the most beautiful in Zululand with its swelling contours and rich colouring. But after it had set in only my thoughts remained, and these I found depressing.

At length I made up my mind that I would go away, for after all what had I to do with this business of the death of Cetewayo, if in truth he was dying? I wished to see no more of Cetewayo of whom all my recollections were terrific or sorrowful. I rose to depart, when suddenly a woman emerged from the hut. I could not see who she was or even what she was like, because of the gloom; also for the reason that she had the corner of her blanket thrown over her face as though she wished to keep it hidden. For a moment she stopped opposite to me and said—

"The king who is sick desires to see you, Macumazahn." Then she pointed to the door-hole of the hut and vanished, shutting the gate of the fence behind her. Curiosity overcame me and I crawled into the hut, pushing aside the door-board in order to do so and setting it up again when I was through.

Inside burned a single candle fixed in the neck of a bottle, faintly illuminating that big and gloomy place. By its feeble light I saw a low bedstead on the left of the entrance and lying on it a man half covered by a blanket in whom I recognized Cetewayo. His face was shrunken and distorted with pain, and his great bulk seemed less, but still without doubt it was Cetewayo.

"Greeting, Macumazahn," he said feebly, "you find me in evil case, but I heard that you were here and thought that I should like to see you before I die, because I know that you are honest and will report my words faithfully. I wish you to tell the white men that my heart never really was against them; they have always been the friends of my heart, but others forced me down a road I did not wish to travel, of which now I have come to the end."

"What is the matter with you, King?" I asked.

"I do not know, Macumazahn, but I have been sick for some days. The Opener of Roads who came to doctor me, because my wives believed those white medicine-men wished me dead, says that I have been poisoned and must die. If you had been here at first you might perhaps have given me some medicine. But now it is too late," he added with a groan.

"Who then poisoned you, King?"

"I cannot tell you, Macumazahn. Perhaps my enemies, perhaps my brothers, perhaps my wives. All wish to have done with me, and the Great One, who is no longer wanted, is soon dead. Be thankful, Macumazahn, that you never were a king, for sad is the lot of kings."

"Where, then, is the Opener of Roads?" I asked.

"He was here a little while ago. Perhaps he has gone out to take the King's head" (i.e., to announce his death) "to Malimati and the white men," he answered in a faint voice.

Just then I heard a shuffling noise proceeding from that part of the hut where the shadow was deepest, and looking, saw an emaciated arm projected into the circle of the light. It was followed by another arm, then by a vast head covered with long white hair that trailed upon the ground, then by a big, misshapen body, so wasted that it looked like a skeleton covered with corrugated black skin. Slowly, like a chameleon climbing a bough, the thing crept forward, and I knew it for Zikali. He reached the side of the bed and squatted down in his toad-like fashion, then, again like a chameleon, without moving his head turned his deep and glowing eyes towards me.

"Hail, O Macumazahn," he said in his low voice. "Did I not promise you long ago that you should be with me at the last, and are you not with me and another?"

"It seems so, Zikali," I answered. "But why do you not send for the white doctors to cure the king?"

"All the doctors, white and black, in the whole world cannot cure him, Macumazahn. The Spirits call him and he dies. At his call I came fast and far, but even I cannot cure him—although because of him I myself must die."

"Why?" I asked.

"Look at me, Macumazahn, and say if I am one who should travel. Well, all come to their end at last, even the 'Thing-that-should-never-have-been-born.'"

Cetewayo lifted his head and looked at him, then said heavily—

"Perchance it would have been better for our House if that end had been sooner. Now that I lie dying many sayings concerning you come into my mind that I had forgotten. Moreover, Opener of Roads, I never sent for you, whoever may have done so, and it was not until after you came here that the great pain seized me. How did it happen," he went on with gathering force, "that the white men caught me in the secret place where you told me I should hide? Who pointed out that hidden hole to the white men? But what does it matter now?"

"Nothing at all, O Son of Panda," answered Zikali, "even less than it matters how I escaped the spear-head hidden in your robe, yonder in my hut in the Black Kloof where, had it not been for a certain spirit that stood between you and me, you would have murdered me. Tell me, Son of Panda, during these last three days have you thought at all of your brother Umbelazi, and of certain other brethren of yours whom you killed at the battle of the Tugela, when the white man here led the charge of the Amawombe against your regiments and ate up three of them?"

Cetewayo groaned but said nothing. I think he had become too faint to speak.

"Listen, Son of Panda," went on Zikali in an intense and hissing voice. "Many, many years ago, before Senzangacona, your grandfather, saw the light—who knows how long before—a man was born of high blood in the Dwandwe tribe, which man was a dwarf. Chaka the Black One conquered the Dwandwe, but this man of high blood was spared because he was a dwarf, an abortion, to whom Chaka gave the name of the 'Thing-that-never-should-have-been-born,' keeping him about him to be a mock in times of peace and safety, and because he was wise and learned in magic, to be a counsellor in times of trouble. Moreover, Chaka killed this man's wives and children for his sport, save one whom he kept to be his 'sister.'

"Therefore for the sake of his people and his butchered wives and children, this wizard swore an oath of vengeance against Chaka and all his House. Working beneath the ground like a rat, he undermined the throne of Chaka and brought him to his death by the spears of his brethren and of Mopo his servant, whom Chaka had wronged. Still working in the dark like a rat, he caused Dingaan, who stabbed Chaka, to murder the Boer Retief and his people, and thus called down upon his head the vengeance of the Whites, and afterwards brought Dingaan to his death. Then Panda, your father, arose, and his life this 'Thing-that-never-should-have-been-born' spared because once Panda had done him a kindness. Only through the witch Mameena he brought sorrow on him, causing war to arise between his children, one of whom was named Cetewayo.

"Then this Cetewayo ruled, first with his father Panda and afterwards in his place, and trouble arose between him and the English. Son of Panda, you will remember that this Cetewayo was in doubt whether to fight the English and demanded a sign of the Thing-that-never-should-have-been-born. He gave the sign, causing the Inkosazana-y-Zulu, the Princess of Heaven, to appear before him and thereby lifting the spear of War. Son of Panda, you know how that war went, how this Cetewayo was defeated and came to the 'Thing-that-never-should-have-been-born' like a hunted hyena, to learn of a hole where he might hide. You know, too, how he strove to murder the poor old doctor who showed him such a hole; how he was taken prisoner and sent across the water and afterwards set up again in the land that had learned to hate him, to bring its children to death by thousands. And you know how at last he took refuge beneath the wing of the white chief, here in the kraal Jazi, and lived, spat upon, an outcast, until at length he fell sick, as such men are apt to do, and the Thing-that-never-should-have-been-born was sent for to doctor him. And you know also how he lies dying, within him an agony as though he had swallowed a red hot spear, and before him a great blackness peopled by the ghosts of those whom he has slain, and of his forefathers whose House he has pulled down and burned."

Zikali ceased, and thrusting his hideous head to within an inch or two of that of the dying man, he glowered at him with his fierce and fiery eyes. Then he began to whisper into the king's ear, who quivered at his words, as the victim quivers beneath the torturer's looks.

At that moment the end of the candle fell into the bottle which was of clear white glass, and there burned for a little while dully before it went out. Never shall I forget the scene illumined by its blue and ghastly light. The dying man lying on the low couch, rocking his head to and fro; the wizard bending over him like some grey vampire bat sucking the life-blood from his helpless throat. The terror in the eyes of the one, the insatiable hate in the eyes of the other. Oh! it was awful!

"Macumazahn," gasped Cetewayo in a rattling whisper, "help me, Macumazahn. I say that I am poisoned by this Zikali, who hates me. Oh! drive away the ghosts! Drive them away!"

I looked at him and at his tormentor squatted by him like a mocking fiend, and as I looked the candle went out.

Then my nerve broke, the cold sweat poured from my face and I fled from the hut as a man might from a scene in hell, followed by the low mocking laugh of Zikali.

Outside the women and others were gathered in the gloom. I told them to go to the king, who was dying, and blundered up the slope to search for some white man. No one was to be found, but a Kaffir messenger by the office told me that Malimati was still away and had been sent for. So I returned to my wagon and lay down in it exhausted, for what more could I do?

It was a rough night. Thunder muttered and rain fell in driving gusts. I dozed off, only to be awakened by a sound of wailing. Then I knew that the king was dead, for this was the Isililo, the cry of mourning. I wondered whether the murderers—for that he was poisoned I had no doubt—were among those who wailed.

Towards dawn the storm rolled off and the night grew serene and clear, for a waning moon was shining in the sky. The heat of that stiffing place oppressed me; my blood seemed to be afire. I knew that there was a stream in a gorge about half a mile away, for it had been pointed out to me. I longed for a swim in cool water, who, to tell truth, had found none for some days, and bethought me that I would bathe in this stream before I trekked from that hateful spot, for to me it had become hateful. Calling my driver, who was awake and talking with the voorloopers, for they knew what was passing at the kraal and were alarmed, I told them to get the oxen ready to start as I would be back presently. Then I set off for the stream and, after a longish walk, scrambled down a steep ravine to its banks, following a path made by Kaffir women going to draw water. Arrived there at last I found that it was in flood and rising rapidly, at least so I judged from the sound, for in that deep, tree-hung place the light was too faint to allow me to see anything. So I sat down waiting for the dawn and wishing that I had not come because of the mosquitoes.

At length it broke and the mists lifted, showing that the spot was one of great beauty. Opposite to me was a waterfall twenty or thirty feet high, over which the torrent rushed into a black pool below. Everywhere grew tall ferns and beyond these graceful trees, from whose leaves hung raindrops. In the centre of the stream on the edge of the fall was a rock not a dozen feet away from me, round which the water foamed. Something was squatted on this rock, at first I could not see what because of the mist, but thought that it was a grey-headed baboon, or some other animal, and regretted that I had not brought a gun with me. Presently I became aware that it must be a man, for, in a chanting voice, it began to speak or pray in Zulu, and hidden behind a flowering bush, I could hear the words. They were to this effect—

"O my Spirit, here where thou foundest me when I was young, hundreds of years ago" (he said hundreds, but I suppose he meant tens), "I come back to thee. In this pool I dived and beneath the waters found thee, my Snake, and thou didst wind thyself about my body and about my heart" (here I understood that the speaker was alluding to his initiation as a witch-doctor which generally includes, or used to include, the finding of a snake in a river that coils itself about the neophyte). "About my body and in my heart thou hast dwelt from that sun to this, giving me wisdom and good and evil counsel, and that which thou hast counselled, I have done. Now I return thee whence thou camest, there to await me in the new birth.

"O Spirits of my fathers, toiling through many years I have avenged you on the House of Senzangacona, and never again will there be a king of the Zulus, for the last of them lies dead by my hand. O my murdered wives and my children, I have offered up to you a mighty sacrifice, a sacrifice of thousands upon thousands.

"O Umkulu-kulu, Great One of the heavens, who sentest me to earth, I have done thy work upon the earth and bring back to thee thy harvest of the seed that thou hast sown, a blood-red harvest, O Umkulu-kulu. Be still, be still, my Snake, the sun arises, and soon, soon shalt thou rest in the water that wast thine from the beginning of the world!"

The voice ceased, and presently a spear of light piercing the mists, lit upon the speaker. It was Zikali and about him was wound a great yellow-bellied snake, of which the black head with flickering tongue waved above his head and seemed from time to time to lick him on the brow. (I suppose it had come to him from the water, for its skin glittered as though with wet.) He stood up on tottering feet, staring at the red eye of the rising sun, then crying, "Finished, finished with joy!" with a loud and dreadful laughter, he plunged into the foaming pool beneath.

Such was the end of Zikali the Wizard, Opener of Roads, the "Thing-that-should-never-have-been-born," and such was the vengeance that he worked upon the great House of Senzangacona, bringing it to naught and with it the nation of the Zulus.

H. Rider Haggard – A Short Biography

Sir Henry Rider Haggard, KBE was born on June 22nd, 1856 at Bradenham in Norfolk, England.

More familiarly known as H. Rider Haggard, he was the eighth of ten children born to Sir William Meybohm Rider Haggard, a barrister (born, incidentally, in St Petersburg, Russia), and Ella Doveton, an author, poet and daughter of a merchant in the East India Trading Company.

Haggard was initially schooled at Garsington Rectory in Oxfordshire where he studied under the tutelage of Reverend H. J. Graham. His elder brothers, who seemed to find more favour with their father, graduated from various private schools whilst Haggard was sent to Ipswich Grammar School, saving his father a considerable sum in fees.

He failed his army entrance exam, and was therefore sent to a private crammer in London in preparation for the entrance exam to the British Foreign Office, which he appears never to have sat. However, it was during his two years in London that Haggard came into contact with a circle of people interested in the study of psychical phenomena and for which he too now developed a life-long interest together with a series of enduring friendships.

In 1875, Haggard's father used his family's connections to send him to Southern Africa to take up an unpaid position as assistant to the secretary to Sir Henry Bulwer, Lieutenant-Governor of the Colony of Natal. In 1876 he was transferred to the staff of Sir Theophilus Shepstone, Special Commissioner for the Transvaal. It was in this role that Haggard was present in Pretoria in April 1877 for the official announcement of the British annexation of the Boer Republic of the Transvaal. The official who had been nominated to read out the Proclamation lost his voice and Haggard was his replacement. It was a moment in history.

Haggard was to remain in the country for six years, during which time he served as Master of the High Court of the Transvaal and an adjutant of the Pretoria Horse.

It was here that he fell in love with Mary Elizabeth "Lilly" Jackson. He hoped to marry her once he obtained more certainty in his career path.

In 1878 he became Registrar of the High Court in the Transvaal and now the time seemed opportune to write to his father to tell him of his hope to marry. The reply from his father was uncompromising. He forbade it until his son had made a proper career for himself.

The following year, 1879, Lily married Frank Archer, a well-to-do banker.

Haggard returned briefly to England to marry a friend of his sister's, Marianna Louisa Margitson, a 21 year old, in 1880, and the couple travelled to Africa together. Haggard's years in Africa had proved, at least on a writing level, rich and inspirational for him, and while still in Natal he wrote two articles for The Gentleman's Magazine describing his experiences.

Moving back to England in (and accounts here differ as to whether it was 1881 or 1882) the couple settled in Ditchingham, Norfolk, Louisa's ancestral home. Later they moved to Kessingland and established connections with the church in Bungay, Suffolk. The marriage produced four children. A son named Jack (who tragically died at age 10 of measles) and three daughters, Angela, Dorothy and Lilias. (Lilias grew to become an author and her father's biographer.)

In England Law was to be the fulcrum of his career. However, although he studied, writing was growing in its appeal to him. His first book, Cetywayo and His White Neighbours, was an account and study of Britain's policies in South Africa.

From this point his career as a writer began to take substantial hold and with it a dramatic shift to fiction. Two years later he published his first fiction, Dawn followed in 1885 by arguably his most popular novel, King Solomon's Mines—detailing the life of the adventurer Allan Quatermain. This was followed the following year, 1886, by She: A History of Adventure, which introduced the female character Ayesha. Both characters, Quatermain and Ayesha, developed a series of books about their adventures.

The study of Law now fell away entirely. He appeared also to have a keen sense of his commercial appreciation. Rather than sell the copyright of his first best-seller, King Solomon's Mines, for a £100 fee he, instead, accepted a 10% royalty. This book is also generally accepted as the first of the Lost World writing genre.

Haggard obviously thought there were many further adventures to tell and it would be hard to find a publisher who would disagree given the start he had made. Sequels soon followed. Allan Quatermain continued his epic and swash-buckling adventures in Africa whilst the sequel to She entitled Ayesha played out her adventures in Tibet. Interestingly Haggard would later extend his characters adventures around the world with Eric Brighteyes, being the basis for an epic Viking romance.

The Haggard family lived at 69 Gunterstone Road in Hammersmith, London, from mid-1885 to mid-1888. It was here that he wrote his most famous works. His time in Africa had given him the experience and atmosphere as well as several observations and friendships of the people who would so influence his fictional characters. Chief among them were the larger-than-life adventurers Frederick Selous and Frederick Russell Burnham. Both were men of Empire and huge ambition as they helped uncover the great mineral wealth of Africa, as well as the ruins of ancient lost civilisations of the continent, such as Great Zimbabwe.

Three of Haggard's books, The Wizard (1896), Black Heart and White Heart; a Zulu Idyll (1896), and Elissa; the Doom of Zimbabwe (1898), are dedicated to Burnham's daughter Nada, the first white child born in Bulawayo; she had been named after Haggard's 1892 book Nada the Lily.

As is typical of the writing of the time his novels contain many of the stereotypes associated with colonialism, yet they also sympathise, to a degree, with the native populations. Africans often play heroic roles in the novels, although the protagonists are more often than not European. The time around the turn of the century was, after all, the great sprint to Empire by many European countries intent on gaining possessions of land, people and resources.

Three of Haggard's novels were written in collaboration with his friend Andrew Lang who shared his interest in the spiritual realm and paranormal phenomena and who was also a greatly admired editor.

Haggard's stories are still widely read today. Ayesha, the female protagonist of She, has been cited as a prototype by psychoanalysts such as Sigmund Freud (in The Interpretation of Dreams) and Carl Jung. Her epithet is, of course, "She Who Must Be Obeyed" and has for decades been used tongue-in-cheek to describe the presumed balance of influence between the sexes.

As a legacy it is easy to establish Haggard, and his pioneering work, as the author of the Lost World branch of writing and its influence of such other writers as Edgar Rice Burroughs, Robert E. Howard and Talbot Mundy. The Allan Quatermain character influenced many 'serials' in Hollywood during the 30s & 40s and can readily be seen as a template for Indiana Jones, the American archaeologist and explorer and huge box office film character.

Years later, when Haggard was a successful novelist, he was contacted by his former love, Lilly Archer, née Jackson. Lily had been deserted by her husband, who had embezzled funds and fled bankrupt to Africa. Haggard installed her and her sons in a house and saw to the children's education. Lilly eventually followed her husband to Africa, where he infected her with syphilis before dying of it himself. Lilly returned to England in late 1907, where Haggard again supported her until her death on April 22nd, 1909.

Haggard also wrote about agricultural and social reform, in part inspired by his experiences in Africa, but also based on what he saw in Europe. By the end of his life, he was adamantly opposed to Bolshevism, a position that he shared with his life-long friend Rudyard Kipling. The two had found friendship upon Kipling's arrival at London in 1889 largely on the strength of their shared opinions.

Haggard was extremely interested in the social affairs of the Country and eager to play a more active part in attempting reform. In 1895 he stood unsuccessfully for Parliament as a Conservative candidate for the Eastern division of Norfolk losing by 198 votes.

Also in 1895 he served on a government commission to examine Salvation Army labour colonies. This, and his heavy involvement in agriculture reform, led to him being a member of several further commissions on land use and related affairs, work that involved several trips to the Colonies and Dominions. This work, in part, helped lead to the passage of the 1909 Development Bill.

In 1911 he served on the Royal Commission examining coastal erosion.

He was an absorbed and dedicated writer of letters to The Times, nearly one hundred were published by them and the bibliography attached below reveals much in the range of subjects he wished to bring attention to.

He was made a Knight Bachelor in 1912 and a Knight Commander of the Order of the British Empire in 1919. Haggard was a member of several clubs including the Athenaeum, Savile, and Authors' clubs.

The district of Rider in British Columbia, Canada, was named in his honour.

Henry Rider Haggard died on May 14th, 1925 at the age of 68. His ashes were buried at Ditchingham Church. His papers are held at the Norfolk Record Office.

The first chapter of his book People of the Mist (1894) is credited with inspiring the 1912 motto of the Royal Air Force (formerly the Royal Flying Corps), Per ardua ad astra. "Through adversity to the stars" (or alternately "Through struggle to the stars") it is also used by other Commonwealth air forces such as the RAAF, RCAF, RNZAF, and the SAAF.

H. Rider Haggard – A Concise Bibliography

Novels
Dawn (1884) Published in three volumes
The Witch's Head (1884) Published in three volumes
King Solomon's Mines (1885) Allan Quatermain series
She: A History of Adventure (1886) Ayesha series
Allan Quatermain (1887) Allan Quatermain series
Jess (1887)
A Tale of Three Lions (1887) Allan Quatermain series
Maiwa's Revenge, or the War of the Little Hand (1888) Allan Quatermain series
Colonel Quaritch, VC (1889) Published in three volumes
Cleopatra (1889)
Beatrice (1890)
The World's Desire (1890) Co-written with Andrew Lang

Eric Brighteyes (1891)
Nada the Lily (1892)
An Heroic Effort (1893)
Montezuma's Daughter (1893)
The People of the Mist (1894)
Heart of the World (1895)
Joan Haste (1895)
The Wizard (1896)
Doctor Therne (1898)
Swallow: A Tale of the Great Trek (1899)
Lysbeth (1901)
Pearl Maiden (1903)
Stella Fregelius: A Tale of Three Destinies (1903)
The Brethren (1904)
Ayesha: The Return of She (1905) Ayesha series
The Way of the Spirit (1906)
Benita (1906)
Fair Margaret (1907)
The Ghost Kings(1908)
The Yellow God (1908)
The Lady of Blossholme (1909)
Morning Star (1910)
Queen Sheba's Ring (1910)
Red Eve (1911)
The Mahatma and the Hare (1911)
Marie (1912) Allan Quatermain series
Child of Storm (1913) Allan Quatermain series
The Wanderer's Necklace (1914)
The Holy Flower (1915) Allan Quatermain series
The Ivory Child (1916) Allan Quatermain series
Finished (1917) Allan Quatermain series]
Love Eternal (1918)
Moon of Israel (1918)
When the World Shook (1919)
The Ancient Allan (1920) Allan Quatermain series
She and Allan (1921) Allan Quatermain series / Ayesha series
The Virgin of the Sun (1922)
Wisdom's Daughter (1923) Ayesha series
Heu-Heu (1924) Allan Quatermain series]
Queen of the Dawn (1925)
The Treasure of the Lake (1926) Allan Quatermain series
Allan and the Ice-Gods (1927) Allan Quatermain series
Mary of Marion Isle (1929)
Belshazzar (1930)

Short Story Collections
Allan's Wife and Other Tales (1889)

Black Heart and White Heart: A Zulu Idyll (1900)
Smith and the Pharaohs (1920)

Publications in Periodicals and Newspapers
A Zulu War-Dance (July 1877) The Gentleman's Magazine
A Visit to the Chief (September 1877) The Gentleman's Magazine
Hydrophobia (letter) (3 November 1885) The Times
The Land Question (letter) (28 April 1886) The Times
About Fiction (February 1887) The Contemporary Review
Mr Rider Haggard and His Critics (letter) (27 April 1887) The Times
Our Position in Cyprus (July 1887) The Contemporary Review
American Copyright (letter) (11 October 1887) The Times
On Going Back (November 1887) Longman's Magazine
Delagoa Bay (letter) (17 December 1887) The Times
South African Policy (letter) (27 December 1887) The Times
Suggested Prologue to a Dramatised Version of She (March 1888) Longman's Magazine
Mr. Meeson's Will (18 June 1888) The Illustrated London News
The Wreck of the Copeland (18 August 1888) The Illustrated London News
Cleopatra (3 December 1888) The Illustrated London News
Hydrophobia and Muzzling (letter) (25 October 1889) The Times
The Annals of Natal (23 November 1889) The Saturday Review
Mummy at St Mary/Woolnoth's (letter) (25 December 1889) The Times
Mummies (letter) (27 December 1889) The Times
The Fate of Swaziland (January 1890) The New Review
In Memoriam (17 May 1890) Thompson's Seasons
American Copyright (letter) (5 June 1890) The Times
Mr Herbert Ward and Mr Stanley (10 November 1890) The Times
Nada the Lily (2 January 1892) The Illustrated London News
A New Argument Against Creation (19 December 1892) The Times
My First Book. Dawn. By H. Rider Haggard (April 1893) The Idler
The Tale of Isandlwana and Rorke's Drift (4 October 1893) The True Story Book
Lobengula (letter) (19 October 1893) The Times
The New Sentiment (letter) (6 November 1893) The Times
Wanted—Imagination   (25 December 1893) The Times
The Fate of Captain Patterson's Party (28 December 1893) The Times
The Three Volume Novel (letter) (27 July 1894) The Times
The Adventures of John Gladwyn Jebb (letter) (30 October 1894) The Times
Agriculture in Norfolk (letter) (30 October 1894) The Times
The Nelson Bazaar (letter) (16 February 1895) The Times
Everything is Peaceful (letter) (20 March 1895) The Times
Lord Kimberley in Norfolk (letter) (17 April 1895) The Times
The East Norfolk Election (letter) (23 July 1895) The Times
The East Norfolk Election (letter) (29 July 1895) The Times
Wilson's Last Fight (7 October 1895) The True Story Book
The Crisis in the Transvaal (letter) (2 January 1896) The Times
The Transvaal Crisis (letter) (13 January 1896) The Times
Jameson's Surrender (letter) (14 March 1896) The Times

The Rinderpest in South Africa (letter) (5 November 1896) The Times
Mr Rider Haggard and Dr Neufeld (letter) (9 January 1899) The Times
Shrinkage of Population in Agricultural Districts (letter) (9 May 1899) The Times
The South African Crisis—An Appeal (letter) (1 July 1899) The Times
Commandant-General Joubert and Mr H Rider Haggard (letter) (8 September 1899) The Times
Anglo-African Writers' Club (17 October 1899) The Times
The War (letter) (25 October 1899) The Times
Farming in 1899 (letter) (22 December 1899) The Times
Farming in 1899 (letter) (1 January 1900) The Times
Settlement of Soldiers in South Africa (letter) (5 May 1900) The Times
1881 and 1900 (letter) (2 October 1900) The Times
Farming in 1900 (letter) (1 January 1901) The Times
Central and Associated Chambers of Agriculture (letter) (6 November 1901) The Times
Small Holdings (letter) (8 November 1901) The Times
Rural England (letter) (4 February 1903) The Times
Mr Rider Haggard on Rural Depopulation (3 May 1903) The Times
Agricultural Distress (letter) (11 June 1903) The Times
The Motor Problem (letter) (24 June 1903) The Times
Fiscal Policy and Agriculture (letter) (16 December 1903) The Times
Telepathy Between a Human Being and a Dog (letter) (21 July 1904) The Times
Telepathy Between a Human Being and a Dog (letter) (9 August 1904) The Times
Mr Rider Haggard on Small Holdings (12 September 1904) The Times
Case L.1139 Dream (October 1904) Journal of the Society for Psychical Research
Mr Rider Haggard on Agriculture (22 October 1904) The Times
Mr Rider Haggard on Rural Housing (27 October 1904) The Times
The Deserted Village (letter) (25 August 1905) The Times
Decrease of Population and the Land (letter) (6 January 1906) The Times
Prevention of Cruelty to Children (3 February 1906) The Times
The New Land and Tenure Bill (letter) (12 March 1906) The Times
Garden City Association (17 March 1906) The Times
Mr H. Rider Haggard on the Zulus (19 May 1906) The Illustrated London News
To Be Proof against British Bullets: A Zulu Incantation (19 May 1906) The Illustrated London News
Housing of the Working Classes (26 June 1906) The Times
Mr Rider Haggard on Small Holdings (4 July 1906) The Times
The Unemployed and Waste City Lands (letter) (19 July 1906) The Times
Mr Rider Haggard on the Transvaal Constitution (7 August 1906) The Times
Vanishing East Anglia (1 September 1906) The Saturday Review
The Land Grabbing at Plaistow (5 September 1906) The Times
The Land Tenure Bill (22 November 1906) The Times
Publishers and the Public (letter) (19 February 1907) The Times
The Careless Children (2 March 1907) The Saturday Review
The Government and the Land (letter) (29 April 1907) The Times
Chambers of Agriculture (2 May 1907) The Times
The Government and the Land (letter) (8 May 1907) The Times
Miss Jebb on Small Holdings (15 June 1907) Country Life
Rural Housing and Sanitation Association (27 June 1907) The Times
St Thomas Hospital Medical School (28 June 1907) The Times
The Land Question (4 July 1907) The Times

A Plea for the Sitting Tennant (letter) (12 August 1907) The Times
A Literary Coincidence (letter) (19 October 1907) The Spectator
Town Planning Conference (26 October 1907) The Times
Dr Barnardo's Homes (16 November 1907) The Times
The Proposed Agricultural Party (5 December 1907) The Times
Mr Rider Haggard and Small Holdings (10 January 1908) The Times
Mr Haggard and Children's Legislation (13 March 1908) The Times
The Drink Trade and Common Sense (letter) (2 April 1908) The Times
The Zulus: The Finest Savage Race in the World (June 1908) The Pall Mall Magazine
Sparrows (letter) (18 August 1908) The Times
Sparrows, Rats and Humanity (letter) (5 September 1908) The Times
The Letters of Queen Victoria (letter) (26 November 1908) The Times
The Romance of the World's Greatest Rivers (December 1908) Travel Magazine
Afforestation. Mr Rider Haggard's View (1 March 1909) The Times
The Late Sir Marshal Clarke (letter) (13 April 1909) The Times
Mr Rider Haggard on Agriculture (27 November 1909) The Times
Mr Rider Haggard on South Africa (11 March 1910) The Times
Why? (letter) (25 April 1910) The Times
Mr Rider Haggard on Irish Agriculture (23 May 1910) The Times
Why Not? (letter) (12 July 1910) The Times
Mr Rider Haggard on Agriculture (16 September 1910) The Times
Mr Rider Haggard on Vermin (8 November 1910) The Times
Danish High Schools (21 December 1910) The Times
Sugar Beet Growing in Norfolk (6 March 1911) The Times
Rural Denmark (letter) (22 March 1911) The Times
Rural Denmark (letter) (3 April 1911) The Times
The Copyright Bill (letter) (6 June 1911) The Times
Mr Rider Haggard on Poverty. The Burden of Civilization (15 July 1911) The Times
Mr Rider Haggard and the Public Records (28 July 1911) The Times
The Farmers' Burden (1 December 1911) The Times
Egyptian Date Farm. The Financial Aspect (11 October 1912) The Times
Umslopogaas and Makokel. Sir H. Rider Haggard on Zulu Types (letter) (16 August 1913) The Times
The Death of Mark Haggard (letter) (10 October 1914) The Times
On the Land. Old Problems and New Ways. The War—and After. (15 March 1915) The Times
Soldiers as Settlers. After-War Problem for the Empire (20 August 1915) The Times
Raids by Air. Zeppelins and Zeppelins (letter) (22 October 1915) The Times
Women's Work on the Land. A Palliative in Hard Times (letter) (29 November 1915) The Times
Women on the Land. Town Girls' Unfitness for Farm Work (letter) (9 December 1915) The Times
Soldiers as Settlers. Sir Rider Haggard's Oversea Mission (2 February 1916) The Times
Soldiers as Settlers (letter) (7 February 1916) The Times
Soldier Settlers. The Future of Rural England (letter) (10 February 1916) The Times
Farewell Luncheon to Sir Rider Haggard (March 1916) United Empire
Soldier Settlers for the Empire. Offer from Victoria (18 April 1916) The Times
Sir R Haggard's Tour. Land for Ex-Service Men (22 July 1916) The Times
Sir H. Rider Haggard's Mission. Land for Ex-Soldiers (1 August 1916) The Times
Land for Ex-Soldiers. Outline of Sir R. Haggard's Report   (12 August 1916) The Times
Empire Land Settlement Deputation to the Secretary of State for the Colonies and the President of the
Board of Agriculture (September 1916) United Empire

Empire Land Settlement by Sir Rider Haggard (December 1916) United Empire
A Journey through Zululand by Sir H Rider Haggard (December 1916) The Windsor Magazine
Mr Wilson's Note. British Publicity (28 December 1916) The Times
Home Produce (letter) (22 February 1917) The Times
The Milk Supply (letter) (11 April 1917) The Times
Corn Production Bill. A National Measure (letter) (13 June 1917) The Times
A Protest and a Plea. Farmers and Meat (letter) (9 October 1917) The Times
Pig-Breeding. A Subject for Municipal Enterprise (letter) (22 February 1918) The Times
The German Colonies. Interests of the Dominions (letter) (5 November 1918) The Times
Light—More Light! (letter) (19 November 1918) The Times
A Great American. Tributes to the Late Mr Roosevelt (letter) (8 January 1919) The Times
Shut the Door (letter) (10 March 1919) The Times
Population and Housing. Emigration v Birth Control (25 March 1919) The Times
The Ex-Kaiser (letter) (11 April 1919) The Times
Empire Birth-Rate. Sir Rider Haggard on Emigration (17 April 1919) The Times
Ex-Service Men Abroad. Warnings from California (letter) (10 May 1919) The Times
Edith Cavell (letter) (16 May 1919) The Times
The Ex-Kaiser. Uncertainties of Trial (letter) (8 July 1919) The Times
Race Suicide Peril. Western Civilization Threatened (11 October 1919) The Times
The British Cinema. Production of Reputable Films (letter) (5 November 1919) The Times
Horrors on the Film. Limits of Publicity (letter) (19 November 1919) The Times
The British Museum (letter) (24 January 1920) The Times
Air Exploration and Empire (letter) (7 February 1920) The Times
The Liberty League. A Campaign Against Bolshevism (letter) (3 March 1920) The Times
Bolshevist Peril. Counter-Propaganda (4 March 1920) The Times
The Empire's Vacant Lands. Settlers and the Food Supply (14 April 1920) The Times
Films and Happy Endings. The Tyranny of a Convention (letter)   (21 April 1921) The Times
Land and its Burdens. Evil of Grinding Taxation (letter) (8 August 1921) The Times
Boy Emigrants (letter) (31 March 1922) The Times
Migration and Morals. Declining Birther Rate (7 April 1922) The Times
Labour Party's Programme. Confiscation and Class Hatred (letter) (28 October 1922) The Times
Efficient Denmark. Keeping the People on the Land (7 December 1922) The Times
The Egyptian Find. Tombs of Eighteenth Dynasty Queens (letter) (19 December 1922) The Times
King Tutankhamen. Reburial in Great Pyramid (letter) (13 February 1923) The Times
The Norfolk Dispute. A Truce while There is Time (letter) (3 April 1923) The Times
Rural Post and Telephone. Minister's Reply to Deputation (19 April 1923) The Times
Liberalism and Land Reform (letter) (1 May 1923) The Times
Small Holdings. Influence of Heredity (letter) (4 July 1923) The Times
Agricultural Parcel Post (26 July 1923) The Times
Country Houses for Sale. Empty East Anglian Mansions (letter) (14 June 1924) The Times
Plight of Agriculture (24 July 1924) The Times
Loans From the British Museum (letter) (30 July 1924) The Times
Zinovieff Letter. Mr MacDonald and a Political Plot (letter) (29 October 1924) The Times
Two Centuries of Publishing. Tributes to Messrs. Longmans (6 November 1924) The Times
Imagination and War (26 November 1924) The Times

Non-Fiction

Cetywayo and His White Neighbours (1882)
A Farmer's Year (1899)
The Last Boer War (1899)
A Winter Pilgrimage (1901)
Rural England (1902)
A Gardener's Year (1905)
The Poor and the Land (1905)
Regeneration (1910)
Rural Denmark (1911)
The Days of My Life (1926)

King Solomon's Mines
This novel has been adapted at least six times. The first version, King Solomon's Mines, directed by Robert Stevenson, premiered in 1937. The best known version premiered in 1950: King Solomon's Mines, directed by Compton Bennett and Andrew Marton, was followed in 1959 by a sequel, Watusi. In 1979 a low-budget version directed by Alvin Rakoff, King Solomon's Treasure, combined both King Solomon's Mines and Allan Quatermain in one story. The 1985 film King Solomon's Mines was a tongue-in-cheek parody of the story, with a 1987 sequel in the same vein, Allan Quatermain and the Lost City of Gold. Around the same time an Australian animated TV film came out, King Solomon's Mines. In 2008 a direct-to-video adaptation, Allan Quatermain and the Temple of Skulls, was released.

She
She has been adapted for the cinema at least ten times, and was one of the earliest films to be made, in 1899 as La Colonne de feu (The Pillar of Fire), by Georges Méliès. A 1911 version starred Marguerite Snow, a British-produced version appeared in 1916, and in 1917 Valeska Suratt appeared in a production for Fox which is lost. In 1925 a silent film of She, starring Betty Blythe, was produced with the active participation of Rider Haggard, who wrote the intertitles. This film combines elements from all the books in the series.

A decade later another cinematic version of the novels was released, featuring Helen Gahagan, Randolph Scott and Nigel Bruce. Unlike the book and the other films, this 1935 version was set in the Arctic, rather than Africa, and depicts the ancient civilisation of the story in an Art Deco style, with music by Max Steiner.

The 1965 film She was produced by Hammer Film Productions; it starred Ursula Andress as Ayesha and John Richardson as her reincarnated love, with Peter Cushing and Bernard Cribbins as other members of the expedition.

In 2001 another adaption was released direct-to-video with Ian Duncan as Leo Vincey, Ophélie Winter as Ayesha and Marie Bäumer as Roxane.

Dawn
The film Dawn was released in 1917, starring Hubert Carter and Annie Esmond.

Jess

This book was filmed in 1912, featuring Marguerite Snow, Florence La Badie and James Cruze, in 1914 with Constance Crawley and Arthur Maude, and in 1917 as Heart and Soul, starring Theda Bara in the title role.

Beatrice
The book was adapted into a 1921 Italian silent drama film called The Stronger Passion, directed by Herbert Brenon and starring Marie Doro and Sandro Salvini.

Swallow
The novel was adapted into a 1922 South African film.

Stella Fregelius
The book was adapted into a 1921 British film, Stella.

Moon of Israel
This novel was the basis of a script by Ladislaus Vajda, for film-director Michael Curtiz in his 1924 Austrian epic known as Die Sklavenkönigin (Queen of the Slaves).